Praise for

"Diana Hawk has crafted a beautiful story of three young women navigating one of the most pivotal times of their lives. Through the power of friendship, these heroines manage with grace, compassion, and laughter. I devoured this compelling story because of how gifted a storyteller Diana is and because it is inspired by true events."

— LINDSEY MORGAN, ACTOR AND DIRECTOR

"Diana connects and confronts the reader with a brilliant depiction of friendship and love that is all too ubiquitous. *As beautiful as it seems* is a charming, humorous, and heartfelt read that serves as an incredible reminder to take a step back sometimes and laugh at the absurdity of it all."

— ZOE HANEY, WRITER

"I didn't even have to correct the grammar that much."

— MY MOM

"I read the entire book in one sitting–I couldn't put it down. It's an epic story about love, acceptance, and a freaking beautiful picture of true, raw, friendship. I cried 3x and felt everything from empowered to sad throughout."

— ALLI SCHAPER, FOUNDER & CEO OF SUPERMUSH

As beautiful as it seems

DIANA HAWK

Artwork by Roberta Zeta.

Created with Vellum

For anyone who's ever felt alone in their struggles.
You are not alone.

* * *

In loving memory of my father, Richard Hawk, and my family: Alexander "Zander" Zehl, William "Billy" Zehl, and Marcia Zehl.

Your stories will live on.

"Frankly, there isn't anyone you couldn't learn to love once you've heard their story."

-Mr. Rogers

Content Warning

This book contains sex, bullying, eating disorders, alcohol and drug consumption, suicide (not on page, only talked about and doesn't happen during the book), death (not on page, only talked about and doesn't happen during the book), and friendship throughout all of this.

CHAPTER 1
Ariana

That *look*.

That look would be her undoing.

Ariana shivered in the memory of Lukas' burning stare from across the cafeteria. The way his lips turned upward into a half-hidden smile when their eyes finally met would undoubtedly keep her awake tonight. But even so, daydreaming of Lukas easily took precedence over the AP History exam in front of her. She tried to imagine what would happen if they found themselves alone together, maybe in a dark, abandoned stairwell at a party. His hand against her waist, pulling her closer and closer to him until...

"Fifteen minutes left!" the teacher announced.

Ariana shook her head and held her hands poised above the keyboard. Essay exams were a piece of cake even if she only half-understood the subject. But before she could type out the first line, a familiar drip of anxiety splashed in her stomach. She shook her head again, choosing to ignore it. There was nothing to be worried about right now. No reason to panic. Ariana touched her fingertips to the keys and began typing, creating her own version of history.

But then there was another drip.

And another.

The drips churned one by one into a medley of panic and despair in her gut. She inhaled sharply. It was as if someone was taking a rake across her brain, stripping out the happiness. She gave up on the exam, grabbing the edges of her desk as her eyes darted around the room. *No, this* can't *be happening now*, Ariana thought, squeezing her eyes shut. She willed herself to calm down, but it was too late.

You're not safe. You're not good enough. Everything is wrong.

A pained gasp escaped her lips. Ariana cursed herself and peeked at her classmates, but no one was watching her for once–they were all too caught up in the exam that would account for ten percent of their grade, due in about five minutes.

"May I be excused?" Ariana's voice broke at the end of the question. She had to get out of there, somewhere safe where she could let the attack play out, away from everyone so she could fully break down.

Several students looked up.

"What about your exam?" the teacher asked.

Tears threatened the corners of her eyes. "I'm finished. Please?"

Recognition flashed across the teacher's face. "Take your things, you're excused."

Ariana let go of her death grip on the desk and slammed the laptop shut. She slung her backpack over her shoulder and raced for the door.

As she ran down the deserted hallway, her choking breaths echoed off the white concrete walls, each reverberation a reminder of how different she was from everyone else. What she wouldn't give to live without erratic anxiety. She was almost to the bathroom, but the edges of her vision were blurring. *Don't faint, don't faint,* please *don't faint*, Ariana chanted to herself.

In what seemed like slow motion, she shoved into the bathroom and sank to the floor. She put her head between her legs and began to sob as the darkness engulfed her.

. . .

Half an hour later, Ariana stepped through the school doors and frowned up at the sun. Another day that she couldn't control a stupid anxiety attack. She sighed, thinking about how she wouldn't be able to mark an X on today's date in the calendar she hid in her dresser. She'd seen psychologists before, but they'd been little help. She knew a couple of friends who had managed to find a good therapist, but that just hadn't happened for her so far. Hers had all immediately tried to get her on some sort of prescription drug, which, although she knew that *could* be helpful, she wasn't ready to resort to drugs yet. She hadn't discovered it, but she just knew there had to be a way to end the attacks on her own, or at least calm them down.

Ariana ran a hand through her golden-brown hair, racking her brain for what the cause might have been. The upcoming cheerleading tryouts came to mind, but she was a shoo-in, so no true worry surrounding that. She'd been getting along with her mom lately, so it wasn't anything at home. Everything with her friends and schoolwork was mostly fine, or at least there was no drama right now, making it hard to pinpoint any particular culprit in her life.

Ariana gulped some fresh air. Sometimes she could swear the attacks came in anticipation of events she didn't know about yet. And although she didn't truly believe it, sometimes she wondered if they acted as a premonition–her instincts picking up on currents of danger only just beginning to form. She leaned against the gridiron gate surrounding the football field and pulled out the latest dystopian book she'd picked up, turning to another reality to soothe the stress of her own.

An overwhelming sensation of being watched brought Ariana out of her reading, and a murmur of her name confirmed her suspicion.

"*That's* Ariana Knight..." the voice said.

Ariana whirled around to find the source, spotting three

guilty freshman boys staring at her and whispering to one another. The tallest of the boys, a gangly redhead with freckles spattering his cheeks, noticed her gaze and nudged his buddies sharply in the ribs. Ariana shot them a knowing smirk. *Caught you*, she thought. The tall freshman blushed a bright crimson and the younger boys shuffled out of her sight.

I wonder what that was about, Ariana thought. Her sophomore year had only started a few weeks ago, but her school wasn't exactly kind when it came to rumors. And although she and her friends were often praised in the whispers, there were many vicious lies spread about them as well.

She closed her eyes, enjoying the natural light after being trapped in fluorescent-lit classrooms for the past seven hours. Most of her friends were still at their usual spot inside, but Ariana hadn't felt like sticking around to talk to everyone today.

The heat from the August sun was causing her to sweat despite the short indigo romper she wore, and a drip slid down her back. She flipped her head over to pull her hair into a messy bun, exposing her neck to the summer breeze.

When she stood again, Ariana smiled as she spotted her two best friends, Jade Pierce and Kiara Lancor, walking toward her and causing a ripple of turning heads after them. Jade wore a black baby tee that stopped an inch above her dark denim jeans, revealing a tantalizing sliver of tanned midriff. Her long, chocolate-brown hair was pulled half up and tied in a bun–a token hairstyle of Jade's that many attempted to replicate, but soon found would never look half as good on them as it did on her. Kiara was the antithesis of Jade in a beige sundress that hugged her body around the waist, her icy blonde hair billowing out behind her.

"Thank God it's Friday," Jade said as they reached Ariana.

A flutter in her peripheral vision caused Ariana to glance around. The freshman boys from earlier had come back with more of their friends and were now staring open-mouthed at them. Kiara and Jade either didn't see them or didn't care, because they continued their conversation as if there weren't a cluster of drooling freshmen following their every movement.

"You act like we didn't just go out last night," Kiara said, laughing.

"Ugh, don't remind me. My head still hurts from sleep deprivation." Jade groaned, squeezing her dark green eyes shut and rubbing her temples.

"I told you I have the remedy for that!" Kiara scolded.

"And I told you I can't just get high whenever like you can! Weed is your remedy for everything Kiara," Jade retorted. "Literally... everything."

Ariana laughed at the honesty of Jade's statement. From looking at Kiara though, she was the last person anyone would expect to be a stoner. She was beautiful in a way that made you want to know her, with blue-green eyes that saw more than they let on and an athletic figure that hid the fact that she ever got the munchies. The only person that possibly smoked more than Kiara was her boyfriend of six months, Teague Alexander. Teague was a grade above them and had been a huge player his sophomore year–his constant shirtless skateboarding and skills as a drummer had given him easy advantages over most of the guys at their school. But his wild days quickly ended once he met Kiara.

"Ian Alkine is looking hot today..." Jade mused, interrupting Ariana's train of thought. Ian and his friends had just finished afternoon football practice and were lingering close to their trucks nearby. The boys' muscles glistened with sweat, visible through their ripped and battered workout tanks. Ian stood on the bed of his truck, squeezing his water bottle onto his head before shaking his wet hair out all over his laughing friends.

"Ian going to be your new flavor of the week, Jade?" Ariana teased.

Jade stretched her lithe arms above her head, her black baby tee lifting to reveal several more inches of midriff. Her movement elicited appreciative looks from the nearby group of boys, Ian included. Jade caught Ian's eye and smiled devilishly, causing

Ariana to laugh again. Jade just had that thing–all the straight guys wanted her, and all the girls either wanted to be her or kill her.

"It's not my fault he looks like that," Jade said, gesturing toward Ian with a flick of her hand. "His body is practically screaming 'come and lick ice cream off me!'"

"And what would Taron think of that?" Kiara quipped. "Or the majority of the junior girls obsessed with Ian?"

"None of the juniors have any claim on Ian. And as for Taron, he knows I don't want anything serious. All we did was kiss, anyway! So, he has no claim on me–he understands that," Jade said as she toyed with the slender black leather bracelet she wore around her right wrist.

"I'm not so sure about that..." Kiara trailed off as Taron Canter approached them, gazing at Jade like he either wanted to kiss her or to eat her and hadn't quite made his mind up yet. Taron ducked behind Jade and wrapped his arms around her waist.

"What's up, ladies?" Taron said with a smile, giving Jade a kiss on the cheek.

Ariana had been attracted to Taron back when she first met him, but then again, it was a little hard not to be. He looked like he had just walked off of a movie set, starring the most typically white, hot teenage male possible. He had blonde hair, blue eyes, and a dazzling smile to match. However, upon spending about five minutes talking to Taron, his personality–or lack thereof–had been enough to turn Ariana off for good. He did have an unbelievable party house though, and his parents were away traveling almost every weekend. But besides that Taron Canter's forte was more or less standing around and looking hot.

After one of Taron's infamous parties the previous weekend, Jade had regaled Ariana and Kiara with a story of how she spontaneously took Taron behind a shed in the backyard and kissed him. This had been due to a bit of boredom on Jade's part and was just a spur-of-the-moment thing, she had explained–an exciting incident not to be repeated.

Ariana looked from Taron to Jade, and then finally to Kiara, catching Kiara's eye as they both smirked–clearly, Taron had not gotten the "spur of the moment; nothing serious" memo. She tried not to laugh at the surprised and disgusted look plastered on Jade's face as she spoke to Taron. "Nothing, we were just saying how thankful we are that it's Friday."

Taron ran a hand through his hair and sighed. "Tell me about it. But you guys are coming to the party at my place tonight, right?"

"Possibly," Jade said as she skillfully sidestepped out of Taron's embrace.

"Probably," Kiara countered with a sympathetic smile. Kiara and Ariana had seen Jade quickly lose interest in many guys before Taron. Fortunately for him, Taron remained blissfully unaware of Jade's discomfort. The thought that *he*, Taron Canter, could possibly be rejected had likely never crossed his mind.

"All right, I'll see you later, babe," Taron said before sauntering off.

When he was far enough away, Ariana and Kiara burst into laughter. Jade crossed her arms and furrowed her arched eyebrows at them.

"Yeah, he really got the message *babe*," Kiara choked out.

"Laugh it up guys," Jade muttered.

Kiara threw an arm around Jade's shoulder. "C'mon. Let's go to my house to get ready. I have some cannabis tea I want you to try."

"Kiara!" Jade said as Ariana laughed.

"Turn it up, Ari!" Jade's muffled voice yelled from Kiara's bathroom. "I love this song!"

Ariana and Kiara sat cross-legged on the plush, cream-colored carpet of Kiara's bedroom as they attempted to do each other's makeup. Ariana adjusted the volume so that Carsen's "You" emanated through the room while taking a sip of her CBD-infused tea. Kiara had given her the option of THC tea, which Ariana had politely declined for fear of heightening her anxiety. No one ever seemed to understand how she could have full-blown panic attacks and not know what they stemmed from, so most of the time she ended up keeping the incidents to herself. Not even Kiara or Jade truly understood–they tried to, but they couldn't.

She took another sip from the teacup, staring above Kiara's shoulder at a painting of a beautiful dark-skinned girl lounging with two lions, her midnight eyes locked on the viewer in confidence. *The girl in the painting probably wouldn't have anxiety attacks*, Ariana thought dismally.

"Hold still, Ari," Kiara said, putting a hand on Ariana's shoulder to hold her in place. "I'm still finishing your left eye."

Ariana did her best to stop fidgeting. She noticed the creamy silk robe Kiara had donned for their make-up session had slipped down her friend's shoulder.

"How'd you get so much more tan than the rest of us this summer, K?" Ariana asked, reaching forward to pull the robe back up, spotting a new spatter of freckles on Kiara's shoulder.

"Lots of time on my roof with Teague," Kiara said, her cheeks glowing pink.

"Oh, I'm surprised you got any sun then since his body was probably on top of yours the whole time," Jade joked from the bathroom.

Kiara let out a faux-shocked gasp. "My goodness gracious, I would never!" she said in a fake Southern accent.

"Sweetheart?" Kiara's mother called from the hallway. There was a soft knock on the door, and Ariana turned down the music while simultaneously sliding her drink into the closet out of habit. But the teacup wouldn't look suspicious, Ariana reminded herself, and besides, Karen Lancor wouldn't care.

"Come in, Mom!" Kiara sang.

Karen opened the door but didn't come through the doorway, leaving the girls their space. Her blonde hair was pulled back into a short ponytail and royal blue reading glasses sat perched on her nose. "Is anyone parking here tonight to walk to Taron's house? If so, I'll pull Jon's car in."

"Yeah, I think so. Thank you," Kiara said.

"And if anyone tries to drink and drive, you know what to do."

"Yes, Mom. Walk them back here, hide their keys in the laundry basket, and throw them onto one of the couches."

"Good girl," Karen said, her blond brows furrowed in concern. "Call me if you need anything. I mean it."

"I will!" Kiara said, sweeping her long blonde hair over her shoulder before adding a finishing touch of eye shadow on Ariana.

"We all will," Ariana chimed in, blinking her eyes open.

Karen focused on Ariana, her face relaxing. "Oh, you look lovely, Ariana!"

Ariana smiled. "Thank you, Karen." It used to be strange for her to be so at ease around parents, but Ariana had quickly learned that Karen and Jon Lancor weren't like the rest.

"Yes, I am quite the makeup artiste!" Kiara said with an accent, taking a small hit of weed from her vaporizer in plain sight of her mother. Ariana's eyes bulged. She still wasn't *that* at ease though.

"Have fun tonight!" Karen said before she swept back downstairs.

Jade popped her head out of the bathroom door. "Has anyone ever told you that your parents are the coolest in all the land?"

"Allllll the time," Kiara said.

Sadness gripped Ariana's stomach. She thought of her own small family–it was only she and her mom. She would have given anything to have her dad back, even for a day. To hear him say he was proud of her, to give her advice, to hold her when she was sad. But that was only a dream now. Luckily, Ariana could commiserate with Jade–both of their fathers had died when they were younger.

Ariana thought back to the first time she and Jade told each other their stories. Ariana had gone first, describing the car accident that had taken her father's life when she was ten years old, and Jade had listened in a way that only someone who had experienced that kind of pain and loss could. When Jade told her story next, Ariana was shocked and heartbroken that this beautiful girl she was coming to know and love had already been through such a tragedy. From the way Jade carried herself though, Ariana never would have guessed her broken past.

"Okay, look at your eyes now," Kiara said.

Ariana turned and studied herself in the full-length mirror leaning against the bedroom wall. Kiara had worked her magic all right–Ariana's eyes were smoldering thanks to some expertly applied smoky shadow.

"I love it. You're a miracle worker," Ariana cooed.

Kiara grinned. "You killed my makeup, too." Ariana had smudged light-brown shadow over Kiara's blue-green eyes and drawn pink stars in liquid liner in the outer corners of each lid. Kiara headed to the bathroom to join Jade, leaving Ariana with her reflection. She was wearing a backless navy silk top and a black skirt that showed off her legs, her golden-brown hair cascading in loose curls that tickled her bare skin. She was a few sizes bigger than Kiara and Jade, and loved the way the skirt hugged her hips and butt. Ariana glanced up at her face. She looked dangerous and confident and brave–much braver than she felt–which was exactly what she needed tonight because *he* would be there. Ariana sighed, welcoming the familiar flutter in her stomach that came whenever she thought of Lukas and fell into the memory of the first time they met.

Two weeks ago, Ariana ditched her homeroom study period to hang out in Kiara's, since Kiara's teacher was lax and her homeroom usually turned into a rowdy gathering of all grades. Ariana had walked from the back of the classroom to get a drink of water from the hallway, passing Lukas along the way.

He had followed her.

"Hey." Ariana heard from behind her. "I saw you last week."

Ariana spun around to find one of the hottest guys she had ever seen in her life standing a few feet away. He was similar in stature to a pro athlete, with black hair that fell in a sort of sexy disarray and bright brown eyes. Lukas' mouth turned upward into a smile and desire streaked through her body, catching her off guard. Ariana was suddenly and acutely aware that they were alone in the hallway.

"I'm sorry?" Ariana asked, confused as to what the insanely hot senior was referencing.

"Last week at the football game. I saw you with your friends. I wanted to know you," he said, taking a step toward her.

The way he spoke was so different from the boys in her year–his words flowed out with the utmost self-assurance and captivated her, like a poem. Ariana hadn't been able to find any words to say.

"I'm Lukas," he said. He smiled again, and she wondered if he could see her heart beating through her chest.

"Ariana," she recovered.

"I'll see you around then, Ariana." He turned and walked away without so much as a glance back.

Lukas had left her there, feeling a stronger attraction to him than she had ever felt for anyone. Ariana hadn't spoken to him since that day–they didn't have each other's numbers and their schedules didn't exactly coincide. Surely he could have found her on social media, but nothing had happened yet. That is, until today. He had strolled through her lunch period and sought her out with his eyes from across the cafeteria, staring at her unabashed while he spoke with a friend. That look had set her on fire.

Jade and Kiara appeared from the bathroom, ready to go. Jade hadn't bothered to dress up at all, wearing the same outfit from earlier that day. Her hair and face looked like she had taken hours getting ready when in reality she had only been in the bathroom for ten minutes. Kiara looked great too, in her usual dressed-down style. She wore a simple white tank top and distressed jeans that cuffed around the ankle. Her light-blonde hair twisted into a fishtail braid that fell over her left shoulder, passing another three pink stars Ariana had drawn on her collarbone. Kiara wasn't wearing a bra, not that she did often. She always said this was one of the perks of having a small chest–she could get away with it.

"Haiden texted me–he's out front waiting for us to walk over," Kiara said.

The girls stepped into the moonlit night and Ariana paused on the stone steps. She took in a deep breath, bringing herself fully into the present moment. The delicious smell of evening air and freshly cut grass made its way into her nose, and a slow grin spread across her face as she basked in the anticipation that rolled around in her stomach. She could hardly wait to see Lukas again.

"Ariana! Get over here!" Kiara yelled to her from the driveway, grinning.

Ariana let out a giddy laugh and took off after her friends. She had a feeling something big was about to happen, and she could hardly wait to see what it was.

CHAPTER 2

J. K. A

Standing near the hot tub and a few feet away from some senior boys playing beer pong, Jade was only half-listening to Alora Menudos and Melodie Baxter talk about a guy from another school that had crashed Taron's party.

"He's so hot though... I wonder if he has a girlfriend. I doubt he would have crashed another school's party if he did," Melodie mused.

"I bet you're going to find out," Alora said with a smirk.

Jade surveyed the scene with a detached sense of awe–Taron Canter's family was wealthy all right. The back deck alone boasted an outdoor kitchen and patio lounge that stood adjacent to the enormous salt-water pool, recently renovated to include a cave and hot tub underneath a waterfall slide. Jade wondered briefly if this opulence was why she didn't like Taron. He was used to having it all and getting whatever he wanted, and something inside of her refused to be added to that list.

If only she had thought of that *before* kissing him.

"So what's up with you and Taron, Jade?" Alora teased. "How's *that* going?"

Jade's thoughts flashed to Ian–she hadn't been able to stop thinking about him since he caught her eye earlier. Jade realized she'd never given him much thought before–she had always known he was hot, but she hadn't *noticed* him like she had today.

"How's what going?" Jade asked with a hint of exasperation in her voice. She wasn't annoyed with Alora, but more so with the topic of conversation. So many people had asked her about Taron in the past week that she wished they hadn't hooked up in the first place. But she *had* to try it out with him, to see if he would be the one to make her feel something. Jade could never quite find that thing that everyone raved about–that feeling that another person was the whole world and nothing else mattered. The answer to that question, she had realized quickly, was definitely not Taron Canter. It all made her feel a bit broken in a way, but she had always secretly suspected that this was the case.

"Oh, like the two of you aren't a thing," Melodie said, letting out a snort while examining her dirty blonde hair between manicured fingers. "I heard it was more than just a kiss."

"Well, you heard wrong," Jade said, narrowing her piercing green eyes. "And we are *not* a *thing*, Melodie."

"Oh my God, Jade! I didn't mean it in a bad way! You two are cute together, just saying," Melodie said, a fake-sweet smile plastered across her face.

Jade didn't bother returning the smile. Melodie sipped her wine cooler and pulled out her phone, trying her hardest not to look offended by Jade's dismissal.

Jade turned her attention back to Alora, noticing that her friend looked particularly luminous tonight. Alora's mane of long, jet black hair was pulled into a high ponytail that spilled over her shoulders and her light-brown face was free of makeup, highlighting her Hispanic features. Alora was a stark contrast to Melodie's blonde locks and overabundance of eyeliner, and Jade found herself thinking it was truly in Melodie's best interest not to stand next to Alora anymore. Although Melodie was considered beautiful by most, Jade didn't see it. She'd thought Melodie was pretty when they first met, but her personality had quickly ruined it.

"Taron and I are just friends. We only kissed once for fun," Jade said.

"I know, I know. K told me. I was messing with you. But maybe I should try that move out sometime... took him behind the shed, eh?" Alora joked.

Jade smirked. "Yeah, and maybe could you try it on Taron so that he'll stop bugging me and focus on you instead?"

Alora let out a snort of laughter right as Taron materialized next to the girls and slung an arm around Jade as if he had somehow known they were talking about him. His ever-present cocky grin hung a little low on his face, and his eyes kept going in and out of focus.

"Ladies," Taron slurred, the smell of beer thick on his breath. "Did you see that last shot I made? The *victory* cup..."

"I'm gonna go find Ari and K!" Jade said. She ducked out from under Taron's arm and made a beeline for the house, hoping to lose him and refill her drink at the same time. Jade heard Alora let out a laugh and she whipped around, exchanging a swift smile with her as she slid in the kitchen door.

The inside of the house was close to deserted and unexpectedly peaceful. Jade checked her phone and discovered a DM from an unknown account on her TikTok. She had posted a video while at Kiara's house, a silly montage of them getting ready and dancing. Someone had responded to it with one word: "Slut."

Jade had gotten better at ignoring the comments, but they still got to her sometimes. Why couldn't she just share a post with her friends in peace?

She opened the fridge as a distraction and searched for something to spice up her drink.

"That would taste a lot better if you let me make it," a deep voice from behind her said.

Jade whirled around to find Ian standing in front of her. *What a corny line*, she thought, but her stomach dropped as she looked at him. Ian was more dressed up than usual in a white polo and jeans, showing off his ripped arms and chest. He somehow managed to be cute and hot at the same time, a combination that made Jade a little weak in the knees, although she'd never let herself show it.

"Hi..." Jade said. She grinned and then pursed her lips. "Hmm... but do I trust your drink-making skills enough to let you?"

"You never know until you try." Ian smiled, and she noticed that his top lip lifted a fraction of an inch higher on the left side. God, it was sexy. Did it do that when he talked as well? She would have to pay closer attention.

"I don't really drink, so juice only."

Ian nodded and extended his hand toward her waist, causing Jade's breath to catch in her throat. Her hopes rose as she imagined his hands on her, pulling her toward him. But then his hand veered to the left and he grabbed the cup instead. Jade smiled, hoping her momentary lapse in cool hadn't shown on her face. She hoisted herself onto the kitchen counter to watch Ian in action, feeling oddly content for the first time all night.

He looked up and caught her eye, still smiling. "Were you hiding out in here?"

Jade looked away. "Maybe."

"I do that too, sometimes. I get to the point where I have to get away from everyone or I feel like I'm going to lose it."

Jade nodded, surprised by his spot-on understanding. She opened her mouth to add on, but then closed it. He wouldn't understand.

"You were about to say something," Ian said. "What was it?"

Jade shook her head and smiled in a way that usually distracted people enough to move their attention from whatever it was she didn't want to talk about.

"No, I want to know," Ian said, his tone breaking her resistance.

"Sometimes I feel like people are always expecting something from me, and I think most of the time they're hoping I'll fail in some way. Like they'd be happier with me if I did." Jade hesitated, thinking of all the negative rumors that constantly flew around about her at school. "I don't know if that makes sense."

"No, it makes sense," Ian said, his eyes melting into hers. "I know *exactly* what you mean."

Something pulled pleasantly in Jade's stomach, like her body was responding to finding understanding in another.

"There," Ian said, handing Jade her cup. "See if you like it."

Jade took a sip and raised her eyebrows–the cranberry, pineapple, and orange juice mixed perfectly. Jade licked her lips and made a noise of approval. She looked up and saw Ian's clear blue eyes trained on her mouth and her pulse sped up.

Ian opened his mouth to say something right as the back door swung open.

"Ian!" The yellow-blonde bob of Kristin Long, a notoriously bitchy junior, popped into the doorway. "We've been looking for you." Her eyebrows furrowed as she noticed Ian's proximity to Jade.

Jade looked Kristin up and down. She wasn't pretty in an orthodox way, but her self-assurance gave her something that translated into a sort of beauty. The respect and space she carried for herself made others revere her.

Jade just thought she was an asshole.

During the girls' freshman year, Kristin spread a rumor that Jade had gone down on a senior named Marx in his car outside of a fast-food restaurant. Kristin swore to everyone she saw the hook up with her own eyes, but when Marx came to Jade's defense stating nothing had happened, Kristin's story conveniently changed to include that she had been drunk at the time so it *could* have been someone else. Even though Kristin changed her story, the rumor had already done its damage. More than one senior had tried to hang out with Jade in the following weeks, asking her if she wanted to "take a ride" with them. Jade could never figure out the source of Kristin's vendetta against her, other than the fact that Jade merely existed.

"Hi, Kristin," Jade said, attempting a smile. Ariana was always telling her to kill Kristin with kindness.

"Hey cutie," Kristin said only to Ian as if Jade were invisible. Jade remembered why she could never follow Ariana's advice for more than a minute.

"What's up?" Ian said, leaning back against the counter next to Jade.

"We need you for beer pong. It's finally our turn to be partners!" Kristin said, bounding over to him. She smelled like beer and overly-fruity perfume, and Jade did her best not to make it obvious as she ever so slightly covered her nose with her hand. Kristin grabbed Ian's arm and began to pull him outside.

"I'll teach you my drink-making secrets another time," Ian said, turning back at the last moment. He winked at Jade and she grinned.

"By the way, Taron was looking for you, Jade!" Kristin pointedly interjected before pushing Ian out the door and slamming it behind her.

"Fan-fucking-tastic," Jade muttered. She hopped off the counter, attempting to quell the rising disappointment in her stomach. She took a swig of her drink and set off to find Ariana and Kiara, knowing they would be able to cheer her up.

* * *

Kiara felt high whenever she was with Teague, even without the help of the joint she had just smoked. They stood hidden from view behind the rock waterfall, with Teague holding her and kissing her slowly in a way that she loved.

"You look beautiful tonight," Teague said, turning her light-blonde braid around his dark fingers.

Kiara smiled up at him but shook her head in disbelief. He tried to argue, but she pulled his face toward hers to kiss him again instead.

Even though they had been together for half a year, Kiara still got butterflies nearly every time she was around Teague. She could vividly remember the first time she'd ever seen him freshman year–her heart had almost stopped. Teague was skating shirtless with his friends in the parking lot after school, V-muscles on full display for all to see. They were surrounded by a gaggle of girls all vying for his attention. The longing Kiara had felt for Teague had been almost painful, but she decided then and there not to be another one of the girls that fawned all over him. So instead, she bided her time.

A few months later, Kiara was at an upperclassmen party with Jade and Ariana, smoking in the backyard with some juniors. She was having one of her giggling fits when Teague wandered over to their group. Kiara flashed a huge smile at him, and to her surprise, Teague took a seat right by her. They were nearly touching. He said "hey" and gave her a smile that melted her inhibitions. For two hours they stayed next to one another, smoking and making idiotic jokes, cracking each other up. At the end of the night when Kiara made a move to leave, Teague followed her.

"Hey," he said, his warm brown eyes shining. "You're hilarious. We've gotta hang out again."

"Okay," Kiara said, and Teague smiled at her for the hundredth time that night, only this time it was celebratory. Kiara's knees went a little weak.

"When can I see you again?" Teague asked.

Kiara looked at him and imagined herself running her hands over his muscular black chest, wondering how it would feel and what he would taste like when she kissed him. Her stomach flipped in excitement at the thought. But then she remembered that Teague rarely had to work for girls, and so why should it be this easy for him?

"Oh, I don't really believe in the construct of time," she said, a light breeze in her voice.

Teague looked at Kiara for a second and then doubled over with laughter. "*Who* are you?"

Kiara laughed. "I'll see you around." She left him standing there, dumbfounded and staring after her.

It had only taken a few weeks after that for Teague to ask her to be his girlfriend.

"Hey," Teague whispered, pulling Kiara back into the present. "I'm so lucky you chose me."

Kiara loved when he seemed to read her mind. He was smiling down at her, the dimples in his cheeks pronounced. She kissed his full lips again, savoring the warmth that spread through her body from their contact.

A loud rustling came from the bushes on the right, and Kiara spotted one of the girls' best friends, Haiden Lee, meandering over, pretending to use his nose to sniff out the source of the weed.

"Whoa, guys, whoa," Haiden joked in protest to their intimate embrace, covering his eyes with a hand.

"Shut up, man," Teague said as he passed Haiden a fresh joint. "Here, light up."

Kiara looked over at her cup of beer sitting forgotten on the waterfall. She'd never been much of a drinker–why waste calories on drinking when it only led to bad decisions and a hangover the next day? Most of her friends just made fools of themselves after the first few drinks anyway.

Haiden took a big hit and passed it to Teague, then started to pull his shoulder-length dark hair into a ponytail when he stopped and looked confused.

"Yo, earth to Haiden," Teague said, shaking his shoulder.

"There was something I was doing before I found you two love birds..." Haiden mumbled. "... but now I have no idea what it was."

"Yeah, well smoking this will do that to you," Kiara said, laughing at him.

"Oh! Right. K–I was supposed to tell you that J and Ari are looking for you," Haiden said.

"Good job, Haide," Kiara said. "I'll go find them now. And

just so you don't forget, you were about to put your hair up into a man-bun before you told me that."

"Ha-ha. It gets me all the ladies though, so the joke is on you."

"Does it though?" Kiara said. Haiden grunted and she poked him in the stomach.

Teague was still laughing when he pulled Kiara close and whispered in her ear, "Don't be gone for too long, baby."

Kiara took a deep breath of Teague and kissed his cheek before wandering off in search of Ariana and Jade. The wind blew an aroma of cooking meat in her direction–someone had grilled and it smelled delicious. She walked toward the scent and saw a plate of hot dogs and hamburgers cooked to perfection, ready to be devoured. Kiara stopped in her tracks, not wanting to get any closer. Her mouth salivated as she peeked back at the hot dogs. With a strained effort, she turned away–those were way over her daily calorie limit.

Cheerleading tryouts were coming up and Kiara was worried about making the team again with her friends. She wasn't an insane tumbler like Ariana or an incredible dancer like Jade, so she wanted to look the part as much as possible. Not to mention she hadn't been feeling beautiful lately, and even when Teague said it, it was hard for her to believe it. As messed up as it sounded in her head, she wanted to feel beautiful enough *for* him. Kiara didn't know how anyone could ever feel beautiful enough these days though when opening any social media meant seeing a slew of girls and models who were too perfect to compete with.

But she would feel better soon, because she had a goal to get herself down to the weight of 110, and she had already dropped a few pounds from her starting weight of 130. About a month ago, she had been talking with another cheerleader, Reigh Maddox, about dieting and had disclosed her weight loss aspirations on a whim. Reigh encouraged Kiara, telling her about a sure-fire way to lose weight: Kiara only had to monitor her calorie intake so she didn't go over a certain amount a day and keep up her workouts, both of which she had been doing for a full month now. Sure, it was difficult, and the food cravings came often, but seeing her weight drop on the scale was exciting.

Kiara gritted her teeth. She had worked hard to eat less today to save some calories for alcohol just in case, and she wasn't about to mess up now. She pulled out her phone, giving up on organically searching for her friends.

9:12 p.m. Kiara: Where are you guys?

Ariana replied within a few moments and Kiara headed toward a secluded bench on the side of the house. She spotted her two best friends sitting close to each other with their heads bowed in conversation. Ariana's gold-streaked hair hung prettily around her face; her cheeks flushed from drinking. Jade looked cool and collected like usual, her dark hair and features wickedly beautiful in the night.

"Kiara!" Ariana shouted. She grabbed Kiara, pulled her down on the bench, and squeezed her in a hug. "There you are, our little pot-head."

"I would've been here sooner, but I couldn't find you guys. Why are we off where no one can see us?" Kiara asked.

"Apparently Ariana has some big news for us, so we had to go where no one could eavesdrop," Jade said matter-of-factly. "Oh, and I'm simultaneously hiding from Taron, or should I say, the 'beer pong champion of the world' as he's taken to calling himself tonight."

Kiara turned her attention toward Ariana, who began a story about Lukas Jansen, a senior Kiara knew because he occasionally smoked with Teague. Kiara had never particularly liked Lukas–he'd never done anything rude to her, but he had an arrogant vibe like he was hot shit and he knew it.

"And I haven't heard from him, but I heard most of the swimmers are coming tonight," Ariana said. Kiara couldn't fully focus. Her empty stomach twisted and growled. She began to think about the food that was only a few feet away, waiting for consumption. *No pain, no gain,* Kiara reminded herself. She giggled as she realized that *that* particular saying wasn't exactly right for the situation.

"Kiara, were you spacing out again?" Jade asked.

"Oh! What?" Kiara said, not quite catching what Jade said.

Jade and Ariana laughed. By now, they were used to her tendency to zone out mid-conversation.

"That could be the title of your memoir, K. 'Spacing Out Again: A tale of only half-listening to my friends, by Kiara Lancor,'" Jade said.

Kiara smirked at her.

"You laughed right after I said I can't tell if Lukas is interested in me or not," Ariana explained.

"That must have sounded bad! Sorry, I was laughing at the joke I made," Kiara attempted to explain. Jade raised her eyebrows, but Kiara continued. "I don't know about Lukas though, he seems full of himself..." she trailed off. "You're sure you like him, Ari?"

"I know I don't know him well, or at all, to be honest. I seriously don't know what's wrong with me," Ariana said, pressing her hands to her temples. "Ugh, and I can't stop thinking about him–it's like I'm possessed!"

"All right, calm down, Twilight," Jade joked, patting Ariana softly on the head.

"I'm serious, Jade. This is bad. I don't ever want to get so obsessed with a guy that nothing else matters," Ariana said, her hazel eyes darkening.

"You're not, Ari," Kiara said. "And don't worry, we'll kick your ass if you ever start to get that way."

* * *

An hour later, Ariana sat between Kiara and a random cute guy from a rival school at the large glass table on the back porch. Ariana was grinning uncontrollably because 1. All the vodka and sugar from the mixers had gone to her head 2. The guy next to her, Sean or Sam or whatever he had said his name was, was hot and clearly interested in her, making him a great distraction from the fact that Lukas hadn't shown up yet, and 3. Kiara's high giggling fits were extremely contagious.

Kiara poked her and made a ridiculous face. They started cracking up as the rest of the table looked on in confusion. Ariana knew it was silly, but they couldn't stop laughing. She wiped a tear from her eye and leaned back to look up at the stars.

The anxiety attack from earlier today was a distant memory now. It was strange how Ariana felt as though she were two people sometimes: one with crippling anxiety that was all-consuming, and the other one upbeat and cheerful–someone who could do things like laugh to the point of tears with her friend over nothing or carelessly flirt with a hot guy from a rival school.

Ariana glanced back down to see Jade gliding over to their table, looking like a goddess cloaked in the moonlight. Jade had slipped off sometime earlier after narrowly escaping Taron for the fiftieth time that night.

"J!" Ariana called out. "Get over here!"

Jade kissed Kiara on the cheek and squeezed into a chair. She nudged Ariana in the ribs.

"Who is *that*?" Jade whispered, looking pointedly at the attractive stranger sitting to Ariana's left.

"Oh!" Ariana exclaimed. "Jade, this is Sam! He goes to Birchmond."

"Jacob... My name is Jacob," the guy replied while laughing, but Ariana could tell he was miffed. He looked like the type of guy who wasn't used to girls forgetting his name and barely paying him any attention like Ariana had been doing for the last hour.

"Right." Ariana cocked her head to the side as she smiled at him, thinking he might be fun for a no-strings-attached hookup. He smiled back, looking as though he had won the jackpot being seated next to them.

Out of the corner of her eye, Ariana spotted a new group of guys arriving at the party. Her stomach tightened when she saw Lukas in her peripheral, looking even hotter than usual. Ariana noticed other girls at the party checking him out too, but his eyes scanned the backyard until they found hers and settled there. He stared at her like no one else mattered and a pulsing heat crept up Ariana's neck and thighs. Desire traced his eyes as he held her gaze.

"So, um, what sports do you play?" Sam/Jacob asked Ariana, attempting to drag her attention back to him.

"...Cheerleading," Ariana barely answered, forcing herself to look away from Lukas' intense stare. Now that Lukas was there, the Birchmond boy didn't interest her in the slightest. Sam/Jacob continued to talk at her as she looked back over to where Lukas and his friends had been, but he was nowhere in sight. Was he not going to say hi to her?

"I'll be back, I have to pee," Ariana said to the table.

She wandered inside, instantly relaxing. She loved Taron's house–it was bright, open, and decorated in almost all white furniture. She wound her way through the house until she reached the master bathroom. She jiggled the door handle only to find it locked.

Damn, Ariana thought. That was her favorite bathroom in the house because it contained a giant white-tiled jacuzzi tub. A faint giggle echoed from behind the door. Ariana thought it sounded vaguely like Kristin Long's annoying tone but she wasn't entirely sure. Ariana sighed. She hadn't needed to go to the bathroom in the first place though–if she was being truly honest with herself, her real intention was to see if she couldn't find Lukas to say hi, or at least to say *something*. She decided to search upstairs instead.

As she climbed the staircase, her phone vibrated in her hand.

10:36 p.m. Unknown: You look pretty tonight.
10:36 p.m. Ariana: Who is this?
10:37 p.m. Unknown: Lukas

Her heart soared. Ariana gripped the banister, stopping in her tracks as she reread the first message while grinning like an idiot. *Play it cool*, she thought.

10:37 p.m. Ariana: How'd you get my number?

She made her way up the stairs and found an empty bedroom to sit in while she waited to see what he would say.

10:39 p.m. Lukas: Where did you go?

Why hadn't he just come up and talked to her?

10:39 p.m. Ariana: I took a break from the party. I'm upstairs.
10:42 p.m. Lukas: I'll come find you.

A wave of excitement rushed over her. Had he been looking for her? Did he ask one of his friends for her number? Did he have feelings for her? She hoped he did because she knew she couldn't just be friends with him.

She had always dreamed of finding someone who could take away her pain. Maybe Lukas was the one. Like in the romance novels she read, he would sweep her off her feet and she would be so filled with love she wouldn't have space for the anxiety anymore. She wouldn't have the capacity to feel the loss or emptiness her father's death had left behind.

Ariana fidgeted with her shorts and took a few breaths, trying to calm her nerves. She couldn't decide if she should sit on the bed or the chair by the computer... or just stand up. But no, that might be awkward. She finally decided to stay on the bed, hoping it wouldn't look like she was being too forward.

The doorknob turned and Lukas entered the room. *God, why did he have to be so attractive?* His shirt hugged his body in all the right places. He raised his eyebrows as he looked at the bed, as if asking about her choice of seat. Ariana blushed.

"Um..." Ariana mumbled, her cheeks burning.

Lukas remained by the door for another moment, observing her, then made his way to the bed. Ariana realized she wouldn't want to be anywhere else in the world at this moment other than sitting next to Lukas, breathing the same air as he was. The right side of her body tingled from where he was almost touching her. She wanted to say something but was uncharacteristically shy now that he was so close.

"So, no one at the party interested you?" Lukas asked.

"What do you mean?"

He hesitated for a moment. "You just seem to have a lot of admirers. I was curious if you were interested in any of them in return."

Ariana cocked her head. Who was he referring to? Sam/Jacob from Birchmond? Had Lukas noticed him flirting with her? She couldn't very well tell Lukas that no one else interested her in the slightest anymore... not since she had met him.

"No, not really," Ariana said instead. She locked eyes with him. "Honestly, I've been a little preoccupied."

There. That wasn't too obvious and it still hinted at how she felt. Lukas grinned and her stomach tightened. He got even more attractive when he smiled like that, and he was smiling because of *her*. Ariana mirrored his grin and laughed a little.

"What are you doing on Thursday?" Lukas asked. His eyes trailed up and down her face as if he were memorizing her. Ariana's breath caught in her throat.

"Thursday? I don't know; we have cheer practice until 4:30," Ariana said, watching him closely still.

"After practice, I want to show you something."

"Okay." She wondered what it could be. Although she didn't care what they did, as long as she was with him again.

"Good. I was actually only stopping by tonight," Lukas said. "But I'll see you on Thursday."

Lukas stood to go, and Ariana scrunched up her forehead. He had to leave this soon?

"Where are you going?" she asked, trying and failing to hide the disappointed note in her voice.

"I've got other plans tonight; I really only came to see you," Lukas said, catching her off guard. "You do look very pretty, by the way. It's no wonder that guy couldn't keep his eyes off of you."

And with that, he left and disappeared down the stairs. Ariana's mouth dropped. What was that about? Was he *jealous*?

She stood, overjoyed with everything that had transpired. She waited a few more moments, basking in the notion of Lukas possibly wanting her back before rushing back to the party to tell Jade and Kiara everything.

CHAPTER 3
Jade

"Jade!! What're you still doing in bed?!" Jade's mother, Lenee Pierce, yelled in alarm. She stood in the doorway of Jade's room, her light-green eyes opened wide in a panic that her youngest daughter was about to be late to school for the umpteenth time. Lenee's dark brown hair fell in tangles down her shoulders and her bangs stuck out in all different directions as if she had only just managed to make it out of bed herself.

"Damn," Jade muttered. She yawned and stretched out in her queen-sized bed, still bleary. She must have slept through her alarms again. "Shit."

Somehow it was already Monday morning. The weekend had flown by entirely too fast in a blur of homework, annoying texts from Taron, occasionally thinking about Ian, and laying out by Kiara's pool. Overall nice, but uneventful.

"Morning, Mom. Your hair looks cute," Jade said. She rolled herself out of bed and onto the floor.

Lenee laughed at Jade's theatrics and smoothed her bangs down. "Thanks, honey."

Jade got up and made a beeline for her mom, hugging her good morning. Lenee kissed her forehead and then leaned back out of the doorway to address Jade's older sister. "Dani, you could have woken her up!"

Jade tensed up. *Oh no*, she thought. *Don't poke the bear.*

"She's not my responsibility, Mom, or my problem," Dani yelled from her room. Jade's stepdad, Vince, was already at work at this time or else Dani would have been slightly less rude, but not much.

"But she *is* your sister. You should help her," Lenee said as Dani walked into the hallway leading up to Jade's room. Jade winced. Not the best thing to say to Dani.

Dani leaned against the wall, crossing her arms over her chest while giving Jade an icy glare. She had long, strawberry blonde hair, an alabaster complexion, and honey-colored eyes. They looked nothing alike. There was even an ongoing joke around their school that Jade and Dani weren't really sisters, which Jade liked to fantasize about when Dani was being particularly mean.

"You have five minutes or I'm leaving without you," Dani said curtly to Jade before turning to address their mother. "See? I'm helping her. I gave her a warning."

As abruptly as she had come, Dani spun around and headed back to her room. Lenee let out a sigh of frustration, gave a weary smile to Jade, then hurried back downstairs.

"Gotta love Mondays," Jade said, sighing. She ran to her closet and pulled on a pair of pale blue distressed jeans and a blush-colored henley shirt. She brushed her teeth, pulled her hair into a messy bun, threw on hoop earrings and a little mascara, and shot down the stairs.

"Here you go," Lenee said while handing Jade an apple and almond butter. "Hurry! Dani is already in the car."

Jade kissed her mother goodbye and ran out the door, hopping into her sister's black SUV.

"You look like shit," Dani spat at Jade as she backed down the driveway.

Jade clamped her lips shut, knowing nothing she said–mean or nice–would do any good. Instead, she checked her phone and tried to make as little noise as possible while eating her apple, not daring to glance in Dani's direction or make any minuscule move that might provoke Dani into berating her.

I might just make it to school without an incident, Jade thought hopefully after some time had passed.

As if Dani could read her mind, she opened her mouth to slur an insult. "I heard a bunch of people talking shit about you over the weekend. You're really making a name for yourself as one of the sluttiest sophomores."

"What? Who was?" Jade asked, wondering if Dani was bluffing to get a rise out of her.

"People. Some of my friends, some of yours."

"But I haven't done anything... I mean, Taron and I kissed but that was it!" Jade said, mostly to herself.

"Yeah right. Everyone is saying you had a threesome with him and his friend from Birchmond at the party."

Jade's stomach dropped. Why did people continuously make up these lies about her? "Who's saying that?" she asked again, fighting to keep her voice calm.

"People. I believe it. And if you deny it, it'll only make you look more guilty."

Jade inhaled sharply. She wanted to kick and scream and punch out the windows. If she had actually done it, then fine, whatever, who cared who knew? It was her choice who she had sex with and she wouldn't be ashamed about it. But she *hadn't*, and that wasn't something she would do, and the lies weren't fair. She decided not to give Dani the satisfaction of a reaction and instead turned to look out the window at the world blurring by, out of her control.

They pulled up to the school and Jade snatched her things in an attempt to make a quick getaway. As she was about to close the door Dani snapped her fingers, effectively grabbing Jade's attention. The girls locked eyes and Dani smirked, knowing she'd won. "Seriously... I would be embarrassed if I were you."

Jade slammed the door shut and clenched her teeth. She took

a deep breath, holding it at the top, and as she exhaled she did her best to expel Dani's hurtful words from her mind. She hitched her black leather backpack up on her shoulder and made her way to the courtyard behind the school where everyone hung out. Jade found Kiara and Ariana easily enough, sitting with a group of sophomores at one of the large circular tables under the lush trees that dotted the lawn. There was no room next to her two best friends so Jade gave them a wave and sat by Aubrey, a former football player turned male cheerleader that had been on the Junior Varsity squad with them last year.

"Hey, J," Aubrey said with a smile. He was wearing a tight-fitting white tee, showing off his strong frame. Jade had met Aubrey their freshman year when he was still on the football team. Most of the girls had a crush on him, but Jade remembered noticing something safe in his smile that told her they would only ever be friends. "You look gorg today."

"Ha-ha, very funny. I overslept and had like five minutes to get ready."

"Well, that's the magic of being as stunning as you," Aubrey said, running a hand through his freshly-colored caramel hair.

Jade shook her head and gave a half-hearted smile. She glanced around the table, wondering who had already heard the rumor about her, and who, if any of them, had been talking shit about her like Dani claimed. Jade sighed and tuned into the conversation to distract herself.

"Well, Ari's a shoo-in of course," Aubrey said, referring to the upcoming cheer tryouts that began after school today. "Didn't you try out with a double-full last year?"

A flicker of nerves flashed through Jade, but she pushed them away easily enough. She knew that what she lacked in Ariana's skill of tumbling she made up for in dance.

Ariana blushed and nodded her head. "I bet we'll all make it again this year. They can't split up the Fresh Six."

The table laughed. Only three or four freshmen usually made the team, but last year she, Ariana, Kiara, Aubrey, Melodie, and

Reigh had all made it, which was a serious feat. They'd given themselves the stupid nickname shortly after.

"Which only leaves three spots for incoming freshmen on Junior Varsity," Reigh said, pushing her reddish-brown hair out of her sharp cheekbones and tucking it behind her ears.

"Jade in that low-cut uniform though! I could barely focus on the ball last season!" the quarterback of the Junior Varsity football team and serious man whore, Weston Kelly, announced.

Weston was as attractive as he was talented, with a cocky personality to match. He excelled in football, baseball, and essentially everything else he tried, including picking up girls. Jade was embarrassed to admit she had had a crush on Weston when they first met but quickly lost interest after learning how many girls he'd already hooked up with. Weston's closely shaven light-brown hair and defined jawline made him appear aggressive and strong, which, in almost all cases, he was. He wasn't used to girls turning him down, so Jade's refusal to fall all over him only seemed to pique his interest in her more. Jade winked at Weston just to screw with him, and his eyes widened momentarily before he shot her a sly smile.

"Man, gross. The girls are like our sisters," Haiden said, swiping a couple of dark tendrils out of his eyes. "The freshmen, on the other hand..."

The guys at the table continued to rate the various uniforms the cheerleaders wore in the past year. Jade rolled her eyes.

Aubrey leaned over and showed Jade a picture of himself in one of the girl's uniforms taken last year at Kiara's house. He was posing seductively, his blue eyes teasing the viewer. "I swear I'm about to send this to the guys–maybe that'll shut down their OBNOXIOUS UNIFORM RATING," Aubrey said, shouting the last few words.

"*Please* do," Jade said.

"Guys," Aubrey called out. "If you don't shut up, I'm going to send you a picture of me in the same skirt and top, forever scarring your minds!"

"Promise?" Haiden said, chuckling.

"He looks insanely sexy in our uniform, I'd watch out," Kiara called over the commotion.

Weston strolled around the table and snatched the phone from Aubrey's hands in one fell swoop.

"Bro, I'm not even gay and I think you look good," Weston said, seeming to know what Aubrey was attempting to do and not taking the bait.

Haiden lifted the phone from Weston, eager to get in on the joke. "Yeah, you look seriously jacked."

"You two are impossible," Aubrey said with a dramatic sigh, grabbing his phone back. With a small smile, he turned to Jade. "Well, I tried."

Jade smiled despite the knot twisting in her stomach that had been growing since the car ride. The guys could be impossible, but she loved how much they had accepted Aubrey's not-so-surprising-in-hindsight news after he came out last year. They were more upset about losing Aubrey as a running back than anything else. As Weston liked to tease, Aubrey batting for the other team only meant less competition and more girls for the rest of the guys, and most importantly, more girls for Weston. Some of the other students hadn't been as welcoming though, and Aubrey had gotten jumped a few times after the news spread. That is, until Weston and Haiden made it publicly known that anyone that messed with Aubrey would be socially ostracized.

Jade looked up and laughed. The boys were now rolling around in the grass, with Aubrey holding Weston in a headlock while Haiden videoed the scuffle and put it on his Instagram story.

"Tag me in that!" Aubrey yelled just before Weston elbowed him in the shin.

"Hashtag idiots," Haiden said under his breath, typing away on his phone.

"Now *that's* a memoir title for the boys," Ariana said to Jade and Kiara.

Jade wanted to talk to Ariana and Kiara about the rumor, but it would be nearly impossible without the rest of the table overhearing. She definitely didn't want to do anything that might spread it further, and there was no point in hanging around to talk about who may or may not make the cheer team. Right now, that seemed trivial. Soon–by the middle of the week probably–everyone, including Ian, would likely hear the rumor that she had sex with Taron and his random friend at the same time. Jade cringed at the thought. She pulled her backpack on, getting ready to head off to her first class early.

At that moment, Melodie's voice rose above the commotion. "I would be pissed if Arica or Lexi made the team... I mean, they *can't* even dance."

Leave it to Melodie to list out the girls she hoped *wouldn't* make the team. Jade was sure her name was also on that list, but Melodie knew better than to say anything in front of the group, especially Ariana and Kiara. Jade's defenses flared. Who did Melodie think she was to bash girls who weren't there to defend themselves? Her fists clenched involuntarily.

"Melodie," Jade said, her stone-cold voice cutting Melodie off mid-sentence. "You're not in charge of who makes the team or not–*thank God*–so what's the point of this? Other than you being a bitch to get attention, of course."

Jade heard a hushed "Oooohhh" from Weston. Before Melodie had the chance to respond, Jade left the table, ignoring Ariana calling out after her. She wound her way inside through the throngs of students, working on slowing her breathing again while she walked, trying to push the entire morning out of her mind.

History was a subject that Jade usually enjoyed, finding the different time periods and ways of the past wild, often wondering what her friends would do in situations like the roaring 1920s and prohibition. Jade also had this class period with Alora, who never seemed to know or care about what rumor was going around.

"Hey, you!" Alora said when Jade sat down, her light-brown

face clear of makeup. Alora did a double-take and quickly changed her tone when she saw Jade's expression. "Oh no, Dani again?"

Alora's glossy black hair fell into her eyes as she leaned closer to Jade to talk.

"Yep," Jade said, looking at the floor. "And I think I just took it out on Melodie a bit."

"Well, let's be honest–Melodie probably did something to deserve that," Alora said with a small laugh.

"Eh... I was pretty harsh," Jade said, biting her bottom lip.

"Want to talk about it?"

"Nope."

"All right, but I do want to say something," Alora looked Jade in the eye. "I know what Dani tries to do to you–Melodie too. But don't listen to her or anybody else that tries to hurt you. You know what they say is more about them than it is about you, right?"

"What do you mean?"

"Whatever they're saying or how they're reacting to you isn't *actually* about you. It's about themselves."

"But it *is* about me," Jade said, confused.

Alora shook her head. "Okay, for example, you wouldn't be upset if I landed the lead role in the play this year, right?"

"No, are you kidding? I'd be beyond happy for you. Just like I was when you got it last year."

"Right, but then there are others who'd be pissed if I got it."

"Sure, but I'm also not in theatre. If they're going up against you for the role I could see people getting jealous."

"I'm not necessarily talking about people who're going up against me. People not in theatre may get upset because, say, they wanted the lead to go to a guy because they think males make better actors or something silly like that. Or someone might get upset because they wanted the lead to be a different ethnicity than me, maybe their own ethnicity because they feel they haven't been portrayed enough in our school plays. I can't help that I'm not a guy, and I can't help that I'm Hispanic and not something else. So, even though they don't want me to be the lead, it's not necessarily about me personally. It's about them and their beliefs."

"I'm still not totally following, A," Jade said, squinting her eyes as if that would help her concentrate. She knew what Alora was trying to tell her was very important, maybe even life-changing, but she couldn't quite grasp the concept. "Dani's calling me a slut for a bullshit rumor going around about me having a threesome. How is that about her, or any of the other people who are saying I had sex with Taron and his friend this weekend?"

"Egh," Alora said, grimacing. "I'm sorry, J. That's so stupid. I know it hurts though. Okay, in your specific example, maybe some people will talk about you and call you a slut for this because their parents raised them to think of women in that way if they're open with their sexuality. Maybe some girls will spread the rumor about you even more because they wish they could be more promiscuous, but they won't let themselves and so they get jealous and want to hurt you. Maybe they get mad just because you're beautiful, and they don't see themselves in that way yet. Dani is a whole other story–she's your sister and there's going to be added competition there. I'm not saying any of it's right, but it's about understanding how others see the world, and maybe even how their parents see the world."

Jade put her head in her hands to think. "Dude. How do you know all of this?"

"I don't know, I listen to a lot of podcasts," Alora said, laughing. She began to play with a gold ring on her finger, twisting it around as her eyebrows furrowed. "Also, last year when I got the lead in the play as a freshman it sucked, because so many people were angry and talking shit about me. I got depressed and I had to find reasoning for it. So even though it was a shitty time, I figured out a lot. It's freeing if you understand that what people say about you isn't actually about you."

"Wait, I never knew that." Jade reached out and grabbed her

friend's hand. "I had no idea you were depressed after you got the lead. I thought you were so happy."

"Yeah, life is funny like that, right?" Alora said. "I didn't want to tell anyone I got depressed after, because I didn't want to seem ungrateful when I had something so many people wanted. But it was hard."

"Wow. So that's why you don't care about rumors. I always thought you were just born that much of a badass."

Alora laughed and shook her head, any trace of leftover sadness leaving her eyes.

"And thank you for telling me," Jade added. For the first time since she woke up today, her body fully relaxed.

"I'm just telling you the truth you can't see," Alora responded. She brushed her hair out of her face and looked down at the assignment on their desks with determination. "Now let's get this fucker over with."

Jade laughed at Alora's quick change from sage advisor to normal high school student, and relief washed over her. She was lighter now, even though she hadn't completely shaken off the weight of the impending rumor mill. But there was logic in Alora's reasoning–she could at least see that. And if Ian happened to hear about her "sexual encounter" with Taron and his friend, well then fuck it. It was probably better that he did.

Then, she could see his true colors.

CHAPTER 4

A, K, J

Ariana pulled out her phone. The final bell had just rung, and there were forty-five minutes of free time until practice for the upcoming cheer tryouts.

3:25 p.m. Ariana: What do you guys want to do before practice?
3:25 p.m. Jade: Ugh bad day. Anything away from school.
3:26 p.m. Kiara: Oh no. What happened?
3:26 p.m. Jade: The rumor is that I had sex with Taron and his friend last weekend
3:26 p.m. Ariana: Oh J...
3:26 p.m. Jade: At the same time.
3:26 p.m. Kiara: Your real friends know that's not true.
3:27 p.m. Jade: Yeah. Still blows.
3:27 p.m. Kiara: Wait. I'm a genius. Let's run to my place and smoke just a little before practice. It'll be fun & get ur mind off things.
3:27 p.m. Jade: Haha oh man. I can't tell if ur a genius or insane but you know what. Who cares? Lets do it.
3:29 p.m. Ariana: Umm...
3:29 p.m. Kiara: Oh come on. Tryouts practice is so fing easy. You could do that shit in your sleep Ari. Plz?

3:29 p.m. Jade: Plzzzzzzz Ari
3:31 p.m. Ariana: FINE. But can we smoke something really mellow K?
3:31 p.m. Kiara: Yes! I've got y'all

Ariana grabbed the aquamarine dolphin-shaped pipe from Kiara, drawing in the tiniest inhale possible. Ariana's relationship with marijuana was a tumultuous one–she had either absolutely the best or the most horrible time ever, depending on if her anxiety decided to make an appearance and take over her mind or not.

Kiara laughed. "Ari, it's such a mellow Sativa. Take another hit, you're not even going to feel that baby one."

Ariana put her lips on the nose of the dolphin. She drew a breath and felt the hot smoke make its way to her lungs. She coughed, her nostrils burning.

"Hell yeah, Ari!" Jade said from the bed, her speech slightly slurred. Jade had already taken three hits and Kiara double that amount.

Ariana rolled onto her back on the bed next to Jade. Jade's arm brushed against hers and her skin tingled with pleasure. "Mmm."

Kiara squished between them and took both of their hands in hers. "This is nice." Kiara shimmied her butt to make more room for herself and the girls burst out laughing.

"Stop, K!" Ariana finally said when she had quelled her laughter. "I'm like... *super* high. Is this normal?"

"Yeah, me too," Jade said, sounding like she needed water.

"I mean, I gave us the most chill strain I have," Kiara said. She stood and absentmindedly picked the canister up, reading the label. Kiara's blue-green eyes widened, then she abruptly set the canister back down.

"Kiara," Ariana said, worried.

"Yes? No. Everything's fine," Kiara said.

"*Kiara...*" Jade and Ariana said in unison.

"So... I may have given us the wrong strain," Kiara said.

"WHAT!" Ariana shouted.

"Yes, um... yep. It's the wrong weed," Kiara said with a nod of her head. "But don't worry chickadees, this bud will open your third eye to possibilities you didn't see before."

"I'm gonna open your third eye, K," Jade said, attempting to reproach her, but then they all burst out laughing again. Kiara laid down and rolled over toward Ariana. A whiff of her vanilla-scented shampoo filled Ariana's nose.

"Dude..." Kiara said to Ariana in what seemed like slow motion. "Your eyes are sooo red."

Kiara's own eyes were barely slivers.

"That's literally not helpful at all," Ariana said. Kiara burst out laughing.

"Eye... eye drops!" Jade struggled to say as she sat up on her elbows. "We need eye drops."

"Aye aye captain," Ariana said, giggling. What were they, sailors? How many times had they all said "eye" in the last minute?

Kiara didn't respond. She had a seriously spaced-out look on her face. Ariana could guess where this was heading.

"Do you ever think that the government–" Kiara began, but Ariana stopped her.

"NO! No conspiracy theories now, K. We have to..." Ariana trailed off, forgetting what she was trying to urgently say.

Ariana looked to Jade for help, but Jade was intently rubbing her hands back and forth across the golden bedspread, smiling to herself. "Ari, this bedspread reminds me of your hair in the sun..." Jade said. "Do you know what I mean? It's not *like* your hair, it IS your hair..."

Ariana could feel her own eyes widen. They were so screwed. Kiara reached over and patted her on the head. "It'll be fine. Just leave everything to me," she said in a consoling voice, seeming to have returned to reality. She glided from the room, smiling and humming. Ariana prayed she was going to procure eye drops.

Kiara came back a few minutes later with a tray of so-called remedies. "Sit up, girls. Drink this tea and take these vitamins." She handed them each a cup and a couple of round pills.

"How is this going to help?" Ariana muttered.

"Just *believe*," Kiara said, leaning Jade's head back to administer eye drops.

After nearly poking Ariana's eye out with the bottle, Kiara held up a mirror. "See? Much better."

Ariana's eyes were still shining and red. She looked like a puffy hedgehog after a long nap.

Kiara took another look at Ariana. "Wait, never mind," she said, cracking up.

Jade burst out laughing from behind them. "Sunglasses?"

Fifteen minutes later they were standing in Kiara's front yard, miraculously dressed and ready for practice in their black workout shorts and white tanks.

"Okay, remember: everyone talk as little as possible once we get there," Ariana instructed.

They set off toward the school with Ariana in the lead. She was so intensely concentrating on putting one foot in front of the other that the sudden outburst of laughter from behind made her jump. She whipped around to see Jade laughing so hard that she was rolling around in the neighbor's yard and Kiara bent over double.

"What!?" Ariana yelled.

"You're walking like a moon man!" Kiara spit out, roaring with laughter all over again.

"What's a moon man?" Ariana asked in confusion. She thought she had been walking fine.

"Like a man on the moon!" Kiara said as if it made perfect sense. When Ariana showed no signs of recognition, Kiara imitated her, walking slowly and picking her knees all the way up every time she took a step.

"Oh my God, I really can't walk!" Ariana said, her heart rate accelerating. "Guys..." she heard the panicked note in her voice.

Jade reacted to Ariana's distress immediately, composing herself and picking her perfect ass up off the neighbor's yard to jog to Ariana's side.

"Just breathe," Jade said. She lifted her aviator sunglasses to sit on top of her head and made eye contact with Ariana. She slid her arm around Ariana's waist, her warm hand touching Ariana's bare skin, and smiled. Her piercing green eyes offered tacit encouragement. "I've got you."

An immediate calm enveloped Ariana–maybe they *could* pull this off. Kiara led the way toward the school. A few minutes later, they stopped outside the doors leading into the gym. "Okay, ready?" Kiara asked.

Ariana and Jade nodded.

They opened the doors, took one step inside, and stopped short. All the cheerleaders had already been put into groups to begin practice. This seemed to be too much for any of the girls' oxygen-deprived brains to comprehend because none of them moved. Ariana's brain was mush. What were they supposed to do now? Everyone was staring at them, including their cheer coach, and Ariana had just remembered they all still had their sunglasses on. Indoors.

Great.

"Greetings, earthlings!" Kiara called out, slowly waving her hand.

Oh. My. God. We're done for–we are dead, Ariana thought. A few of the cheerleaders started laughing; some of the bitchier older girls simply glared at them. Reigh and Aubrey seemed to realize the situation was about to become dire if someone didn't step in to help them because at the same moment they both sprung into action.

Reigh called out for the girls to stop goofing around and trying to delay practice, while Aubrey jumped up and went to them, guiding them back to where he and Reigh were sitting.

After taking a seat, Ariana looked toward their cheer coach, Coach Krall, to see if she had noticed anything off, but the coach's attention seemed to be elsewhere as she talked to a Varsity cheerleader on the other side of the gym.

"Thank you... you saved us," Ariana said gratefully to Reigh and Aubrey.

"Sure. But Ari, why were you walking like that?" Reigh whispered so that only they could hear.

"Oh no," Ariana said, feeling like a complete idiot. "I was doing it again?"

This sent Jade and Kiara into another fit of hysterical laughter.

Aubrey looked at them like they were half insane. "I don't know what y'all are smoking, but I want some," he said with a laugh.

* * *

Kiara watched Jade gracefully float through the motions of a cheer while looking only slightly spaced out. She giggled, causing Jade to stick out her tongue pointedly in Kiara's direction. Ariana shushed the girls, shooting them a warning glare. They had placed themselves in the back row during practice, staying out of everyone's way as they attempted to look and act normal while waiting for the effects of the weed to wear off.

Ariana pulled Coach Krall to the side and spoke in a hushed tone. "I don't know how I did it, but I was practicing so much that I hurt my knees. I know all the cheers already–can I go ice in the sports doctor's office?" Ariana rubbed her knees as she spoke.

"Oh good for you, Ari. Yes, go! I hope you feel better," Krall gushed.

Sucker, Kiara thought.

Coach Krall, or simply "Krall" as she insisted they call her, was an easy target for Ariana's influence. She was only ten years their senior and had an odd obsession with popularity and the girls' lives, which, although it freaked Kiara out, worked in their favor as she, Ariana, and Jade were some of Krall's favorites.

Ariana smirked at Kiara on her way out of the gym, and Kiara bit her tongue to keep from laughing while Krall's eyes were still on her. Kiara admired Ariana for being so quick on her feet–metaphorically of course in this scenario–Ariana had just covered why she was walking so weirdly *and* managed to get herself out of practice at the same time.

Kiara returned her attention to practice, thinking of how boring their cheers were. She had once seen a show in which a woman made up interpretive dances to poems–now *that* was interesting. Kiara shrugged to herself. Why not? She closed her eyes and began an interpretative dance version of the classic "Be Aggressive" cheer they were taught each year. She let her limbs move freely to the beat of the other cheerleaders' claps and got lost in the rhythm.

A minute or two later Kiara heard Jade's chiming laugh and opened an eye. Jade had her hands on her knees as she watched Kiara, who was now crawling on the ground like a tiger.

"Kiara!" Krall shrieked.

Their friends laughed while the freshmen looked around, confused.

"Should we be doing that?" a young-looking freshman with strawberry-blonde hair asked, a serious expression on her face.

"No, please, please do *not* do that," Krall said, changing her tone to playful when the seniors behind her began to laugh.

"Thank God this is what you normally act like," Jade whispered to Kiara.

"Thank you for the break in seriousness, Kiara," Krall said. "But everyone, go back to work on your cheers now. K, please stick to the normal cheers."

"Back to the boring stuff, got it," Kiara said through a smile. She imagined a squad of interpretive dancers at the games instead of cheerleaders. What a fun world that would be.

As the monotonous drills wore on, Kiara let her mind drift

farther away from Krall and cheer practice. She thought back to last night when Teague had come over for dinner. Her parents had prepared steaks for the main course, with salads and steamed veggies for sides.

"I'm giving up meat," Kiara said when her mother went to serve her. "Put it on Teague's plate, Mom."

"Since when?" her dad asked.

"Since I don't want to kill the planet," Kiara said.

"Well, that's definitely a good reason," her dad said, laughing.

Eating only salad and veggies for dinner would keep her a little below her allotted daily calorie intake. Encouraged by the pounds she had already lost in the last month, Kiara would try to dip under her number as often as she could. When she ate fewer calories than she had planned, she considered that a *very good* day.

After dinner, Kiara and Teague excused themselves at the chance to be alone. They made their way upstairs to Kiara's room, climbing out of her window and onto the flat portion of her roof to look at the stars. Kiara laid down to get a better view of the sky while Teague kept his eyes trained on her.

"Don't you want to look?" Kiara asked, taking in his dark, angular face and dimples.

"I *am* looking," Teague said. "You're a better view than the stars."

He smiled at Kiara like he had the first time he asked her out, making her insides twist in a delicious way. Teague's expression was a mixture of desire and cockiness, like he already knew her answer to some question he hadn't asked yet. He ran his fingers from her stomach up to her chest and back down again, each time stopping a little further down in her shorts, turning Kiara on more with each sweep of his fingers. After a few minutes, Kiara's groin was on fire and she felt like ripping her clothes off and telling him to take her, right there.

But, her parents were home and she didn't exactly want her mom walking in on *that* sight. Instead, Kiara grabbed Teague's hand and pushed it down her shorts, a devilish grin on her face.

Teague let out a groan in surprise. She linked her arms around his neck, pulling his face to hers and kissing him deeply until he finally had to go. Kiara knew she was ready to have sex with Teague, she just didn't know when or where.

A flurry of activity in the gym brought Kiara out of her memory. Practice had come to an end and everyone was collecting their belongings.

"Why are you smiling like that, K?" Jade nudged her with a knowing grin. "Were you fantasizing about T?"

Kiara grinned back. "Maybe."

Ariana walked into the gym toward them, normally this time, with a scowl on her face. Kiara couldn't help but giggle.

"Never. Again." Ariana said sternly.

"Oh, it was fine!" Kiara protested.

"You got out of practice altogether and didn't even break a sweat Ari–look at how well you made out in the situation," Jade joked. A light layer of perspiration shone on Jade's brow. Of course she still looked like a supermodel, but that wasn't the point.

"I don't think you realize how much deep shit we were almost in... what we did was so stupid," Ariana said.

"What was stupid?" Krall asked, popping up behind the girls and putting her arms around Jade and Ariana.

"Nothing!" Ariana and Jade chimed together.

Jade trailed behind Ariana and Kiara as they walked through the back parking lot by the football field, letting her cheer shoes scrape against the concrete with each step. Tryouts were such a bore–if she had her way, they would have practice outside so she could ogle the football players as they raced across the field in their tight-fitting athletic pants.

Jade tried to spot Ian on the field. She wanted to feel his eyes on her again; she was craving that feeling he had stirred in her on

Friday night. But she also wanted more than that–she wanted him to get to know her before he knew her through other people. Would he like what was underneath her looks? She thought of Dani's eyes when she had called Jade a slut this morning. They had been so cold. So sure of it. This was probably around the fifteenth rumor about her supposed sexual escapades since Jade had started high school, so others would be sure of it as well.

A loud smack on the field and a grunt from one of the players caught Jade's attention. She whipped around to spot Weston standing over a player twice his size.

"OOOOH!" Kiara yelled in awe. Ariana laughed automatically and then clapped her hand over her mouth.

"Holy shit. Was that West?" Jade asked.

"Yep," Kiara answered. "That's our West all right."

"Damn," Jade said, her voice giving away a note of awe. Kiara smirked at her and then continued walking a few steps ahead with Ariana. Jade watched Weston help the larger player up. They bumped fists and the larger player ran down the field. Weston took his helmet off and turned, looking directly at Jade. He smiled while running a hand over his head. Jade grinned back at him and shook her head.

Before their eye contact lasted for too long, Jade turned on her heel and jogged to catch up with Ariana and Kiara. "Hey," she said, having a burst of inspiration. "Want to watch the rest of football practice?"

"Why not?" Ariana said, squinting up at the sky. "We can get some sun."

"Doesn't matter to me," Kiara said.

Jade grinned–now she could spy on Ian easily. And maybe he would see her too. She had worn one of her favorite teal sports bras today, and she couldn't help but wonder what he would think of it.

The three girls walked along the backside of the field to the bleachers and plunked their bags down, claiming a spot toward the middle. There were a few groups scattered around the bleachers. Jade recognized a brunette with freckles dotting her face from an algebra class they had taken together last year, sitting with a group of sophomore girls Jade only vaguely knew. The brunette's name was Holly, and they had been friendly enough. Right as Jade was about to wave, Holly scrunched up her nose and turned to her friends, seemingly to tell a story. The girls laughed as Holly spoke, turning to sneak glances at Jade every few moments, their eyes judging and sizing her up. Jade's insides boiled–Holly and her friends had better chill out unless they wanted Jade to come down on them. Her muscles tensed as she got ready to stand up. If that little scene was what she thought it was...

"Ahh, isn't this nice?" Ariana said, breaking Jade's train of thought.

"AAAAAHHHH," Kiara let out a ridiculously loud sigh of pleasure in agreement. Despite herself, Jade laughed, effectively cooling the rising anger in her bones. She turned back to the group of girls, who were now focused on the football field, giggling any time one of the players ran close to the bleachers.

Why should I worry about what they think? Jade thought. It's not like she would change their minds by yelling at them. And besides, she wanted to enjoy this moment, not spend it worrying about some girls she didn't even know, and that didn't truly know her. *And if they don't know me, then maybe it is more about them than me,* Jade thought as she stretched out and scanned the field, determined to spot Ian's butt in football tights.

A few minutes later she found him and her stomach did a flip when she saw that he was staring directly at her. He was tall and lean in his uniform but built at the same time. Ian's lips slowly parted into a sexy smile as he continued to stare, and Jade returned his smile, her head woozy like she had a slight buzz. After a moment, Ian turned and ran back down the field, leaving Jade smiling at no one with her cheeks burning. She checked herself, glancing at Ariana and Kiara to see if they had noticed, but Ariana was busy reading 1984 by George Orwell and Kiara had laid out on the bleachers with her eyes closed, her headphones surely spouting some Krishna chanting music.

Relaxing, Jade smiled again and fished her phone out of her bag, searching through her music for a song that sounded like Ian until she stopped on "Awake and Pretty Much Sober" by The Violents and Monica Martin. Ian was entertaining to watch–he was quick yet graceful on the field and no one seemed quite able to catch him. The plays slowly moved toward the bleachers, and Ian looked up at Jade now and again, each time smiling a little more when he saw her looking at him, too.

Kiara sat up. "I'm getting hot," she said, wiping her glistening forehead. "Are you both ready?"

Jade nodded reluctantly as Ariana packed up her books. The girls began their descent with Ariana in front when Holly stood up and blocked their path as her friends looked on.

"Hey, Ari," Holly said.

Jade's insides were immediately boiling again. This girl thought she could talk shit and then come up and speak to her friends minutes later with no repercussions?

"Only our *friends* call her Ari," Jade said, her voice as sharp as a razor.

The color drained from Holly's face. She glanced back at her friends, looking embarrassed. Ariana shot Jade a look but Jade didn't move her eyes from Holly. Funny that the girl's freckled features seemed sweet and innocent up close.

"Sorry. I mean, I meant, Ariana," Holly stammered.

"Hey Holly, don't worry about her," Ariana said in a coaxing voice. "What's up?"

"Nothing," Holly said, barely audible.

"Hi, Holly!" Kiara said brightly from behind Jade. Jade felt a sharp pinch on her back, but she didn't give in and apologize.

"Hi, Kiara. Um, I wanted to say good luck with cheer tryouts. And I'm having a party in a few weeks that I wanted to invite you all to," Holly said, keeping her eyes on the ground.

"Oh, that's sweet, thank you," Ariana said, smiling. "We'll try to stop by."

"Okay," Holly said, looking up again. She didn't meet Jade's eyes. She seemed like she wanted to say something else but then muttered a hasty goodbye and quickly sat down with her friends.

"What was that, Jade?" Ariana asked once they had descended the bleachers.

"What's your read on her, Ari?" Jade asked, ignoring the question.

"Holly? Why?" Ariana asked, her head tilting in surprise.

"Yeah." Jade ignored the question again.

"I think she's a little lost right now. I heard she's going through a rough time at home. Her dad turned to drinking and messing with pills after losing his job and her mom is trying to help him but also get a divorce at the same time. It'd be nice if we went to her party... and were nice to her in general."

"Shit," Jade said.

"Yeah," Ariana said. Her eyes ran over Jade's face, then turned soft. "Are you okay?"

"Yeah. I just fucked up, is all," Jade said.

Jade's mind raced. The girl hadn't deserved that. Not that Holly's behavior should be excused, if it had even been what Jade had thought it was, but at least Jade understood now. She knew what it was like to have chaos at home and have the anger and emotions bleeding uncontrollably into school.

Jade decided to be nicer than usual when she saw Holly now. She let out a breath as a little weight lifted off her shoulders. She followed Ariana and Kiara away from the field, but not before turning to look for Ian one more time.

The players were further down the field again but she could have sworn she saw Ian following her with his eyes, watching her leave.

CHAPTER 5
Kiara

Kiara sat on the edge of her gold comforter on Wednesday night, listening to Vallis Alps as she pondered what she was about to do. She took a deep breath, inhaling the candles lit around her room before chuckling to herself. Teague was going to lose his mind. She rubbed her hands over her goosebump-dotted legs. Her phone vibrated from the bedside table, kicking her nerves into full gear.

8:28 p.m. Teague: I'm on my way over baby girl. Can't wait to see the surprise.

Oh, he was in for a surprise all right. Her parents had gone out for dinner and Kiara had decided on a whim that she and Teague had done enough waiting. And why not just do it on a random school night? Kiara didn't want to plan it all out and try to make it perfect. Life wasn't perfect. Life was about seizing opportunities and having fun along the way. She also thought it would be way more fun to catch Teague off guard, which was why she'd told him she had a "little" surprise for him, when in reality she planned on greeting him completely naked and letting him figure out the rest from there.

8:30 p.m. Kiara: Just come in when you get here!

Kiara stripped off her clothes and pushed them under the bed. Now what? She shifted her weight from one foot to the other–she'd waited so long for this. She grinned to herself. She couldn't believe was about to have sex with Teague, the boy who had seemed so unattainable when they met, the boy who had captured her heart from their first interaction. Now, here they were. She lay back on her bed, stretching her arms out behind her head. Normally she might smoke to calm her nerves, but she was enjoying the excitement coursing through her body too much. Plus she didn't want to be high for their first time. She wanted to be fully herself and feel and remember every moment of it.

Kiara glanced at her phone. Jade and Ariana didn't know her plan yet–she'd wanted to keep it to herself for a while, but now she couldn't wait. She grabbed the device and started typing in their group text.

8:33 p.m. Kiara: So... quick heads up–I decided to have sex with T tonight! Lol he's otw over
8:33 p.m. Jade: OMG What?!! Does he know yet?
8:34 p.m. Ariana: Use protection!

Kiara laughed and some of her nerves disappeared–of course *that* would be Ariana's first thought.

8:34 p.m. Kiara: T doesn't know yet. Answering the door naked and let him figure it out ;) will use protection mom.
8:35 p.m. Ariana: v funny. But holy shit! So excited for you
8:35 p.m. Jade: Hell yes! Love the delivery haha
8:36 p.m. Kiara: Ok I have to go. He should be here any minute. Love you guys
8:36 p.m. Jade: We love you!! Tell us all about it after! xx

Kiara slipped her phone back onto the bedside table after

putting it on silent. "Young" came on her speakers–one of her favorites from Vallis Alps. She heard the front door open and her heart began to sprint.

"Kiara?" Teague called from downstairs. A sharp pang of adrenaline shot through her at the sound of his voice.

"Up here!"

Teague's footsteps echoed down the hallway. Kiara gulped. She stood and took one last glance in the mirror, thinking how wild it was that the next time she looked at her face, she would know what it felt like to have sex. She had let her long, ash-blonde hair down and it almost fully covered her small breasts. Her blue-green eyes were glowing and her cheeks flushed–she looked like a siren, waiting to seduce Teague for her own benefit.

Kiara took a long drag of air to steady herself and put her hands on her hips. Teague pushed through the door, but he was looking at his phone, distracted.

"Eh hem," Kiara cleared her throat playfully.

She stared at the top of Teague's head until he looked up. His reaction was almost cartoon-like: his mouth dropped just about as quickly as his phone fell to the floor; his eyes looked like they were about to pop out of his head. Kiara laughed at Teague as his eyes devoured her body.

"Hi," Kiara said, her voice shaking and betraying her composure.

"Oh. My. God," Teague mumbled, grabbing for her and kissing her hard, holding her head with one hand while the other slid down her back. Kiara was greedy for his touch; she wanted his hands to explore the rest of her body. She realized Teague didn't know he had permission yet, so she took a step toward the bed, bringing him with her.

He stopped abruptly and pulled away, his deep brown eyes locking with hers right as they lit up as if he'd solved a riddle. "You're ready? Now?"

"Now," Kiara whispered. As Teague started to undress, her excitement elevated along with her nerves. Teague had done this before with a few different girls. She must've frowned at that thought because Teague stopped unbuttoning his pants and sat her on the bed.

"Hey," he said softly. "This feels like my first time, Kiara, because it's with you." He lifted her chin and kissed her. "Honestly, I bet I'm more nervous than you are right now." He let out a laugh.

Kiara's heart sang and her groin twisted with a delicious sensation. She tackled him onto the bed, all inhibitions long gone. She wanted this with him so badly. Teague finished taking off his pants as she grabbed a condom from her bedside drawer. She'd known this would happen soon and had prepared.

With a ripping noise, Teague opened the condom wrapper and slipped it on. He positioned himself over Kiara with one muscular arm on either side of her. She couldn't believe this was it–she was about to do it in a matter of seconds. She looked up at his face and her mind quieted. Everything just made sense with Teague. He stared down at her, half-smiling, and Kiara gave a little nod.

"Tell me if it hurts," Teague said seriously, and then slowly eased himself inside of her.

"Oh!" A few moments of sharp, searing pain overwhelmed her.

Teague stilled, but Kiara nodded at him to keep going. He kissed her shoulder and then began carefully pushing deeper inside of her, creating a new, odd sensation in her abdomen. She felt full–overly full even. It was uncomfortable but not too painful.

Teague kissed her on the lips, pulled himself out, and then began to push in again. He let out a slight groan this time and the noise spiked her arousal.

"Faster," she said, her voice breathless. She wanted to feel him, all of him. He sped up his pace and began to groan with almost every thrust into her, each time turning her on more. Kiara was getting used to the full feeling, and it was beginning to feel good in a way that she'd never experienced before. She had a small bullet vibrator and was used to getting herself off with it, but Teague was hitting a spot inside of her that felt completely different. Kiara moaned and wrapped her legs around him, pulling him further into her.

"Kiara, you're going to make me..."

"I want you to," Kiara whispered and pulled his face toward hers to kiss him again.

Teague thrust into her all the way and held himself there, letting out a moan as he came. He stayed still for a moment, breathing heavily, then slowly pulled himself out and laid his slightly damp head on her chest. Kiara cradled his head with her arms, doing her best to memorize everything about the moment.

"I'm sorry that was so fast," Teague said a little timidly. "That was so different from any other time Kiara. That was incredible."

"No! Don't be sorry," she said, tracing her fingers over his back and smiling. "That was perfect."

"Did it hurt?" he asked.

"It only stung every once in a while," Kiara said. "And it felt uncomfortable, but it wasn't overwhelming pain. Only a little at the beginning."

"Hmm. I'm glad," Teague murmured. "I love you."

"I know," Kiara said, happiness humming through her. "I love you, too."

Kiara's mind wandered. She remembered reading in an article that only about 30% of women under the age of 25 could reach climax from the G-spot during intercourse. She thought that was a terrible statistic, and who knew if it was true or not, but she decided not to be one of the 70% that couldn't do it. "Hey," she lifted Teague's chin with her hand. "Are you up for round two?"

Teague's eyes lit up like he'd won the lottery. "You can't be serious," he said. "You really want to go again?"

"Yep," she said, sitting up and twisting her blonde hair into a bun.

"Okay, I'm going to need some water and... I don't know, a

protein bar or something?" Teague laughed. "You're gonna wear me out!"

"Come on." Kiara grabbed Teague's hand and pulled him out of bed. "Let's get you hydrated."

They stumbled around each other, not caring that they were naked and not being able to stop touching one another. Teague kissed every exposed part of her bare skin he could. Kiara's body tingled with electricity. She'd never felt closer to Teague. She grabbed a bottle of coconut water from the kitchen and tossed it to him. Teague took a few huge gulps and set it on the coffee table before pulling Kiara to him. Her body ached slightly, but not so much that it was painful. Teague sat her down with him on the couch and held her in his lap as she turned and kissed his neck. He let out a moan and turned her face to his, the passion reignited. She grabbed at his face, trying to get as close to him as possible.

"Whoa... yep, I'm ready!" Teague scooped Kiara in his arms and brought her upstairs again, kissing her forehead, cheeks, lips, and neck all the while.

"Mmm, you always smell like vanilla," he said. "How did I find you?"

"We were best friends in a past life," Kiara said, certain. "We found each other."

Teague kissed her nose. Kiara couldn't stop smiling–she never imagined life could be this good.

CHAPTER 6

A, J, K

"You had an orgasm your FIRST TIME?!" Ariana yelled across the lunch table on Thursday afternoon. She laughed and brought a hand over her mouth after realizing how loud she had been. "I didn't even know that was possible," she whispered.

"Well, technically it was my second time..." Kiara trailed off. She wore an oversized white tee that kept slipping down her shoulder, giving a peep of the mint-colored lacy bralette she wore. Ariana didn't know if it was because she knew Kiara had now had sex, but she thought Kiara looked more experienced somehow, and maybe a little older.

Ariana, Jade, and Kiara had gotten to lunch a few minutes early and were huddled together at their usual table in the cafeteria, taking advantage of what little time it would be just the three of them. Ariana normally took this time to get some reading in, but today was a special occasion. She loved that Kiara had surprised Teague without planning any of it. It was totally Kiara. There was also a hint of jealousy resting in her stomach–she'd never been anywhere near that level of intimacy with anyone.

Ariana wasn't a virgin, but it had never been *intimate*–like totally in love, can't get enough of each other, passionate sex. The first time she had been tipsy and sad after having to sit out of a father-daughter dance at a cheer banquet and wanted to do something to distract herself. The guy was a junior she had thought was hot at the time, and although he was kind, she didn't have any real connection with him. Ariana wondered if he could help to ease some of her pain, so she had sex with him at a moonlit park down the street from the banquet.

It was exciting for a few minutes and took her mind off the feeling of loss, but her grief came back with a vengeance the next day.

She never regretted doing it, because she'd been curious about sex and they were completely safe, but she also knew it was nothing near what she wanted to experience. She definitely didn't have an orgasm. She'd spent most of the time staring up at the moving clouds while he pushed into her at random intervals. After that, she'd tried it out with a girl from her cheer gym who was fun and sweet–they were both curious about what it would be like with another girl. She had brought Ariana way more pleasure than the guy had, actually being able to bring her to orgasm. Ariana had since then been with one other girl from another school, because although it always came back, those moments of being so close to another human helped her to pretend she didn't have a constant fear of the world closing in on her. She knew deep down that she was self-medicating in a way, and that it wasn't exactly healthy, but she still hadn't found whatever it was that could heal her.

Ariana wondered for a split second if she and Lukas would ever reach that level of intimacy, or if they would ever be anything at all. She knew it would be different with him. It had to be.

"That's impressive, K," Jade said, leaning over the table on her crossed arms. Ariana looked at Jade, who had left her long, velvety dark hair down and wavy today. She wore a tight-fitting gray shirt and looked like a magazine ad. *Jade never had to worry about whether or not a guy liked her*, Ariana thought, disheartened.

"How did it feel?" Ariana asked, turning her attention back to Kiara.

"Um, the first time I felt very full, too full even. But it was only wincing pain every once in a while. I was relaxed though, so I think that helped it not to hurt."

"No, the orgasm!" Jade exclaimed, laughing.

"Oh! Incredible. Different from when you do it yourself," Kiara said with a grin.

Aubrey, Reigh, and Melodie walked up and filled in the seats around them.

"Why do y'all look so secretive?" Aubrey asked as he set down his lunch tray, which was overflowing with a massive mound of curly fries.

Ariana noticed Kiara become distracted by the fries for several moments. She nearly laughed out loud, wondering if Kiara had the munchies at school yet again.

"Well, Teague and I had sex last night," Kiara said after a beat.

Aubrey's mouth fell into an "O". Melodie coughed into her water and Reigh gasped. Ariana chuckled at everyone's shocked faces. Kiara's candor never disappointed.

"What!? How long were you planning that?" Melodie asked, her blond eyebrows rising. Ariana could only guess she was upset about the amount of attention that would be on Kiara for the next few days.

"I didn't plan it, per se. I just let it happen," Kiara said with a serene, far-off look in her eyes. Ariana knew she was replaying the scene in her head. Kiara giggled. "I mean, I did greet him naked, but other than that..."

"Memoir title!" Jade yelled out.

Aubrey cracked up and Reigh shook her head, smiling. Only Kiara.

"Oh, that sounds like when Darren and I did it," Melodie said loudly, running a hand through her dirty blonde hair.

"Didn't you do it on a scratchy blanket in a field somewhere?"

Jade asked. "How could you greet him naked? Didn't you have to get to the field first?"

Ariana bit her lip to keep from laughing.

"Jade, it's okay that you haven't done it yet. Don't worry–the entire school thinks you have anyway," Melodie said and smiled at Jade, malice flashing in her eyes.

Jade pursed her lips and glared at Melodie.

"Okay, enough," Ariana said, shooting Melodie a warning glare. Did Melodie know that was a tender spot for Jade at the moment? Jade did prod the girl though.

"Tell us about it, K," Reigh said, changing the subject.

As Kiara recounted her story to the others, Ariana rose from the table and walked over to the lunch lines to grab some food. As she walked, she adjusted her light-violet sweetheart top that showed off her full-size C chest. She wasn't thin in the way that Jade and Kiara were, and she took pride in her curves.

Ariana had picked this top specifically because today was the day she and Lukas were supposed to hang out after school. She hadn't checked her phone since this morning, and she was hoping to have a text or two from him waiting for her. She'd refused to let herself reach out to him after their rendezvous at the party, not wanting to come off as eager, but she'd gone so long without hearing from him that she was beginning to think their plans weren't going to happen. It was almost as if Lukas enjoyed keeping her waiting.

As she walked, Ariana anxiously pulled her phone out and checked the screen. She had messages from her mother, Haiden, and a ton of group texts, but none from Lukas. A wave of disappointment crashed down on her. Had he changed his mind?

"Hey, Ari!" a voice called from a table behind her.

Ariana spun on her heel, causing her cascading hair to fan out. She grinned. Daire, one of her favorite seniors, was waving her over to his table.

"D!" Ariana strolled over and threw her arms around Daire's neck. His mirroring grin enveloped her in a cloud of comfort.

Last year, a varsity cheerleader had taken her, Jade, and Kiara to an upperclassman party. Ariana first saw Daire in the kitchen, commentating on a beer pong game in an Australian accent, pretending the players were wild animals. Daire had everyone around him doubled over with laughter, and Ariana was instantly attracted to him–he was tall, handsome, and hilarious–the life of the party and exactly her type.

Toward the end of the night, Ariana had wandered outside and found Daire smoking by himself on the side of the house. Her imagination had run wild at first, envisioning the two of them kissing, pressed up against the brick wall and hidden away from everyone. But soon enough she realized that Daire had actually been hiding out, too distraught from a recent breakup to be around the party anymore. Ariana and Daire had talked through the night until the early hours of the morning, and she'd helped to soothe him as he spoke of the girl who had broken his heart. Ariana realized that although Daire hadn't had the same feelings toward her as she initially had for him, he was an incredible friend, and over the past year she'd lost the romantic feelings for him and instead come to cherish their friendship immensely.

"You look like a supermodel, Ariana," Daire said. "Hot date tonight?" He reached out to grab her hand, attempting to make her do a spin. Ariana blushed and laughed, swatting his arm away.

"No," she said, not *fully* lying... at this point, she had no idea whether or not she had any plans tonight. "Just cheer practice today. We have tryouts soon."

"Ohhh, right! Well, good luck, even though you don't need it," Daire said, throwing a wink at her. "By the way, I'm having a party next weekend and I'd better see you there."

"Sounds like a plan," Ariana said. If Daire were to have a party, surely Lukas would go.

She never heard much about Lukas–he mostly hung out with the swimmers (whom Ariana didn't know) and only a couple of her older friends, so her sources were limited. Although she knew Daire and Lukas had grown up together, she didn't feel comfortable trying to get the scoop on Lukas so soon from one of his close buddies. It just didn't feel right, and also she was embarrassed. Lukas did occasionally hang out and smoke with Teague, but Kiara said it was a surface-level relationship–they were acquaintances more than anything else. Lukas rarely ventured out to parties, and that pretty much summed up what she knew about him.

"Good," Daire said, grinning again. "I miss you, Ari! Come and hang out anytime. You know where I live."

"Will do, D," Ariana said. "Food is calling my name!" Ariana walked backward toward the lunch line, flashing Daire one more grin before she spun around, feeling one hundred times better than she had a few moments ago. Why couldn't Lukas be as inviting as Daire?

Fuck it, Ariana thought. She would text him first and find out what was going on.

12:39 p.m. Ariana: Are we still meeting up today?

She waited a few minutes, expecting to feel the familiar buzz indicating she had received a message, but nothing came. Ariana flipped through her social media, liking a few videos and the silly memes Haiden had tagged her in, barely registering anything as she thought up reasons why Lukas hadn't reached out already. Had he changed his mind?

As if on cue, Ariana felt her phone vibrate and her heart sped up. She grinned and looked to see who it was, but her heart deflated as she read "Mom" on the home screen.

"Ugh," Ariana cried out, not caring who heard her. Determined not to let her mood sour anymore, Ariana hastily ordered and went back to her table, not even bothering to read her mom's text.

* * *

Jade watched Ariana nearly stomp back to their table holding a sandwich, her gold-streaked hair flying out behind her. Ariana sat down in a huff–quite comically, Jade thought–with a scowl on her face. Jade couldn't help it, she let out a laugh and Ariana squinted her eyes in Jade's direction. Jade loved it when Ariana got angry. It was like watching a kitten turn into a mountain lion.

"Hey!" Jade said, the hint of a smile still playing on her lips. "I'm sorry. I just don't understand how a falafel sandwich could make you so angry." A single-sided smile crept onto Ariana's face for a moment, but she quickly pulled her mouth back into a hard line.

"What's wrong, Ari?" Jade asked, leaning her head down in front of Ariana, forcing her to look into her eyes.

"Ugh Jade," Ariana moaned. She turned and looked around the table for a moment, making sure no one was eavesdropping.

"They're not listening," Jade said. She drummed her magenta-coated nails on the dark cafeteria table. "They're all too engrossed in Kiara's retelling of her first time... First *times*, I mean."

Ariana sighed and began to explain her situation, giving Jade a whiff of her Amor Amor perfume when she leaned in to talk. Looking slightly embarrassed, Ariana finished with, "You would never have this problem. Guys trip over themselves just to say hi to you."

"Hah." Jade snorted. "Not the ones I want," she said, thinking of Ian. After all of their flirting from afar, she figured he would've said something by now. Ian sat a few tables away with some juniors at this very moment and could easily come over and talk to her if he wanted. "Anyways Ari, from my experience, the less you care about the guy–or the less you make it seem like you care–the more they'll be interested in you. That's just the way it works."

"I didn't even text him until just now!"

"Yeah, but a guy like Lukas–he probably knows he has you already. And he's right, he does." Jade saw Ariana wince slightly but she continued. "So stop thinking about him and start thinking about yourself and having fun with your friends instead. Seriously, this'll only help you no matter what way this thing goes. Make a game out of it–you're an actress now, and Lukas is the furthest down on your list of guys you have a thing for. Make him *see* that. Okay?"

"Okay... but there is no list of guys."

Jade laughed. "I know. That's why I said to be an actress."

Ariana smiled. Jade put her arm around Ariana's shoulder and kissed her cheek.

"Oh and by the way, Ian probably isn't coming over to talk to you because he's confused as to whether you're taken or not," Ariana reassured Jade. "But I do have to tell you something, and you're not going to like it."

Jade grimaced. "I can almost guess what it's about."

Ariana gave Jade a sympathetic look. "I heard some freshmen talking about how 'the Jade Pierce' had sex with two guys at once at Taron's party. I told them it wasn't true though."

Jade's stomach fell. She'd been waiting for this–it was inevitable, but it still hit her like a bag of bricks. Who was spreading it this quickly?

"People talked about me behind my back when I first started having sex, but then everyone eventually got over it," Ariana said.

"I know, Ari, but you actually did it, and you wanted to. I've never even gone down on a guy and the whole school thinks I'm like a nympho. It just sucks because that's not me. And no one believes me when I tell them it's not true."

"We'll stop it, Jade. Don't worry." Ariana continued to reassure her, but it was no use.

Jade looked over at Ian's table and saw that Kristin Long and her posse had sat down next to him. Kristin must've been watching her because she immediately caught Jade's eye and glowered at her. After a moment, Kristin's face shifted and she smiled pointedly at Jade–a foreboding, nasty smile–and turned to whisper in Ian's ear. Ian looked around until his eyes met Jade's, and then he looked... confused. Jade dropped her eyes to her food.

That bitch! If Ian hadn't heard the rumor before, he probably knew it now.

Tears stung the corners of her eyes. Jade never cried–she had cried so much when her father died that she felt there wasn't much left in her. And nothing compared to the pain of her dad's absence or the way he had died. Not much warranted her tears after that. But these weren't tears of sadness. They were from rage. The prickling intensified and she fiddled with her slender black bracelet, willing herself to calm down. She took a deep breath into her belly, held it for five seconds, then slowly let it out. She continued to focus on deepening her breathing until she wasn't thinking about all the ways she could get revenge on Kristin, like dragging her by her ponytail across the cafeteria...

Instead, Jade let herself peer up at Ian again. He wasn't talking to Kristin anymore but looking at his lunch, picking at his food a little. His overgrown chestnut hair hung in front of his eyes, making half of his expression unreadable, but it looked like he was frowning. Jade silently willed Ian to look up at her so she could see those blue eyes and somehow let him know she hadn't done it. But he kept his head down, staring at his food.

A yearning she was unfamiliar with crept up in her belly. Jade put a hand over her stomach. Was she losing her chance with him? He'd been friends with Kristin and her clique for years and years, while he hardly knew Jade at all. Of course he would believe whatever Kristin told him about her.

In a flurry of motion, Weston and Haiden strode up to the table and plunked themselves next to Jade and Ariana, sending food flying when they slammed their overflowing trays onto the table.

"Careful!" Ariana yelled as she shot backward out of her chair. The conversation stopped with the chaotic arrival of the boys, and Weston took advantage of the attention.

"My bad, Ari," Weston said, and then continued without missing a beat. "So, bets on who's going to get with the freshman meat!"

"Do *not* call them meat, Weston," Ariana hissed at him.

"Sorry, Ari. The beautiful freshman *ladies*," Weston corrected himself.

"Dibs on the blonde one that's trying out for cheerleading," Haiden announced, his long hair pulled half back today. Haiden looked handsome with his hair out of his face; his angular features not half-hidden by dark locks that were normally falling into his eyes.

"What makes you all think that just because they're freshmen, they're going to hook up with you?" Jade asked.

Jade was really talking to Haiden–not that Haiden wasn't attractive, but there was a certain quality to Weston that got girls to fall for him, a dangerous concoction of cockiness and swagger that couldn't be replicated, no matter how hard the other guys tried.

"*Jade,*" Weston scoffed, sounding almost disappointed with her questioning. "Just watch."

Weston stood up and sauntered by the table full of freshmen, including the "little blonde one", who was a sweet girl named Mara they had met at cheer practice earlier in the week. The animated conversation at the younger girls' table abruptly stopped, and all of their heads turned to watch Weston saunter past. Jade let out a dramatic sigh, shaking her head. Weston went to the water fountain, took a drink, and walked back, lifting his t-shirt to wipe his face right as he walked by the young girls' table, exposing his chiseled six-pack. Jade and the rest of her table laughed as Weston flashed a smile at the table of swooning freshmen.

Jade rolled her eyes at Weston as he sat and put his arm around her. "See?" he cooed. "This'll be easy."

Jade started to shake his arm off but then turned to look at him instead. Kiara and the rest of the table were back to talking about their various sexual adventures so Jade figured she could talk to Weston with no one hearing.

"Hey, Weston," she began.

"What's up?" he inquired, mirroring her somber tone.

"Have you heard anything, you know, when you're in the locker room or whatever, about me from this past weekend?" Jade whispered quickly, looking into his brown eyes. They had flecks of amber in them that were only visible if you were inches away from his face.

Weston clenched his angular jaw. "Yeah, I heard some guys talking. And, no–" He jokingly covered her mouth with his hand as Jade opened it to protest. "You don't need to defend yourself. I know you didn't do it." He pulled his hand away and stopped for a second, then continued. "By the way, I made sure none of them will talk about it again."

"What? How?"

"I just took care of it," Weston said with a smile.

"It was pretty funny," Haiden piped in, making it clear he was listening. "West ended up putting this junior in a chokehold against the lockers. That shut 'em up."

"He was trying to talk back to me," Weston said with a shrug.

Haiden laughed and the corner of Weston's mouth twitched upward. Jade couldn't help the grin that flooded her face. Weston was the ultimate guy's guy, but he had a soft side too and was extremely protective of the girls in their group. Half of the time Jade found it insanely attractive to see the lengths he would go to defend the girls, and the other half of the time she questioned whether it was just because he wanted to bang them himself.

Either way, she was moved by his actions.

"Thank you, West," Jade said earnestly. "But how did you know I didn't do it?"

"Well one, because I know you–you're not like that–and two, because I was with Taron on Sunday. A bunch of football players went to grab beers and he drunkenly spilled to me how you came onto him and then backed off for no reason at all. He's so confused Jade; it's hilarious. He was asking me for advice since he knows we're close. I told him he didn't stand a chance."

Jade knew she had inadvertently given Weston a great gift in having a senior come to him, a sophomore, groveling for advice. As overly cocky and obnoxious as Weston could be sometimes, he made it hard not to love him. Jade smiled, remembering why she'd liked him early on last year, but then caught herself before she could think any more about it.

Instead, she looked back over at Ian who was now staring at her, and of course, Weston's arm was still around her shoulders.

"Ah shit," Jade said as she shrugged Weston's arm off of her.

"What? What happened?" Weston asked.

"Nothing." Jade sighed. "Just my life."

* * *

"Remember that party at my place last winter? Arica and I almost had a threesome in my parent's bed that night," Reigh said, stealing the attention of the table.

"What! With who?" Melodie said.

"With *whom*," Kiara heard Ariana say under her breath.

Kiara took this opportunity to check her phone.

12:46 p.m. Teague: was last night even real?

Kiara grinned, her heart filling with joy. She missed Teague already–even more so now that they had done it, if that were possible. Teague had photography during her lunch period and if she left a little early she could usually stop in to say hi to him. Rushing High's photography teacher, Mrs. Nolty, was an instructor known for her leniency. The students could basically come and go from the class as they pleased within reason.

"Kiara, you're not eating lunch?" Ariana asked, her hazel eyes wide with concern.

Kiara cringed internally–she hadn't expected anyone to call her out. "I'm not hungry today. I had a big breakfast," Kiara lied as she put her hands over her stomach.

Ariana stared at her quizzically but said nothing else. Kiara had never been one to tell lies, and she didn't like doing it. But she didn't want Ariana of all people on her case. Ariana, who could occasionally tell when people were lying just by watching them.

Kiara smiled and shrugged. Before Ariana could study her body language any further, she took off toward Teague's classroom, convincing herself that Ariana hadn't realized anything was off. She looked down at her white tennis shoes hitting the linoleum floors and caught sight of her thighs jiggling.

Her stomach turned. Each step set off ripples that made her wish she had covered up more today. She squeezed her eyes shut and let out a sigh–at least she'd skipped lunch. Sure, she'd lost a few pounds since beginning her diet a little over a month ago, but the visible results were taking longer than she thought. *I could drop my daily calorie intake again*, Kiara thought. *I could sacrifice another hundred calories. The results would be worth it*. With that decision, she smiled. Thinner thighs were coming.

As Kiara approached the hallway leading to Mrs. Nolty's room, she sent Teague a text letting him know she was about to be outside. As soon as she spotted his dark, handsome head pop out of the doorway, Kiara quickened her pace. She couldn't wait to be back in his arms.

But then another head appeared behind Teague, and Kiara recognized the spiky dark hair belonging to Lukas Jansen. Her pace slowed.

"Hi, baby!" Teague said with a smile as she approached the two boys. Teague pulled her into a hug and kissed her temple.

"Hi," Kiara said, eyeing Lukas over Teague's shoulder. "What're you doing here?"

Teague released Kiara from their embrace.

"I hang out here every once in a while," Lukas said. "I left my phone at home today and Ariana and I are supposed to hang out later. Could you tell her I'll be waiting to pick her up after practice? I'll be in the back parking lot. I drive a white truck."

Kiara didn't know why this annoyed her so much, but it did. Or maybe it was merely Lukas that annoyed her. Sure, he was good-looking and all, but he was way too cocky about it. He seemed like he was used to everyone doing whatever he asked of them.

"Why don't you go tell her yourself? She has lunch right now. You can't miss her," Kiara said, moving her eyes from Lukas back to Teague.

"I can't, I've gotta get back to my class. I've been gone too long already. Please, just let her know for me? See you, Teague," Lukas said and then took off before anyone had time to respond.

Kiara grunted, crossing her arms at Lukas' retreating back.

"Is someone in a bad mood?" Teague said, laughing at Kiara's sour face.

"No, Lukas just annoys me. Why can't he take care of his own shit?"

"Whoa!" Teague took a step back and put his hands up in defense.

"Sorry. I didn't get a lot of sleep last night." This was true. She had been so hungry it had been hard for her to fall asleep. Maybe that was why she reacted badly to Lukas.

"It's okay," Teague stepped back in to take her in his arms. "I'm sorry though. Lukas was here hanging out with some of the guys and asked me if he could talk to you. I figured you wouldn't mind."

Kiara gave in and smiled. "It's all right. Cheer me up?"

Teague grinned and dipped her backward, one hand behind her head and the other behind her waist. When she was nearly vertical, he kissed her.

"Of course, baby girl," Teague said in a deep, playful voice, making her grin and forget the rest of the world.

CHAPTER 7
Ariana

"So I talked to Lukas earlier today," Kiara said, sounding bored while she bent over on the locker room bench to tie her athletic shoes.

"What!?" Ariana whipped around, nearly taking Jade's eye out with her elbow.

"Sweet Jesus!" Jade exclaimed. She had one leg in her jeans and one out and nearly fell over trying to duck out of the way.

"Why didn't you tell me earlier?" Ariana demanded, uncharacteristically not saying sorry for nearly knocking Jade over.

Kiara peered up at her but didn't stop tying her shoes. "I kinda forgot," she shrugged. "Lukas annoys me so I think I pushed it to the back of my mind. Anyway, he said he'll be waiting for you after practice in the parking lot. Look for a white truck."

Ariana stood there feeling ecstatic, bewildered, and only slightly peeved at Kiara's nonchalance. How Kiara could ever think Lukas was annoying was beyond her. Ariana wanted to spend hours with him, preferably laying in a bed somewhere, barely clothed, talking about their lives while exploring each other's bodies...

"So hot date after practice then," Jade said with an exaggerated wink. She twisted up her shirt and whipped it out in Ariana's direction. "Ow owww!"

Ariana shook her head, unable to stop a giddy grin from stretching across her face. She would be with him again. Alone. A delicious shiver ran down her spine as she let her mind wander to Lukas. With the earlier apprehension now gone, she could think about him without anxiety. She wondered if Lukas ever got anxiety over girls but couldn't picture it. Ariana was incredibly attracted to this at ease quality of his, and yet it also unnerved her on some level. Not only was she afraid he wouldn't like her as much as she did him, but she also knew that if a single conversation with him could cause her to have feelings, there was no way she was the only girl who had noticed him.

She let out a sigh, a bubble of uneasiness rising in her stomach at that last thought. She strained to push it out of her mind. She had better things to focus on, like how there were only about two hours left until she would be with him.

After practice, Ariana changed back into her creamy violet top and somehow made her long, light-brown hair flow nicely around her face after being in a ponytail for the last hour.

"How do I look?" Ariana asked Kiara and Jade, who lay sprawled on the bench next to her, taking selfies while making the worst faces possible on Kiara's phone.

"Oh my god, how did you make yourself have so many chins?!" Jade squealed and then burst into laughter at the picture.

Kiara snorted. "Let's send this to Teague."

"Wait no, let's airdrop it to everyone nearby," Jade said excitedly, grabbing Kiara's phone and hitting random airdrops.

"That last one was a teacher!" Kiara howled, cracking up all over again.

"Guys!" Ariana said. "C'mon, I'm nervous."

Jade and Kiara looked up. "Oh Ari, you look beautiful, you

know that!" Kiara said, almost scolding. "He doesn't deserve you."

Ariana smiled, placated. She said bye to the remaining cheerleaders and set off to find Lukas. As she crossed the second large gym where the dance team tryouts were going on, Ariana realized she hadn't been this excited in an extremely long time–Lukas had such a hold on her already. Ariana waved at some girls she knew trying out for the dance team and then headed out the door.

Once outside, Ariana searched the rows of cars until she spotted Lukas' truck parked toward the back. Her breathing accelerated as she made her way to the shiny white truck and hopped into the front seat.

Immediately she was greeted with the smell of mouthwatering cologne and Lukas in a dark blue t-shirt and a backward baseball hat. His posture was more relaxed and at ease than usual, and Ariana's heart squirmed as if trying to wiggle its way out of her chest. She was getting to see him with some of his guard down, she realized, in a way that others didn't.

"Ariana." Lukas' voice wrapped around her name and made a certain muscle in her stomach tighten. She automatically crossed her legs.

"Hi," she said. "So... where are we going?"

"I thought we could go to the lake in Windsor Hills–I have this spot there that I go sometimes."

"That's my neighborhood!"

"Oh, is it? Do you want to go somewhere else?"

"No, I love the lake," Ariana gushed, smiling. The lake had picturesque waterfalls and a three-mile trail circling it that Ariana sometimes ran to work out. It was beautiful; a welcome break from the highways and traffic. She and her friends used the covering of the woods surrounding the water to get away from their parents and indulge in not-so-legal substances at night, although with Lukas she could think of a few other things she would like to do.

"Good," Lukas said, grinning as though he could read her thoughts.

As Lukas started up the engine, Ariana leaned forward and turned up the music. He was listening to a Dave Matthews Band live playlist in which the instrumentals made her feel as though her very soul were being lifted. She took in a deep breath of fresh air from the rolled-down window and appreciated the moment. The day was perfect, with clear blue skies and the smell of freshly cut grass mixing with Lukas' cologne. She wanted to pinch herself–she was going somewhere secluded with Lukas Jansen, the hottest senior in the entire school. Ariana felt like she had a buzz, but better. She snuck a glance at him. He looked so sexy she wanted to scream.

"That's a good look for you," Lukas said after a while.

"What is?"

"Your hair blowing in the wind like that–wild. It suits you," Lukas said.

"Thanks," Ariana murmured, not understanding exactly what he meant by his observation. "Do you think I'm wild?"

"I've heard stories."

Ariana's heart stopped for a moment. For the first time, she felt a sense of shame for her meaningless hookups. Lukas didn't yet understand that the others didn't mean much to her, yet they helped to fill a void.

"You were the one that jumped off that office building for the hell of it, weren't you?" he asked, teasing her.

Ariana let out a breath of relief. "Oh, *that* story."

Last summer, Ariana, Jade, and Kiara had been hanging out with a bunch of the upperclassmen in a parking lot of some abandoned office buildings. They were out on a back road, so there wasn't a high probability of the cops showing up, but Ariana had wanted to make sure she knew all possible escape routes just in case.

The main office building was two or three stories high and the roof was accessible by a metal ladder attached to the side. Ariana had scaled the building, convincing Daire to go with her. When they made it to the top they laid on their backs, cracking up and watching the sky. Ariana was a few beers in so she decided to try an alternative way of getting down. There was an awning that hung over the front entrance to the building, so she climbed onto it. Without a moment's hesitation, she leaped off onto the grass below. Luckily her years of gymnastics had taught her how to soften a hard landing, or else she probably would have broken some bones.

"I lived, didn't I?" Ariana said indignantly. It was fun for her to scale buildings and test her limits, but she was sure others regarded her daredevil-esque acts as sheer stupidity. Which, in that particular case, it had been. It was funny, although she generally had heightened anxiety, she found when she was doing the more dangerous things she became calm. Maybe that's why they appealed to her.

"Yeah, and also made Daire unable to stop talking about you," Lukas said quietly.

"What?"

"I can see why he has trouble stopping though."

Ariana blushed. Did Lukas mean that? She closed her eyes to take in the music and the moment, pushing away the thoughts of Daire possibly having feelings for her. She would deal with that some other time.

When they pulled up to the lake, Lukas turned to her. Ariana fidgeted with a gold ring on her finger, flustered under his gaze.

"Um, should we go?" she asked.

"Sure." He smiled, anticipation etched around his eyes. Her heart stilled for a moment. Was there any way she affected him even a tenth of how much he affected her?

They climbed out of the truck and walked side by side onto the trail encompassing the lake. They were close to each other but not quite touching, which was driving Ariana a little wild. Normally, she would have made the first move and closed the space between them, but she was uncharacteristically shy and awkward around Lukas, not knowing what to say or do next.

"It's a little further out here," Lukas said. "Off the trail and back into the trees, there's a pond. Have you ever seen it?"

"I think so," Ariana replied. She couldn't believe Lukas liked to hang out so close to where she lived and she had never known. That fact made the woods seem that much more magical somehow.

"You're always reading," Lukas said out of the blue. He was a couple of steps ahead of her and Ariana couldn't make out his face to see his expression.

She laughed. "Yes, I am. I love reading. What brought that to mind?"

"It's interesting. Everyone is usually on their phones all the time. So it's refreshing to see you reading," Lukas said.

How did he know the exact right things to say? She was usually self-conscious about her reading. She felt like one of the few kids left in her generation who enjoyed reading an actual book more than being glued to a phone, agonizing over their latest social media post.

Ariana glanced at his profile. "Well, reading calms my anxiety; my phone and social media heighten it."

"Hmm. What do you like to read?"

"Anything and everything. I love dystopian stories though. Oh, and anything with a good romance in it," Ariana said, blushing slightly.

"A good romance, huh?" Lukas said. He turned for a moment to look at her, his eyes landing on her lips. Desire hit her like a tsunami and she bit her bottom lip unconsciously. Lukas sucked in a small breath but then turned forward, walking on. Ariana had to remind herself to breathe–something had definitely just passed between them.

"I *have* been here before," Ariana said as they neared the pond. "Haiden and I found this place last year. We carved our names into this tree–here." She found the spot where they had marked "Ari" and beneath it, "Haid" into the trunk of a tree closer to the pond.

"Are you and Haiden... is there something going on?" Lukas asked.

"What?!" Ariana almost cried out. "No way. He's like my brother! We've lived down the street from each other since we were kids."

"Oh," Lukas said, sitting down on one of the large rocks. "I'm just trying to figure you out, that's all." He motioned for Ariana to sit next to him. Her arm brushed against his and sent a soft vibration of pleasure through her. "I'm wondering what makes me different, if I am, from the rest of the guys you always seem to be hanging out with."

Ariana took a moment and stared at him, then looked out onto the pond. They were so close to each other that it was making it hard for her to breathe properly. Should she tell him how she felt? Would that be too much too soon?

"You are different," Ariana admitted finally. "You have a pull on me already that I can't explain."

Lukas sat still, looking off into the distance–his profile was beautiful. Ariana could hear herself breathing. The longer he sat there unmoving, the louder her breath seemed to get. Ariana cursed herself. Had she conceded too much?

After what felt like an eternity, Lukas turned toward her and spoke. "You're different for me, too. It's like everyone else is on mute, but I hear music when I'm around you."

An uncontrollable grin engulfed Ariana's face. She had wanted this so badly, and had been so unsure of how Lukas felt about her, that for him to confirm he had feelings... She was flying. Lukas moved his leg slightly so that they were touching.

"So, what now?" Ariana asked in an excited whisper, her leg humming from where it was touching his.

"Let's just get to know each other, and see where it goes," Lukas said, his eyes melting into hers.

Ariana smiled again. "Okay."

. . .

"It's getting late, I've gotta head home soon," Lukas said, interrupting their conversation after glancing at his phone. It had gone off a few times while they were talking, but he had ignored the calls and texts, much to Ariana's pleasure.

The sun was setting and her mom would be expecting her home soon. They'd been there for a couple of hours, yet not a single part of Ariana wanted to leave. This afternoon had been perfect. Something about being with Lukas made even the most ordinary of things seem dreamlike. They had talked without pause–about their childhoods, their dreams, where they wanted to end up. Every once in a while, Lukas would reach over and pull a fallen lock of gold-streaked hair out of Ariana's eyes, tucking it behind her ear. Each time he did so, she would inadvertently stop talking, hardly breathing as he touched her face.

"One last question," Ariana said, pursing her lips. She had been mustering the courage to ask him all evening.

"Yes?" Lukas leaned forward to trace his fingers along her arm, causing her to have a momentary lapse in memory.

She stared at his hand. "Um. I forgot."

Lukas laughed and stopped his hand by her wrist and then laced his fingers with hers.

Ariana smiled down at their entwined hands and found her courage. "Have you ever been in love?"

Lukas stilled, looking uncomfortable. He sighed before answering. "I thought I was once. Do you know Laura Keaton?" Ariana nodded her head yes while her stomach fell through the earth–Laura Keaton was one of the most gorgeous seniors at their school. "Anyway, we had a thing last year. I was really into her at first, but then the initial reaction to her wore off and I realized she was just a pretty face for me. There was no personality or brains underneath the looks. I want someone with depth."

Ariana glanced over to see him looking pointedly at her and happiness bubbled back up in her veins.

"And to be honest, she was kind of a bad person," Lukas said with a mischievous smile, causing Ariana to let out a laugh.

"I want to see you again soon," he said.

Ariana wanted to shout in happiness. Even those few words held so much promise. "Me too."

Lukas stood and walked to the tree with the carved names. He took a pen out of his pocket and carved an "L" below "Ari" and right above "Haid".

"Now I'm on there with you, too," he said.

Ariana smiled at Lukas and traced her finger along the L. "I like that." Her voice was slightly husky, giving away the desire that had been rising in her all afternoon.

Lukas seemed to catch it because he took a step toward her, causing Ariana's back to press up against the tree. He traced his fingers along her neck and she let out a breath as they locked eyes. Lukas stopped his hand on her collarbone and then slowly pulled it away, leaving her momentarily unable to move.

"I like it too," Lukas said, his words dripping with promise.

Lukas backed away and started for the trail, leaving Ariana nearly gasping for breath. That had hands down been the most erotic moment of her life and they hadn't even done anything! Ariana took a deep breath, trying to gain her sanity back. She caught up with Lukas and they walked in comfortable silence through the woods to the street. Ariana wondered if he was dreading leaving her as much as she was him.

Once they were back by the truck Lukas turned to her. "Let's keep this quiet for a while. I don't want everyone in our business and this is too good. I don't want it to get ruined."

Ariana nodded even though she didn't want to keep it quiet. She understood what Lukas meant though and knew he had a point. The gossip everyone spread when a romance sprang up unexpectedly was ridiculous. Ariana was also afraid someone might try to screw them up before they'd gotten to know each other. It was better this way.

Lukas' phone started ringing again and they both jumped. "I really can't ignore this anymore. I'll talk to you soon."

Lukas stepped into his truck and Ariana frowned. *He shouldn't have left yet*, she thought. She shook her head, wondering where the errant thought came from. She hugged her arms around her stomach and began walking toward her house, trying to shake the feeling of desertion. *I'm being silly*, she thought. The engine rumbled down the road and Ariana retreated into her head, replaying all the wonderful moments from the afternoon, trying to get rid of the pit in her stomach from Lukas' abrupt departure. How did everything feel so right with him? How could such a simple afternoon make her feel as though her life was forever changed?

Ariana's phone vibrated in her hand. Her heart leapt when she saw his name on the screen.

8:38 p.m. Lukas: Watching you walk away in my rearview mirror was hard. I wanted to come after you. Sorry I left so fast.

Ariana grinned from ear to ear. After this, after *him*, nothing would ever be the same.

I'll make him wait, she thought, deciding not to answer just yet. She put in her headphones and turned her music app to the same Dave Matthews Band station Lukas had on earlier, again losing herself in the memories of the afternoon and fantasizing about what their future might hold.

CHAPTER 8

J, K, A

On Friday afternoon Jade sat in the back of cheer practice with Kiara, watching with disbelief as Ariana flitted around the gym. Jade had never seen her this exuberant, playful, and over the top happy before. Kiara let out a snort of laughter as they witnessed Ariana volunteer to help the younger girls who couldn't quite get their cheers right.

"Oh dear God," Jade said in a mock horror voice. "The girl really is in love."

"She's done for," Kiara agreed, laughing.

Jade pulled her dark ponytail in front of her shoulder and began to braid it. Ariana had told them all about her afternoon with Lukas, and while Jade was happy Ariana had gotten to hang out with Lukas alone, a small knot of jealousy sat in her stomach. What would it be like to get a few minutes alone with Ian? Jade burned with the desire to find out.

Ariana trotted over to them and Jade couldn't help but smile. The pure bliss radiating from her friend was contagious. Her features even seemed to glow, her honey-colored eyes glittering and cheeks flushed a pretty pink. Jade put a mock-serious look on her face and held up her hand, pretending to take Ariana's temperature from her smooth forehead.

"Yep, we've lost her, Kiara," Jade said in a stern tone.

Kiara giggled as Ariana swatted Jade's hand away.

"Guys!" Ariana said, pouting but unable to stop smiling. "Quit making fun of me!"

Jade nudged Ariana's arm. "You're making it too easy, Ari."

Kiara frowned at her phone and an uneasy zip shot through Jade's stomach. "K? What're you looking at?"

"Kristin put you on her story..." Kiara said, sounding apologetic as she handed over the phone. "...It's weird."

Jade braced herself and watched. There she was, in the background of a video Kristin had shot, but it soon became apparent that Jade was the intended subject as it zoomed in on her talking with Haiden. Jade's stomach turned. She remembered talking with Haiden earlier today, but why had Kristin decided to film this moment?

Then she saw it.

Haiden had his arm around Jade's waist as she leaned in to whisper in his ear. It looked like they were flirting. As Jade leaned more of her weight on Haiden, Kristin zoomed in on where his hand fell down her back, near her butt. Text appeared. "Another one" it read. Jade wanted to scream. How had Kristin managed to turn an innocent moment into something gross?

Jade whipped her phone out and looked for Kristin's story, but there was nothing. Of course. Kristin had hid the story from certain people strategically.

"Ari? Can you see it on your feed?"

Ariana furrowed her brows but shook her head. "She must have forgotten to hide it from Kiara."

"Fuck her, dude," Kiara said. "She's just jealous."

"Easier said than done," Jade said with a sigh. Who knew how many of these she was posting without Jade knowing? She and Haiden had only ever been platonic friends, but now people might think otherwise. Who all had Kristin let see her story? Had Ian been one of them?

From across the gym, three of the younger girls made their

way over to where the group was sitting, bumping into one another as they walked. Jade recognized the petite blonde one as Mara, but she didn't know the names of the other two. One had dark, almost black hair, done in a long braid down her back. The braid had pieces of pink, blue, and teal intertwined in it, and the other girl had light-red hair that was almost strawberry blonde, but not quite.

"Hi Ariana," Mara said. "These are my two best friends, Lyric and Everly. Can we sit with y'all for a minute?"

Ariana smiled and nodded, gesturing for them to sit.

Jade moved over a few inches to make room for the girls and smiled. "I'm Jade."

"We know," Lyric said quickly, blushing. Jade studied the younger girl's vibrant braid.

"I love your hair," Jade complimented Lyric. "You'll have to tell me your secret on how you got those colors to stay so well."

"Sure!" Lyric nearly shouted, her face flushing from Jade's compliment. Lyric's eyes took on a dreamy look, like she had just been kissed by her crush. Ariana gave a small cough to get Jade's attention and playfully rolled her eyes.

Everly cleared her throat and began stammering, "So, we were wondering, Krall said if we needed help with the cheers, we could ask the older girls, and yeah, so, we were just wondering..." Everly stopped talking, her cheeks turning red. She was smaller than her two friends in stature and looked down while she spoke.

"Do you guys want to come over to my house this weekend to practice with us?" Kiara said.

The younger girls looked at each other as if they couldn't believe their luck.

"Yes! Oh my gosh, thank you!" Mara exclaimed. She and her two counterparts were all grinning now, and Kiara pulled out her phone to get their numbers.

Well, this should be interesting, Jade thought. A similar thing had happened to the three of them when they were only freshmen. The cooler upperclassmen girls, whether or not they were fellow cheerleaders, picked out a few freshmen every year to bring into their world and take to the older parties. It was a corruption of sorts, and an honor at the same time. Jade wouldn't be surprised if Kiara had a plan to do the same with Mara, Lyric, and Everly.

"So, you'll show me how you do your hair this weekend?" Jade said as she winked at Lyric.

* * *

Kiara smiled as she exchanged numbers with the younger girls. They were naïve and sweet, and Kiara wanted to help them while showing them some fun at the same time.

Krall came over to their group. "Ari, J? Help me pack up the cheer equipment?"

"I'll text you later," Kiara called after Mara. The girls went back to sit with the other wide-eyed freshmen who'd been watching the interaction. Mara spun around to acknowledge Kiara's statement with a little wave, looking overjoyed.

"Oh my God, I have such a girl crush on her!" Kiara overheard Mara exclaim as she sat down.

Kiara laughed a little to herself and fell back into a memory of when she, Ariana, and Jade were approached by the reigning upperclassmen last year, Nali Gray and Tae Everett. Nali–blonde, beautiful, Barbie-esque Nali–was a cheerleader on the Varsity team and had taken a liking to Ariana and the girls. One Friday last year when Kiara, Jade, and Ariana were leaving school, Nali and her best friend Tae had been waiting for them in Tae's red convertible in the parking lot.

"Hey," Tae called out from behind the wheel. She lifted her aviator sunglasses to the top of her bangs, her raven hair falling in a stick-straight bob. "Wanna go to a party?"

They had only been a few months into their freshman year, but Kiara already knew this was an opportunity that they should *not* turn down. Nali and Tae were the talk of the school–together they were loved and hated, sought after and feared, idolized and demonized.

Kiara exchanged an excited nod with Ariana and Jade before letting out a whoop and hopping into the car. Nali smiled back at them, her blonde, sleek hair flowing in the wind as they drove. Kiara was ecstatic the top was down–she prayed everyone in her neighborhood would see them. Tae blasted her speakers as they rode to Marx Woods' house for their first senior party while Nali passed around a bottle of champagne.

Nali and Tae took the girls around the party and introduced them to everyone. Kiara had never felt cooler in her life. They played drinking games, took shots, and ended up streaking through Tae's neighborhood at one in the morning. She and Ariana had even kissed as a dare at one point, or was it from a game? She couldn't remember the exact details of the night. She'd puked the entire next day, and even though that night caused her to swear off shots (and alcohol for the most part) forever, it had been one of the best nights of her life.

"Hey, Kiara," Reigh said, appearing beside her and pulling her back into the present. "How's your diet going?"

Kiara glanced up at Reigh. Her high cheekbones protruded from her face more so than they ever had before. Reigh seemed to get thinner every day and Kiara wondered what exactly she was doing to lose weight so quickly. *She must restrict herself more than I do,* Kiara thought.

"I'm trying," Kiara said. She sighed, attempting not to get jealous of Reigh's stick-thin legs. "It's so hard sometimes."

"Yeah I know, but being skinny is worth it. You have to fight through the cravings," Reigh said in a low voice that only Kiara could hear.

"You must have more willpower than I do. I don't think I'll ever be as thin as you."

Reigh looked at Kiara for a moment, seemingly mulling something over. "Will you come with me to the bathroom?" Reigh finally said. "I want to show you something."

"Yeah, sure." Kiara stood up and followed Reigh to the single bathroom down the hallway from the gym.

Reigh locked the door behind them and turned to look Kiara in the eyes. "Okay. I want to tell you something, but you have to swear–*I mean swear*–not to tell anyone, okay?"

"I swear."

"EVER, Kiara. You can never tell anyone."

"Reigh! I said I swear. You know you can trust me." A smirk rose to Kiara's face. "Remember Weston's party freshman year when you–"

"Yes, yes! Okay. I know I can trust you," Reigh blurted out, cutting Kiara off.

Reigh had kissed Weston while her girlfriend at the time had been in the very next room. It had been the first time for a lot of their friends to get drunk, and Weston didn't remember most of the night, including that particular incident, to this day. However, Kiara had been sitting right next to him when Reigh came over and drunkenly told Weston how hot she thought he was, sat in his lap, and made out with him right then and there. Weston had obliged without question, of course. And since he didn't remember, Kiara and Reigh remained the only two souls who knew about the incident.

"Okay," Reigh began. "So you're serious about losing weight, right?"

"...Yes." Kiara's eyes narrowed. She was a little afraid of where the conversation was heading.

"Have you ever thrown up?"

"You mean on purpose? No!"

"It's not that bad..." Reigh said quietly, looking at the toilet as she spoke. "You can eat anything and everything you want again. You just have to throw it up after. *Anything* you want. It's amazing."

A pang of longing struck Kiara. She hadn't eaten a slice of pizza in over a month. She hadn't eaten sugar in two months. The thought that she could eat those things again and not gain any weight seemed almost too good to be true. And she *was* having increasing difficulty restraining herself from eating the foods she used to enjoy all the time. Hell, she was having difficulty stopping herself from eating, *period.* It was so hard to lose weight, and Kiara had already been eating a lot fewer calories than she'd originally planned. As much as the thought of making herself sick disgusted her, the reward for doing so was deliciously tempting. Kiara weighed this in her head–back and forth, back and forth she went until finally, she decided.

Kiara took a deep breath. "All right. Show me."

* * *

"Jade, could you give me and Ari a moment? You can head to the locker room early," Krall said. They had just finished putting the cheer equipment away in a room adjacent to the gym.

Jade gave Ariana a quizzical look but then smiled. "I won't turn that offer down!" she said before running off.

Krall motioned for Ariana to sit next to her on one of the folded up mats.

"So," Krall began, pushing her dirty blonde hair behind her reddened ears. "I have something I want to talk to you about."

Ariana smiled politely and waited. Was she in trouble?

"As you know, junior varsity's head cheerleader has to be nominated by the varsity squad," Krall said while making intense eye contact.

Ariana's hopes rose. She thought she might get nominated, but she hadn't been sure.

"Nali nominated you, and you got enough votes to run for the position," Krall said, letting the corners of her mouth turn up into a smile. "Congratulations."

Ariana nearly jumped up in excitement, but then remembered something. "But I haven't made the team yet. Is this how it normally works?"

"Some years we wing it," Krall said, shrugging. "And let's face it, you're a shoo-in. Melodie is most likely going to be your competition, so I would start preparing your speech now. I know she's been working on hers all summer."

Ariana blinked. She'd forgotten about the speech part. "Wow, thanks, Krall. I appreciate it."

"Your skills earned it, Ari. And it's not a bad thing to have Nali on your side. Just make sure to keep this between us for now." Krall gave her a meaningful look.

"I will," Ariana said. "Wow. Thank you!"

She walked the hallways in a partial daze–she had dreamed about making cheer captain since her first day of high school. And how comforting to know that Nali had her back. It was funny to think that she'd been intimidated by her when they met last year. Ariana had taken one look at Nali's figure-eight body, with her perfectly straight, waist-length blonde hair and baby doll eyes and automatically assumed she would be a complete bitch. Yet Ariana couldn't have been more wrong–Nali had taken her, Jade, and Kiara under her wing, showing them the ropes and making sure they didn't do anything stupid when she and Tae took them to the upperclassmen parties. This year Nali was a senior, and it definitely didn't hurt to have her vote.

Ariana turned into the locker room and sat on one of the benches to wait for Kiara and Jade. She checked her phone and a rush of happiness flowed through her body when she saw a text from Lukas.

3:20 p.m. Lukas: I can't stop thinking about you

A goofy grin stretched across her face and Ariana knew she would get shit for it if Jade or Kiara saw. She didn't care though–she knew now that Lukas liked her back. Last night, after a few hours had passed and Ariana hadn't responded to his messages, Lukas called her and they stayed on the phone until they fell asleep.

Ariana quickly typed a response.

4:12 p.m. Ariana: Well I definitely can't concentrate anymore
4:13 p.m. Ariana: Will I see you this weekend?

Ariana waited with her phone in her hand for a few moments to see if Lukas would respond right away.

4:14 p.m. Lukas: Yes. I'll see you tonight

Ariana pressed her phone to her heart and clenched her eyes shut. *I'll see him again tonight*, she thought. She could hardly wait.

CHAPTER 9
Jade

Jade stood in her bedroom Friday evening, studying her reflection in the gilded full-length mirror hanging on her bedroom wall. She'd decided on a sultry black dress that hung off both of her shoulders and exposed her neckline and part of her back. She'd taken her time to get ready for the party at Weston's tonight since Ian would be there.

She traced a dark red fingernail along the smoky shadow surrounding her eye and Kristin's video flashed in her mind. A dark thought took hold of her: she looked like someone who could have done all the things said in the rumors. Would people assume she had sex with anyone and everyone like Kristin tried to portray? Like someone who would sleep with random guys at a party, sometimes two at a time? *The way humans look on the outside compared to what's actually on the inside can be so different,* she thought. Why did people assume they knew what she was like just because of the way she looked?

She pulled her hair up into a messy bun, twisting a few small braids in. Long, gold string earrings hung from each ear, reaching almost to her bare shoulders. There was nothing she could do about the assumptions others made about her, and she liked the way she looked tonight.

So screw it, let them talk, Jade thought as she smiled in the mirror, her glittering green eyes twinkling back at her.

Kiara wandered into Jade's room and let out a whistle of appreciation. "It's a good thing you don't dress up often. None of us would stand a chance."

"That's not true," Jade said, but smiled at the compliment. What would Ian think when he saw her? And more importantly, would he still like her after he got past the looks? Then again, maybe she wouldn't let him fully get to know her. Maybe she didn't want him to see how messed up she sometimes felt inside.

Ariana walked into the room while frowning down at her phone. Jade thought she looked exceptionally pretty tonight; her tan body glowed under her white halter dress and showed off her cleavage and curvy hips.

"Why the long face?" Kiara asked.

Ariana looked up from her phone. "Haiden's already there, and he said Kristin and her girls are for sure coming."

Jade groaned in apprehension. "Well, you know what they say–murder them with kindness."

"That is not the saying at all," Ariana said, a smile creeping to her lips.

"Eh," Jade shrugged, causing her gold earrings to brush her shoulders. "Brutally murder them with kindness?"

"Let's stick to killing them with kindness?" Kiara said. She wore her ice blonde hair down and wavy tonight, and a few pieces fell into her face as she laughed. Kiara was dressed up by Kiara standards in a gray, low-cut shirt dress. She'd drawn geometric shapes around her eyes with white liner and covered them with a shimmer, giving her an angelic glow.

There was a loud bang from Dani's room, followed by a burst of shrieking laughter. Kiara raised her eyebrows. Jade groaned and rolled her eyes. Her parents were out of town for the weekend, but unfortunately, they hadn't taken Dani with them.

"Let's go before Dani can wreak havoc on our night," Jade said.

They strolled outside to Kiara's retro white convertible, gifted to her one month ago on her sixteenth birthday. Kiara tapped her fingers on the steering wheel, as if impatient to get her pride and joy onto the open road.

Jade climbed in the front while Ariana walked to the back passenger side. Jade reached over to fiddle with the seatbelt and jolted forward as Kiara began to back down the driveway. Jade whirled around to see an empty backseat.

"Ariana!" Jade shrieked and then roared with laughter. "You forgot Ariana!"

Ariana was still standing in the driveway, bent over double and laughing.

"Oops!" Kiara said bashfully, joining in on their laughter.

"Really, K?" Ariana scolded when she'd caught up with the car, and they all erupted into fits of laughter again. "Are you sure you didn't smoke anything before you came over?"

This wasn't the first time Kiara had accidentally taken off before everyone was fully in the car, and Jade was sure it wouldn't be the last. She just hoped they would make it to Weston's without any incident, like Kiara backing the car into a dumpster because she was high and thought she saw a bat in the backseat, which had happened a couple of weeks ago.

"No! After that last time... I will not endanger my baby," Kiara said while patting the dashboard.

"Yes, never mind about the humans inside the car," Jade mumbled.

Weston's house wasn't far, but they were also picking up Mara, Lyric, and Everly on the way. Kiara had told them about the party, and they hadn't hesitated when she'd invited them. Jade was sure Weston and the rest of the guys wouldn't mind in the slightest that they were bringing three cute freshmen with them, but she planned on making sure they all knew what the boys' main intentions probably were.

As they pulled up to Mara's house, Jade couldn't help but get swept up in a wave of nostalgia. Kiara honked her horn and almost immediately Lyric, Mara, and Everly appeared, wearing nearly identical dresses in teal, pale yellow, and coral. Jade laughed into the wind, remembering the times that she, Ariana, and Kiara had matched their outfits last year. They hadn't been as obvious about it, but it was still pretty embarrassing by any standard.

The young girls jumped into the convertible, talking over one another.

"Oh my gosh, this is such a cool car!" Lyric squealed. Her hair was down tonight and the pink, teal, and blue streaks peaked out every time she moved her head.

"Thanks so much for bringing us," Everly gushed, her light-red hair highlighted by the coral dress.

"Which boys are going to be there?" Mara asked.

"All of them," Kiara said with a smirk as she started up the engine.

Jade looked back at the girls, thinking of what advice would help prepare them for the night. "Just remember, you hold all the cards. The boys will try to make it seem like you don't, but you do. If you feel uncomfortable about anything at all, I don't care how small of a deal you may think it is, walk away and come find one of us."

They all nodded furiously from the back seat.

"And stay away from shots," Kiara added. Jade wanted to laugh, knowing exactly what night that piece of advice came from. It had been the same night Kiara and Ariana had kissed–Jade couldn't even remember if that had been a dare or not anymore.

They made it to the house just as it was getting dark outside. Weston's home sat on a large lot of land and along the perimeter of the house they had a wraparound porch, a fire pit, a swing set from when Weston was younger, and a gazebo. Weston's father and his new fiancé were away for the weekend, so naturally Weston was taking advantage of the situation.

Kiara parked the car and they headed into the massive kitchen with the younger girls trailing behind them like nervous ducklings. Melodie squealed when she saw them, running to throw her arms around Kiara and Ariana's necks and drunkenly gushing about how beautiful they looked. Jade stood back with the younger girls, trying to think of the best way to avoid a hug from Melodie.

"Who do we have here?" Weston said, walking up to assess the freshman. Mara ever so slightly stuck out her chest and pouted her lips as she introduced herself to him. His eyebrows raised for a moment and then he smirked. Jade cleared her throat, attempting to disrupt whatever playboy-esque thoughts were bubbling up in his brain.

"Jesus, Jade," Weston said when his eyes landed on her. Jade was still standing a few feet away from the crowd, leaning in the doorway a safe distance from Melodie. "Are you trying to give us all a heart attack?" Weston walked over and hugged her, holding on for a second longer than was necessary.

"What, I can't get dressed up every once in a while?" Jade teased back. She noticed Mara looked a little miffed by the amount of attention Weston was giving her.

Haiden sauntered into the kitchen, looking handsome in a white button-down and his hair pulled back into a bun.

"Haide, you know the girls, right?" Jade said, diverting the attention from herself. "This is Mara, Lyric, and Everly."

"I do now," Haiden said, wiggling his eyebrows at the girls, which garnered a few laughs. He began to pour beers for everyone as Jade pushed Weston to the side against the kitchen wall.

"Do *not* pull any moves on these three," she whispered to him, gesturing back with her hand. "I'm serious. I will come for you if anything happens to them."

"I'm harmless." Weston put his hands up in defense. "I do kinda like it when you're rough with me, though."

Jade made a gagging noise and Weston grinned before turning his attention back to the party. Jade squeezed out of the kitchen and made her way into the game room, where she found Aubrey and Alora standing by the pool table, talking animatedly. Aubrey wore a blue button-down adorned with tiny green anchors and dark gray shorts that were just a little shorter than the usual length that most of the guys wore, showing off his toned legs.

Alora looked beautiful as usual with her long, jet black hair cascading freely down her back. She wore a pair of white shorts overalls with a crazy patterned black, red, green, and yellow print V-neck tee that showed off her ample cleavage. She looked insanely cool–Jade never would have thought in a million years to attempt to pull off that look, but Alora looked like she had just left a magazine photoshoot. Jade warmly hugged them hello.

"What are you two gorgeous creatures talking about?" Jade asked.

"We want to try something," Alora said, grinning. "And we wanted to see if you, Ari, and K want to join us."

Aubrey smiled wickedly and clapped his hands. "We're going to try MDMA!" he exclaimed.

Jade was caught off guard momentarily. "Molly?"

"Yeah! Maybe after cheer tryouts are over for you guys?" Alora said.

Jade considered this for a moment. Their school seemed to be going through some sort of MDMA phase because she had been hearing about more and more people trying it every weekend. She was curious about the effects of the drug herself. Jade was always down to try new things, granted she was safe about it, and MDMA sounded like fun. Plus, she would be doing it with people she trusted, and they would all look after each other.

"I'm in," Jade said.

"Yes!" Aubrey shrieked with excitement.

"Let me see about Ari and K," Jade said. She reached down to pull out her phone, stopping abruptly when she realized she'd left her bag in Kiara's car. She headed back to the kitchen where she found Ariana and Kiara hanging out with the younger girls–Kiara was in a conversation with Mara and Haiden, but Mara's eyes were trained on Weston. *Oh lord*, Jade thought. It would be interesting to see how that one played out.

"Can I grab your keys, K? I left my phone in the car," Jade said. "And when I get back, we have to talk."

Kiara nodded distractedly and handed her keys over. Jade slipped out of the kitchen and into the foyer, only to be stopped in her tracks. There was Ian, looking as hot as ever, walking into the party right as she was walking out.

"Whoa," Ian blurted out, looking momentarily stunned. "Jade," he said, his voice rough.

Her chest constricted at the sound of her name coming from Ian's lips. Jade realized she had never heard him say her name before. Or maybe she had just never paid attention to him the way she was now... but she loved the way it rolled off his tongue.

"Are you here by yourself?" she asked without thinking.

"Not really," Ian said, shaking his head. "My friends are on their way in, but you know what? Come with me."

He took Jade's hand and led her out to the backyard. Jade grinned at Ian's back–maybe her luck was turning around. They both instinctively let go of the other's hand as they came into view of the party outside.

"Where are we going?" Jade asked, laughing at his urgent manner.

"Away from everyone," Ian replied with a grin, making Jade's heart speed up.

Ian finally stopped when they were at a bench around the back of the gazebo, out of view of the patio.

"Wait here, I'll be right back," Ian said, and he rushed off again.

Jade couldn't stop smiling; Ian had practically read her mind. They were about to have an actual conversation. And she wondered if she would still like him after they did. A couple of minutes later, Ian returned carrying a beer and a cup filled with reddish-orange liquid.

"I got you your favorite drink," Ian explained.

"*My* favorite drink?" Jade said, scoffing at him.

"Yeah, the one I make," Ian said and grinned again, holding up the cup.

Jade laughed as she swiped the cup out of his hand. "Thank you." After a beat, she said, "So, why did you pull me away?"

"I've wanted to talk to you for a while, but it seems like other people are always vying for your attention," Ian said, his clear blue eyes finding hers.

"More like your attention," Jade said half-jokingly, half-angrily. "Tell me, does it ever get tiring being constantly surrounded by your admirers?"

Jade heard the bite in her question and was puzzled by the swift change in her mood. It wasn't that she was mad at Ian, she was more so frustrated with the situation, and that Kristin had more of a bond with Ian than she did. Kristin and Ian had known each other for years, while she and Ian had barely had a handful of conversations. Jade felt like she hadn't been given a fair chance–that Kristin had already dug her claws and lies so deep into him that they weren't coming out.

"Ha!" Ian exclaimed. "And what about you? Are you seeing Taron?" His expression was serious now.

"No! I was never *seeing* him."

"Are you guys hooking up?"

"Did you hear that we were?"

"Yeah, I heard a few things," Ian said, and Jade's stomach coiled. "But I wanted to ask you for the truth."

Jade let out the breath she had been holding. Ian was asking her, rather than immediately believing the rumors. It was almost too good to be true. "No, we never hooked up. I kissed him once, and it was a mistake."

Ian stood still for a few moments, his mouth twitching at the corners. Jade crossed her arms, a scowl on her face. Ian's face broke into a grin and he let out a laugh. For a second Jade bristled, her defenses up. Having rumors spread about her wasn't funny. But then she looked into Ian's eyes and saw no malice there, only joy. She let out a laugh at the situation–how long had she ruminated over this, and for what? Ian hadn't believed the lies.

"Why are you laughing at me again?" Jade asked, happiness billowing up through her body.

"It just made me happy how pissed you got when I asked about Taron–I couldn't help it. I was about to start hating life if I had to be jealous of a guy like *Taron Cantor*," Ian said, grimacing as he said Taron's name.

Jade was caught off guard by Ian's sudden confession. She looked into his darkening blue eyes and imagined herself kissing his neck and running her hands over his chest. A delicious thrill jolted through her at the thought.

Ian gave her a sexy, somewhat cocky grin, as if he could read her thoughts. "I want to take you on a date. Will you go out with me?"

Jade let out a surprised laugh. She tried to remember if anyone had ever asked her out on an official date that wasn't a school dance or something else school-related. Weston had asked her to dinner once freshman year, but she had already been over him at that point and turned him down. How different this was!

She nodded her head yes. Ian grinned again and grabbed her face, leaning down to kiss her in one swift move, catching her off guard for the fiftieth time that night. Jade's heart leapt into her throat, and she found herself pleasantly surprised at how well he could kiss. He was gentle yet rough, and his lips were cool from his drink. Ian pulled back and Jade looked up at him through her long, dark eyelashes.

"Sorry, I–" Ian began, but Jade cut him off.

"Don't be," she said.

They stared at each other for a few moments, something electric passing between them. Jade saw a world of possibilities opening up that she hadn't deemed conceivable only a few moments ago. Ian's eyes shined with excitement and Jade was sure her expression mirrored his.

"Can we... Can we keep this a secret for a little while?" Jade asked. "I don't want to deal with the wrath of Kristin and her gang until I know what this is."

Ian studied her. "Oh, they're not that bad. They're just... they can get a little heated sometimes."

"You only think they're not that bad because you're a guy and half of them are in love with you," Jade responded. "Just... for me, okay?"

Ian gave her a nod of solidarity that made Jade's knees go a little weak. It was like they had a secret now, their own pact.

"Okay, so let me get this straight–if you decide you like me enough, we can do that in public?" Ian asked.

Jade laughed happily. "Yes. But let's keep it behind closed doors for now."

"So I just have to find more ways to sneak off with you from now on?" Ian asked, his question filled with promise. Jade's insides buzzed; she had never been more attracted to anyone. A strong desire to kiss him again overwhelmed her momentarily, but she decided it would be more fun to leave him wanting more.

"Mhm. Look for me later," Jade said mischievously, beginning to walk backward. She took a mental picture of the sexy way his mouth was still partially open while his eyes stayed on her. She turned back toward the house, knowing he would still be watching her as she walked away.

CHAPTER 10

K, A, T

After introducing the freshman girls to enough people that she didn't feel the need to babysit anymore, Kiara snagged some cookies from the kitchen and made her way to the back patio. She took a seat on Teague's lap, planting a kiss on his dark, smooth cheek. His arms slinked around her waist and Kiara stilled for a moment, fear gripping her by the neck. Did he feel the fat on the sides of her stomach?

"Mmm," Teague murmured against the bare skin of her back.

Kiara relaxed at the sound. She took a deep breath, enjoying the weight of Teague's head on her shoulder. A cool evening breeze swept across her legs, providing relief from the end of summer heat. Kiara looked down at her plate of cookies and grinned, a peculiar calm tinged with excitement taking over her–this was it. She was about to test out Reigh's miracle method. She grabbed a frosted cookie from the plate and held it to her lips, letting the sugary sweet smell fill her nose. Kiara sunk her teeth into the cookie, salivating as it melted in her mouth.

How she had dieted for this long without throwing up she didn't know. Thank the heavens she could eat desserts again without having to worry about the sugar turning into fat and going straight to her thighs. And the fact that she wasn't counting each calorie was enough to be pure bliss in itself. Before even finishing the first bite of the sugar cookie, Kiara popped half of an oatmeal raisin into her mouth. She turned and gave Teague the other half with a smile–she had four more on her plate, anyway.

Ariana, Haiden, Alora, Melodie, and Aubrey all lounged nearby, discussing what they thought it would be like to try MDMA for the first time.

"I mean, it's like nothing else you'll ever feel in your life–but the comedown can be horrible," Teague said.

Jade wandered over and found a seat with the group, a sheepish grin on her face. Kiara caught her eye and imitated her grin for no reason, feeling the effects of the sugar rush. She picked up the cookie and frosting sandwich she'd been saving for last and closed her eyes as she took an enormous bite.

"Kiara," Melodie called suddenly, loud enough so that everyone could hear. "I'm so jealous of you–your metabolism must be incredible if you can eat that much!"

The color drained from Kiara's cheeks as she opened her eyes and stared at her nearly empty plate, mouth still full of cookies. She wished she could punch Melodie in the face. She placed the rest of the cookie sandwich down and did her best to avoid eye contact with everyone.

"Melodie?" Jade called sweetly. Kiara looked up at Jade, surprised by her kind tone, but then saw the malevolence flashing in her dark green eyes. *This is not going to be pretty*, Kiara thought.

"Mhmm?" Melodie said, picking at an imaginary piece of lint on her dark pink wrap dress.

Aubrey took a swig of beer, his eyes dancing between Melodie and Jade, eyebrows raised to the sky.

"Are you counting how many cookies Kiara is eating? Because that's fucking weird," Jade said flatly while staring Melodie down.

"No," Melodie said with a scowl. "Lay off me Jade, it was just a question."

Jade gave a disbelieving laugh. "Sure."

Kiara's chest swelled with pride. She could always count on Jade to call out backhanded compliments.

"I just have the munchies," Kiara lied to the group. She hadn't smoked at the party because she was driving the girls home later, but figured that was a solid excuse.

"You eat as much as you want, babe. You know I wouldn't mind if you got curvier," Teague told Kiara while patting her hip.

Kiara cringed. She knew Teague meant to be reassuring, but his statement had the opposite effect. Kiara didn't *want* to get any curvier. She stood abruptly and excused herself to the bathroom. As Kiara traipsed through the house, she noticed Ariana had followed and was walking closely behind her.

"Hey, I have to pee too. Mind if I come with you?"

"No!" Kiara yelped, panic seizing her. "I mean, I think I may have to go to the *bathroom*-bathroom."

"Oh!" Ariana said and laughed, her cheeks turning slightly pink. "Yeah, I don't want to be in there for that!"

Kiara smiled weakly and ran upstairs to one of the lesser-used bathrooms. She locked the door and took a few gulps of water from the sink. Slowly, she took off the rings on her right hand, secured her hair in a bun, and turned on the faucet to create covering noise. This was the first time she was purging alone. A terrifying thought gripped her mind for a moment: *What if she couldn't get all the food to come back up?*

Kiara knelt next to the toilet as if to say a prayer. She closed her eyes and stuck her finger down her throat, engaging her gag reflex as Reigh had taught her. She heaved, ugly noises escaping from the depths of her stomach. She squeezed her eyes shut and wished she could drown out the sounds. If anyone were outside, they would surely hear her.

After a few agonizing moments she finally vomited, all the sweets and some of her dinner from earlier coming up and filling her mouth with bile as she involuntarily bit down on her hand.

"Ugh!" Kiara yelled out in disgust.

She rushed to the sink to wash off the vomit and looked in the mirror. Her eyes were bloodshot and shiny, her nose was running, and her mouth was an angry red around the corners. In that one flash of a moment, Kiara was disgusted with herself. But as soon as the feeling had come, it was gone and morphed into satisfaction. She had gotten to enjoy all of that dessert and now she wouldn't have to worry about any of the calories! Kiara searched through the cabinets for some mouthwash and swished it around in her mouth, spitting out the taste of regurgitated food. She took out her makeup and did her best to cover up the signs of irritation and redness on her face.

As Kiara reapplied her brown eyeliner, she thought through her alibi. She could blame the bloodshot eyes and earlier overconsumption of food on being high, the runny nose on allergies, and she could easily say her stomach was upset if she was asked why she was in the bathroom for so long. The signs of bulimia were pretty easy to cover up, she realized.

"Wow," Kiara said out loud, freezing in place.

That was the first time she had thought of this as bulimia. It was so strange, how she had fallen into it. Almost as if she hadn't noticed it happening. But the warning movies about eating disorders they watched in health class were so extreme, showcasing women whose bones protruded from their bodies as if they were about to poke through their skin at any moment. What she was doing wasn't like that at all. She was only throwing up occasionally, and only until she reached her goal weight.

Kiara nodded to no one, satisfied with her reasoning. She reached down to unlock the bathroom door, only then noticing the bite mark indented on the top of her right hand that was already beginning to bruise.

* * *

Ariana checked her reflection in the soft light of Weston's bathroom. Her hair hung in loose spirals around her face and the golden shadow she had applied earlier highlighted her hazel eyes, making them appear larger than they were. *Damn, I look* good, she thought to herself drunkenly. Ariana hiccuped and then laughed with her reflection. God, she loved it when the anxiety was absent. But where was Lukas? She missed him. She wanted to see him. Why hadn't she heard from him yet? She checked her phone but had no missed calls or texts. She would call him if he didn't text within the next ten minutes, she decided.

Ariana wandered back outside to the group. Right as she was about to sit, her phone vibrated in her hand. *Please be him, please be him*, Ariana chanted in her head before checking. The familiar thrill ran down her spine at the sight of Lukas' name on her screen. She rushed away from the party to a more private area by some bushes.

"Hey," she said breathlessly. "I was just thinking about you." The rest of the words came out in a rush; all the liquor she'd taken down had gone straight to her head.

"Hey," Lukas said. "Are you still at that party?"

Something in his voice was off. He wasn't coming. She knew it. "Yeah. Aren't you coming?"

"No... I don't think so."

Ariana's mood deflated like a pricked balloon. She hated that another person had so much control over her emotional state. She leaned against the side of the garage and attempted to relax.

"Oh? Why not?" she asked, trying to keep her voice light.

"I'm just not feeling it tonight." He was being exasperatingly vague.

A surge of anxiety pummeled through her chest. What was going on? "So, what are you going to do instead, Lufas?" she asked, annoyed that she felt like she was prying and irritated that he wasn't exactly making the conversation easy.

"Are you drunk?"

"*No*, are you?" she asked accusingly.

"Well, you just called me Lufas, so..."

Ariana's cheeks burned. Shit. "I'm *not* drunk," she said, her tone indignant. "Your name is hard."

Lukas sighed into the phone. "I'm going to hang out with some friends. I'll text you later, okay? Have fun."

"Well, I guess that's that then," Ariana said and hung up.

That was it? She couldn't tell if she was overreacting or not, but they had made plans for tonight, hadn't they? Ariana sniffed. She was pissed, disappointed, and most of all, angry with herself. She didn't want her mood to be so dependent on someone else's whim.

"Ariana!" Weston yelled from the back patio. "Shots?" He held up a bottle of tequila and grinned.

"Yes!" Ariana yelled and hurried over. She threw one arm around Weston's neck and grabbed the bottle from him with her other hand, putting on what she hoped was a good act of being happy so no one would ask her what was wrong. Right now, she decided, she would drown her feelings and forget all about Lukas. Tomorrow she would have hell to pay–her anxiety usually shot off the rocker after a night of drinking–but in her booze-laden mind, the payoff was worth it. "Can we do half-shots though? I may or may not be a little tipsy already."

Weston laughed and began to pour the liquor. Haiden, Jade, Melodie, Alora, Teague, Aubrey, and the three freshman girls gathered around, holding their overflowing shot glasses up as Weston cleared his throat to make a toast. Ariana glanced around. Where was Kiara? What was taking her so long in the bathroom? Her thoughts were sidetracked as she watched Ian walk up and brush behind Jade, who stood slightly away from the group. Ariana could swear she saw him linger by Jade's side before pouring himself a shot. Jade looked like she was holding back a smile, and Ian's eyes stayed on Jade's as he stood on the other side of the crowd. It seemed like something had happened between them, and Ariana wasn't surprised in the least. Jade looked like a goddess tonight–Ian had probably been a goner from the moment he laid eyes on her.

"I'll make this short and sweet," Weston announced. "Here's

to beautiful women." He raised his glass pointedly in Jade's direction and Ian's back stiffened.

Ariana frowned as she thought of Lukas ditching her tonight. Maybe he didn't like her as much as she thought after all. She never would've passed up an opportunity to hang out with him. A stab of sadness sliced through her gut. She threw the shot down her throat and immediately grabbed the bottle to pour another one. Screw the half-shot. "Who's game to take another one with me?" she asked, her eyes darting from person to person, daring everyone around her.

"I'll take one!" A voice called from behind her. Ariana whirled around to see Daire walking across the yard with a group of his friends. She was so excited and surprised to see Daire that her mood lifted all over again.

"D!" she yelled. She ran to him without thinking. He was so tall that she had to jump and stretch her arms up to hug him, but he caught her mid-leap and swung her around.

"It's good to see you, too," Daire said with a laugh. After a beat, he let her down and Ariana gave quick hugs to the rest of the seniors in his pack.

"I'm so glad you're here. I've missed you!" Ariana said, pouting. The shots had definitely gone to her head.

"Yeah, football practice has been crazy," Daire said, a large grin stretching across his face. "But we'll start hanging out more, I promise."

It was so easy to be around Daire compared to Lukas. "Okay," she said, looking up at him through her eyelashes.

Daire smiled down at her. He was warm and genuine, and Ariana couldn't help but smile back. She didn't know what it was about him, but everything didn't seem so bad when Daire was around. And if anyone could take her mind off of Lukas, it was Daire. Ariana grabbed his hand and dragged him back to the table where the bottle of tequila and shot glasses rested.

"Are y'all ready?" Ariana asked the group with a devilish grin.

* * *

Jade had been watching Ian's figure out of the corner of her eye for a while now, waiting for an opportunity to grab him and take him somewhere private. She stood on the opposite end of the room with Aubrey, who was spilling about his crush on a new guy that had transferred to their school this year. Jade couldn't fully focus, which seemed to be fine, as Aubrey was mostly talking *at* her at this point.

"He's so confident. Like, he doesn't care what people think, Jade. It's so attractive. Not to mention his cheekbones! I could dream about his cheekbones all night," Aubrey said, his hands fluttering to his face.

Jade glanced in Ian's direction again. He locked eyes with her and a tingling sensation ran down her legs. Ian looked her up and down pointedly, his eyes devouring her body and causing her to burn with desire. She yearned to feel his lips on hers, his body pressed up against hers...

Ian looked into her eyes again and smiled, then returned his attention to a conversation with Daire, who had an arm swung casually around Ariana's shoulders. Jade thought about inviting Ian back to her place after the party but then decided against it. If Dani were to see them together, everyone would probably hear about it, and that was the last thing she wanted. She also wasn't sure she trusted herself to take it slow with Ian if they were alone together, in her room, with a bed...

Suddenly, Jade couldn't stand not being close to him for another moment.

"Aub, I'll help you come up with a game plan to get his number, okay? He sounds incredible." Jade squeezed Aubrey's hand. "I've gotta go check on Ariana though."

Jade walked over and hugged Ariana, grazing her hand against Ian's as she did. Ian grabbed her for a quick second, letting go before anyone saw.

"Ian," a girl's shrill voice called out from behind them.

Jade clenched her teeth involuntarily. There was no mistaking that voice: Kristin and her group of followers had arrived.

"Jade, we're not at a nightclub. What're you wearing?" Kristin said with a giggle as they approached. Jade narrowed her eyes. Kristin was wearing a white silk tank top with floral print and jean shorts, her thin lips painted a peach color to match the outfit. It wasn't flattering.

"Honestly, I don't even need to say anything about what you're wearing," Jade said with a smile.

Ariana was quick to Jade's side, intervening before Jade and Kristin had time to exchange anything more than passive-aggressive greetings. "Jade? Comenside with me?" Ariana asked, slurring her words slightly while looping her arm through Jade's.

"Thanks," Jade whispered. They left Kristin to fall all over Ian as they pushed their way inside. Jade half-figured Ian would follow them, but he didn't.

Ariana stumbled over the living room rug and practically fell onto the couch. She laughed, pulling Jade on top of her. "Ari!" Jade said, snorting with laughter.

"I'm sorry," Ariana said, still giggling. "I just wanted to cuddle you. I'm clearly the only one around here not getting any action."

Jade sat up and raised her eyebrows. "What do you know?"

"I am assuming that *someone*," Ariana said, placing her finger on Jade's nose, "...may have had a little rendezvous with Ian earlier?"

"How did you know that?"

"I'm a wizard," Ariana said, shrugging.

Jade laughed and Ariana joined in, laughing hard at her own stupid joke.

"Yeah, Ian kissed me. And he wants to take me on a date."

"Aww, I'm so happy for you. Where and when did it happen?"

"Outside by the gazebo earlier. He just grabbed me and kissed me, Ari! It was so hot." Jade could feel her face flush with color, but she didn't care.

"Well, I love that for you, but Lukas won't even come hang out with me at a party apparently," Ariana said with a hiccup.

"Oh. That explains why *someone*," Jade mimicked Ariana, placing a finger on her nose, "is a little tipsy. Why won't Lukas come?"

"I don't know. Maybe he doesn't feel like it. I think he's hanging out with his friends tonight." Ariana picked at the couch.

"But aren't his friends here?" Jade asked.

"I'm guessing some of his other friends in swimming or something. The ones who don't party."

Ariana bowed her head further, looking defeated. *This is not good*, Jade thought. She wondered if perhaps Lukas was the one person who Ariana couldn't see clearly.

"Hey Ariana," Jade said softly. "It's time for some tough love. Remember when you said you never wanted to be the person who got so obsessed with a guy that nothing else mattered? I'm not saying you're at that point, but he's got a lot of control over your emotions. And I think I remember Kiara promising to kick your ass if you ever started to slip. So you have two options–either cheer up, or I'll go find Kiara."

Ariana burst out laughing and Jade joined in, smiling at her best friend.

"That's better," Jade said. "Where is K anyway?"

"The last I saw her she was going to the bathroom. She *has* been missing for a while..."

"She's probably in there taking a few hits or something," Jade joked distractedly. She was beginning to wonder where Ian was as well. Surely Kristin couldn't monopolize his attention for the entire party?

A loud shriek boomed from outside and Jade turned to see the back door fly open. Daire strolled in, followed by a stoned-looking Haiden.

"Ari, J!" Haiden called out, walking over to them with his arms outstretched before collapsing on the couch. Jade cracked up as Haiden rolled his head onto her lap, his reddened eyes barely slivers.

"I'll make us some drinks in the kitchen?" Daire said.

"Yes, please," Ariana said sweetly, standing to follow Daire and stumbling slightly as she did.

"Ohhh no. None for you, drunky," Jade said, grabbing the hem of Ariana's dress and pulling her back down to the couch. Ariana giggled and buried her face in Jade's shoulder. "D, will you get her some water instead, please? For both of these hoodlums?"

Daire nodded and bent over to search the fridge.

Jade stroked Haiden's hair. "What was that loud scream by the way?"

"Oh, Weston accidentally spilled some tequila on Kristin or something," Daire said with feigned nonchalance, barely holding back his laughter.

"That was just the distraction we used to get away from them," Haiden said. "It was West's idea. Those girls have too much drama for me, man."

"Wow. What did she do to piss West off?" Ariana asked, sobering up momentarily.

"Just trying to start shit, as always," Haiden shrugged. "West always seems to find a way to shut people up when they go after the ones he cares about, doesn't he?"

Jade looked down at Haiden in surprise. He was staring pointedly up at her from his spot on her lap, and Jade was about to ask him about the comment, but Ian walked in. Jade sat up straight, her mood immediately lifting at the sight of him and all thoughts of Weston gone.

"Water is served," Daire said, spinning two glass bottles out onto the counter with a flourish.

They wandered into the kitchen and Jade pushed herself up to sit on the counter. She felt Ian's presence beside her before she saw him.

"Meet me upstairs in five minutes," Ian whispered as he walked by.

Jade couldn't focus as everyone talked enthusiastically around her. She was in her own world where it was only she and Ian. She watched him slip away, and then after waiting several minutes, did the same.

Jade wandered up the staircase and paused by the first bedroom with the door open. Weston's mahogany king-sized bed waited for her in the darkness. Her heart beat in her throat as she remembered last year when she yearned to be alone with Weston in a scenario just like this. And now here she was, looking for Ian instead. She couldn't make out much as she walked down the dimly lit hall, but suddenly a hand reached out and pulled her into a bedroom. Ian swiftly shut the door behind Jade and pushed her up against the wall, kissing her hard. Jade drew a quick breath out of surprise as Ian's mouth closed over hers, her libido instantly on fire. Ian pulled her arms above her head as their kissing intensified. Jade pressed her body against his, causing Ian to let out a groan against her mouth.

The sound of footsteps coming up the stairs made them both freeze. Jade clamped a hand over Ian's mouth to silence his heavy breathing. His eyes searched hers, and Jade took a mental picture of the unguarded expression in them. She knew she would want to remember this moment. Ian licked her hand, causing her to laugh. She clamped her free hand over her own mouth. They stilled, listening as the footsteps headed away from them toward the bathroom. When they finally heard the door open and close, Jade let her hands drop. They grinned at each other.

"To be continued?" she asked.

"Wow," Ian said breathlessly. "Yes."

Jade ran from the room, leaving Ian staring after her again. Who knew sneaking around would be this much fun?

CHAPTER 11
Kiara

Kiara didn't want to rejoin the party. She stood at the bottom of the stairs, watching her friends laugh and flirt with one another in the kitchen without a care in the world. She could easily walk back in, fake some laughter, and pretend like everything was okay–she knew that's what she *should* do to keep up appearances. But she was too far away from them tonight. A rift had been cemented with her decision to purge; the secret acting as an invisible wall between herself and everyone she loved. Kiara sighed and turned, wandering outside to the lesser-occupied part of the backyard toward the aging, paint-chipped gazebo.

"Hey, can I have one of those?" Kiara asked an army boots clad boy walking by.

The boy raised his eyebrows and pointed to the cigarette in his mouth as if in question. Barely anyone smoked real cigarettes anymore. Kiara nodded her head, doing her best to give a captivating smile despite the feeling of despair in her stomach. The boy smiled back and acquiesced, handing Kiara a long, thin cigarette and a lighter. Kiara said thanks and turned on her heel before any further conversation could happen, making her way into the abandoned gazebo.

She lit the cigarette and took a long, deep drag. She leaned back on the bench seat and listened to the night, alive with chirping and humming insects. She tried to smile and appreciate the beauty around her but to no avail. Her brain wouldn't shut off. She thought of what throwing up could do to her teeth, since she was bringing up acid and eroding the enamel each time she puked. She wrestled with the jealousy of girls who were naturally skinny and didn't have to go through what she did to lose a few pounds. She anguished over what would happen if anyone found out what she was doing. And on top of everything, she was hungry again. She had cleared out her stomach, including what little food she had eaten for dinner. But since nothing was labeled, she couldn't count the calories of any food at the party and therefore wouldn't be able to eat. A dark dread pooled and bubbled in her gut.

Kiara checked her notifications to distract herself. Alora had posted a photo of the group from earlier and tagged her in it. Kiara skimmed over everyone's smiling faces, finally landing on her own. She looked happier then, the excitement of the binge and purge still looming. But her arms... they squeezed against her sides and looked gigantic. They were *way* too big. She went to the profile of one of her favorite fitness models and checked the girl's arms. They were taught and muscular, and even when they were at her sides they looked lean. Not an inch of fat anywhere. Kiara flipped back to Alora's photo, comparing. She shuddered at her appearance and slammed her phone down, turning her head away to look at the moon. She needed to lose weight faster.

"Hey there," Teague's voice rang out in the dark.

"Oh, hey," Kiara said, her voice dragging.

"What're you doing? You hate those," Teague said as he appeared in the gazebo, his dark brown skin glowing in the moonlight.

"I know," Kiara said, looking at the cigarette. "I just needed something. I didn't feel like hanging out with everyone."

"I feel you, baby. Was it what Melodie said?"

"No," Kiara lied, suddenly feeling like she needed to get out of the conversation. "We all see a lot of each other already with cheer. I just wanted some time to enjoy nature without the constant chattering."

Kiara never lied to Teague, and the pressure of not telling him what was eating at her was almost palpable. A strange silence hung in the air, as if he could sense her omission. Teague looked away from her, and Kiara wondered if he was putting together the pieces of the puzzle.

She hurried to fill the quiet. "But I should go look for Mara and the girls. I want to make sure they don't do anything they'll regret or drink too much."

"You're a good friend," Teague said, not turning to meet her eyes. "I'll find you later."

Near 1 a.m., and right around the time Lyric attempted to do a keg stand with no assistance, kicking her legs in the air and nearly face-planting on the kitchen floor, Kiara announced it was time to go home. She ushered the young girls outside and into her car, where they clambered in the back seat and promptly began declaring their love for each other. Kiara shut the door, laughing a little despite herself. How many times had she, Jade, and Ariana done the same thing?

"I'll see you later?" Teague asked as he kissed her goodbye.

"I can't wait," Kiara said, doing her best to smile at him. She *was* excited for tonight–she was. Teague smiled back before turning toward the party. "Don't forget to send Ari and J out!" she called at the last second.

Minutes later, Daire ducked out of the house, carrying a laughing Ariana in his arms like a damsel in distress while Jade floated along behind them.

"She, uh, refused to take her shoes off, but they were hurting her too much to walk anymore," Daire said as he approached

Kiara. His cheeks were flushed and a huge grin was plastered on his face.

"Oh my god! Where were you ALL night, K?" a drunken Ariana shrieked as she was being placed in the car. "So much has happened!" Ariana got in the back with the three freshmen who were giggling hysterically. Jade climbed into the front and gave Kiara a look.

"Oh yeah, you missed all of this all night," Jade said and gestured her hand toward the backseat. "Someone has had a *little* too much liquor."

"Let's get the girls home. Is everyone staying at Mara's?" Kiara asked.

"Yes!" all three chirped at the same time.

"Everyone buckle up!" Jade said while reaching back into the tumble of limbs and helping to fasten seat belts.

Kiara put on some throwback Britney Spears for the hell of it and cranked up the speakers. She and Jade cracked up as ecstatic screams erupted from the backseat, followed by loud, off-key singing. Jade threw her arms up and began to dance, and a modicum of happiness crept back into Kiara's bones.

When they pulled up to Mara's house Jade and Kiara forced Ariana to stay in the car while they got the younger girls inside. Lyric and Mara incessantly spilled their thanks up to the very last second.

"It was the best night of our lives!" Everly screamed before the door shut, causing Jade and Kiara to erupt into laughter all over again.

"Ten bucks says Everly will puke tonight," Jade said once they had gotten back in the car.

When they finally parked at Jade's house around 2 a.m., Kiara perched on the trunk and lit her first bowl of the night. Jade wandered over to take a seat beside her while Ariana remained in the backseat with her face glued to her phone, giggling as she texted away.

"Where were you tonight?" Jade asked her. "A lot did

happen." Jade's hair was messy and blowing across her face in the wind. Her lips were slightly swollen and chapped and her eyes wide and beautiful. She looked like she had definitely been up to something.

"I just got away from the party for a bit," Kiara explained. "But every time I looked, you were MIA too."

Jade leaned forward with a secretive smile and told Kiara everything that had happened with Ian, and then proceeded to explain Ariana's predicament with Lukas.

"Do you think he cares about her?" Kiara whispered to Jade.

"Honestly, I don't know. From the way he talks to her, it seems like he does. But I've never really spoken to him, so how would I know?" Jade whispered back.

As if on cue, Ariana's head popped up. "Lukas is going to come by! Is that all right?" She looked so hopeful it scared Kiara a little.

"*Now* he decides he has time for you?" Kiara snapped. Ariana was allowing Lukas to set the tone of their relationship–how did she not see that?

"He was just busy earlier and didn't feel like partying. It's a *good thing* he's not wild," Ariana said.

"Yes, it's fine Ari," Jade said. "Teague is still spending the night, right?"

"Yeah, he's coming over soon. Thanks again for letting him," Kiara said, relaxing at the thought of Teague's presence.

"Just clean up any messes you make!" Jade said, jokingly poking Kiara's ribs. "You know what I mean..."

"Gross!" Kiara swatted Jade's hand away. The weed was starting to hit her–a familiar fuzzy, relaxed feeling was crawling over her brain, making her smile. Kiara took a deep breath and tilted her head back, pondering her change in lifestyle. She would only keep throwing up until she got her weight down to where she wanted it, then she would stop–it wasn't as if she would do this forever, so what was the harm in keeping this one tiny secret from everyone? It did feel weird though. Jade and Ariana always told her everything, and the same went for her with them. But she had to keep the throwing up her secret if she wanted to continue to have a way to eat whatever she wanted while still losing weight. Ariana and Jade would undoubtedly try to stop her if they knew, so as much as she loved them, she couldn't let them know.

It'll be over soon, Kiara thought, reassuring herself again. *It's not like I'm going to do this forever.*

Kiara sat on the edge of the pool in Jade's backyard, swinging her bare legs around in the water. She'd taken off her gladiator sandals and flung them onto one of the beige lounge chairs where Jade and Ariana were perched nearby. Kiara watched how the water's reflections played with the appearance of her legs with each kick. One kick up and they looked thinner, one kick down, fatter. Fascinated, she watched her legs change kick after kick, thin to fat, fat to thin, and back again. *My legs are disgusting*, Kiara thought. She shuddered and pulled them out of the water, seizing a towel nearby to cover herself.

An engine rumbled in the driveway and Kiara got excited thinking Teague had arrived, but then remembered he was skateboarding over. It must be Lukas. She looked over at Ariana, who was grinning like an idiot, which confirmed her suspicion.

Lukas stepped into the backyard with only the slightest hesitation, dressed in his usual muscle-hugging type of shirt with a backward baseball cap. *He* is *an attractive guy*, Kiara thought, but he had a calculated look that she didn't like. Kiara could just picture him picking out t-shirts at the store that hugged his muscles perfectly, while trying his hardest not to make it obvious he was attempting to do so. Lukas walked over and sat next to Ariana, taking her hand in his.

"You look beautiful," he said to her.

A flush of awe and excitement took over Ariana's face. *You would've thought she'd just seen a unicorn*, Kiara thought. *Do* I *look like that when Teague comes around?* Ariana leaned her head onto Lukas' shoulder, a dreamy smile on her lips.

Oh god, I hope not, Kiara thought, making herself laugh out loud.

Lukas gave Kiara a quizzical look.

"She does that sometimes," Ariana said with a warm smile.

Lukas turned to face both Kiara and Jade. "I'm sorry I missed tonight. Those kinds of parties aren't really my thing." Lukas waved his hand as he spoke. "Sometimes I feel like I see all those people way too much and I have to take a break. Know what I mean?"

"I know *exactly* what you mean," Jade said, nodding her head.

Kiara narrowed her eyes at Jade. *Don't get suckered in by him*, she wanted to say. Kiara found it strange that Lukas had apologized to them about missing tonight and not Ariana. She decided to stay out of the conversation, still trying to figure out exactly how she felt about him.

"Kiara," Lukas said abruptly, holding out a bag of bud to her. "I brought over some Willie Nelson–I thought you might want some."

"What!" Kiara shouted, forgetting that she was weary of Lukas momentarily and grabbing the bag. "That's one of my *favorites*!" Lukas grinned at her, and Kiara understood Ariana's view for a split second. Lukas was turning his charm on for them, she realized, and he wasn't half bad at it. *Fine*, Kiara conceded to herself, *I'll be nicer for tonight*.

"Thank you. That was thoughtful," Kiara said. "I'm sure T will appreciate this too."

"Speak of the devil," Jade said as Teague opened the back gate, sweaty from the ride over on his skateboard.

"What up," Teague called out while peeling his sweat-soaked shirt over his head, revealing an impressively toned stomach. Kiara's heart leapt into her throat as she glimpsed Teague's V-shaped muscles in his lower abdomen–sometimes she still couldn't believe that he had wanted to be with her over all the others that threw themselves at him. "I just gotta wash off real quick!" Teague tossed his cell phone and keys onto the deck and dove into the pool, splashing Kiara as he did. She laughed and leaned down to kiss his reemerging head.

"Hi baby," Teague whispered when he came up for air. "I get to spend the night with you tonight."

Kiara giggled at Teague's shining eyes and excited expression. "Yes, you do," she whispered back. "Wanna dry off?"

Teague nodded and Kiara left her spot on the edge of the pool to grab a towel and settle in near Jade on one of the lounge chairs. Teague took a seat beside her, his half-naked body acting as a pleasant reminder that they would be alone together in a bed soon. She grazed her fingers along Teague's leg and he leaned in to give her a discreet kiss on the ear that sent shivers down her spine. She smiled, wondering if this time would feel any different from their first time.

"I don't understand why some people are still against medical marijuana when the science coming through is backing up all the benefits," Jade was saying as Kiara tuned back into reality.

"It's like how people are still freaked out by psilocybin," Ariana chimed in. "When the government decides to campaign against a beneficial drug for so long, it becomes ingrained in peoples' minds and becomes a part of their values. It's fear. It'll just take time and more leaders speaking out to hopefully change the perception."

"And people not misusing those drugs and being idiots," Lukas added on.

"Yeah, but people misuse alcohol every day," Teague countered. "It's arguably the worst thing for you."

Ariana shifted in her seat, pulling her hand out of Lukas' to take a large gulp of water. Kiara knew Ariana relied on alcohol to take away her anxiety at times, and that she wasn't proud of it. Teague's comment probably made her nervous about the resurgence of anxiety that would come in the morning. Kiara made a mental note to check in on her tomorrow.

Kiara sat back and studied Ariana and Lukas' interactions. Every once in a while, when Jade or Teague were talking or telling a story, Ariana and Lukas would look at each other. It wasn't a glance or anything flirtatious, Kiara realized. They were staring at each other like they were connected, like they were talking to each other through their eyes. Those looks made Kiara doubt her earlier assumptions about Lukas' feelings–those weren't any normal stares.

Teague slid his hand into Kiara's lap, diverting her attention. He grabbed her hand and squeezed it, smiling at her. Initially, Kiara smiled back as she looked at their entwined fingers resting on her lap, but then she noticed that her dress had ridden up to her mid-thighs, and her face fell into a frown at the sight of her legs. Her thighs were engulfing the patio chair. She panicked, trying to remember if they had looked this fat all night.

She sucked in small bits of air, finding it hard to breathe normally. Surely everyone had seen her huge, bulging thighs–and not just now, but earlier at the party too. Was that why Melodie had made that comment? Was she trying to warn her? She let go of Teague's hand and shifted her weight so that her thighs weren't touching the chair, trying to calm herself and slow her quickened breaths.

"Everything okay?" Teague said to her quietly.

Kiara put her hand to her face, unconsciously touching her lips. "Yeah, I'm just tired. I think I'm going to head up to bed."

"Okay, I'll be right there after I dry off," Teague said as he took her hand again and kissed it. Kiara couldn't even look him in the eyes–he must have seen how fat her thighs were. There was no way he hadn't. She hurriedly said goodnight to everyone and headed to the guest bedroom where she and Teague were staying. Dani and her friends hadn't made it home yet, leaving the house empty.

Kiara pulled shorts and a t-shirt out of her overnight bag

and stripped down to her underwear, catching a glimpse of herself in the full-length mirror. She grimaced at her reflection: her thighs looked too wide, and even with the weight she had lost her stomach was still soft. Her boobs looked small and disproportionate on her body. What was truly astounding to Kiara though, was how she had never noticed all of these flaws before she'd started dieting. She used to love her boobs. It was like she'd been blind to the flaws, and only now could she truly see.

How had I walked around looking like this all the time and never realized how many problem areas I had? she thought to herself, a tear sliding down her cheek. Kiara had also begun to notice flaws in others she had never seen before. Sometimes it felt as though everywhere she looked was a reminder of weight and size. She knew now that she wouldn't be happy until she got her body slimmed down the exact way she wanted.

She had to lose more weight–that was the only answer.

"Hey," Teague said softly from the doorway. "Man, do I love that view."

Kiara spun around, her hands flying to her stomach and chest.

"Teague!" she yelled, her voice harsh from humiliation. "Don't you knock?"

"What's the big deal? No one's up here. It's just us."

Teague moved across the room and put his arms around her waist, causing Kiara to stiffen. His hands were resting on her hips–her pudgy, too wide hips. She took a step away from him and Teague let his hands fall to his sides. Kiara grabbed her pajamas and threw them on.

"Why are you putting that on?" Teague teased her, but she could hear the caution in his voice. "I'm just going to take it all off you again."

Teague looked as sexy as ever, his eyes traveling up and down her body. Yet, instead of this turning her on, Kiara could only think of every single flaw he must be seeing. She hastily got into bed and pulled the sheets up around her, trying to shield herself and cover the imperfections.

"No. I don't feel like it," Kiara said.

"Are you not feeling well?" Teague asked with concern in his eyes.

"No, I just don't want to! Jesus, can you get off my back?" Kiara lashed out.

Teague took a step back and ran a hand over his head.

"What's wrong Kiara?" he asked. "What did I do?"

The hurt in his voice unraveled her anger in a split second. What was wrong with her? That rage had come out of nowhere. She would *have* to get a handle on her mood swings. She reached up and pulled Teague to her so she could wrap her arms around his warm body.

"I'm sorry," she said, her voice shaking. "I don't know what came over me. Can we just go to sleep and forget about this?"

"I guess so." Teague climbed into bed, turning his back toward her. Kiara knew this wasn't good. She wanted to make things better, but there was nothing she could say right now. How could she explain to him that she didn't want him to see her naked because she looked disgusting without clothes on?

"You know, I thought tonight was gonna be amazing because we have this room to ourselves. No parents, no interruptions, no nothing–just you and me... What happened?" Teague said, his back still facing her.

Another tear rolled down her cheek. "I'm sorry," she repeated lamely.

Teague turned his head toward her slightly, as if to wait for her to say more. After a few moments of silence, he let out a sigh and turned away from her, settling back into the bed.

Kiara stared at Teague's muscular back in the darkness. What had she done? Her mind began to race to the worst possible scenarios that could come from this fight, and she imagined losing him. What if they broke up and he started seeing someone else? She tried to push the unwanted thought from her mind. That would be devastating. She loved him too much. With that thought, Kiara couldn't stand to not be touching him.

"Teague," she almost cried. "Come here. Please..."

Teague rolled over instantly, looking alarmed at the sound of her voice. But her lips closed over his before he could say anything, and she was relieved when he gave in and kissed her back. It was dark enough in the room that she figured he wouldn't see that much of her. She pulled her shirt over her head and grabbed at his boxers, knowing in the back of her mind that this wouldn't fix anything.

CHAPTER 12

A, J, K

Ariana leaned back in her chair during sixth period AP English on Thursday, a smile hanging on her face that she hadn't quite been able to shake all week. Nothing could throw off her good mood, not even cheer tryouts today. Before Lukas left Jade's house on Friday night he had taken her to the side of the garage where they were hidden in darkness. He had pushed his body close to hers and ran his lips along her jawline in between a whispered apology for missing the party, nearly making her lose her breath. Why he hadn't kissed her yet was beyond her, but she had to admit she loved the anticipation. They'd spent the rest of the weekend talking on the phone and texting in their spare moments.

When Ariana had arrived at school on Monday, she'd wanted to shout to the world that she and Lukas were together. He'd asked for her schedule and throughout the week had been showing up to her classes randomly, texting her to come outside and meet him. Ariana never remembered school to be so exciting; they were in their own world when they walked the empty hallways, talking about nothing and everything at the same time.

Yesterday, Ariana experienced her most exciting Chemistry class to date–during a boring lecture about the elements of the periodic table she felt a single vibration from her phone and automatically checked the window. When she saw Lukas' figure leaning against the lockers waiting for her, a certainty solidified in her soul that was terrifying and exhilarating at the same time: she was falling in love with him. As shocking as it was, as soon as the thought appeared in her mind she knew it was true. How could it have happened this fast?

"I can't stop thinking about you," Lukas said when she slipped into the deserted hallway to meet him. "Do you know how beautiful you are, inside and out?"

Ariana wore a loose-fitting white tee with black jeans and a thin, gold necklace with a crescent moon resting on her collarbone. Nothing special, but she might as well have been dressed for a gala with the way Lukas looked at her.

Ariana shook her head in embarrassment. She wasn't the best with compliments, especially from him.

"You *know,*" Lukas said, certain. He took her wrist delicately in his hand, guiding her body back against the wall.

Ariana's breath caught in her throat.

Lukas leaned forward, his brown eyes clear with intention. Ariana couldn't move; she could barely breathe. "I have to actively stop myself from staring at you," he said in her ear.

Ariana bit her lip. She had never wanted anyone more than at that moment. She wanted to feel his body against hers, his bare skin on hers in the dark. She wanted him to touch her where no one ever had before. She looked into his eyes, her want unmasked, and Lukas let out a short breath. The intensity of his stare made her certain he was thinking the same thing.

A locker slammed shut down the hallway and caused them both to jump, the spell broken. *Damn it,* Ariana thought. She'd been sure he was about to kiss her. They parted ways after that, and even though it had only been a day since she'd seen him last, it felt like a lifetime.

An excited shiver ran through her at the memory. She could relive their moments again and again and never tire of them. They had plans to hang out again tonight, so Ariana only had to get through a few more hours before they were together again... then maybe she would finally see what it felt like to kiss him.

A whisper from the seat beside her brought Ariana back to reality.

"What're you grinning about?" Alora whispered, raising her eyebrows.

"Nothing," Ariana answered, trying and failing to pull the smile off her face.

"Yeah, bullshit," Alora said, her soft laughter chiming.

Ariana let her grin spread. "I've kinda been seeing Lukas lately. We're hanging out again tonight and I'm just excited. I like him a lot."

Alora scrunched up her tan face. "Lukas Jansen? Doesn't he have a girlfriend?"

A strange pit began to form in Ariana's stomach. "What? No. I know he used to date Laura Keaton, but that was last year."

"No, not her, that girl on the dance team. Um... Olivia, I think."

"Olivia?" Ariana said skeptically, heat rising to her cheeks.

Ariana didn't need to ask which Olivia she was referring to. Olivia Bellepoint was a junior–she wasn't one of Kristin's clan but was well known nonetheless. Olivia always seemed to have a smile on her face, like nothing bad had or could ever happen to her. She seemed, to Ariana at least, to effortlessly float through the halls, leaving a trail of admirers in her wake. Her long, wavy black hair, olive skin, and natural beauty made a lot of girls jealous, but she was so sweet that no one could hate her for it. Ariana doubted Olivia ever had to deal with anxiety.

Did Lukas have a thing with her? Ariana thought back through all of their conversations, looking for clues. She knew Olivia and her girlfriends were close with Lukas' friends on the swim team, but he'd never said anything about her.

"I think they're just friends. What made you think that?" Ariana said.

"I feel like maybe I heard it somewhere or something? I'm not sure if that's right at all though–you know me."

Ariana smiled at Alora, but a simmering pulse of anxiety still jumped in her bones. Being with Lukas was so perfect that all along Ariana had been waiting for something to go wrong. Was this it?

"GIRLS," Mrs. Havardly, their stern and perpetually aggravated teacher interrupted them. "You'll have time to talk once you've completed your assignment and I've finished handing out your graded exams."

Mrs. Havardly placed a folded paper onto each student's desk with a clack of her blood-red fingernails as Ariana's mind raced out of control. She tried to calm herself–there was no way Lukas was seeing anyone else. It wasn't like he was very active on social media, but Ariana was sure she would've seen something to give her a hint if he were dating someone.

Clack.

She remembered that Lukas was in some group pictures with Olivia on Instagram, but they weren't ever near each other or anything. The only thing that nagged her was that if he were seeing someone else... if he were seeing Olivia–*perfect* Olivia–too, then his slightly erratic behaviors would make a lot more sense.

Clack.

Lukas' excuse for his absence from the party this past weekend came to mind, and Ariana realized he had never told her who he'd been with that night, and nearly all of his friends had been at the party. But he *had* come over to see her later on in the night. There's no way he was with another girl.

Clack.

It was just like when she was ten years old, one minute she had her dad and everything was fine and safe, and then a few sentences from her mother had ripped the world out from under her: "He's gone, Ariana. He's never coming back."

Ariana's breathing picked up and dread poured over her. Was she going to have an anxiety attack over this? Here, and now?

Fuck, Ariana realized, the panic hitting her like a bus–*I am*. Her hand shot up as she squeaked out a quick plea to Mrs. Havardly to use the restroom.

The tall, crow-like teacher turned to glare at Ariana with beady black eyes. "Maybe you should've thought of that *before* you spoke out of turn in my class."

"Please," Ariana pleaded. "It's an emergency."

"I doubt it." Mrs. Havardly turned her back on Ariana and continued passing out the exams.

Ariana concentrated on keeping her hyperventilating quiet. The dizziness was beginning. She looked at her hands, which were turning pink and white from squeezing the desk so hard as she tried to steady herself. She had to keep herself from falling over the edge into the attack.

"Ari?" Alora said quietly.

Ariana turned to look at her friend, her eyes widened with fear.

"Oh my god, fuck her, GO!" Alora shout-whispered.

Ariana stood and bolted from the room. Alora was right–fuck it–this was an emergency. She ran through the hallway and skidded into the bathroom. She leaned against the wall, her labored breathing picking up. The sides of her vision began to go dark, so she carefully slid to the floor in case she fainted. She put her head between her knees, crying and fighting to get back in control of her thoughts.

When her breathing finally slowed and she was certain the worst was over, Ariana shakily went to the sink and splashed water on her face.

I've got to figure out some way to help myself with these, she thought, looking at her blotchy face and red eyes. Ariana pulled out her phone and began to search. She stumbled upon a famous psychologist's social media page and found a breathing technique she hadn't tried before. Her name was Dr. Nicole LePera and she had some pretty good content; Ariana found herself relating to it in a way she never had with anything else. Dr. LePera recommended slow, deep belly breathing in through the nose and out through the mouth.

Ariana tried it for a few rounds and felt calmer. Or at least she felt like she wasn't going to lose it again. She made a mental note to check out more of Dr. LePera's stuff at home. Ariana looked in the mirror and saw that the signs of crying had close to disappeared, so she made her way back to the classroom, steeling herself for the repercussions.

Upon opening the door, she found the way to her desk blocked by Mrs. Havardly.

"I don't know who put it in your head," Mrs. Havardly spat so the whole class could hear, "that the world waits on Ariana Knight, but in my classroom, it does not."

"I don't think–" Ariana began, but Mrs. Havardly cut her off.

"Detention this Saturday Ms. Knight. Your parents will be so proud."

"Parent," Ariana corrected, unable to stop herself.

"Make that two detentions," Mrs. Havardly said, leaning closer to Ariana and dropping her voice. "I'll give you the second one at another time this year when I feel like it. Let your *parent* know to call me if they have any questions."

Ariana's anger burned through her remaining anxiety as she returned to her desk. Fuck Mrs. Havardly for thinking she knew her. Fuck her for assuming Ariana thought the world waited on her. How was it that some teachers could be just as presumptuous as the students?

Ariana looked around the classroom, half expecting her classmates to be eyeing her, but most of them had distracted and worried looks on their faces as they stared down at their exam grades, which Ariana had all but forgotten about. It had been the first test of the school year and would account for a large chunk of their grade–an essay exam that covered material that they, as advanced placement students, had been expected to learn and read on their own over the summer. Ariana flipped over her paper and saw a large 98 drawn in red. She tucked her exam into her backpack and put her head on the desk, wishing the school day would just be over already.

* * *

"How do you half-ass all of our workouts and still look like you skip a couple of meals a day, Jade?" Melodie shouted across the girl's locker room.

Jade barely glanced up from her phone.

Final period had just ended and all of the girls were changing out of their clothes and into their cheer tryout uniforms, pretending as though they weren't secretly ogling each other's bodies. The upperclassmen always claimed the preferred section of the locker room next to the bathrooms while the sophomores and freshmen changed in a separate area by the hallway doors. It was one of those rituals that everyone just sort of accepted and passed on through the years–a rite of passage given through seniority.

In the sophomore and freshman section, Jade had just taken her shirt off and was absentmindedly checking her phone for any new texts from Ian while standing in her teal and blue 34 C bralette and dark denim jeans. It was her favorite bra at the moment, not that she liked to wear bras at all, but at least it had a cool design on it that reminded her of the ocean. The younger and older girls alike gossiped as they changed and not so discreetly shot jealous glances at Jade's glorious half-naked body.

"You look like a mermaid right now in that bra, J," Ariana said, smiling up at her from a bench by the lockers.

Jade smiled back at Ariana and blew her a kiss, making it clear she wasn't going to answer Melodie's noxious question.

"It's not what she eats or how much she works out, Melodie, so don't get your hopes up–you'll *never* look like Jade," Kiara said bluntly from her spot next to Ariana, startling everyone.

They were all used to the happy-go-lucky, giggling-at-her-own-jokes, zoned-out-to-all-drama Kiara. Jade tried to make eye contact with her, but Kiara's eyes were trained on her shoes so it was impossible to tell what she was thinking. Kiara finished tying her laces in the silence she had created and then, without another word, stood and swept out of the locker room.

"What's *her* problem?" Melodie sneered as soon as the doors closed behind Kiara. Melodie was fussing with her freshly colored blonde hair, pulling it up into a ponytail. When no one jumped in to talk shit about Kiara, Melodie continued. "She's probably just being a bitch because she pukes up everything she eats now."

A few of the freshmen let out audible gasps. Melodie stood in the center of the locker in her bright pink sports bra and turned slowly, reveling in the uncomfortable silence, almost as if she were on a stage. "What? I heard her after lunch," Melodie said faux-innocently, putting her hands on her hips.

Jade felt her feet carrying her over to Melodie before her mind comprehended that she was moving, although she didn't know what she was going to do once she got there. As Jade walked at her, Melodie lifted her arms as if to deflect a blow if one came. Jade halted abruptly in front of her as Ariana began to speak.

"Melodie," Ariana hissed, her voice slicing through the air. "I would suggest you stop talking now."

"This is low, even for you," Jade said, her hands balled into fists. "Who makes up a lie like that?"

"I mean, it's not that big of a deal," Melodie said defensively. "I've done it before, and I know some of you have done it before–"

"You're out of your fucking mind, Melodie!" Jade yelled. "That is a BIG deal! And even if it were true about Kiara, which it is NOT, you don't fucking announce it to the entire fucking locker room!"

Some of the upperclassmen stopped what they were doing and made their way over to the scene. Nali hurriedly asked Ariana what was going on in a hushed voice, and the two carried out a quick conversation that Jade couldn't hear because

Melodie was loudly and insincerely apologizing for "just being honest".

Nali came to Jade's side and put an arm around her shoulders. "Come on, J. Why don't you and Ari finish changing with us? I've been dying to catch up with you guys anyway–I have to tell you about the new guy I'm seeing!"

Jade snatched up her bag and allowed herself to be pulled away from Melodie and over to the upperclassmen's territory. Nali strolled to her locker and pulled her jeans and dark purple V-neck shirt off, revealing that she hadn't worn a bra to school that day.

"Don't let Melodie get to you," Nali said, still completely nude except for a small black thong. She grabbed a hair tie from her locker and pulled her stick-straight blonde hair into a high ponytail, her perky 34 C's brazenly on full display. "Trust me. From experience, it's better to let it go and not waste your time worrying about her spreading a stupid rumor."

"Yeah, and I feel like telling Kiara would just make it worse," Ariana said, taking a seat on the bench.

"I guess if it's not spreading, there's no reason to upset her. But if we hear anyone else talking about it, that'll be a different story," Jade said.

"Agreed," Ariana said. "I am a little worried though. Kiara *has* been eating less. It wouldn't hurt to talk to her and make sure she's alright."

Jade nodded and focused on changing, eager to get out of the locker room. Her mind drifted to the rumor going around about her and her stomach dived. Why did people cause others so much pain? Why couldn't everyone just stop talking about each other and chill out? As if on cue, Jade heard a disgruntled laugh from the corner lockers and turned to see a few juniors eyeing her body. They began to whisper to one another pointedly and Jade sighed. *Looking like me doesn't make your life perfect; it won't heal your pain,* Jade wanted to say.

"Case is so hot," Nali was saying to Ariana. "I met him when I went to one of the Birchmond parties last weekend. And he has some really cute friends!"

"I'm gonna head to the gym early to stretch," Jade said, excusing herself from the conversation. She liked Nali, but she wasn't close with her like Ariana, and there was no way she could focus on trivial small talk about some guy Nali would probably be over in about two weeks.

As she walked down the hallway, Jade replayed what Melodie had said in her head. I *heard* her, she'd claimed. A pit formed in Jade's stomach. It was one thing for people to spread nasty rumors about her–she was used to it. Well, as used to it as a person could get. But Kiara? No way was Kiara bulimic. She was athletic and strong! Ariana was even a few sizes bigger than Kiara and Ariana loved her body. If Kiara had been that troubled about her weight, surely she would have told them or at least talked to them about it.

Jade continued the attempt to talk herself down as she walked, but she didn't feel any better about the situation. She was mainly pissed at Melodie, and the feeling was taking on the form of a throbbing sensation in her body, keeping her antsy and agitated. She turned at the end of the hallway and was about to head into the gym when the voice of a guy calling out her name stopped her in her tracks, her stomach dropping in a good way this time.

"Jade!" Ian yelled as he jogged in from the doors leading to the football field. He was wearing his battered workout tank and shorts, showing off his muscles. "Hey," he said as he caught up with her, his wide smile reaching to his clear blue eyes.

"Hey." Jade breathed out. Her whole body relaxed in Ian's presence; her hands unfurled. She hadn't realized she had still been clenching them into fists. Before she could change her mind, Jade looked up and down the hallway and then grabbed Ian and pulled his head toward hers. She breathed in the smell of the sun on his skin and shivered. As she kissed him, that jolt of electricity ran through her body again, just like the first time.

Jade pulled away after a few seconds and looked up at Ian, laughing at his slightly shocked expression. "Were you looking for me?" she asked, her voice light and airy now.

He ran a hand through his unkempt chestnut-brown hair and smiled down at her, regaining his composure. "So, you can kiss me here now too? I'm making progress."

Jade playfully raised an eyebrow at him and waited.

"Okay, yes. I was looking for you. I wanted to tell you good luck on cheer tryouts in person. And, I'd like to take you on the date you promised me this weekend. If you're up for it."

Jade's stomach flipped. He looked so hot in his workout tank–it was ripped on both sides, giving her a clear view of his abs. She wanted to say yes immediately, so she did the opposite.

"Hmm," Jade said, toying with him. "I don't know..."

"Oh come ON," Ian said, laughing. "You literally just kissed me. You know you want to."

A junior boy burst through the same doors Ian had come through only moments earlier. "Ian, Coach is looking for you, man! He's pissed. You better get back out here!"

"Alright!" Ian began walking backward. "So, yes then?"

"I'll think about it."

"By the way, you look hot as hell in those shorts!" Ian shouted before taking off into a sprint.

Jade heard laughter coming from the opposite end of the hallway and turned to see that Ariana and Nali had walked out of the locker room just in time to witness the last part of their exchange. Jade burst into laughter and slipped into the gym. Maybe today didn't have to end badly after all.

* * *

Kiara stood by the full-length mirrors lining the back wall of the gym, pretending to fix her ice blonde ponytail when in reality she was studying every inch of her body in cheer attire. She hadn't eaten over her calorie limit since Saturday, and if she'd messed up and eaten a little too much, she'd gone straight to the nearest bathroom and thrown it up. She realized, with wholehearted satisfaction, that she could see a slight difference in the size of her arms. And were her legs getting thinner too? Kiara grinned at herself in the mirror, and then spun around when she saw two bobbing heads approaching her, one dark-haired and one golden-brown.

"Hey, K," Ariana said. "You would tell us if something was bothering you, right?"

Kiara paused for a beat, startled. She stared at her friend while blood rushed to her cheeks, and did her best to keep a calm, collected mask on her face. She glanced at the bruise on the top of her right hand without thinking, then thrust her hands behind her back. "What do you mean?"

"You know I love that you called Melodie out for me, but you've seemed a little stressed out lately–not your usual, cheerful self," Jade said. "We wanted to make sure you were okay, that's all."

"Oh! No, just stressed about tryouts, but that'll all be over after this week, right?" Kiara said quickly. She let out a little sigh of relief–she had been worried that maybe Ariana and Jade had noticed her bizarre eating patterns.

"Okay good. It's not like you don't already know this, but remember, you can tell us anything. We're always here for you, and we would never judge you," Ariana said, her hazel eyes glowing with concern.

Heat crept up Kiara's neck. That was a strange thing to say out of the blue, and Ariana was using that coaxing voice she used when she had a hunch someone wasn't telling the full truth. Maybe they *had* noticed something... or worse yet, maybe they had heard her in the bathroom earlier this week when they'd been practicing? She'd been worried about that. But she couldn't let them know. She just couldn't. Kiara took a deep breath and did her best to channel the demeanor Ariana took on when she was telling a lie with confidence to get them out of trouble.

Best to keep it somewhat close to the truth, she thought. *Best to add in specific details.*

"I, um, I have been keeping a little something from you, but only because I was embarrassed and I knew y'all would be angry with me. I've been trying to lose a few pounds so I've been eating better and getting in extra workouts whenever I can, but losing weight is so hard! So I did something kind of stupid," Kiara said, making sure to look into each of their eyes. "I took these diet pills I bought online and they made me sick. I was having trouble keeping food down. I learned my lesson though, and before you say anything Ari, I know how dangerous diet pills are. I won't do it again."

Kiara surprised herself even–she had no idea the lie would come out so effortlessly, but maybe it was because she knew what was at stake if her secret was found out.

"I would never be angry with you for that. Only worried about you!" Ariana said.

"K, it's okay. We've all done stupid shit before," Jade said, sounding relieved. "But you should've told us. We would have talked you out of taking the pills."

"I know," Kiara said. "That's probably why I didn't say anything."

"And you don't need to lose any weight, seriously. You look great. You always do. But it's always good to try and eat healthier! We can start eating healthier with you," Ariana said while nodding in solidarity.

Jade let out a long and playful groan but then acquiesced. "I guess I could eat a little healthier too," she said. "But from now on, *tell us* what's on your mind. We can't help if we don't know what's going on in that beautiful head of yours."

"I will. I promise," Kiara lied, feeling like a horrible friend. They were being so supportive and had believed her so easily. But then again, she'd never lied to them before. "Okay, enough about that! How was everyone else's day?"

"Well, Mrs. Havardly gave me Saturday detention," Ariana said, her mouth falling into a hard line.

Kiara shook her head while letting out a surprised laugh, her body relaxing. "What did you do? Make too high of a grade on your English exam?"

"No, I was having an anxiety attack and she wouldn't let me use the bathroom, so I went without permission," Ariana explained with a shrug.

"Wow," Jade said, crossing her arms. "She gave you detention for that? Did she know you were having an attack?"

"No, but she hates me, J. She thinks I think I'm the shit or something and that normal rules don't apply to me. She's attempting to teach me a lesson apparently," Ariana vented.

An ember of indignation flickered inside Kiara. Why would she pick on Ariana of all people? Mrs. Havardly was sadly another member of the school staff that seemed to have taken a teaching job so she could use her authority to lash out at students. The yearning to protect Ariana from wrong-doers was taking over, and it felt good for Kiara to have a noble outlet for her intense emotions. Mrs. Havardly was known to pick out a few favorite students right as classes started and spend the rest of the semester rewarding them while simultaneously shitting on everyone else. For some reason, Mrs. Havardly had picked Kiara as a favorite, but that wouldn't last for long. Not anymore, at least.

"Well, apparently she doesn't know you very well," Kiara said with a disdainful snort. She smiled as she concocted a plan in her head to get a point across to Mrs. Havardly. "Good thing I have her for English."

"Kiara... What do you mean? What're you going to do? You've got an evil grin on your face," Ariana said, her arched eyebrows rising.

"EVERYONE LINE UP! TRYOUTS ARE STARTING IN FIVE MINUTES!" Krall shouted from across the gym.

"Shit, we better get over there," Kiara whispered, using the distraction to avoid Ariana's question.

"K!" Jade said while laughing. "Don't change the subject! What're you going to do?"

Kiara looked back–Jade and Ariana hadn't moved and were adamantly waiting on her to explain her motives.

"Oh nothing," Kiara said vaguely. "I've just decided that you're not going to Saturday detention alone, Ari. I'm going to be right there with you."

* * *

Hours later, Kiara slammed her front door shut and slung her bag into the foyer, mentally and physically exhausted from the day. Tryouts had gone well–she hadn't messed up the cheers or her tumbling at all, so she should've been celebrating. Instead, she was agitated and jumpy. Something was off, but she just didn't know what it was. Her phone vibrated in her hand and she groaned.

4:35 p.m. Teague: Can I swing by? We need to talk.

And there it was. Kiara didn't know if there were four more terrifying words he could have said. After last weekend she and Teague had been in a weird funk, getting onto each other for insignificant things and talking only on a surface level. Well, Teague was more so refusing to talk to her, stating he was sure she was hiding something. And it didn't help that Kiara's restricted calorie intake was giving her increasingly severe mood swings.

"Honey, would you like a snack or something?" Karen Lancor called from the kitchen.

"Oh hey, Mom! I didn't realize you were home," Kiara called back. "No, I'm good, but thank you!"

"Come in here for a moment, will you?"

Kiara's eyes widened. She didn't necessarily want to be in the kitchen surrounded by food right now. She was starving after practice, but hell-bent on not eating anything before dinner to save the calories. Kiara walked slowly toward the kitchen, steeling herself for the hunger pangs.

"What's up, Mom?" Kiara said as she did her best to sit normally at the counter, all the while combating thoughts of crackers and cheese and chips dancing in her mind. Karen chopped some onions for the guacamole she was preparing, and Kiara's mouth watered. She tried to breathe in and out of her mouth so she wouldn't smell any food.

"I wanted to check in with you. You've seemed a little distracted at dinner lately–not quite yourself. Is there anything you want to talk about?" Karen asked, concern clouding her blue-green eyes.

Twice in one day she was getting called out? What was happening? Without warning, Kiara's eyes welled up. She bowed her head to hide the tears, staring at the tiny purple bruise on her hand. She desperately wanted to tell her mom everything, she realized, just so she would have someone to talk to about it all. The secret she carried got heavier each day, and she was now acutely aware that something not so normal was happening in her thoughts.

But it'll all be over soon, Kiara reassured herself, *just as soon as I lose like ten more pounds*. Then she could relax and go back to living her normal life.

Keep the lie close to the truth, she reminded herself. *Add in details.*

"Oh, no Mom. I'm just worried about tryouts. I've been stressing about making the team again–I'm not an insane tumbler like Ari or a dancer like Jade, so I'm a little scared. But I should be better soon! We'll find out if we make the team or not tomorrow," Kiara said, surprising herself with the ease of the lie for the second time that day.

"A little anticipation is normal, honey. Relax and enjoy the process, it'll all turn out alright whatever way it goes," Karen said with a relieved smile.

Kiara moved the corners of her lips up automatically, unfeeling. "Thanks, Mom. I love you." It was almost too easy to convince everyone she was okay. It was like they wanted to believe it more than they wanted to see the truth.

Kiara winced at the sound of the doorbell ringing moments later, signaling Teague's arrival. *Time for round three of the defending*, she thought. She let Teague in and attempted a smile at him but his face was set in a frown, his eyes distrustful. He had never looked at her like that before–it broke her heart. Her stomach twisted and she fought back tears as they made their way upstairs to her bedroom. She plopped on the bed and took a deep breath.

"So what's going on with you K, *really*?" Teague said abruptly, cutting through any small talk. He stood in the doorway with his arms crossed over his chest.

Kiara blanched. "Jesus. Okay, truthfully?" she began, formulating her next sentences carefully. "I've been freaking out about cheer tryouts. I'm worried I'm not going to make it, and it's driving me crazy, and I didn't want to tell you because it sounded so stupid. I didn't think you'd understand. Like, it's been keeping me up at night."

"*That's* why you've been so moody?" Teague asked, narrowing his eyes.

"Yeah. If I don't make the squad but Ari and J do, I'll be devastated."

"It seems like it's something else," Teague pressed. Kiara was breathless and dizzy for a moment, anxiety gripping her stomach. How close was he to seeing the truth? "I just don't see how something like cheer tryouts could make you this different with me."

"See?!" Kiara cried. "This is how I figured you'd react. Why'd you even make me tell you if you're just going to judge me?" Kiara had never been more of an actress in her life. Luckily, her moods were so volatile the wild reaction came easy. Tears rolled down her cheeks and she sniffed indignantly.

Teague looked like he was about to say something but then hesitated, his forehead scrunching up. He sighed. "I'm sorry, babe.

I've just never seen you get this worked up over anything before." His face softened. "Is there anything I can do?" He opened up his arms and she went to him, nuzzling against his shoulder.

Now that her face was hidden, she let the horror she was feeling play out across her features. She didn't even know who she was anymore–how could she have so blatantly lied to everyone she cared the most about in the world in a few hours flat? She definitely couldn't tell the truth now, not after this. They would never forgive her. Never trust her again. She was a liar.

"No, I don't think so. It'll be over soon," Kiara said, desperately hoping that was true.

CHAPTER 13

Ariana

Ariana walked into the cheer gym on Friday afternoon and immediately looked around for Kiara. Mrs. Havardly had been in an odd mood today; her usual demeanor of contempt and thinly masked resentment had been replaced by an air of controlled bitterness, which, for Mrs. Havardly, was a huge improvement. Ariana immediately put two and two together–Kiara must have done something.

She spotted Kiara and Jade seated with a group of sophomores and freshmen. Jade was leaning back on her hands with her long, tan legs stretched out in front of her while Kiara's head rested on them, her ash-blonde hair spilling onto the blue gym mat. The younger girls watched Jade and Kiara with admiration in their eyes while her two best friends remained oblivious, talking and laughing seemingly without a care in the world. From where she stood, Ariana could understand why other people resented them and spread rumors. They made life look so easy. Jade never had to worry about a guy wanting someone else and Kiara never really worried about anything at all. Neither of them understood what it was like to have debilitating anxiety.

It wasn't fair.

Suddenly, Ariana was filled with resentment. She wished one

of them would have a full-blown panic attack, and then maybe they could see how devastating it was to lose control. Maybe they could understand that it isn't so easy to just live without anxiety. Ariana inhaled a sharp breath and shook her head, startled by her spiteful thoughts. She took a step back, not wanting to go near them, lest they somehow read her mind.

She reminded herself: Jade has been through so much. And Kiara *chooses* not to worry about anything.

Ariana leaned against the gym wall as shame momentarily overwhelmed her. She remembered the deep belly breathing she learned to calm the nervous system and did a couple of rounds with her hand on her heart. *Take it easy, you're not a bad person because you had a little jealousy toward your friends*, she thought.

She took a tentative step forward, testing her thoughts, and then made her way over to the group. The younger girls hastily shuffled aside to let her sit.

"What'd you do to Mrs. Havardly, Kiara?" Ariana said.

"I just gave her a taste of her own medicine," Kiara said. She grinned and sat up. "By the way, I officially have Saturday detention with you now."

Aubrey burst into laughter from his seat next to Everly. "It was hilarious, Ari," he interjected. "We were reading some boring grammar lesson, the classroom dead silent and everything, and then Kiara jumped up and announced that everyone should stop what they're doing because she had to use the bathroom and we all *had* to wait for her to get back to continue, then ran out the door. Mrs. Havardly didn't know what to do–she was beside herself. She still didn't know what to do when Kiara stormed back in and announced that everyone could now carry on because she was ready."

"So I let her know to give me Saturday detention with you, because I *definitely* think the world waits on me," Kiara finished. "I think she got the point."

The younger girls' eyes traveled from Kiara's face to Ariana's, waiting for her reaction. Ariana lurched at Kiara and pulled her into a hug. She couldn't believe only moments ago she had wished anxiety upon her.

"Oh my god, K! You didn't have to do that," Ariana exclaimed, kissing Kiara's cheek. "I love you so much."

"I know. You would do the same for me though," Kiara stated, wiping a smudge of lip gloss off her face. "Probably in a more sophisticated and eloquent manner, but still."

"I would do that for y'all," Lyric said to Mara and Everly. Her black hair was done up in a bun with the teal and blue streaks twisting into the center. The girls all nodded at one another in agreement and Kiara laughed.

"I can't tell if we're being good or bad influences," Ariana whispered through a smile.

"Definitely good," Jade whispered back.

"Krall is handing out the letters!" Aubrey shouted.

The conversation died down while Krall made her rounds, handing out the letters that would confirm or deny their spots on the cheerleading team. Ariana picked at her tie-dye sports bra, surprised at the nerves jumping in her stomach. She was, yet again, the only girl to try out with a round-off back handspring double full, and she'd stuck it perfectly. The rest of her routine had gone off without a hitch, but her palms were still sweating by the time she received her envelope. What if she didn't make it?

"Fuck it," Jade said next to her, and they all ripped open their envelopes at the same time.

Ariana's eyes immediately found the word "Congratulations" on the letter and she did a silent cheer in her head. She read over the few extra lines at the bottom, which told her she'd also been nominated for cheer captain and the guidelines for her speech, which she would give this coming Monday. She turned to look at Jade and Kiara, who both smiled and nodded.

"YES!!!" Lyric yelled. Ariana turned around to find Mara, Lyric, and Everly all hugging each other while jumping and screaming. Ariana was happy their three protégés had made the team. Melodie, Aubrey, and Reigh talked excitedly nearby, and

Ariana could only assume that meant they'd made the team as well.

Krall wandered over to Ariana and slinked a pudgy arm around her shoulders. "It's going to be a good year," Krall said quietly. "I made sure you got all of your girls."

Ariana smiled, confused by the comment. "Um, thank you, Krall. For all of your coaching."

Unsure of what else to do or say, Ariana shimmied out of the awkward embrace and ran straight to Jade and Kiara, who were the only people she truly wanted to share the moment with.

"I'm nominated for cheer captain," Ariana said when she made it to them.

Jade whooped loudly and Kiara playfully spanked her butt while yelling, "YAS!"

Ariana laughed. "Melodie is the other nominee."

"Oh Lord help us all," Jade said, putting a hand to her head.

"Don't worry. I'll work on my speech this weekend. I'm going to kill it," Ariana said.

"Of course you will, Ari," Kiara said.

"And if you don't, I'm moving schools," Jade said.

Several hours later, Ariana sat on the plush, beige carpet in her bedroom in front of her mirror, getting ready for her date with Lukas. She had let her hair dry naturally after her shower, leaving it extra wavy, and was now deciding whether to give up trying to tame it by putting it up or just leave it down and wild. She ran her fingers through the gold-streaked waves one more time before giving an exasperated sigh and turning her attention to her wardrobe instead. She'd decided on white high-waisted jeans and a tan, off-the-shoulder top paired with white sneakers. Ariana swept a line of creamy white eyeshadow on her inner lower lids that illuminated her soft brown eyes. She stood and took a step back, assessing herself. She was glowing, her summer tan contrasting beautifully with the light colors. And her hair would look better tumbling over her bare shoulders, she decided finally.

She fidgeted with a thin rose gold ring on her finger, thinking about what was yet to come tonight. What Alora had said was still bothering her, and she planned on asking Lukas about Olivia to sort the entire thing out for good.

"Baby," Ariana's mother, Athena, said as she appeared at the door. Athena's light-brown hair was styled to frame her face and she wore a red dress that was a little short for Ariana's liking. Athena's features were smaller than Ariana's, but other than that, they looked incredibly similar. "I'm going on a date tonight, will you be okay?"

Ariana's stomach lurched. "Who's the guy, Mom?"

"Oh, someone from an app. His name's Mike. You haven't met him yet."

Ariana wondered if anyone else she knew got worried sick about their parents the way she did for her mom. The anxiety strangled her for a moment. "Are you sure he's a good guy? Will you text me and let me know where you are and when you're going to be home?"

"Yes, Ariana." Her mom gave a playful sigh. "It's okay for you to be the daughter sometimes, you know?"

Ariana turned back to her reflection. "Is it, though?" she said under her breath, trying to get a handle on her emotions.

"You look beautiful," Athena said as she appeared behind her and kissed her on the head. "Have fun tonight."

Ariana leaned into her mother and sighed. "Thanks. Just share your location with me."

Athena retreated downstairs, leaving Ariana to her thoughts. She used to wish for a little sister or brother to make their family bigger than just the two of them, but without her mom having a steady man in her life, Ariana didn't see that happening. It was hard for Ariana to accept any of the men her mother dated–she never found them good enough. And it made her almost sick when her mom didn't come home after her dates sometimes. The first time that had happened back in the sixth grade was the first time Ariana had ever had an anxiety attack. Athena hadn't meant to leave her alone for the night, but had accidentally gotten so drunk she stayed the night out. Ariana couldn't remember her life without anxiety attacks after that.

"Thanks for asking where I'm going," Ariana muttered. She knew her mother trusted her to be responsible so she didn't question her much, but still. It would've been nice.

A soft vibration from Ariana's pocket redirected her focus. She looked down and welcomed the euphoria she'd come to know and love whenever she saw Lukas' name on her screen.

7:48 p.m. Lukas: I'm down the street. I'll meet you at the lake?

Ariana wondered briefly if she would always feel this way from something as simple as a text from Lukas. Her insides flitted as she hesitated a few seconds before responding, swimming in the anticipation of the night.

7:49 p.m. Ariana: Meet you there.

Ariana picked up the red glass perfume bottle from her dresser and sprayed it on her wrists. With one last glance in the mirror, she ran downstairs and out her front door while yelling goodbye to her mom.

It was a clear, cloudless evening and her neighborhood was surprisingly quiet. Only a soft hum from restless bugs made any background noise. Ariana walked quickly, not wanting to waste a single moment she could be with Lukas. When she turned the bend of her street, she saw him leaning against his truck wearing a black tank top that showed off his tanned muscles. Ariana almost laughed out loud at the sight of him–he looked like a male model standing there, posed with one leg kicked back on the truck and sunglasses shading his eyes.

She slowed her walking, wanting to prolong the moment: this

feeling of excitement, this feeling of being so alive. Ariana watched as Lukas' mouth stretched into a sexy grin when he finally saw her. It was in moments like this that she wondered if all of this was really happening to her–how could her real life be better than her dreams?

Picking up her pace again, Ariana playfully bounded up to Lukas and stopped inches from his face, smiling. "Hey," she said breathlessly.

Lukas' grin disappeared, as if her sudden closeness had startled him. Desire flashed in his dark brown eyes. Lukas reached up and brushed a strand of hair behind her ear, letting his hand linger there. "You catch me so off-guard sometimes," he said. She thought she heard something almost defensive in his tone.

"I've missed you," Ariana said honestly.

"You have no idea how much I've missed you."

Ariana's heart rate picked up at his response. There was something about the way he said the words, like there was much more meaning behind them than what he merely stated.

"But I see you even when I'm not with you," Lukas continued.

"What do you mean?"

"You're in everything I see and do," Lukas said, trying to explain. "I was at the park the other day and I saw this beautiful red robin that kept toying with the dogs. She would land briefly, the dogs would run to where she was, sure they were going to catch her this time, but then the robin would gracefully take off again, leaving them all chasing after her. The way the robin flew reminded me of you."

Ariana's cheeks burned. Who said things like that?

"Then the robin came and landed on the bench next to me," Lukas said quietly, his eyes on hers. "And she was so wild and beautiful."

Ariana looked away, the intimacy of his comment overwhelming her for a moment. They were standing very close, and she was afraid that if she looked into his eyes much longer she would lose all self-control and finally kiss him.

"I think I know what you mean," Ariana said to fill the space.

A car passed by with a group of kids whooping and hollering out of the rolled-down windows, breaking the electric moment. Lukas tore his eyes away from her and watched the car pass.

"Who was that?" he asked.

"Who knows. A lot of people from our school live in my neighborhood."

"Come on," Lukas said, motioning for her to get in the truck. "Let's get out of here."

She walked to the passenger side, preparing herself to question him about Olivia. Ariana was fine with him having a past; she had had a few flings herself freshman year. But what truly worried her was if Lukas *still* had feelings for any of the girls from his past. That is, if Olivia was even *in* his past...

"So," Ariana began once she'd buckled in. "I overheard someone talking about you the other day. They were saying something about you dating Olivia Bellepointe? Did you used to be together or something?"

Ariana cringed. She hadn't meant to be so accusatory, and the questions at the end had sounded unnatural, but she'd decided that was the best way to ask him–phrased as if she'd overheard random people she didn't know talking about it. Ariana kept her eyes on Lukas, watching for any visible signs of deception in his body language, but he seemed at ease.

"Olivia used to date one of my best friends, Marx Woods. I think Jade used to hook up with him?" Lukas said.

"That was just a rumor," Ariana chanted automatically.

"Oh. Well, either way, Olivia used to date Marx, so my friends and her friends all hung out a lot. Now that he graduated, we all still hang out. Maybe that's where the confusion was," Lukas said simply.

Relief flooded through her–nothing was going on between them. She tried to hide the huge smile threatening to spread across her face by turning to the window before she spoke again.

"I guess I forgot about Olivia dating Marx. When the rumors about Jade and Marx started circulating and Jade got all of that backlash for it, Olivia was probably one of the only girls who *didn't* come after her," Ariana admitted, feeling magnanimous now that Olivia wasn't a threat.

"Yeah, Olivia isn't like that. She's a gorgeous girl, inside and out," Lukas said, a note of reverence in his voice.

Ariana's stomach recoiled. At his statement, she immediately wished she could take back her last comment. All at once, she began to experience violent jealousy toward this girl, a girl she had probably never exchanged more than a few words with. Ariana shot a sideways glance at Lukas, trying for the billionth time to figure out what he was thinking. It almost hurt to look at him now. His ability to make her feel so alive, how much she was attracted to and drawn to him, the almost ethereal way he spoke to her–everything about him that brought her pleasure and delight would only bring her pain if she lost him.

With a sigh, Ariana turned her body away from Lukas, crossing her arms. If Olivia was *so* gorgeous, inside and out, why didn't he just go and hang out with her? Ariana watched the cars passing, trying to spot the facial expressions of the riders. Was anyone dealing with a situation similar to hers right now? She gritted her teeth–she despised the inner monologue going on in her head. She wasn't the girl that disliked girls she didn't know over a guy.

Having been distracted by the conversation and her thoughts, Ariana hadn't been paying attention to where they were going and only now realized that they were off the main roads. She saw her high school zoom by the window and noted that they were surprisingly close to Kiara's house. Ariana wanted to ask Lukas where they were headed but didn't feel like speaking to him again just yet. Every once in a while he would glance over in her direction, but the silence continued to hang in the air.

A few minutes later the car slowed and Lukas pulled over.

"Hey," he said softly, turning to her. Lukas waited for her to look into his eyes before he spoke again. "I want to be exactly where I am right now. Here, with you. I wouldn't want to be anywhere else." He reached over to take her hand, letting his face slide into a grin. "By the way, you're about to meet my mother, so you may want to cheer up a little."

Ariana let out a gasp of surprise. "You didn't tell me I'd be meeting your mom!" She exclaimed, instantly nervous and extremely pleased at the same time. Her doubts and worries about Olivia vanished, and she couldn't stop the corners of her mouth from turning up into a smile to mirror his. Lukas was taking *her* to meet his mother. "Am I dressed okay?"

"You look beautiful and comfortable," Lukas said as he slowly let go of her hand and climbed out of the truck. "I love your style."

Ariana stepped onto the stone pathway. She was surprised that Lukas lived in Kiara's neighborhood, but then again, a lot of their friends did. Lukas' home was further back than Kiara's, in an outer area of the neighborhood that just so happened to be seated on a lake.

Ariana inhaled, taking in the smells of nature around her. Lukas' lake was different from hers–the calm blue body of water was larger and much more overgrown. Each homeowner managed their yard space and most of them liked to have privacy and coverage from the hedges and trees. Lukas' house was one of the newer ones on the block, with large glass windows in front and back, so you could practically see straight through the house to the water. It was beautiful, and Ariana envisioned them spending lots of time here. She would wear her new white strapless bikini to sunbathe in as Lukas swam laps in the lake, shirtless....

Lukas moved toward her, interrupting her thoughts. "Do you like it?"

"I love it," Ariana said.

He grinned and led her through the spacious white flagstone

entryway into the house. It was a mostly open floor plan, with the living room, kitchen, dining room, and back porch all visible from where she stood in the foyer. Lukas motioned for Ariana to wait as he walked down a hallway to the left, calling out to his mom as he went. His mother emerged, and Ariana heard her explain to Lukas that she'd been reading in her room. Lukas waited until she finished talking to redirect her attention to where Ariana was standing. Her eyes lit up as she registered Ariana and they came over.

"Mom, this is Ariana," Lukas said, a smile playing on his lips.

"She was *so* sweet," Ariana gushed as Lukas lit up a joint and inhaled. They had just left Lukas' mom in the house and were seated on the secluded wooden dock that peeked out into the lake. Lukas' mother had politely asked Ariana all about cheerleading and how she and Lukas knew each other before Lukas had ushered Ariana outside.

"Yeah, I think so too. Do you want some?" Lukas said between exhales.

"Nah, I already feel amazing right now," Ariana said, really meaning it. She felt too good almost, if that were possible. She lifted her toned arms above her head to stretch and then let her body slowly rock back on the dock until she was lying down. She sighed happily and looked at the sky, listening to the sounds of crickets chirping mingling with the lapping water. She took a breath and started giggling for no reason at all–apparently she didn't need drugs to get her high when she was with Lukas.

Ariana never could have imagined that merely being around someone could make the entire world seem better somehow. She turned toward him, studying his handsome profile until he glanced over. When they locked eyes, Ariana's stomach dropped. Lukas looked at her lips and her breath caught in her throat while a delicious heat crept between her legs.

Seeming to sense her thoughts, Lukas leaned over her, placing one arm on either side of her body. Ariana stilled, her heart pounding against her chest. Was he about to kiss her? She'd yearned for this moment since the day they met.

Lukas leaned down and stopped when his mouth was less than inches from her lips. She laughed out of nervousness and closed her eyes. Lukas breathed into her, and she began to grow impatient and overflowing with excitement simultaneously. His lips brushed the right corner of her mouth, and then the left. It seemed as though he was enjoying teasing her, and she wanted to scream and laugh at the same time. He stilled again, poised over her, every inch of his body electrifying hers where they touched.

She opened her eyes to see that his eyes bore into hers as if he were looking for an answer to a question he hadn't asked. Ariana was reminded of being at a standstill at the top of a rollercoaster, teetering, just waiting for the inevitable fall. She shivered from a sudden gust of wind and without warning Lukas' lips came down on hers. Ariana's body responded before her brain did, and she kissed him back hungrily, knotting her hands in his hair and pulling him closer, although she knew she would never be able to get him close enough. Something inside Ariana shifted. Every other kiss, every other hook up, every other crush, every other boy–period–melted away. Nothing and no one could compare anymore.

Lukas' breathing turned ragged as their kissing grew more intense by the moment. She had never wanted anyone as much, or in the way that she wanted Lukas. After a few minutes he stopped suddenly. "I have to tell you something."

"What?" Ariana asked, her voice so low it was barely audible. She was terrified of what he was about to say. If it was something good, something like what she was feeling right now, then she was scared that once she opened that door she wouldn't be able to close it. At the same time, she was afraid that if it were something bad she'd be devastated, because now she couldn't imagine life without Lukas–without these feelings.

"I know I shouldn't say this but..." he trailed off.

"Lukas, what?" Ariana asked, trying not to hyperventilate.

"I can't help it," he said fervently, his brown eyes meeting hers. "I'm falling in love with you."

Ariana's heart nearly came out of her chest and she squeezed her eyes shut, trying to freeze the moment in time. Opening them again, she found his gaze still on her.

"I'm falling for you, too," she whispered.

CHAPTER 14

J, K, A

"Do you want my napkin to cover your legs?" Ian asked, concern flitting in his handsome features. He was dressed up in a black long-sleeved button-down that hugged his arms and chest. "I would give you my shirt but I don't think they'd like that..."

Jade laughed and shook her head. The fancy Italian restaurant Ian had picked was stunning and the food fantastic, but the main dining room was freezing. Jade grabbed the white linen napkin gratefully and tucked it around her thighs where her black leather miniskirt had ridden up. She was probably underdressed, but the young male servers had been clamoring around their table anyway, seemingly eager to catch her eye.

"Better?" Ian asked as a server took their plates and lingered by Jade's side for a moment too long.

"Yes," Jade lied, pushing a wave of chocolate-brown hair behind her ear.

Ian smiled, visibly relaxing. The amount of effort he'd put into the date was charming the pants off of Jade, metaphorically speaking, but she didn't have the heart to tell him she would've been fine with, and maybe even preferred, a casual restaurant where they could've ordered burgers and fries without a dozen servers hovering over them.

"So, what would you do in life if you could do anything?" Ian asked.

Jade didn't have to think about this one. "I'd create an app that rewarded people for being vulnerable and kind to each other rather than only showing their best moments and trolling the comments." She bit on her nail. "Or be a comedian. Or both."

Ian smiled. "Does that mean some sort of web developer for the good of the internet?"

"That could be cool. Or learn UX UI to support myself while I build the app. *And* while I make people laugh with my hilarious standup."

Ian laughed. "Can I tell you something?" He rested his elbows on the table so he could lean in closer to her. "Something about a time at one of Taron's parties you probably don't remember."

"Oh no, which party?" Jade said, cautious. What was he about to bring up?

Ian laughed. "Don't worry. It's a good thing. The '*Rita* of Passage' party at the end of last year when Taron invited a bunch of freshmen to get drunk for the first time before becoming sophomores."

"God, how could I forget?" So many people puked it was a little hard *not* to remember. Taron must've been feeling generous because he'd bought a margarita machine specially for the occasion. Jade leaned forward on her elbows, mimicking Ian's posture. "You have my attention."

"I wanted to tell you about that night because that's when I realized I had a thing for you," Ian said, his eyes warm and smiling. "We'd hung out a few times in groups, and I always thought you were attractive and funny, but this is the thing that really got me." He looked away, as if watching a memory play out in his head. "Everyone was pretty smashed because Taron made the margaritas too strong, and this freshman girl who'd never been to a party with all of us tripped and fell up the patio steps in front of everyone. So many people were laughing at her. She was mortified. It looked like she was about to cry, but then you got up from your seat and sat next to her. You crossed your legs over hers and said the best of us fall down sometimes and then laughed. The two of you stayed there, talking and laughing until no one was paying attention anymore. You helped her save face and you didn't even know her."

Jade's eyebrows raised high as she processed Ian's story. She actually did remember that, she just didn't think anyone else had cared. "Wow, so *that's* what made you like me?"

"Yeah. It's easy to be beautiful and a bitch. You were kind. You *are* kind."

Jade furrowed her eyebrows. Was she kind? She was pretty sure she'd almost gotten physical with Melodie in the locker room. And she wasn't kind to Holly the other day. She'd embarrassed the poor girl in front of her friends. She still needed to apologize to Holly, in fact.

"I don't know if I am," Jade said, wanting to be honest. She looked away. "I try to be. I want to be. A lot of the time my anger gets the best of me."

"You don't have to be a saint, Jade. We're all human, we make mistakes." Ian put his hand on her wrist and touched her black leather bracelet.

She blushed and looked into his eyes as the exhilarating rush from his words coursed through her body. A delicious tension had started to build between her legs, and at that last statement Jade couldn't wait to get Ian out of the confines of the restaurant.

"Let's get out of here," Jade said, letting a devilish smile inch over her lips.

"You don't know what you're doing to me right now," Ian said, his voice low and hoarse.

Jade squirmed in her seat. "Likewise."

The server brought their check and Ian took care of it, causing Jade to smile. She wouldn't have minded going half in, but it was nice of Ian to treat her. They made their way outside to his black

SUV and Jade stretched her arms up to the setting sun, welcoming the warm evening air. Without warning, Ian walked to Jade and pushed her against the car, kissing her hard. He ran his hands through her hair and Jade let out a small groan.

Ian pulled back, cupping her face with his hands. "You do something else to me, Jade."

"I'm sorry?" Jade said, shrugging unapologetically.

Ian smiled and opened the car door for her before walking around to his side. Glass Animals' "Heat Waves" started playing and Jade grinned. What a perfect song for the longing she was feeling for Ian at the moment.

"Mmm, I love this song," Jade murmured.

Ian reached over and turned the speakers up, grinning at Jade as he did so. His expression was enough to keep her lying awake at night, replaying his slow, sexy smile over on a loop in her head.

Ian hit the gas and the wind whipped Jade's long dark hair around her face. She laughed out the window as he hit the gas again, purposefully speeding up to give her a little thrill. Ian was proving himself to be a bit of a daredevil, and thankfully she hadn't begun to get bored with him yet. Jade looked over and let her eyes explore his face, imagining what it would feel like to call Ian hers.

Ian seemed to sense her gaze and turned toward her, his clear blue eyes embedded with a craving that sent a jolt through her stomach. Why should they keep their relationship, whatever it was or would be, a secret any longer just because some mean girls were going to come for her? Jade realized with sudden clarity that she didn't care anymore who saw them together, or what it might bring.

Excited by her change of heart, Jade leaned over the middle console to tell Ian what she'd decided but then hesitated, thinking it would be more fun if she surprised him by showing him with her actions instead. Jade had only slid back down an inch into her seat when Ian's hand sprung out to catch her face and pull her into a kiss.

"Hey! Where do you think you're going?" Ian asked as he pulled her to him again, kissing her deeply for a brief second before letting go.

Jade's breathless laughter rang out through the car. She pulled her mini skirt down the short distance it had ridden up her thighs and settled into her seat as they arrived at her house.

"I'm going to miss being able to kiss you whenever I want at Daire's party tomorrow," Ian said.

He put the car in park and absentmindedly ran a hand through his hair; tousling it and inadvertently making Jade's stomach do a little flip. He was so sexy without even trying. In the flash of an eye, Ian reached over and pulled Jade into his lap, cradling her in his arms. Jade opened her mouth to protest, but her breath caught in her throat as Ian reached out his hand and began to trace his fingers down her chest from her collarbone. He looked into her eyes while his fingers slowly made their way further and further down, finally reaching where her top clung to her chest. Something about his eye contact made the moment surprisingly intimate, and Jade heard a small gasp escape her lips as Ian's hand abruptly stopped its movement. He smiled at Jade's reaction as she struggled to regain her composure.

"You might be pleasantly surprised," Jade said. She breathed in Ian's usual scent of crisp cologne.

Ian bent his head to Jade's ear and lightly kissed her earlobe, sending shivers down her neck. "What does that mean?" he whispered.

Jade could hear the wonder in his voice and realized that as much as Ian appeared to have control a few moments ago, he was affected by her as well. His eyes were wide and his breathing irregular. Jade leaned in and kissed his cheek, enjoying the way he stilled when she got close to him. She slowly ran her lips along his jawline, paying close attention to the way he reacted to her. His breathing was beginning to slow now, and his lips were slightly parted. Jade pulled back, relishing the moment. She couldn't believe how good it felt to just be with him.

"You'll see, soon enough," she murmured. With one swift movement, she untangled her long legs from Ian's and slipped from the car, pulling him out behind her. The muscles on the sides of Ian's arms flexed as he closed the door and turned to face her. She looked him up and down, thinking of how hot he looked in dark colors. Jade couldn't believe that only last week she'd been worrying that he didn't care for her.

A contented silence fell over them and Ian grabbed Jade's hand, pulling her closer to him. The cautious yet intense way he was looking at her made her shift her weight from one foot to the other, surprised to find herself thinking that Ian may possibly wind up being her first. It was an errant thought, but Jade slowly turned it over in her mind. How was it possible that she felt so comfortable around him already that she was considering having sex with him?

Maybe it was that Ian's words felt different than anyone else's before him. He wasn't just saying the same old lines about her beauty to try and score points with her. He'd paid attention and looked beneath the surface. He truly wanted to know her.

Jade put her hands on his chest and reached up to kiss him. A low groan came from Ian's throat and Jade smiled into his lips.

"Thank you for tonight, and for everything you said," she whispered. He couldn't have known how much it all meant to her, and that she might have needed to hear it. "I'll see you tomorrow," she said, her body still on fire where it had been pressed up against his.

"I'll see you tonight in my dreams," Ian called back.

Jade laughed as she reluctantly turned away from him, wondering how it was possible that he always managed to pull off the corniest lines.

* * *

Kiara lay on her bed with her fingers laced together on her stomach, staring at the ceiling. She was fully dressed and ready to go out for the night, but she had just canceled her plans with Teague and their friends five minutes ago. Now she lay unmoving, trying to untangle herself from the array of distressing thoughts that ran amuck in her head.

The problem was that no matter what any of her friends were doing, it involved consuming calories in some way and she was already too close to her maximum for the day. Her chest constricted with anxiety just thinking about it. She couldn't risk going over the allotted amount by going out because she didn't want to throw up again today. She stared at the tiny inconsistencies on her ceiling, her vision blurring around the edges from going so long without blinking. Why wouldn't the thoughts stop? She had decided to sacrifice going out–she thought that would've helped.

Kiara sighed. She needed to vent somehow, she realized. She reached for her bedside drawer and grabbed her journal–almost a relic at this point, since she hadn't written in it in close to a year. She stared at the blank pages and froze. There was so much going on in her mind that she wanted to get out but she was afraid to give it life–like if she didn't talk or write about it, it wouldn't be real and couldn't hurt her. But she was being suffocated by her own mind, and this was the one thing she thought might help.

She held the pen poised above the page, wondering where to start.

"*I don't know when my dieting got so out of control,*" she wrote, and almost instantly tears began to drip down her cheeks at the confession. "*But I threw up my lunch today and blood came up. It scared the shit out of me and I can't tell anyone. I guess I could tell Reigh, but she would probably just say that's what happens if you want to lose weight. How is this something that people keep up? It's affecting every aspect of my life... and my thoughts scare me the most. As soon as I eat something and I can't count the calories I get an insane urge to throw it up as soon as possible. And the anxiety doesn't go away until I do. I literally can't think of anything else or even hold a conversation properly until I get the food out of my body.*

It consumes me. It IS consuming me. Every thought I have now is somehow about my weight, or other people's weight, comparing myself, counting calories, wondering how many I'm burning, and so on. I have to put concealer on my hand every day to cover up the bruise from biting down on it when I throw up. How fucked up is that? It's like I don't have my life anymore. I feel so out of control and I think Teague is going to break up with me if I don't tell him what's going on, but I can't. I just can't. I miss my old self. I miss my old mind. When did I get so far from everything and everyone?"

Kiara put her head on her arms as the tears poured out. Loud, strangled noises came from her throat as she broke down into a million pieces. The fear, anxiety, and overwhelm from the past few weeks crashed down on her as she realized just how serious of trouble she was in.

I'm just not going to throw up anymore, Kiara thought. But almost immediately, despair washed over her–she didn't want to give up that control. She couldn't. Not yet. Not with the thoughts. Kiara let out a wretched groan, turning to the side to hug her knees to her chest. There was no way out of this. She felt like she was trying to hold on to something–*anything*–that would keep her grounded as she battled the anguish barreling through her. Her phone vibrated on the nightstand but she ignored it, too far gone in her misery.

Hours later when Kiara had no more tears or strength, all that was left for her to do was fall asleep. She was depleted and her mind exhausted, but she had one last thought. It was a bittersweet but victorious one, though it made her want to weep all over again: she had been so preoccupied with her misery that she hadn't eaten any dinner.

The following morning, Kiara sat across from Ariana in the library in Saturday detention, pretending to study for math while Ariana recounted her first kiss with Lukas.

"I've never felt that before K, like I would never get enough of someone, even if we had all the time in the world…" Ariana trailed off, her eyes unfocused. Her wavy hair cascaded onto her bare skin and she looked so… content, dressed in a pale yellow sundress that showed off her bronzed shoulders and back. Kiara, on the other hand, had rolled out of bed this morning in her baggy sweatpants and oversized t-shirt, hastily thrown her hair up into a disheveled ponytail, grabbed her glasses and messenger bag and ran out the door. She almost let out a sour laugh–how different their nights had been. Jealousy stung Kiara's stomach; Ariana never worried about what others thought of her looks. She owned her curves and loved her body. Why couldn't Kiara be like that? What was wrong with her brain?

"He told me he's falling for me," Ariana said carefully, watching Kiara as Kiara watched her.

"WHAT?" Kiara yelped, completely ruining their studying façade. She was a little off from her breakdown last night; her emotions were out of whack.

"Shhh!" Ariana shot at her. "We'll get another detention stacked onto this one if we're too loud!"

"Ariana," Kiara said in a lower voice, trying to hide her annoyance. "*What* did he say exactly?"

"Why do you seem so angry?" Ariana said defensively.

"I'm not. I'm sorry. Go ahead," Kiara said, clamping her pale lips shut in subdued compliance.

"Basically, he kissed me and told me he loved me. Well, he told me he was *falling* in love with me. I can't even describe to you how it felt. I was beyond."

Kiara involuntarily clenched her jaw, realizing too late that Ariana would see it in her face. But this was exactly what she'd feared for Ariana–she was enamored with Lukas, despite his shifty behavior. Kiara couldn't put her finger on exactly what was off about him. "Ariana, I'm happy for you if you're happy, but that was really fast… I know you're smart enough to see that."

"Trust me–I know. But I can't help what I already feel," Ariana said, fear flashing across her flushed face.

Kiara softened. She knew that feeling all too well from her relationship with Teague–she had fallen for him so quickly–it had been terrifying and exhilarating at the same time. She took a deep breath. "I know what you mean. And I'm sorry for reacting like that at first." Kiara reached across the table to put her hand over Ariana's. "I know what that's like, to fall even when you're afraid."

Ariana nodded, her eyes wide.

"Just take it one day at a time and come to me or Jade if you're ever worried about anything," Kiara said, reassuring her friend with a smile.

Ariana's face fell for a tenth of a second but then she smiled back at Kiara and bent her head over her schoolwork just as the assistant principal walked by their table. Ariana looked up at the AP and smiled while jotting down notes. The aging male AP nodded at her, pacified, and walked away again.

Kiara doodled in her light-blue notebook, waiting for Ariana to become distracted by her schoolwork. After a few minutes, she double-checked that Ariana wasn't paying any attention to her, then began tallying how many calories she'd consumed this morning. Breakfast was one egg- 70 calories, one piece of vegetarian bacon- 45 calories, and gummy vitamins- 15 calories each, so 30 total. It was 11:30 a.m., and she was only at 145 total calories, so she decided she could have a tiny snack. Kiara's stomach ached from hunger as she reached into her messenger bag and pulled out a bag of seeded crackers. They were only about ten calories each, so she figured she would give herself five and call it an even 250 calories, just to round up.

Kiara noticed a movement in her peripheral vision and looked up. Ariana's hazel eyes were on her face, studying her. Kiara gave a little jump like a kid caught misbehaving.

"So, are you coming to Daire's party tonight?" Ariana only asked.

"Oh, um, yeah. Of course," Kiara said, slowly moving her arm to cover up the calorie math on her notebook. She continued to talk out of nervousness. "I love Daire. He's such a good guy."

"I know! We should set him up with one of the freshmen. He and Lyric would be great together."

Kiara laughed with relief. Ariana wasn't acting like she'd seen anything after all. Kiara rolled her eyes pointedly at her friend. "Yeah, Ari, I'm not sure that's what, or *who*, he wants."

"*Whom*," Ariana corrected, then laughed at the petulant face Kiara made. "Um, I think you forget I liked Daire when I first met him and he wasn't into me. We're just good friends now."

Kiara knew that was true–but she'd also seen the way Daire had started to look at Ariana. He definitely realized what had been right under his nose the entire time.

"Okay, whatever you say, Ari," Kiara teased. She stretched her arms out and crossed them behind her head. "Is lover boy coming tonight?"

"Umm, I'm not sure actually."

"Don't you guys talk, like, almost every night on the phone?"

"Yeah, for hours," Ariana said dreamily.

"And you didn't ask him what he's doing tonight?"

"No, I did. He just doesn't know yet."

"Okay... well, let me know when you know, I guess. Do you want to go with T and me? I think Jade is going with Ian tonight."

"Actually, Daire invited me over to help him set up and grab dinner beforehand," Ariana said, looking down guiltily at her notebook. "So I'll be in the same neighborhood as you!"

"Ari!" Kiara laughed. "Those both sound like very girlfriend-y things! Does Daire know anything about you and Lukas, considering they're close friends and all?"

"No, but it's not like that with me and Daire. We have a lot of fun together and I feel comfortable with him. He's become one of my closest friends."

"Okay, and how does Lukas feel about you and Daire doing a solo dinner? Not that you can't have dinner with another guy, but

I'm curious since it's pretty obvious to everyone that D has a crush on you."

"I don't know," Ariana said. "He should know that I only care for him though. Jesus, I just told him I'm falling for him! Besides, it's not like Lukas made any plans with me tonight."

"You can't make plans with him?" Kiara snapped. "He's not the only one in control, remember."

Ariana looked angry for a moment, but then smiled sadly and sighed. "I know, I know. It's fine though, I promise. You don't see what it's like when we're alone together."

"Mmm," Kiara answered, biting her tongue. She looked at Ariana's face. Happiness radiated from her friend like sunshine on a summer day. *Doesn't this feel off to you?* Kiara wanted to say. *He has you, but do you have him?*

But Kiara was so emotionally exhausted she chose not to say anything, thinking that now was not the best time to bring up Ariana's dwindling resolve to not become "so obsessed that nothing else matters" with Lukas.

Ariana was perfectly at home at Daire's house. She sat cross-legged on his brown suede couch with a pillow in her lap, petting his two Great Danes, Willy and Wally. Daire was at his desk across the room, getting her opinion on the playlist he'd created for the party. They'd eaten dinner at Carmine's earlier, a popular restaurant that served as *the* go-to place for her high school. You couldn't dine at Carmine's without seeing at least five people you knew from school, which was either really fun or really annoying, depending on what mood she was in.

"How about this one?" Daire asked her, putting on "Recurring" by Bonobo.

Ariana had heard the song before, although she couldn't place where or when. It filled her with a nervous, excited energy, like she was waiting for something to happen, but couldn't figure out exactly what it was.

"I like it," she said. "Really, they're all good D, but shouldn't you go and change? It's almost nine. I'm pretty sure everyone's going to get here soon."

Daire was still wearing a pair of workout shorts and a tank, the same clothes he'd worn to dinner with her. That was another thing she loved about Daire: he was always relaxed–from his demeanor to his clothes.

"Oh shit, you're right. I always lose my sense of time when I'm with you," he said as he wandered into his room to change.

Ariana stiffened at the offhand comment. Daire had said it innocently enough, but she couldn't help thinking of Kiara's commentary on their friendship. That remark had sounded *very* boyfriend-y, all right. Ariana shifted her weight, suddenly uncomfortable in her cross-legged position on the couch, and tugged her pale yellow sundress down from where Wally had scooted it up her leg with his nose.

She patted the giant dog away and reached for her phone to text Lukas.

9:06 p.m. Ariana: Hey! Over at Daire's. Are you coming tonight?
9:07 p.m. Lukas: Yeah I heard. Otw with the boys
9:08 p.m. Ariana: Ok see you soon xx

Oh shit, Ariana thought. What did that mean? She prayed Lukas didn't think anything was going on between her and Daire. She sat still for a few moments, letting the anxious thoughts take over her mind. Why hadn't Lukas just told Daire about them, anyway?

Ariana wandered into the kitchen and poured herself a beer, figuring the alcohol would help to calm her nerves. She hoisted herself up on the dark marble countertop just as she heard the back door swing open. A group of senior boys entered the house, greeting her as they charged through the kitchen to the beer. Lukas filed in last, looking mouthwateringly handsome in a white henley shirt. Her heart lurched. He wasn't looking at her. Actually, he was looking everywhere *except* at her. It hurt knowing that she couldn't run to him and kiss him like she wanted. That, in fact, no one had any clue about what they had together at all.

Instead, Ariana stayed put on the counter, calmly sipping her beer and acting as though Lukas was simply another guest, greeting him with the same polite enthusiasm she'd used to greet everyone else. Lukas leaned in to hug her and she stilled, instantly drunk from his touch. He held her for a moment before releasing her and immediately looking away. Ariana's body stung from where his skin had touched hers–his sudden withdrawal burned.

Lukas moved to the opposite corner of the kitchen, the farthest away he could possibly get, and picked up a conversation with Taron. *I'll have to warn Jade that Taron is here*, she thought, attempting to distract herself. Her mood was falling fast. Was Lukas angry that she'd been here alone with Daire?

As if on cue, Daire emerged from his room, showered and clean, wearing a form-fitting white V-neck shirt and dark blue shorts. He looked refreshed and handsome, towering over mostly everyone as usual. Ariana watched him say hello to the guys and then finally to Lukas, who regarded him coolly.

"What's up, man?" Daire said. "You look like you need something stronger than a beer."

Lukas looked at Ariana, his eyes distrusting. Daire followed Lukas' gaze and grinned.

"Ari, you're down for a shot, aren't you?" Daire called out to her.

"I could definitely use one," Ariana responded, hopping off the counter and making her way to them. She hated to be the one to go to Lukas first, but it was as though a magnet were pulling her in. Daire casually slung an arm around her shoulder and Lukas' face shifted into a grimace for a moment, but he quickly regained his composure.

"Yeah, I'll take one," Lukas said.

Daire grabbed a bottle of vodka from the cabinet and hastily poured everyone a shot. They threw them back and Daire wandered off to greet a wave of juniors. Ariana found herself being pushed closer to Lukas as the kitchen filled up.

"So, you and D?" Lukas shot at her in a whisper when they were nearly touching.

"What the hell are you talking about Lukas?" she shot back. "You didn't know what your plans were for tonight and Daire invited me over to hang out in a friendly, *platonic* way. Well, it's platonic for me. And I'd think you'd trust me after..." She broke off, trying to find the Lukas she knew and loved in his eyes.

"This is what I meant about you, Ariana," Lukas said, his eyes distant. "You're always with a different dude. Maybe it's just too much for me. Maybe I can't handle you."

"What?" Ariana almost dropped her drink in shock. "But you *just* told me that you..." she trailed off. She was having trouble remembering how to breathe properly and the feeling of needing to escape had taken hold of her. Tears stung the corner of her eyes, but she refused to retreat so easily. "I'm not the one insistent on keeping this so fucking secretive anyway," she spat at him. "Maybe if you would tell your friends about us, they would stop hitting on me."

Lukas' mouth fell open. Ariana whirled on her heel and walked out the back door, barely keeping her increasingly panicked breaths hidden. She was vaguely aware that someone was calling her name, but she didn't turn around. She squeezed through the gate and pulled out her phone to text Kiara, letting her know she was about to walk over to her house, and then set off into the grim night without another look back.

A car drove by with kids hollering at her out of a rolled-down window. Ariana flipped them off without thinking as she strode on. She'd never been more grateful and annoyed that nearly everyone lived in the same god-forsaken neighborhood.

CHAPTER 15

Jade

Jade paced back and forth in her room, furiously trying to come up with a plan. Ian was on his way over to pick her up for Daire's party and simultaneously meet her mother, but Dani was still home–*not* according to plan. Dani was *supposed* to be at dinner with her friends, yet had canceled at the last minute because she wasn't feeling well. Even though Jade was planning on showing everyone she and Ian were together at the party tonight, that didn't mean she wanted Dani to see him over beforehand. Who knew what Dani would do or say?

Jade checked her messages again, her nerves climbing while she waited to hear from Ian. He said he would be there within the hour about fifty minutes ago, so Jade could only imagine that he was down the street. Dani was in her room, doing whatever she did in there–Jade had no idea since she stayed as far away from Dani as possible at all times.

A wave of nostalgia hit Jade unannounced, and she remembered when they used to spend hours playing dress-up and telling fairy tales in Dani's huge closet when they were young, making each other laugh so hard they nearly peed their pants. She'd felt so safe when it was just the two of them in there, like nothing bad could ever touch them. But then the incident happened, ripping their family open and leaving holes in each of their hearts in peculiar ways. A long time ago, before everything, Dani had loved Jade–Jade *knew* that she had–but that Dani was long gone.

Jade also knew in her heart of hearts what the real problem was, but no one in her family ever talked about it anymore. She never spoke of her family's past either, except to Ariana and Kiara, and even so, it wasn't often. Not that she didn't want to talk about it, but the subject was difficult for most people to swallow. No one ever knew what to say. Jade played with her bracelet, twisting it around her wrist again and again, toying with the idea of telling Ian about herself. She wanted to be closer to him, but also didn't want him to look at her differently.

Jade's phone vibrated in her hand and she jumped, but then saw it was Ariana and relaxed. Ian wasn't there just yet.

"Hey Ari, I'm so glad you called–" Jade started to say, but was cut off as Ariana began racing through her story. Ariana sounded like she was close to tears.

"What the fuck?" Jade exclaimed after Ariana finished. "You did the right thing. Fuck him. He can't *handle* you? Do you want me to *handle* him for you?!"

Jade listened to the laughter coming from the other end of the line and smiled. *This is a good thing for Ariana*, she thought. Clearly, Lukas was only interested in himself and Ariana would be better off without him. She ended the call by promising she and Ian would stop by Kiara's and they would all go to the party together. After hanging up, Jade saw she had a text from Ian–he was five minutes away.

"Ughhh," Jade groaned as she prepped herself for Ian to meet her mom while Dani was there to wreak havoc on it all. She took one last look in the mirror, happy she had dressed down in a white V-cut top and a pleated maroon tennis skirt with black sneakers. Her hair fell in shiny waves around her chest, and her dark green eyes were luminous in the reflection.

"Bring it on, Dani," Jade said quietly to herself, then she

walked out of her room and shouted down the stairs, "MOM! He'll be here any minute!"

Dani's door cracked open and Jade stiffened. She took a breath to steady herself as Dani slowly swung the door open and slithered toward her. Dani's strawberry blonde hair was pulled back into a tight bun, her face clear of makeup. Jade would've told her she looked pretty if Dani hadn't looked like a cobra ready to strike.

"Who's coming over?" Dani asked, her voice silky and venomous.

"Just Ian," Jade said, attempting to say as little as possible. She stared at her navy blue coated fingernails, hoping she appeared nonchalant.

"Ohh," Dani said, smiling. Warning bells blared in Jade's head as her sister's lips continued to turn up and her smile widened. "Ian Alkine?"

"Yes. And it would be great if you weren't rude to him," Jade said, fighting to keep her voice calm.

"Aw, how adorable. You're really sticking up for him?"

"Yeah, I am, Dani. I like him, so please, please don't sabotage this," Jade gave in and begged. "Please, for me?"

Dani stared at her for a moment, and then her face twisted. "Jade, you idiot. Why would I need to sabotage this for you when Ian did that himself? You know he's been fucking Kristin Long right?"

Jade's mouth dropped, all of her bravado evaporating in that instant. This, she had not seen coming. A hot pit began to form in her stomach.

"Dani... please. Are you lying? Or is that true?" Jade asked, her voice breaking.

"Oh my God, why are you upset? You're so weak. You're seriously pathetic. You were really starting to like him? You trusted him? And all this time he's been fucking Kristin Long?" Dani said in rapid fire, laughing all the while.

"WHY DOES IT HAVE TO BE THIS WAY DANI?!" Jade

screamed. Her heavy breaths filled the heightened silence following her outburst. She'd lost control and Dani knew it. "Why do you hate me so much?"

Dani smiled a tight-lipped, belittling smile and shrugged her shoulders. "There's nothing to love."

With that, she swept by Jade, purposefully shoving her into the banister. A pricking sensation stung the corners of her eyes.

"Ow!" Jade yelped, but she made no move to retaliate. Jade rubbed her ribs where the banister's edge had smashed into them. The shove came so quickly that she hadn't had time to defend herself.

Jade shakily retreated to her room and leaned against the wall, pushing her hands against the sides of her head. *If I were normal,* she thought, *tears would come now.*

Dani was right–she was pathetic. Ian had fooled her, and she'd stupidly trusted him. She couldn't believe she'd been considering having sex with him. He was like any other guy, and she hated herself for thinking differently. And he didn't actually think she was special at all. If he had, he wouldn't have lied to her.

Jade gave into the dejection. Her back slid down the wall until she was crumpled in a ball on the floor with her face smushed into the carpet, feeling how utterly pathetic she was.

After a few minutes of what could only be described as crying with the absence of actual tears, Jade started to breathe normally again, staring at the close-up fibers of her beige carpet as they swayed from her breathing. *I am on the floor right now because of some guy,* Jade thought. *A guy that would choose Kristin Long over me.*

So, she knew now. What was the point of wallowing in it? If he wanted Kristin Long, he could have her. She wouldn't be a part of that. She was too strong for that. Jade decided she would allow herself to feel the loss–to fully revel in it–for thirty more seconds, and then she would move on. She began to count down, slowly writing Ian off with every second that passed.

With four seconds left her phone rang.

Ian's name lit up on the screen and her stomach turned. She already missed him, even before she'd let him go. *Focus,* she thought, angry that she still had any longing for the liar. She answered the call and spoke clearly, refusing to allow her voice to waiver. "I know about you and Kristin. You should have told me. You and I are done."

"Shit. Jade, I was going to tell you–"

But she hung up before he could finish his sentence. Ian called several more times, one right after another, and each time his name came on the screen Jade had to avert her eyes so she wouldn't answer.

Finally, after the fourth or fifth call, the ringing stopped. Jade ran to the window and searched the street for his car. She saw the retreating tail lights as a text came in.

9:27 p.m. Ian: I'm sorry I didn't tell you. I'm so sorry.

Jade deleted the text, her insides twisting. He didn't deny it.

She called Haiden, who said he could be over in ten minutes to pick her up. Jade changed her outfit–why not hurt Ian back a little if she could? She pulled off the top and skirt she'd been wearing and donned a dark green silk dress that pooled around her cleavage. It was sexy and looked incredible on her figure.

Deal with this, Ian, Jade thought. She pulled on a pair of heels and made her way downstairs, quickly telling her mom that she wouldn't be meeting Ian tonight.

"What happened, sweetie?" Lenee asked in concern. "And when I was in the shower earlier, I thought I heard yelling. Were you and Dani arguing again?"

"He's just a stupid boy, Mom. You win some, you lose some, you know? I love you!" Jade said, rushing for the door.

Lenee sighed, seeming to catch on that Jade was avoiding her question about Dani. "I wish the two of you would get along. We're all each other has. And when Vince and I are gone, it'll just be you and Dani. You have to look out for each other."

That's such a destructive thing to say, Jade thought. *Way to tell me to get closer to someone who torments me.* But she knew her mother was blinded by her love for both of her daughters and didn't see what Dani was really like. "I have to go, Mom. Haiden is almost here–I'll tell him you say hi. I'm spending the night at Kiara's, and you can call her mom to check. I'll see you tomorrow morning."

Jade kissed her mother on the cheek and stepped outside.

"And the stupid boy?" Lenee called after her, "Will I ever meet him?"

"Nah, he was just a fling!" she yelled back, forcing a smile. When Jade turned around she let her face fall. A "fling" was the farthest thing from the truth.

Jade hopped into Haiden's hand-me-down jeep with ease as all the doors were missing. Haiden called this "part of the charm," even when it was storming outside. He'd saved up for the car after long summers of lifeguarding and it was his pride and joy. Haiden waved furiously at her mother through the window before peeling out of the driveway.

"What's up, dude?" he asked. "You look down."

"You know Ian Alkine right?"

"Yeah, who doesn't know Ian Alkine? But yeah, he's cool."

"Well, we kind of had a thing..."

At this, Haiden let out a loud laugh. "Nice, J!" he said, reaching out to fist bump her. When Jade made no move to return the gesture, Haiden turned serious again. "Oh. What happened?"

"I heard he's been hooking up with Kristin Long," she said, the words stinging her tongue.

"Oh shit, I didn't realize you actually liked him. I'm sorry." He ran a hand over his hair, thinking. "Damn, that girl is non-stop trouble for you."

"Tell me about it." Jade sighed. "Actually, don't," she said a moment later. Haiden laughed, and she let herself laugh at the absurdity of it all. It was so ridiculous how much Kristin was a source of misery in her life that it felt kind of good to laugh about it. "Just, help me think about something else right now?"

"Oh, I can do that. Why don't you take a break from your life and think about my *awesome* speakers!" Haiden yelled as he cranked up his EDM music, playfully swerving the car to the beat. Jade let out a squeal and laughed into the wind. They drove the entire way like this, Haiden swerving periodically to the music and Jade cracking up. She was surprised they didn't get pulled over, but she honestly couldn't have cared less if they had. Once they got to Kiara's house, Jade sent Ariana a text to let her know they were out front. Ariana and Kiara traipsed outside, looking defeated.

"Whoa!" Haiden yelled, standing on the side of his jeep. "What's going on here? Why the long faces from everyone?"

"Where's Teague?" Jade asked Kiara.

"He's... He's going straight to the party," Kiara said, her blonde hair hanging in front of her face. "I think he's mad at me again, but I don't know why."

Something looked off about Kiara, Jade realized. Her mouth had blotchy red marks around the edges and her eyes were more distant than usual. Was that from crying? The situation with Teague must've been worse than she was letting on. Jade reached out and grabbed Kiara's hand, squeezing it tightly.

"Where's Ian?" Ariana said.

"He's been fucking Kristin Long. It's over," Jade said.

Ariana and Kiara reacted with shock, a small gasp escaping each of their lips.

"Oh, Jade," Ariana said as she threw her arms around her. Jade put one arm around Ariana's shoulders as she reached her other arm to Kiara again, who grabbed her hand and squeezed back. Jade took a deep breath, overcome with gratitude for her friends, and instead of feeling bad, she smiled.

"You know what? Fuck them. Fuck all of them. Let's just go be ridiculous at this party," Jade said.

Haiden jumped up, pumping the air with his fist. "Hell yeah!"

he yelled. He pulled the three of them into a semi-bear hug, and then, unable to maintain his balance while they all laughed and squirmed, pulled the girls with him as he fell over onto the lawn.

They lay there for a while, sprawled out and laughing crazily. Jade loved moments like this. No matter how many times she played out what could or might happen in the future in her head, these unplanned moments were always the best.

"Shit! Jade... I forgot to tell you. Taron is there tonight, too," Ariana said.

"Perfect!" Jade exclaimed, and they burst out laughing again. "Can my night possibly get any better?"

Daire's house was overflowing by the time they arrived. Jade pushed her way through the crowd straight to the kitchen, dragging Ariana and Kiara behind her. She was vaguely aware of several pairs of eyes on her, one of those belonging to Ian. Jade would be lying to herself if she didn't admit she had known exactly where he was from the moment she stepped into the party, but she refused to make eye contact with him or even look in his general direction. At least he was over in the living room a safe distance away. Several girls were surrounding him, and Jade involuntarily clenched her fists when she saw that one of them was Kristin. The thought of them naked and sweaty together made Jade sick to her stomach. She needed to focus on something else.

"Daire!" Jade shouted over the crowd to Daire's towering figure. He could always be counted on to lighten the mood. "D!"

Daire made his way into the kitchen, grinning from ear to ear as he stopped in front of them.

"Three of my favorite girls," Daire said, hugging them simultaneously. He was already pretty tipsy. "Seriously, you guys are like Charlie's Angels or something."

"Aww, thank you D," Ariana said, laughing. "I think."

Kiara nudged Jade softly on her side. "I'm going to find Teague and try to patch things up."

Jade gave her an understanding nod before turning back to Ariana and a drunken Daire. Anything to distract her from the thoughts of Ian and Kristin that were threatening to resurface.

"Lukas!" Daire yelled suddenly, calling over her shoulder into the connecting den. "Come here!"

Jade crossed her arms. She looked back at Ariana, who stood frozen in place with a look of dread in her eyes. Jade decided she would need to *handle* this situation for her friend. A severely stoned Lukas sauntered into the room, looking like he had just taken a huge hit off the bong. Sure, he was still good-looking, but Jade felt as though she was seeing him in his true form for the first time: eyes bloodshot and unfocused, mouth hanging slightly open, hair smashed down on his head. He didn't look like he could handle anything.

"Don't Ari, J, and Kiara remind you of Charlie's Angels?" Daire slurred to Lukas, who stopped dead in his tracks at the sight of Ariana.

Jade raised a perfectly arched eyebrow as they waited for him to respond.

"Hello? Is anyone home?" Jade snapped at Lukas, waving her hand in front of his face. He was standing in stunned silence, either from seeing Ariana again or from how much he had smoked, Jade didn't know. What she did know, though, was that she was tired of these boys. Ian was a liar and Lukas was a flake who had hurt her friend, and that was that.

She turned to Ariana and spoke loud enough for everyone in their general vicinity to hear. "I don't think Lukas can *handle anything,* Ari." Jade spun back to Lukas, who was still staring stupidly. Daire seemed extremely confused by the turn of events, but looked down at Lukas expectantly as well, waiting to see what his buddy had to say.

Jade refused to wait around on Lukas for another second. She took a step toward him and leaned in until she was only an inch from his ear, making sure only he could hear her. "You can't even handle your weed, Lukas. Of course you can't handle Ariana."

She gave a small laugh. "You're pathetic. Now, stay away from my friend."

"I don't know what you're talking about..." Lukas mumbled.

Ariana gave her arm a gentle tug. Jade threw Lukas one last glare before facing Ariana, who was shaking her head as if it were no use even talking to Lukas. Ariana's eyes were sad, but she was smiling.

"Don't bother," Ariana said. "He's too high right now to know what's going on."

Jade glanced back to where Lukas had been but he'd already disappeared into the crowd.

"By the way, this song always reminds me of you, J," Ariana said softly, and for the first time that night Jade noticed the music playing in the background. Halsey's vocals echoed through the room, and the music inspired Jade.

She searched the crowd for Kiara, whom she found in the back corner of the kitchen with Teague. Kiara's eyes were misty and even though Teague was standing close to her, they weren't touching. Jade dived for Kiara, and after shouting an apology to Teague, pulled her and Ariana to the bar separating the kitchen from the living room.

"This is *not* how our night is going to go," Jade told them. "Let's forget about all of it." She closed her eyes and let the music fill her mind, tuning out everyone except for her two best friends. She stepped onto the bar, bringing Kiara and Ariana with her. She put her hands above her head and began to dance, a smile on her lips.

CHAPTER 16

K. A. J

After a good hour of dancing, Kiara was dying of thirst. "I'll be right back!" she shouted to Jade and Ariana.

She didn't know if they heard her or not–Jade's eyes were closed while her hips swayed to the beat. Ariana was dancing with two blonde girls from another school, her head thrown back in laughter.

Kiara hopped off the counter and wandered into the kitchen to grab water but got distracted by an ice cold beer sitting unopened, seemingly waiting for her. *Fuck it, I haven't drank in forever*, Kiara thought. She was pretty low. Maybe the beer would help.

As she chugged it, Teague spoke from behind her. "Kiara, we really need to talk."

At the tone of his voice, Kiara snapped back from the reality break she had taken for the last hour. And her reality at the moment wasn't pretty: she and Teague had never truly healed from the night at Jade's house when she snapped at him for merely coming on to her. They had only continued to put Band-Aids on the situation, the last being her blaming cheer tryouts for her moods. Teague wasn't an idiot–he could tell she was keeping something from him. They'd kept up their dance of Kiara lying and Teague pretending like he believed her for a while, but they were both tired.

Kiara wanted to tell him everything, she really did, but at this point she would rather die than tell the truth. And what was she supposed to say? That her eating habits had gotten so out of control that she was now beginning to get truly worried? That she was at the point where she felt the urge to throw up every meal she ate because she could swear she was getting fatter, although she was barely eating anything at all? That she had thrown up blood more than once now and was scared out of her mind, but she couldn't tell anyone because no one knew the depths of her situation?

No, she couldn't do that. She took the last swig of beer and grabbed another one, feeling less like herself than she ever had in her life.

"Kiara," Teague said again.

She finally turned to face him. "Hey." She trained her eyes above his right shoulder at the old-fashioned clock on the wall, watching the rhythmic ticking rather than looking at Teague's face. It was like the clock knew. Kiara had ticked down all the moments she had left before the inevitable.

"Come talk to me, please?" Teague said.

Kiara's stomach started to fall, but she nodded anyway and let Teague lead her outside. They found a secluded area and sat on a stone bench by the back gate. Kiara took a huge swig of beer to ready herself for what was about to happen. She looked Teague in the eyes. His deep, brown eyes. The eyes she trusted but that didn't trust her anymore.

"Kiara... I know, and you know, that there's something going on that you're not telling me. I love you. You know that I love you and I would never judge you. But we can't have a relationship if you don't trust me. I'm starting to think maybe you don't love me anymore, and if that's the case, then you owe it to me to let me know."

Kiara dropped her gaze as her eyes teared up. She couldn't see any way out of this without telling Teague the truth. And as much as she hated to admit it, everything would be much easier to hide if they weren't together anymore.

"Teague, I love you. You know I do. I just... I don't want to hurt you anymore." Her voice was trembling.

"It doesn't have to end like this, just tell me what's going on with you!" Teague's eyes searched hers. "And don't tell me there's nothing wrong. I know there is. Is it another guy?"

"NO!" Kiara yelled, outraged at Teague for jumping to that conclusion. She was tired all of a sudden, so tired that she couldn't think of anything else to say. Her brain was scrambled and she could barely focus. Kiara tried to think back and remember if she had eaten anything since detention, but her head was too foggy.

"Well, what do I do Kiara!? Tell me what to do, *please*! Because I don't know what to do other than break up with you! Is that how I have to get your attention?"

"Teague! Please!" She stood up abruptly; she had to get some blood flowing to her head so she could think. "Teague," she began again, but stopped as her legs gave out for a split second. "Whoa," Kiara said as her vision started to swim.

"Kiara?" Teague said in alarm. He stepped toward her.

Kiara grabbed onto his arm with a weak grip, attempting to regain her balance and sight. She tried to look at his face, but it was too hard to focus her eyes. She was nauseous. Teague's voice was all around her, but she couldn't understand what he was saying.

"Teague," Kiara whispered, and then her vision went black.

Jade placed her hands on Ariana's waist, moving her hips to mirror her own. They had everyone's attention. Guys had stopped their conversations to stare, while more and more girls were climbing onto the countertops to join them. Ariana had already forgotten the names of the other two blondes dancing with them–Karen and Georgia, maybe? The blondes were fun and all, but Ariana wanted Kiara to be with them for this moment.

Ariana turned on the countertop to look for Kiara at the same moment that Haiden ran in the back door, his face ashen and in shock. "Ariana! Jade!" he yelled.

Ariana sobered up immediately. Before Jade had even registered that there was trouble, Ariana was already halfway to Haiden.

"Kiara fell or something, I don't know, I think she may have fainted. Teague just said to find you," Haiden said, his eyes dazed.

Ariana put a hand on his arm. "Where?"

"Outside."

They rounded the house to where Kiara was slouched over on a stone bench, her face as pale as the moon. Teague had his arm around her, trying to get her to take slow sips of water. Jade called out Kiara's name and Teague looked up at them, defeated.

"Guys," Kiara slurred. "I'm okay, I just got dehydrated from all the dancing. I forgot to drink water."

"I... I don't know what happened," Teague stammered in a stunned voice. "We were arguing and then she started swaying so I grabbed her and she couldn't focus her eyes..." Teague's voice was breaking slightly. "And then her legs gave out, and she just went limp in my arms."

"Teague... I'm okay," Kiara said.

"Kiara," Ariana said. "When's your birthday?"

"I'm okay. It's in July. July 13th," Kiara said, lifting her head to look Ariana in the eyes.

"Are any parts of your body tingling? Do you feel tired?"

"Seriously, Ari, I'm fine. No. I just can't handle my alcohol," Kiara said with a forced laugh.

"You fainted," Teague said, his jaw clenching. "Don't joke about it. It wasn't funny. It *isn't* funny."

Ariana stilled. Something wasn't right. Kiara was being

strangely defensive and trying weirdly hard to be upbeat. Ariana was almost one hundred percent sure she was hiding something. And something big was hanging on the edge of Ariana's consciousness; it felt like it was something she'd caught glimpses of in Kiara, but hadn't been paying close enough attention for it to register.

Kiara shuddered again and Ariana was brought back to a memory of gymnastics and a girl in her level who used to act strange around lunchtime every day, similarly to how Kiara was always staring at other people's food now. The little girl had been as thin as a skeleton, even for a thirteen-year-old. One day, after fainting at practice, the girl's mother had gone into her room and found bottle upon bottle of stored vomit underneath her daughter's bed. Only then did the parents realize their daughter had been hiding an eating disorder. It was a horrible memory, and one she hadn't thought about in ages, but Ariana knew it had resurfaced for a reason. Keeping the emotions wiped from her face, Ariana slowly replayed the last few weeks in her mind. To her horror, she began to see patterns she hadn't spotted before.

Teague pulled his arm from around Kiara and let Jade sit in his place. She brushed Kiara's hair off her face and kissed her forehead.

"T, I'm sorry," Kiara said, her blue-green eyes welling up around the edges.

"No," Teague said curtly. "You're lying."

Teague took one last look at Kiara and walked off into the party. Haiden gave Kiara a hug before he trailed after Teague, giving the girls some space.

Ariana ran her hand through her hair, trying to think. She didn't want to make it obvious that she was onto something, so she sat on the grass next to Kiara's legs with her arms resting on Kiara's lap, facing slightly away from her.

"That was scary for a second, K," Ariana said. "What do you think happened?"

Ariana felt Kiara's leg twitch against her, but she stayed perfectly still.

"I have no idea, I think I just fainted because I didn't drink enough water, you know? And then we were dancing and all of that beer... Everything combined made me dizzy," Kiara said.

"Mmm." Ariana stared off into the distance. That was a lot of excuses.

"Ariana?" Kiara asked, surely feeling discomfort in the silence.

"Just thinking."

"I mean, you know, it could've been anything really... also I think I might be anemic, so that could have something to do with it," Kiara continued.

"Or maybe it was something you ate?" Ariana asked.

Kiara's leg twitched ever so slightly against Ariana's body.

"No, I don't think so," Kiara said.

"Well, let's go through it," Ariana said, needing to know if she was right. If Kiara really had an eating disorder, and it was this out of control, she would have to find out now even if Kiara would hate her for a while because of what she was about to do. "What'd you eat today?"

"Oh my God, Ariana," Kiara said, her voice raising. "I don't know, can you remember what you ate today?"

"Yes, breakfast was eggs, lunch after detention was a sandwich and fruit at home, and I had grilled eggplant salad at dinner with Daire," Ariana said, not missing a beat.

"What're you doing, Ari? She just fainted, leave her alone," Jade said.

"No, seriously, we need to know what she ate," Ariana insisted. Her cheeks were burning; she was so scared she would push Kiara away, but she didn't know if Kiara would tell them the truth if she didn't push her. "Kiara, I saw you snacking in detention, but you barely ate anything. What'd you eat after that today? Are you not eating enough?"

"I told you I don't know! Back the fuck off me!" Kiara shouted.

"It's not that hard, Kiara. What'd you have for lunch? What'd you have for dinner? It really shouldn't be that hard!"

"Ari!" Jade interjected again.

"What is your problem!?" Kiara yelled, her voice breaking.

Ariana got on her knees before Kiara so she could look her in the eyes, but Kiara wouldn't look at her. *Another sign that I'm right*, Ariana thought. She grabbed Kiara's hands.

"...Unless you didn't eat anything after detention today. Unless you haven't really been eating anything at all," Ariana said.

Jade sucked in her breath.

A single tear escaped Kiara's eye and trailed down her cheek. She opened her mouth to speak, but a look of worry flashed across her features and she clamped it shut again. Kiara hung her head and began to sob. Jade looked up at Ariana in alarm, and Ariana gave a small nod. Jade put her arms around Kiara.

"Let's get you out of here," Ariana said softly.

* * *

Jade rocked Kiara in her arms while Ariana grabbed their stuff from inside. She stroked Kiara's pale blonde hair rhythmically, the way Dani used to do to her when they were young. Jade mulled the revelation over in her mind, trying to make sense of it. How could Kiara have an eating disorder? Jade saw her eating all the time! What about at Weston's party? Jade had stood up to Melodie for making fun of Kiara for eating *too* much!

A dark wave of understanding washed over Jade. After the incident with Melodie at Weston's party, Kiara disappeared into the bathroom for a long time. They hadn't been able to find her for the rest of the night. Had she been throwing up all the food she'd eaten? Jade blanched. How had she not noticed that her best friend was in this turmoil?

"I love you, Kiara," Jade said, keeping her voice strong.

"I love you too; I'm sorry for lying," Kiara said in a quivering voice. "I was getting so scared Jade... I've thrown up blood."

Jade wanted to laugh bitterly. There she'd been, so worried about Ian and Kristin, when Kiara was truly suffering.

"Well, Ariana and I know now. We'll figure this out together," Jade said, although she didn't know the first thing about eating disorders. She also had absolutely no idea what to say in this type of situation. She wanted to ask Kiara a million questions but held her tongue, choosing instead to share the silence in solidarity with her.

Ariana reappeared carrying all of their bags and a bottle of water. "I tried to call a car but they're taking forever. It'll only take a few minutes to walk." Jade lifted Kiara off the bench, keeping an arm around her waist. Ariana took the other side and they set off for Kiara's house.

Kiara's parents were asleep by the time they got back at midnight. Both Jade and Ariana's phones had been going off on the walk home, but they hid them in the other room without even bothering to check them. The three of them curled up on Kiara's massive bed, covered themselves in blankets, and snuggled in together.

"What am I going to do?" Kiara whispered. "I can barely eat anymore without throwing up afterward."

Jade cringed internally. She wanted to cry. How had it gotten this bad?

Ariana reached out to put a hand on Kiara's arm. "Kiara, I've seen people get through this before in gymnastics. People that had been doing it for years. You're going to get through it too."

"But what do I *do*?" Kiara asked desperately, looking to Ariana for an answer. "My mind is so fucked up now. I can barely think about anything else. It's even come to take precedence over Teague. Every little thing I do is somehow related to my weight, and I can't stop the thoughts–I've tried and tried. I can't stop," Kiara's voice broke at the end of her speech, and she started sobbing hysterically.

Jade put her arms around Kiara and began stroking her hair again. Kiara cried into her neck. Jade knew, from doing this with Dani after everything that had happened to them, that sometimes another human's touch and presence was the best answer.

"I'll do some research," Ariana said after Kiara began to breathe evenly again. "We'll see what options we have. Probably a therapist of some sort."

"So I have to tell my parents?" Kiara asked, sniffling in between words.

"Yeah, I think you should," Ariana said, her hazel eyes stern.

Kiara groaned. "I don't want them to know. They're going to be so freaked out."

"We don't have to decide on anything tonight," Jade chimed in, skimming her navy blue nails over Kiara's scalp.

Ariana shot Jade a warning glare and Jade narrowed her eyes in dissonance. She knew Ariana was just doing and saying what she thought was best, but Kiara had been pushed enough for one night. After a little while, Ariana relaxed her face and gave Jade a barely noticeable nod of agreement.

Jade watched as Ariana entwined her fingers with Kiara's on top of the covers. For the second time that night, amidst all the chaos, Jade felt a deep understanding of how lucky she was to have Kiara and Ariana in her life. And if anyone could figure out how to help Kiara, it was Ariana. With that peaceful thought, Jade drifted into a deep sleep.

Ian stood about thirty feet away, smiling his goofy grin at her. He was so cute. Jade's cheeks flushed and her body hummed with excitement. She'd missed him so much. She looked at her shoes, embarrassed by her immediate and obvious reaction to him. She looked back up, opening her mouth to ask why they had split in the first place–she couldn't remember–but stopped abruptly. Kristin was on his arm now, snarling at her, while Ian had the same smile on his face, unnoticing. How had Jade not seen that

Kristin had always been there? Her stomach fell, but she knew she had to save Ian. She reached out her hand, wanting desperately to pull him out of Kristin's grasp. He reached out to her in return and Jade's hopes rose. She would free him and he could be with her then. *Really* be with her. But Kristin turned his face toward hers and kissed him, clawing her arms around his neck.

"Hey! Wake up!" Ariana's voice called in her dream.

Jade woke with a start to the sound of fingers snapping by her ear. Her eyes adjusted to Ariana's face only inches from hers. Jade's reality came crashing down–the overwhelming sadness she felt at the absence of Ian was alarming. She clutched her stomach to try and stop the hurt, reminding herself that there were more pressing matters at hand.

"What's up?" Jade asked a wide-eyed Ariana.

Ariana shushed her and tilted her head toward Kiara and then back toward the guest bedroom where they had stashed their phones.

"Did I make the right decision?" Ariana asked frantically as soon as they shut the bedroom door.

"What?" Jade asked, wiping the sleep from her eyes. She could still feel Ian's presence, or the lack thereof. She wrapped her arms around her stomach again.

"Jade. Wake up. Wake *fully* up. Did I make the right decision? Do you think we should've taken Kiara to the hospital? She *fainted*–and she hasn't been eating. Her body could be eating itself! What if that's *why* she fainted?!"

Ariana was pacing the room at an alarmingly fast speed. Jade caught her wrist as she walked by and pulled her into a hug.

"Hey, calm down," Jade said softly. She had no idea what the right thing to do was or wasn't. She hadn't even thought of taking Kiara to the hospital. Of course Ariana would think of that and freak out over it, but Jade thought they'd done the best they could in the situation. "We didn't know what to do. But it's close to 3 AM. Let's monitor her for the night and tomorrow morning everything will be clearer."

"I don't know..."

"Ari... I know you're trying to make the best decision, but we haven't slept and I don't know what the answer is. I'll take shifts with you watching over her and she'll never have to know, okay? We'll find some way to convince her to tell her parents in the morning, and then the three of them can decide on whether or not she needs to go to the hospital. This isn't all on your shoulders, okay? And since you clearly haven't slept yet, I'll take the first shift," Jade said, surprising herself with how calm and collected she sounded.

"What if you fall asleep?"

"I just had a dream about Ian and I've realized that now even my dreams of him will be nightmares. Trust me, I won't fall asleep again for a while," Jade said. She glanced over at her phone, wondering if Ian had been one of the people trying to contact her earlier.

Ariana hugged her and Jade could feel her exhaustion. She guided Ariana back into bed with Kiara.

"Put that big beautiful brain of yours to rest. We've got work to do tomorrow," Jade said quietly.

"Love you," Ariana murmured, already half asleep.

Jade went back to the guest bedroom, unable to stop herself from checking her phone. There were texts from Haiden checking in, Daire had asked in a group message where they'd gone, and Lyric had texted her for advice on a girl she'd met at the party. Although she wouldn't have answered it, her stomach still dropped when she saw there was nothing from Ian.

And then, as if on cue, her phone vibrated.

2:53 a.m. Ian: I can't believe I lost you.

CHAPTER 17
Kiara

Kiara blinked her eyes open, feeling as though she'd been asleep for a very long time. The sun filtered in through the blinds, casting thick rays of light over her room. She turned her head to find Ariana perched on the edge of the bed with her golden hair spun into a bun, typing furiously on her laptop.

Kiara almost made a move to sit up, but was immediately hit by a truckload of sobering memories from the previous night. *Oh no*, she thought, terrified–*they* know *now*. She must have been drunk when she told them last night; she never would've confessed to that sober. Panic flooded her system as she thought about the repercussions of sharing her secret. She wouldn't be able to throw up anymore. She would gain back all the weight she'd worked so hard to lose. All the calorie restriction, all the workouts–they would all be for nothing. But how could she continue? It had gotten so out of control already, and it had only been a few months. And Teague... were they done? Were they really over? She let out an involuntary sob, causing Ariana's head to snap up in alarm.

"Kiara," Ariana said, her voice breaking.

Kiara let out another loud sob as Ariana moved to hold her.

Jade rolled over and blinked her slightly swollen eyes open. "Hey," she said with a raspy voice. "It's okay Kiara, we'll help you."

"Maybe that's *why* I'm scared. The craziest part..." Kiara said, trying her best to explain the irrational fear. "The craziest part is that I know how bad it is for me and how trapped and miserable I feel, but I'm still so terrified of stopping because I don't want the weight to come back." Kiara hung her head, letting the tears stream down her cheeks while Jade and Ariana tried to console her.

Despite the alcohol, why did *I give in and tell them last night?* she wondered. *Because I knew how out of control I was getting*, a voice in her head answered. She had to stop what she was doing to herself and she didn't think–no, actually she *knew*–that if someone else didn't know about it, then nothing could stop her, especially not sheer willpower. There had to be another way to lose weight. A healthy way. Surely people didn't really live like this? Throwing up after every meal? Constantly counting calories and restricting so much that it hurt? Kiara looked back over the last few weeks of her life. It was as though an alien had taken over her brain. Had she really put her relationship to the side to keep these secrets and remain thin? Teague meant the world to her. She wanted to change; she wanted to stop this and get her life back.

"So what's the plan?" Kiara asked in between little gasps. She'd gotten her crying under control for the moment, but only just barely.

"We–well, you... need to tell your parents," Ariana said.

Kiara sucked in a breath, her eyes filling with tears again. If she told them, they would know to look for the signs. What if she needed to throw up again in the future?

"Kiara, this is serious. It concerns your health. You should probably see a professional to make sure you get the proper information and help you need. So your parents will have to know," Ariana said.

Kiara raised her eyebrows. "A professional?"

"Yes. They'll help to get you freed from this."

"Really, Ari?" Kiara knew how adverse Ariana normally was to "professional help". Psychologists had almost always jumped to putting Ariana on pills right away, numbing her to life instead of trying to work through the underlying issues. *She must think my situation is really fucked then*, Kiara thought.

"Yeah, I know. But just because I've had some bad experiences doesn't mean there aren't good therapists out there. Plus, we've learned from what I went through. When they immediately try to put you on antidepressants or downers and tell you pills will fix you... you run."

"Unless you have a medical condition that requires meds," Jade interrupted.

"Right, of course. But in cases like prescribing high doses of Xanax to a girl that's barely a teenager, you run," Ariana corrected herself.

Kiara sat back and thought about this. Could another human actually help her out of this misery? If there was even the slightest possibility that someone could, she had to take it.

After a few moments of silence, Jade's stomach growled, reminding Kiara of her own hunger.

"I'm hungry..." Kiara whispered. The terror of gaining the weight back slammed into her mind. "I don't think I know how to have a meal without counting calories anymore. And if I can't count my calories, I'll want to throw it up."

Kiara looked up and saw a look of shock cross Ariana's face that she felt sure she wasn't meant to see. Regret and anger ran through her, pulsing stronger as she saw the shock transform into pity behind her friend's eyes. Ariana had *forced* her to reveal her secret when she hadn't been ready yet. She didn't *want* to stop counting. She didn't want to lose that control.

"*What* Ariana? Don't look at me like that! I shouldn't have fucking told you anything," Kiara spat.

"Kiara please, I... We only want to help you," Ariana stuttered, looking like she was about to cry.

"Really!? How could either of you help? Ari, you've always

been comfortable in your own skin. Jade doesn't ever have to worry about what she eats and she's always thin. You don't have to diet; you don't have to restrict yourselves. It's just SO easy for you both. You wouldn't understand and you *couldn't* understand, so how could *you* possibly help me? And don't you *dare* cry, Ariana."

Kiara heard her mother's voice calling from downstairs but ignored it. She wanted Ariana to feel how painful it was to have thoughts constantly choking her; every thought a comparison to others and how much better they looked than her, every plan revolving around how many calories it would cost her, everywhere she went knowing exactly where the bathroom was located and whether the stalls were public or private.

"Kiara..." Ariana said softly. "Of course I think about my weight and sometimes wish I could be skinnier like you guys. With all of the bullshit we consume from social media showing us girls that are ten times as beautiful, ten times as skinny, cool, and rich, and so on than we are, how could I not? I just choose to love myself and how I look. I could just as easily say the same to you. I'm three times your size. And I do know something about hiding a problem from the world. I do know what it's like to have scary thoughts that people don't understand. That you yourself can't even understand. I know how painful that is and I don't want you to have to go through that alone anymore."

Jade squeezed her leg and Kiara felt like she was being pulled back to reality. She blinked and let her face fall slack, the anger rolling off her features.

"I know it doesn't feel like it now, but it *can* get better," Ariana said.

"But how do you know?" Kiara asked.

"Because I have faith in you, and I've seen it done before," Ariana said adamantly.

"And we'll be here for you," Jade piped in, breaking the tension. "Even if you need to yell at us some more."

Kiara let out a short, embarrassed laugh.

"I know this is an emotional rollercoaster for you right now," Ariana said. "But nothing worthwhile is ever easy."

"Come on," Jade said, sitting up. "Let's go have a good, healthy breakfast. We'll stay with you and make sure you're okay. Then you can decide when and how to tell your parents. Although from my experience, it's best just to dive right in with the harder shit."

Kiara nodded, her determination back again. The mood swings would be one thing she wouldn't miss. *I can do this*, she thought resolutely again and again: *I can do this*.

After breakfast, Jade and Ariana made their way upstairs under the pretense that they were packing their things to go home. Kiara hung back, fiddling with the napkin next to her plate, steeling herself for what was about to come next.

"Mom? Dad?" Kiara said quietly. "Could you come back to the table for a second? I wanted to talk to you about something."

Karen and Jon sat down, looking expectant and slightly concerned. Jon was tall and broad-shouldered, which made Karen Lancor look smaller than usual when they sat side by side. Jon put his book aside, a slight wrinkle resting on his forehead. Kiara had never asked her parents to sit and talk so formally before.

"What's that, Kiara?" her dad asked.

Kiara opened her mouth, then closed it again. How did she even begin? How could she tell them that she couldn't stop throwing up her food and make them understand the thoughts? She wanted to bolt upstairs to the safety of her room, dive under her covers and hide from the entire world. But Jade and Ariana were upstairs. She'd insisted that they stay for this part since she wasn't sure she would tell her parents unless they held her accountable.

She picked at her napkin again, calculating how many calories her breakfast contained. She had consumed eggs, half a gluten-free English muffin, two pieces of vegetarian bacon, and coconut yogurt. Normally, she wouldn't have eaten so much, but Ariana reminded her she had passed out last night, so she figured she could cut herself some slack. Now all Kiara could think about was that the food had been way over what she would normally consume for one meal, and at the beginning of the day, too. The more she thought about it, the more the fainting didn't seem like that big of a deal. It was probably just dehydration, anyway.

"Um, I just need to tell Ariana something real quick," Kiara said as she slid her chair back abruptly. A harsh screech came from the legs sliding across the wooden floor and made them all flinch.

Kiara raced upstairs and rushed through her room, knowing that Jade and Ariana would know what was happening but not caring.

"Kiara?" Jade called out in alarm from her spot on the bed.

Ariana began to shout in the background, but Kiara couldn't make out what she was saying. Everything was blurring, and the only thing that mattered was making it to the toilet before her stomach absorbed too much food. Through Ariana's protests, Kiara dashed for the bathroom, imagining the sweet relief that would overwhelm her once she got the breakfast out of her system. She yanked open the door, adrenaline flowing through her body. She ran inside and started to spin around to slam the door shut when arms clasped around her waist, stopping her dead in her tracks. She let out a small yelp of surprise as she heard Jade's steady voice by her ear. "I'm not letting you do this to yourself."

"Let me go, Jade. This will be the last time. I promise," Kiara swore, not knowing if it were true.

"You never let anyone make you do anything you don't want to–that's something that I've always admired about you. What makes this any different? Don't let the crazed part of your brain take over. *You* are still in control here," Jade said.

"And you won't gain back pounds from one breakfast. Weight loss and gain don't work like that. Whatever thoughts are going on inside your head–they're not true. They're not *real*," Ariana said from behind them.

Kiara squeezed her eyes closed as tight as she could and put her fist into her mouth, biting down. She wanted someone to dissect her brain and take out the thoughts. She wanted to go to sleep for a very long time and wake up as someone else. Someone without *this*. She turned around and let out a muffled cry into Jade's shoulder, her body shaking.

"The thoughts aren't true," Jade repeated, her voice heavy with emotion. "Just breathe."

Kiara took in a huge breath, held it, and then let it go. Her body relaxed a little in Jade's arms. Jade pulled her over to the bed and Kiara sat while taking deep, even breaths.

"Try four counts each for your inhale, holding at the top for six or seven counts, and then seven for the exhale," Ariana murmured. "Do longer if you can."

Kiara kept breathing deeply. She stared at a glow-in-the-dark star that had been stuck to her ceiling since she was a kid and tried her best to think of nothing else for the next few minutes. How many times had she looked at the star before, at different time periods of her life? How many moments of love, laughter, anger, joy, and sadness had that star seen? Whether wonderful or painful, all of those moments were fleeting. With that thought, Kiara realized this pain would eventually end too.

She came back to her current situation and watched the movie that was playing in her head about the weight coming back. If this feeling would eventually end, why not help it along? She made the movie smaller, shrinking it until it looked like it was floating far away from her. It was strange–she could still feel the war inside her mind raging on, but it was further away now, and it wasn't as loud or as bright. When she stopped and took a step back, it was easier to listen to the logical side.

I don't have to throw up my breakfast and I'll still be okay, she thought, trying it out in her head. To Kiara's surprise, she didn't feel the urge to go to the toilet. *Was it working?*

"Thank you for stopping me," Kiara said. "I think I'm okay for now. I'm going to get under the covers."

Jade gave her arm a little squeeze and scooted beside her on the bed. Kiara pulled the silky sheet over her body, feeling exhausted all of the sudden, but knowing she wasn't quite done with what she needed to do.

"Can one of you grab my mom?" Kiara asked. "I'm ready to tell her now."

"This is really brave of you," Ariana said, her hazel eyes shining.

"It's not brave, I'm scared as shit," Kiara said, letting out a sad sigh.

"Being brave doesn't mean you're not scared. Being brave means doing the hard thing, or the right thing, even when you're scared," Ariana said. "*Especially* when you're scared."

Kiara nodded, her throat tight.

"Do you want us to be here when you tell her?" Jade asked.

"Yes," Kiara answered without hesitation.

Jade nodded and climbed under the sheets with her, grabbing her hand and holding it while Ariana stepped out of the room. Jade stroked her thumb over Kiara's knuckles as they sat in silence, waiting for Ariana to return with Karen. A couple of minutes later, they heard footsteps approaching from the stairs, and Kiara squeezed Jade's hand so tightly it almost hurt.

I'm brave enough, Kiara thought. She nodded to herself and took another deep breath, readying herself as the door opened.

CHAPTER 18

A, J, K

Ariana sat in 5th period History class on Monday, jiggling her foot to a song that was stuck in her head, feeling surprisingly free and upbeat. She figured she would feel more depressed since she still hadn't spoken to Lukas since Daire's party, but the fact that he hadn't even *attempted* to contact her had turned her sadness into a humorous indignation. She would hold onto that for now, or for as long as she could to keep her strong, because anything was better than succumbing to the sorrow.

At the thought of Lukas, Ariana automatically looked to the classroom window, sighing at the sight of the empty hallway. She would be lying to herself if she didn't admit that she looked for him outside of her classrooms throughout the day, wondering if he would show up like he used to and apologize, taking her into his arms and kissing her until everything was right in the world again. But this wasn't like a movie, where the boy suddenly realizes how wrong he is and rushes back to declare his everlasting love. This was high school, and more often than not it was a jarring reality check, like a swift punch to the gut.

Ariana felt a light tapping on her shoulder but didn't make a move to turn around. Melodie sat behind her in this class, and

Ariana wasn't exactly jumping to see what she had to say. Melodie had kept her distance since the incident in the locker room, but Ariana could tell she hoped they would talk again soon. Every time Ariana turned her head or opened her mouth to speak in class, Melodie would perk up, nodding profusely in agreement with whatever Ariana had to say.

Melodie gave a small pointed sigh, and Ariana reluctantly swiveled around in her seat.

"Hey," Melodie whispered, tucking her blonde hair behind her ears. "You look cute today."

This morning Ariana had chosen to show off her figure and dressed in a maroon V-neck bodysuit with dark denim jeans and sneakers. Her hair was loosely pulled half back with a few tendrils framing her face. She wanted to be as comfortable as possible today while still looking good. *Ugh*, she thought. *Comfortable and beautiful* was the way Lukas described her style. Ariana hated being reminded of him in unexpected moments.

Ariana gave her a small smile of thanks–she was still weary of how much Melodie knew about Kiara's situation. She was hoping Melodie hadn't heard about Kiara's fainting episode, but then again, she'd been pleasantly surprised to find that almost no one knew about it except for those who were involved.

Taking care of Kiara had helped to keep Ariana's mind off of Lukas this weekend; Kiara's situation made her own boy troubles seem minuscule in comparison. Melodie opened her mouth to say something more, but Ariana wordlessly turned her attention back to the front of the classroom.

Ariana immediately felt another tap on her shoulder. "What's up, Mel?" she whispered, a note of exasperation chiming in her tone.

"Did you think of what you're going to say today?" Melodie whispered.

"About what?" Ariana's annoyance level was rising by the second.

"For cheer captain. Did you think of your speech? I must have practiced mine like twenty times last night."

Oh shit, Ariana thought, momentarily blind-sighted. The speech for cheer captain.

"No, I figured I'd just wing it," Ariana recovered, lying through her teeth. If Melodie hadn't heard anything about the tumultuous events that had taken place over the weekend, Ariana surely didn't want to be the one to say anything, even if it had been the reason she totally forgot about the speech she had to give to the entire squad in... oh, about an hour. How was it possible that her life had been such a whirlwind lately that she had forgotten about something she'd wanted for over a year?

"Well, that's brave."

Ariana nodded, a knot forming in her stomach. "Sure," she replied to the ever-so-slightly passive-aggressive remark.

"By the way, where's Kiara today?"

Ariana tensed up for a second, but saw that Melodie seemed to be asking innocently enough. "She caught a bug over the weekend–she may be out tomorrow too."

Ariana turned to face the front again and her stomach dropped to the floor, along with her heart. Lukas was outside the classroom in direct view of the window, standing in the far corner of the hallway. Ariana thought her mind was playing tricks on her, but then they locked eyes. Her breath left her body as Lukas gestured for her to come outside and then disappeared.

Ariana had thought she was fine with not seeing Lukas anymore, but her feelings betrayed her now. At the mere sight of his face, the yearning came back tenfold. Her arm shot up in the air and she excused herself to the bathroom. She found Lukas out in the hallway, standing near the double doors that led to the football fields. Her breath caught in her throat as he opened one, stepped outside, and waited for her.

Like a moth to the flame, Ariana had no choice but to follow. Lukas turned to face her and the moment their eyes made contact all of her resolve melted away. If he said he wanted her back she wouldn't resist. Her heart raced with how badly she wanted to kiss him. His face and arms were deeply tan like he'd been outside all weekend, and a brief pang of jealousy ran through her gut toward whoever had been with him. She wondered what he'd been doing. Above all, she just missed being near him.

Stay strong, Ariana thought, attempting to recall her anger. She crossed her arms and looked him square in the eye.

"Look, I..." Lukas began, but then let out a frustrated sigh and stopped.

She raised an eyebrow and waited for the apology. She watched his face as he thought through his words and ignored a yearning to touch him.

Lukas reached out, seeming to read her mind. He grazed his fingers along her cheek and tucked a lock of golden hair behind her ear, his touch like cool water after wandering dehydrated in the desert for days. Her face relaxed but she didn't dare move a muscle; she knew she would betray her resolve if she did.

Lukas' hand dropped. "I had to see you," he said, causing Ariana's heart to flutter. "I'm sorry I didn't say anything after Friday night. Something happened."

"What was that? And that was completely unfair to me, what you said."

"I know. But it's true. I get jealous when I see you with other guys."

Ariana almost smiled. She liked that she could make him jealous. "Wait, but *what* is true?" Was he talking about the part where he said he didn't think he could handle her, or that what he had said was unfair?

"Look, I don't think we should continue..." Lukas said, gesturing back and forth with his hand between them. "...This."

Ariana's chest went cold and hollow.

Lukas ran a hand through his hair and sighed. "It's not working."

"What?" Ariana lost her breath momentarily as shock flooded her system. She thought he was coming to apologize–no, to *beg* for her forgiveness, and he was breaking it off? She didn't... she *couldn't* understand what caused such a turn in their relationship. How could he do this? *He must not* really *love me*, Ariana thought sadly. He was just stringing her along. But, for what reason? No one knew about their relationship, so it wasn't like he was doing it to brag to anyone, and he'd stopped before he had even gotten her to give it up. Hell, they hadn't done anything except kiss!

"I can't do this anymore. I'm sorry," he said. He looked concerned for her, which just pissed her off. After all, he was the one causing her pain. She could scream at him. She wanted to push him or shake him, anything to try and bring back the Lukas who looked at her like she was the only girl in the world. The one who had so truthfully told her he was falling for her.

Instead, she decided not to say anything at all. She didn't want to give him the satisfaction of her words or a reaction. He didn't deserve that kind of attention from her. She shook her head in disdain and turned on her heel, walking back to the classroom and half expecting him to follow, but not surprised in the least when he didn't.

* * *

On Monday afternoon Jade stopped by the common area where her friends hung out before they went on to their various clubs, sports, and after-school activities. She stood a short distance away from the group, not having the energy to fully engage with anyone, but wanting to be near them nonetheless. Haiden dipped out of the circle and came to her side, his kind face wrinkled in concern.

"Is K okay?" he asked in a whisper.

Jade felt a rush of love for Haiden–he was protecting Kiara by keeping the fainting a secret.

"She will be," Jade said, putting a hand on Haiden's shoulder and squeezing it. "Thanks for being there for her. For us."

"I'd do anything for Kiara," Haiden said, pushing his hair out of his face. Jade thought she saw a flash of emotion cross Haiden's expression, but he was probably just worried. "And yeah, dude. Of course."

Haiden took back his place in their circle of friends, bumping fists with Aubrey. A chill ran down Jade's neck, and she looked toward the back of the room instinctively. Piercing blue eyes met hers. She sucked in her breath, her body instantly reacting to Ian's eye contact. His eyebrows knitted and sadness dotted his face. He took a few steps in her direction and Jade turned around so quickly she almost knocked over a freshman.

"Sorry!" she shouted to the freshman as she took off for the locker rooms, not daring to look back but feeling his eyes on her all the way down the hall. She couldn't talk to him now. She didn't know how she'd react if he was within arm's reach, and it was hard enough to ignore him as it was.

After changing at lightning speed, Jade walked into the gym and took a seat toward the back, away from the pre-cheer-captain-speech excitement. She already missed Kiara, who had skipped school today to go to the doctor with her mom and get a full checkup–they wanted to make sure she hadn't done any damage in the past month from the anorexia and bulimia. They were also taking Kiara to a nutritionist she found through a podcast to go over some different and *healthy* weight loss and maintenance methods.

Jade was beyond relieved she was getting help, but she still wished Kiara were there with her, especially on a day like this. Ariana took this stuff more seriously than the both of them, so for such occasions they usually sat in the back together, giggling over how wound up everyone got over matters like cheer captain. Jade had faith Ariana would get it, but she still felt a slight uneasiness about Melodie going for the position too. If Jade had to take orders from Melodie... well, she would probably lose her damn mind.

Jade's phone vibrated in her pocket. She pulled it out, her

heart speeding up and sinking simultaneously as she saw Ian's name on the screen. She opened the text and read.

3:10 p.m. Ian: Can we please talk?

With incredible determination, Jade deleted the text. She had to believe the pain would get easier with time.

Ariana plopped down next to her with a groan and dropped her head onto Jade's shoulder. Jade laughed and wiggled her arm, jostling Ariana's head up.

"Aren't you going to sit up there with Melodie?" Jade asked, inclining her head.

"Nah, I didn't even write a speech or practice anything because of this weekend. Oh, and Lukas just broke everything off with me. So I don't really care right now. About any of it."

Jade's mouth dropped into an O. Fucking Lukas. "What the fuck? Why?"

Ariana shrugged. "Not sure."

Oh man, Jade thought, *this is not good*. Ariana was acting like it was no big deal when it clearly was. Jade was about to open her mouth to speak again when Krall waddled up to the podium they had wheeled into the gym for the occasion.

"As you all know, today we'll hear from our junior varsity captain candidates," Krall began in an unnaturally high voice. "After the speeches, we'll have an anonymous vote and I'll announce your new captain on Friday. I wish you all good luck, and with that being said, do we have a candidate who'd like to go first?"

Without a moment's hesitation, Melodie's hand shot up in the air. Jade and Ariana groaned simultaneously, causing Ariana to giggle. Jade studied her for a moment, puzzled. Ariana had to have been devastated when Lukas told her it was over, but she wasn't showing it.

"...and I have a great new cheer in mind! I think it will be a great rendition of our old one. In conclusion, I think I would make a great captain for our junior varsity team!" Melodie finished. Both squads clapped politely; a few of the varsity cheerleaders were nodding to one another. Jade's hopes fell a bit.

"Do you think it'll be great, or is it going to be great?" she joked to Ariana. Krall stepped back to the podium to ask for Ariana's speech.

Jade did a silent prayer as Ariana strode to the front of the room, her high ponytail bobbing.

Ariana put her hands flat on the podium and took a deep breath. "Basically, I've been doing this shit my whole life," she began. The crowd let out a collective, hushed gasp, but Ariana didn't seem to notice.

"Oh *fuck,*" Jade murmured.

"I was a gymnast for ten years, then a cheerleader for the past two, and I've learned a lot. I've listened, and I know many of you want to focus more on your tumbling, so I'm going to help with that. My goal is for you all to have AT LEAST a roundoff back handspring layout by the end of this year. We'll accomplish this by solely focusing on tumbling Tuesdays and Thursdays. I believe this is doable if we work hard and push one another, and I can promise you I'll be there every step of the way to support every one of you. Which brings me to my next point–I want to make sure I'm always here for my team. Whether it's a problem concerning cheer, school, or your personal life, my figurative door is always open, and I promise to keep whatever you have to say confidential. Let's kick some ass this year!" Ariana concluded with a huge grin.

The cheerleaders were stunned into silence for a few moments, and then the applause erupted. Jade burst into laughter as she saw Krall's jaw hanging open in shock. Nali was nearly rolling on the ground in tears of laughter with most of the varsity squad, and the freshman looked as though they had just witnessed a legend in the making. Ariana skipped away from the podium and blew everyone a kiss.

She nearly ran to Jade, her grin spreading so wide that it

covered her entire face. Jade pulled her down into a hug as soon as she was close enough, causing Ariana to lose her balance and sprawl on top of her. They burst into laughter and rolled around on the floor, tears streaming from Ariana's eyes. Who gave a shit if they were making a scene? Jade was so proud of Ariana. Not only had she delivered a charismatic as hell speech, but she'd done so right after Lukas had broken her heart. They didn't need the boys. They had each other.

"What the hell was that, you badass?" Jade asked when they finally got their laughter under control.

"I guess I was inspired," Ariana said, her hazel eyes shining with excitement. "Also, it makes life a little easier when you stop worrying about every little thing."

"Well, it was amazing. Even with the cursing, I'll be damned if you don't get it. Seriously, where did that part about the tumbling goals come from?"

"Oh. I really have been thinking about this, because I actually do listen to everyone. And I do truly want to help if I can by being another ear and support if anyone needs it. I think that could help, especially with the freshman and everything they're going to go through in their first year of high school."

"Of course it would. People would be stupid not to vote for you."

"Thanks, J," Ariana said with a smile.

"Poor things, though. No one is ever going to be able to top that," Jade mused, smiling back.

* * *

Kiara ran her hand along the smooth bookshelf of the self-development aisle in the quaint bookstore. She read title after title, each one adding to the cloud of overwhelm hanging over her head. She didn't know anything about this stuff. How was she ever supposed to know which one would help her?

"Oh, that's a good one," Karen Lancor said from behind her.

She reached around Kiara and pulled a thick book off the shelf. "I never told you this before, but when I was around your age I had a period where I worked out all the time and got pretty restrictive with my dieting."

"What?" Kiara said, her mouth falling open. Her mom loved cooking and food and never seemed to be uncomfortable around it. Could that mean it was possible Kiara really could get out of this? "You did?"

"I did. A lot of people go through it, unfortunately. So don't ever feel like you're alone. Or that you'll never be rid of the headspace you're in now."

"But how'd you get out of it?"

Karen ran a hand through her short blonde hair. "I stopped going to the gym where I developed obsessive workout patterns. I made some new friends that weren't worrying about their weight all the time. I realized that I could change my thoughts, and therefore my life. That was the biggest step. Just realizing that I could change my own mind was revolutionary. Most people never even take the time to notice what they're telling themselves."

Kiara shook her head in disbelief. She didn't know if she could change or fight with the thoughts in her head. She usually lost.

"We're all telling ourselves stories, Kiara. You just have to figure out what yours are and then change them to something empowering. This is your life. You're the creator. You can make it miserable for yourself or you can help yourself. It's time to choose."

Kiara stared at the book in her hands. It's not like trying this stuff could make things any worse. "I'll try, Mom. I might as well, 'cause I can't keep living like this."

"And remember that everyone is different when it comes to what works best for them. I was able to help myself by doing those things but it'll vary from person to person. The most important thing is to keep trying things until you find what works for you.

I've found that massive action makes for the biggest results–like when I changed my gym or the people I hung out with."

Kiara nodded, lost in thought. A question circled around in her head: what were some changes she could make immediately to help herself?

When they had made it back to the car, Kiara whipped out her phone and unfollowed close to twenty fitness model and influencer accounts. She unfollowed anyone she saw who gave her even a tinge of an anxious feeling. She was ruthless.

Then she typed out a message to Reigh.

4:04 p.m. Kiara: Hey! I decided I'm done with the dieting stuff. I'm happy where I am w my weight so no need to check in on me anymore. I'll keep everything you showed me a secret tho, don't worry.
4:05 p.m. Reigh: Ok... Everything ok?
4:05 p.m. Kiara: Yep! All good.

It might have been a lie, but Kiara felt like that was the right way to go for now. She didn't have to explain anything to Reigh. Kiara began to check her texts from earlier–Ariana and Jade had blown up her phone, detailing the spectacle that had just taken place during the cheer captain speeches. Kiara had completely forgotten they were today and had a momentary flash of regret that she hadn't been there for Ariana. *But*, Kiara thought, remembering something she had just gleaned from one of the books–*I need to take care of myself first so I can fully be there for my friends.*

3:54 p.m. Jade: The only thing missing was Ari dropping the mic after she finished! Lol
3:54 p.m. Ariana: The mic was connected to the podium haha
3:55 p.m. Jade: Seriously, you would have been so proud of her K. It was epic
4:07 p.m. Kiara: I am SO proud!!

Ariana texted one more time, saying she had more news but that it could wait. Kiara sat there for a moment, turning the phone over in her hand. She had just lied again. She didn't feel proud, she didn't feel excited, she didn't feel anything at all right now. She stashed the phone in her tan messenger bag alongside her untouched schoolbooks. Concentrating on any schoolwork had proved impossible today. She tried to remember the last time she was able to concentrate on anything that she used to find important and came up blank.

"Hey, Mom," Kiara said, her voice barely a whisper.

"Hey, sweetie. How're you doing?" She glanced over at Kiara and smiled, the worry only slightly shining through her blue-green eyes.

Kiara couldn't speak; she was overcome by equal parts sorrow, disbelief, and pain. She looked into her mom's eyes, not knowing how to describe the feeling that had engulfed her.

Karen reached over and grabbed her hand. "Kiara, I know it may be hard to believe now, but you're going to overcome this. You're so strong."

"Mom," Kiara said, her voice breaking. "I may not be strong enough for this." She bent her head as the tears started. Kiara honestly didn't know. Everyone kept saying how strong she was and that she would get through it, but she didn't feel strong. She felt like she wanted to run to the restroom and throw up the lunch that they'd enjoyed a half hour ago. Her mood kept swinging from feelings of premature triumph–of somehow knowing that she could overcome this–to absolute despair and wondering how she would ever fully defeat the thoughts.

"Oh, honey," Karen squeezed her hand. "We never know how truly strong we are until we *have* to be strong."

Kiara nodded her head. They pulled into the driveway and Kiara's phone vibrated. She expected to see more messages from Jade and Ariana, but instead saw Teague's name. Her heart pounded wildly–they hadn't spoken since Friday night. Teague had made it clear that he only wanted to talk to her if she was going to be honest with him, and she just didn't know if she could be.

4:03 p.m. Teague: Saw u weren't at school today. Just wanted to make sure ur ok

Even though it wasn't much, Kiara rejoiced in the fact that Teague had sent anything at all. She realized Teague must have gone out of his way to check her classes and know she hadn't been at school. Kiara had been so worried that she'd pushed him away to the point that he didn't give a fuck anymore, but maybe that wasn't the case. What would she tell him though? *I have to be strong and done with lying if I want to keep Teague in my life,* Kiara thought to herself with determination. She had already told Jade, Ariana, and her parents... What was one more person?

4:05 p.m. Kiara: Hey, it's good to hear from you. I'm not okay yet, but I think I will be.

Although her answer was cryptic, she hoped that Teague could appreciate that she was trying to be honest. Could she tell him now? Did she have that courage already? Teague had never given her a reason not to trust him, but this wasn't so much about trust. She loved Teague, looked up to him even, and she didn't know if she could stand him knowing how out of control she'd gotten with this. Or that she'd been throwing up when he'd been in the very next room on several occasions. Or that she'd been so ashamed of her body that she would put herself through this hell to change it.

4:06 p.m. Teague: Alright. Good to hear. See u around

Kiara stared at the text. She couldn't bear not knowing when she would talk to him again, and that thought made up her mind.

She hopped out of the car and walked to her mother, wrapping her arms around her.

"I'm going for a walk," Kiara said into her mom's shoulder. "And I'm going to tell Teague."

"Proud of you," her mom said.

This was one of those moments when she would have to be stronger than she thought she was. She took a deep breath and opened up Teague's contact info. Her finger hovered over the call button for a second, but then she pressed it before she could change her mind. He picked up on the first ring.

"Hi," she said.

"Hi," he said back, guarded.

"I want to tell you what's been going on with me, if you still want to hear it."

"Oh, Kiara," Teague said, relief clear in his tone. "Of course I want to hear it. Now?"

"Yes. Now."

CHAPTER 19
Ariana

After the natural high from her outrageous cheer captain speech on Monday wore off and Ariana had come home, away from all the background noise from cheerleading and school and her friends, the realization had finally sunk in that she and Lukas were over. Anguish slammed into her and Ariana crawled into bed to cry for hours, unable to eat dinner and barely able to sleep. The next couple of days had been more of the same: her waking moments filled with agony at the loss she felt and even her dreams haunted by images of him. She hadn't seen him around at school, almost as if he were avoiding her, which almost hurt more than him calling it off.

Almost.

Ariana couldn't understand how Lukas could so abruptly turn off his feelings for her when she found traces of him in everything she did and everywhere she went. She spent half of the time wishing she'd never met him–that she'd never experienced what it was like to live with love like this illuminating her world. The other half of the time she knew that she would rather have fallen in love with him and gotten to feel it–to fully feel the ecstasy of it–than to feel nothing at all. And as sad as it was, whether or not he loved her back, she still loved him.

. . .

On Thursday, she woke in the middle of the night with a start. Tears streamed down her cheeks as the absence of Lukas overwhelmed her. She dreamt he had come back to tell her he loved her. Even in the dream, her stomach twisted in a delicious way when she saw him. The dream Lukas said he was sorry for making such a stupid mistake; that he would never hurt her again. It felt so real that waking up to her harsh reality was jarring: she was alone, crying in her bed, and there was no reason to think Lukas would ever come back.

Ariana grabbed for her phone with every intention of calling him–she couldn't take not talking to him for another *second*. But then she forcefully stopped herself, thinking better of it. If Lukas had changed his mind or felt any remorse at *all* he would've tried to contact her.

She blinked the tears out of her eyes and checked the time on her phone. It was 3:24 a.m.. Her mind flashed back to the nights she and Lukas had talked until four or five in the morning, staying on the line just to sit in comfortable silence. Ariana let out a small cry. She couldn't imagine ever feeling this way about anyone else. She buried her head in the pillow and clenched her jaw, bracing herself to make it through the oncoming feelings of loss and emptiness.

Just then, her phone began to vibrate in her hand. Ariana thought it was a text at first, then realized someone was calling her... But who would call at this hour?

Ariana turned over her phone, and upon seeing Lukas' name on the screen her heart nearly gave out. She continued to stare blankly at the screen until the ringing stopped, thinking it must be a mistake. She stayed still, unblinking. Moments later, he called again. Ariana hastily picked up the phone and held her breath. She didn't know what to say. She was furiously angry, yet so relieved he'd called that she didn't want to accidentally blurt out how much she missed him. ...Or that she still loved him.

"Ariana?" Lukas' quiet voice echoed on the line.

Ariana came alive again at the sound of his voice. The relief that flooded through her body just by hearing him say her name was pleasantly and frightfully overwhelming.

"Why are you calling me?" she demanded, her voice breaking.

"Are you... were you crying?" Lukas asked, sounding pained.

Ariana didn't answer. She didn't want to give him the satisfaction of knowing how deeply affected she'd been by the absence of him.

"Hey," he said quietly. "I've missed you. I've missed you so much."

Ariana's head was spinning, she was drunk from his words. She didn't know what was going on or where this had come from. Hadn't he been the one to call their relationship off? She was confused by the exhilaration she felt, knowing in the back of her mind that none of this made any sense.

"What?" she asked incredulously. "I can't keep up with you." Ariana clamped her mouth shut before she said anything more. She was at war with herself–one half wanted to tell him to come over now, that she *had* to see him, *had* to kiss him again. The thought that he'd been completely done had pained her so much that she was awash with longing now–maybe they still had a chance. The other half of her knew this was dangerous. How could he change his mind so quickly? What could make him be *this* fickle, especially when claiming it was love?

"I'm sorry. I never meant to hurt you. I feel like I've made a huge mistake because I can't stop thinking about you. Ever since last week, I feel like a part of me has been missing."

Ariana's heart soared. That was it–he said he'd made a mistake like she'd hoped and prayed he would; he'd realized he couldn't be without her.

"But why did you cut it off in the first place?"

Lukas stayed silent for a few moments and Ariana realized she was holding her breath again, waiting for him to speak.

"I got jealous of you and D," Lukas said finally.

The simplicity of his statement was like a slap in the face. "So you just *dropped* me? That's fucked up."

"Ariana," Lukas pleaded. "Take it as a compliment. I didn't think I could stand getting any closer to you if I knew you had feelings for someone else."

"I don't have feelings for him!"

"Look, I don't want to argue with you," Lukas said, his voice hushed again. "I just had to talk to you tonight. No matter what happens, I wanted you to know that when you came into my life, you caught me off guard. I didn't realize someone could mesmerize me like you do. I think I'll always love you."

With those words, all of Ariana's self-preservation evaporated into thin air. The misery of their break up faded into the dark distance. Lukas loved her; he would always love her. Ariana heard a soft knock on her door and cursed. Her mother must have heard her and come to check what was going on.

"I have to go..." Ariana couldn't stand not saying it back. "I love you, too."

"Ariana," Lukas said, urgency in his voice.

"Yes?"

"Don't forget what I said tonight. It's the truth."

"I won't," she replied, a grin spreading so far across her face that it hurt.

"I love you, Ariana Knight. Sleep well."

Ariana floated through the empty, cream-colored hallways toward the cheer gym on Friday afternoon, free from nerves even though cheer captain would be announced within the hour. She was flying today, her lust for life revived from Lukas' declaration of love the night before.

"What're you doing out of class?" a passing Assistant Principal snapped as he attempted to stop her.

Ariana gave him a serene smile, lifting a hall pass signed by Krall in the air as she breezed by. As soon as she was out of sight of the AP she checked her phone. Still nothing from Lukas, but she wasn't bothered. How could she be, after what had transpired? She knew now, beyond a shadow of a doubt, that he loved her. Ariana sent him a quick text asking him to wish her luck and hurried into the gym.

She spotted two heads toward the back wall–one icy blonde and one a dark chocolate brown, and took a spot beside her two best friends. Jade threw her arms around Ariana's neck.

"You'll get it," Kiara said, a twinkle in her blue-green eyes. "I just know."

A hush fell over the crowd as Krall appeared, shuffling her way to the front of the gym. She waited for the group to reposition themselves until they sat facing her, then cleared her throat and began. "I want to start off by saying thank you to all the candidates–your hard work and dedication to the team are sincerely appreciated."

The girls shifted in their seats, waiting for the important part.

"So without further ado, for varsity this year, your cheer captain will be.... Nali Gray!" Krall bellowed.

Ariana whooped loudly–at least if she didn't make junior varsity captain, they would have Nali looking out for them. Krall paused and waited for the cheering to subside, then continued on. "This was a tough decision, as we had great candidates this year for junior varsity. However, we felt that one stood out with her determination to better the team as a whole while also showing strong leadership abilities and empathy."

Ariana looked at the floor, her cheeks burning. Was Krall talking about her?

"For junior varsity, I'm pleased to announce that your new captain will be.... Ariana Knight!"

Jade and Kiara tackled Ariana, both girls squealing in her ears while she laughed out loud at their zeal. A smile stretched across her face–she'd done it! Even with all the chaos in their lives, she'd done it. Jade and Kiara let go of their grip on her and started dancing ridiculously in triumph while the squads watched and laughed. Krall came over to personally congratulate Ariana, followed by the rest of the varsity team.

Nali put an arm around Ariana's shoulder and leaned into her ear. "You deserve this."

And Ariana smiled, believing her.

Ariana, Jade, and Kiara left the gym in a flurry of excitement as the final bell rang. Aubrey and Reigh walked with them while Melodie slunk off after spouting a forced congratulations.

They found their way to their group of friends in the middle of the cafeteria with Kiara running ahead. "GUESS WHO'S THE NEW CHEER CAPTAIN!? ARIANA KNIGHT MOTHA-FUCKAS!!" Kiara shouted to their crowd.

"No shit!" Weston yelled. He grabbed Ariana, spinning her around in a hug.

"Ari! Ari! Ari!" Haiden and Alora started to chant, galvanizing the others to join in.

Ariana took a step back, embarrassed but proud. She couldn't remember ever feeling this happy before. The only thing missing now was Lukas. Ariana snuck a glance at her phone, but nothing new had come in from him.

She knew Lukas and his friends sometimes stood toward the far corner of the cafeteria when they didn't have practice, so she scanned the crowd in that direction, but only saw Daire and a few others. Daire caught her eye almost immediately and smiled. Anxiety spiked in her stomach–she had the sneaking suspicion that Daire must have been watching her, or at least looking her way to have caught her gaze so quickly. She would deal with that later. Ariana turned her attention back to her friends. Alora was now at her side, pulling her into a hug.

"I'm so proud of you," Alora gushed. Ariana closed her eyes, pride swelling in her chest.

When she blinked her eyes open, her heart lurched at the sight of Lukas. Over Alora's shoulder, Ariana had a clear view of him, standing with the junior girls. But no, he wasn't standing with the group, Ariana realized. He was standing *next* to the group *with* Olivia Bellepoint, staring at Olivia in adoration. In what seemed like slow motion, Ariana watched as Olivia reached up to Lukas, her hand sliding behind his neck as she pulled his head down for a kiss, as if it were the most natural thing in the world, as if they had kissed a million times before. If Alora hadn't still been hugging her, Ariana's legs would have given out. She tasted bile as she watched Lukas kiss Olivia back with fervor. Her world closed in around her and a hot pain seared through her body.

Her stomach continued to fall, a wretched, miserable hollow taking its place. Ariana's brain still hadn't fully processed what was happening when Lukas looked up, somehow straight into her eyes. His eyebrows furrowed as a flicker of guilt flashed across his face, but then he turned his attention back to Olivia, and Ariana felt as though someone had slashed her open with a scorching blade. She gasped involuntarily, but she couldn't pull her eyes away. It was like watching a train wreck–a train wreck that would leave only her dead, and everyone else would walk away unscathed. The pain was worse than the first time Lukas had merely cut it off with her–this was final and she knew it. Alora pulled back, her face falling when she met Ariana's eyes. Ariana could only imagine what her expression must have looked like.

"What's wrong?" Alora said.

Ariana couldn't answer. She could only stare at Lukas, who was focused entirely on the one in his arms–on *Olivia*. Ariana's stomach coiled as she thought of what Olivia and Lukas must do alone together if they were this affectionate in public. She let out another pained gasp–she was having trouble breathing, fighting through the sensation of her intestines being ripped open one by one. Alora followed Ariana's gaze to the other side of the cafeteria and drew a sharp intake of breath.

"Oh, no," Alora said. She grabbed Jade's arm, who was busy jumping and dancing around in the middle of their circle of friends–someone was now blasting music from a portable speaker. Jade spun around, still grinning beautifully from the madness, but her smile faded when she saw Ariana's expression. Alora nodded her head toward Lukas, and Ariana watched Jade take in the unfolding catastrophe. Jade's expression hardened. She walked to Ariana and put her arm around her shoulder.

"Come on, let's go," Jade said fiercely in her ear. "Kiara!" she yelled.

Ariana didn't know how much longer she would make it before the onslaught of tears came. She took in a shaky breath and Jade tightened her hold on her body. Kiara turned away from Haiden, leaving his side without saying a word after seeing their faces. Alora nodded her head toward Lukas again. Kiara looked back at Ariana, her blue-green eyes showing concern and a twinge of anger. Kiara began to push through the crowd, making a path for Jade, Ariana, and Alora to follow. Ariana tried her best to judge how long she would have to last before they made it outside–she figured about 20 seconds.

She only had to hold it together for another

19...18...17...

Don't think about how much he lied.

16...15...14...

Don't think about how it felt when he kissed you.

13...12...11...10...

Don't think about him with her alone.

9...8...7...

Kissing her, touching her.

6...5...4...

Whatever you do, don't think about how much you love him.

3... 2...1...

And will never be with him.

Jade shoved the door open and Ariana stumbled outside, falling to her knees on the grass.

And then she lost it.

CHAPTER 20

J, K, A

Jade pushed a lock of hair out of her face while filling up a glass of water from Kiara's kitchen sink. The dim light of the slowly sinking sun filtered in through the window, warming her bare skin. She was wearing a borrowed pair of Kiara's white pajama shorts and a teal tank top, which she had donned this morning following a quick shower. After the Lukas incident at school yesterday, the three girls had made a beeline straight to Kiara's house and hadn't left since. Kiara's parents knew Ariana was going through a break up and had been nice enough to allow an all-weekend slumber party to take place, even though it was a three-day weekend and they'd left town for a friend's wedding.

Jade opened their friends' group text. Tonight was the MDMA night. Ariana had actually been on the fence and was leaning toward not doing it since there were some pretty scary possible side effects, but that was before yesterday happened. Post the Lukas catastrophe, she was all in.

6:31 p.m. Haiden: We'll be at K's soon with the goodies ;)
6:33 p.m. Alora: I can't WAIT. Otw too
6:34 p.m. Aubrey: Me either but I'm kind of scared tho!

6:34 p.m. Weston: Fuck being scared! Gonna be the best night ever
6:36 p.m. Kiara: Come over whenever, front door is open :)

Jade shivered from excitement. It'd been a long time since she'd experienced this feeling–one of equal parts uncertainty, fear, and eagerness, like the first time she'd kissed a boy back in seventh grade. She hadn't even liked him that much, but she'd loved the novelty of kissing.

She knew it wasn't a miracle drug, but she was secretly hoping the MDMA would help her to erase any lingering thoughts of Ian. Jade could only imagine how Ariana must be feeling–shit, she was *in love* with Lukas. Jade had known that Lukas was flaky, but she never would have imagined he had a girlfriend, let alone a girlfriend that they *knew* and went to their school. That took serious balls.

Jade let out a sigh as she thought about how ridiculous this past month had been. She, Ariana, and Kiara had been through the wringer all right. Whoever said that high school was supposed to be the best years of life had clearly never gone to high school.

Jade laughed out loud at her own joke, causing Kiara's dog, Bob, to waddle up and lick her leg. "If you can't laugh at life, Bob, what's the point?"

Bob stared at her expectantly and wagged his whole butt, causing Jade to laugh again.

She took a drink of cool water before hopping up the stairs, her long ponytail swishing against her shoulder blades as she went. She kicked the door open to Kiara's room and found Ariana smoking a cigarette out the window that led to the roof. Full Empty Heart by Lexie Lowell flowed from Kiara's speakers.

"Hey rebel," Jade said, laughing at the notion of Ariana smoking. "How're you holding up?"

Ariana looked at the cigarette burning in her hand and scoffed. "I think I'm still partially in shock. It was right under my nose. Literally, everything he did was a sign that should've pointed to what he was doing."

"I mean, *none of us* guessed what he was doing–we didn't know he was capable of being such a rat. Seriously, no one could've expected him to so blatantly lie about everything–and to everyone! He *had* to be lying to Olivia too. She just doesn't know it."

"I almost wish I never found out either," Ariana said so quietly that Jade could barely hear her. "I can't decide if it hurts more or less that I haven't heard from him since."

"What *I* can't believe is that he would call you, at 4 in the morning, like the little chicken shit that he is," Kiara announced while climbing back inside the window from the roof, "and tell you AGAIN that he loved you! Like what the actual fuck?!"

Jade would have laughed at Kiara's wording if the entire situation weren't so vile. Lukas was a piece of shit all right. He must've known Ariana was going to see him and Olivia together the next day. Why else would he have said, "*No matter what happens...*" before declaring his love to her again?

Jade noticed Ariana looked like she was about to cry and decided it was time to change the subject. "Why don't you just smoke an e-cig like the rest of the idiotic population?"

"This feels more dramatic," Ariana replied, holding the cigarette near her eyes to scrutinize it. "And hopefully it'll kill me faster."

"Ariana, you are not serious," Jade said, laughing at her banal tone.

Ariana shrugged her shoulders and took another long drag from the cigarette. Kiara looked at Jade and they exchanged an "Oh shit, we need to do something about this" look.

"I'll call the crew and see where they are," Kiara said before descending from the windowsill and stepping into the hallway.

"Hey," Jade said softly to Ariana. "What can I do to help?"

"I don't know," Ariana replied miserably. She stamped her

cigarette out on the windowsill and watched as the smoke curled and twisted in the evening air. "I don't know anymore."

Jade frowned. Why couldn't she take away pain from the people she loved? If she could have one superpower, that would be it.

"That was actually really gross. I remember now why I don't smoke," Ariana said, making a face. Jade let out a laugh and the corners of Ariana's mouth turned up ever so slightly.

"It'll get better," Jade said. "In the meantime, we should have some fun. Also, there are a million other guys out there. I should start looking around again too, to be honest."

Jade had a feeling she'd said the wrong thing because Ariana's eyes welled up with tears. Before she could say another word, from somewhere downstairs Kiara shouted, "They're here!"

"Okay, look at me Ari," Jade said, deciding to try again. Ariana looked up at her through misty hazel eyes. Grief radiated from her friend. "You're beautiful, intelligent, kind, and a better friend than I could've ever asked for. You're Ariana Knight, damn it, and you are not going to let some *toolbag* stop you from missing out on one of the best nights of our lives, alright?" Ariana let out a small giggle and Jade grinned. "There's my girl."

There was a flurry of motion in the hallway and Weston came bursting into the room a couple of seconds later, nearly ripping the door off its hinges. "I heard someone is in need of a little pick me up?" he announced. Weston grabbed Ariana and picked her up, spinning her around while she laughed.

"Put me down, West!" Ariana squealed.

"Alright!" Weston said with a grunt, playfully throwing her on the bed. "You're next, J!" Weston growled. Jade screamed involuntarily and tore down the hallway with Weston chasing behind her. Jade laughed as she ran, feeling like a kid again.

"Noo!" Jade shouted as Weston reached her. He grabbed her by the waist and they went tumbling down on the carpeted floor. Jade flipped over to get a better angle to push him off of her, but found herself momentarily flustered by how close their faces were.

It was hard to *not* find Weston attractive. His brown eyes were softer up close, and she could just make out the first signs of scruff beginning to grow back in from his last shave on his chiseled, angular jaw. Jade got a strange urge to reach up and run her hand over his toned chest.

"Whoa," Weston said quietly, causing Jade to wonder if he'd just felt the same thing she had.

He held her eyes for a moment, and Jade found herself thinking of what it would be like to kiss him.

"Guys?" Kiara yelled up the stairs, breaking the moment.

Jade pushed Weston off of her and stood. She almost held a hand out to help him up, but then reconsidered, not knowing what would happen if they made physical contact again. Weston stood slowly, never taking his eyes off Jade.

"Well, that was interesting," Jade said under her breath.

Weston chuckled and maintained eye contact with Jade while yelling back to Kiara, "We're coming!"

What was it with him today? Jade wondered.

"Come on, let's grab Ariana," she said, rolling her eyes.

* * *

Kiara held seven small, oval pills in her hand. She couldn't stop shaking them, as if something magical would happen at any minute, like light beams shooting out from the rounded edges. How could something so plain looking possibly have the insane effects people told her about? Although she was trying not to think about it, Kiara was grateful that Molly suppressed appetite and that the pills weren't going to add any calories for the day. She knew she shouldn't be thinking like that anymore, but she couldn't stop the thoughts from crossing her mind.

Alora laughed in Kiara's direction. "They're not going to float away K, you don't have to stare at them like that."

Kiara smiled over at Alora, who looked beautiful as usual in blue jean cutoff shorts and a tight-fitting gray-blue tee. She sat between Aubrey and Haiden with her long, light-brown legs tucked up beneath her.

"I'm so happy it's a three-day weekend," Aubrey said, resting a hand on Alora's leg. "This is the perfect time to try this. K, do you have any electrolyte water? We need to make sure we're hydrated."

Before Kiara could answer, her attention was diverted. Jade and Weston came down the steps with flushed faces while Ariana traipsed behind them. Pinched anger ran through her at the sight of Ariana's despondent face–Kiara had known Lukas was bad news all along.

"Why don't we just take them now?" Kiara said, inspiration hitting her. "Like, right now. Let's just do it."

"Down!" Haiden shouted, jumping up from the couch.

"Down," Weston said. Alora and Jade nodded in agreement and Kiara turned to Ariana expectantly.

Ariana kept her face steady as she walked to where Kiara was standing. Without missing a beat she grabbed a pill from Kiara's hand, popped it in her mouth, and swallowed. "Yep. I'm down," she said with a little smirk.

"OOOOHHH BIG LEAGUES!" Weston shouted, praising Ariana. He grabbed a pill from Kiara's hand and threw it in his mouth. Kiara and the group were laughing as they took their pills one after another, ginning wide.

"Now we wait," Aubrey said, settling back into the couch with the others.

Kiara turned on some lofi music and glanced at her phone, checking to see if she had anything new in from Teague. To her delight, she did. She hadn't realized how much she needed to tell Teague what had been going on in her head. She thought he would've gone running for the hills, freaked out by the fact that she had willingly made herself throw up. But he hadn't. He had wanted to help the entire time–she just never gave him the opportunity to do so.

Admitting to her problem had been one of the hardest things

Kiara had done in her life to date. She still wasn't one hundred percent cured–she didn't even know if there was a certain "cure". But for the past week she'd worked on her thoughts every single day, noticing when the harmful ones surfaced, like how fat she was getting or that she *needed* to vomit, NOW. After catching them, she'd remember that they weren't truthful and that her mind was playing tricks on her. She would take four deep breaths and change her focus to the ways in which certain foods nourished her body and healed her instead. If that didn't work, she called her mom or Ariana or Jade immediately and told them what she was thinking about doing. They would help to talk her down when she couldn't help herself.

As silly as it sounded, she found talking to herself helped too. "I'm beautiful as I am. I am enough. I'm loved. I'm strong enough to overcome this. The mean thoughts aren't real. The mean thoughts aren't the truth," had become her daily mantra. She said it to herself every morning and every night and every time she felt like she was starting to slip. Hell, she even had to make herself get up and dance and cry through it sometimes—often at the same time—but she made sure to tell herself with conviction each time. The truth was she was all of those things, and she wasn't going to let this take over her life.

Kiara read the text from Teague.

7:08 p.m. Teague: Y'all should come over to Taron's place. I promise it's really chill. Only like 10 people here
7:09 p.m. Kiara: I'll run it by everyone. We just took the stuff!
7:09 p.m. Teague: Oh shit! I can't wait to see you... come soon

Kiara grinned. It felt like she and Teague were just beginning again. They were taking it slow for now, which they'd agreed upon since Kiara had a lot of work to do on herself before anything else.

"How long does it take for these to kick in? Kiara! Come back over here!" Jade shouted. Kiara hadn't heard the relentless laughter coming from her friends–thinking of Teague could cause her to tune out the world accidentally. How had she ever thought she could give him up?

"Should we go to Taron's? By the time we get there, we should feel it. Teague said there's only ten people there, so nothing too wild," Kiara said as she wandered over and sat on one of the couches by Aubrey and Alora, who had begun to braid Ariana's hair. Kiara noticed Jade and Weston sitting incredibly close to one another on the opposite couch.

"Why not?" Ariana said. "But we have to get ready first if you guys don't mind waiting."

"Only if I get to pick out what you're wearing..." Weston said with a devilish smile.

"West, we can't go to the party naked, so that's out of the question," Jade retorted, causing everyone to laugh.

Kiara watched as Weston seemed to become lost in thought, probably imagining Jade naked. A sudden surge of excitement and love for her friends rocketed through her body. Not that that wasn't normal, but it was definitely heightened. Could that be the Molly kicking in already? "Okay, J, Ari, Alora, you come upstairs with me so we can get ready. Everyone else stay here and do whatever! We'll be back in 20 minutes."

"You're leaving me here with these idiots?" Aubrey pleaded in a mock tone.

"Here," Kiara said as she pulled out her gaming system and tossed it at the boys. "There's Overwatch and all sorts of games–go crazy."

The boys hollered in delight and scrambled for the controllers, shoving and smashing each other out of the way.

"Aubyyyy!!" Weston taunted. "Remember that one time freshman year when I destroyed you like twenty times in a row in Overwatch after our first football game?"

"Was that before or after Haiden was too stoned to figure out how to even use the controller?" Aubrey countered, successfully transferring the teasing to a different subject.

"Aw c'mon, that was my first time ever ripping a bong! I was on a different planet!" Haiden moaned.

Kiara left the room, content and smiling to herself. That would buy them at least a half hour. She found Alora, Ariana and Jade back in her room, talking about the different feelings they were experiencing from the MDMA. Kiara ran to her closet and began to rummage through a multitude of outfits.

"I'm going to pick something out for each of you, and if you don't like it you don't have to wear it–but at least try it on," Kiara said.

Alora, Jade, and Ariana consented and splayed out on the bed. Kiara turned her attention back to her closet–this was going to be fun. The girls weren't the same size, but she had all different types of clothing and fits.

After several minutes of browsing through her wardrobe, Kiara came to her decisions. For Alora, she pulled a brilliant lime green low-cut top that had always been a little too big to fit her own chest, but she figured would fit Alora like a glove. For Jade, a tan high-waisted skirt and simple white spaghetti strap that would only come down to her midriff. For Ariana, she pulled a dusty gold wrap dress that would show off her curves. Kiara displayed the choices on the bed and waited for the others' reactions.

"These are PERFECT!" Jade squealed as she began stripping down to change.

Alora clapped her hands with excitement and whipped off her shirt, pulling the lime green top over her head. It fit her perfectly and the color of the top made her skin glow. "This is beautiful, K," Alora complimented after assessing her new look in the full-length mirror. "My turn to pick out something for you!"

A momentary wave of panic seized Kiara as she watched Alora hunt through her summer clothes. She would probably look chubby in whatever Alora pulled, which would be humiliating. This was supposed to be fun and yet her mind was taking the experience away from her.

"Agh," Kiara said, shaking her head.

"Hey," Ariana said, coming over to sit next to her on the bed. "Is it the thoughts?"

Jade stopped admiring her outfit and walked over, taking the spot on the other side of Kiara. "Just let it out."

"I'm embarrassed," Kiara admitted. A tear ran down her face as she tried to explain. The shame knotted in her throat and tore at her stomach. "You're all so beautiful and I still don't fully see my body in that way. I'm trying... but the pressure to have a perfect body is overwhelming."

Jade picked Kiara's chin up. "Kiara, do you want to know a secret? None of us see our bodies as perfect. Also, there's *no such thing* as a "perfect body". Even if there were, your body doesn't define you or make you an amazing person–which you are already. I mean, just look at Melodie–she's got a great body, and she's an asshole." Kiara let out a small snort of laughter at Jade's point.

Ariana smiled and shook her head, then picked back up where Jade had left off. "You're a beautiful person, inside and out, period. You care about your friends and family, you're kind and inclusive to everyone you meet, and you crack people up–us especially. You're a source of light for a lot of people in your life. A body can't do that, only a heart can."

Alora stepped out of the closet and walked to them with a gorgeous but casual white off-the-shoulder dress in her arms. "What's going on?"

"I've been having some trouble with body image lately... it just took over me for a second there," Kiara said truthfully.

"What?" Alora said, her eyes dancing wildly between the girls. "You? You've got to be kidding me."

Kiara looked away from Alora before she spoke again. "Yeah, it started a couple of months ago and got serious pretty quickly."

"Wow," Alora said in amazement. "I'm sorry. I never would've thought... you're in such great shape though." Alora shook her head as if in denial and then began again. "Kiara, I hope you know you're not alone. I know a lot of people who struggle with body image. There's actually a support group for it that one of my friends goes to. I could get the information if you want," Alora said.

"Really? That would be great," Kiara said. A surge of hope swelled up inside her. She wasn't the only one... Of course she'd known that, but for some reason, and perhaps it was the MDMA coursing through her system, she felt more connected to the others that were suffering in the same way that she was at that moment. And why should she keep suffering? If Alora never would've guessed she had a body image problem, and hell, her own best friends hadn't known... Maybe it *was* just all in her head. With that simple yet profound epiphany, Kiara shot up off the bed.

"It's just in my head," she exclaimed, not sure if she was making sense to anyone else but not caring. "It's all me–it's all mental. Teague never cared, you guys never cared... who cares how much I weigh?"

Jade whooped and Ariana clapped her hands. Kiara whipped off the comfy shorts and t-shirt she'd been wearing and pulled on the white off-the-shoulder dress Alora had picked out. As simple a thing as it was, being comfortable enough to be naked in front of her friends again was extremely empowering. She looked in the mirror and made sure to *not* examine every little detail of her body.

"I love it, and I love you guys," Kiara said resolutely. "Thank you."

The girls beamed at her.

Kiara grinned back. Fuck this body image bullshit. It was all in her head, and it was driving *only* her crazy–she wasn't going to do that to herself anymore–she was going to love herself. Kiara took one last look in the mirror and complimented herself. *I look beautiful*, she said in her head, truly believing it.

And she did.

* * *

Ariana's body and mind buzzed pleasantly from the MDMA as her group of friends walked up the driveway leading to Taron's backyard. It was a pleasurable, exciting, wonderful feeling that she could have used a million different words to describe–but mainly, she just felt *good*. Beyond good, actually. Ariana loved the clothes Kiara had picked out for her. The pale gold dress hugged her hips and chest, and it was the kind of dress she loved–one that would only look good on someone who wasn't stick thin. She wondered what Lukas would think if he saw her in it.

"Ugh," Ariana said under her breath. She cringed involuntarily and shook her head. Every time she thought of Lukas, which had been nearly every other minute since Friday, she became overwhelmed by sorrow and her eyes were constantly welling up with tears–she couldn't help it–she'd been so sure this was a forever type of thing. Perhaps one of the saddest thoughts Ariana had that she couldn't shake was that maybe Lukas was, in fact, the love of her life, and now that it was over, nothing would ever compare. This thought was what had crossed her mind when Jade brought up looking for other options. Ariana couldn't imagine any other options. There was only Lukas.

Haiden strolled up to Ariana and threw an arm around her shoulder.

"Hey dude," he said, pushing his long, dark hair out of his face with his free hand. "I don't really know the full story of what's got you so upset, but the tide always churns, you know? You think you're going to be worried about this forever? You're not man, trust me."

"Thanks, Haide," Ariana said with a laugh. "Even though you didn't *exactly* get the saying right, that was scarily intuitive."

"Whatever. Either way, I'm taking that as a compliment," Haiden responded.

Ariana grinned. She could think of a million different reasons as to why Lukas did the things he did, why everything turned out the way it had, and the differences between herself and Olivia, but that would drive her insane. This night was to get her mind off of all that. Besides, although it didn't feel like it, she was almost sure Haiden's simplistic advice was right–the tide always turns, and so maybe she wouldn't always feel this way.

The group stepped into the backyard to a stunning view. The pool danced with color-changing lights that slowly rotated from royal blue, to purple, to fuchsia, to teal, and back again. Tiny gold lanterns hung across the patio and looked like twinkling stars in the clear night sky. Thankfully, the party was quiet and small. Only Taron, Melodie, Reigh, Teague, some junior girls–although no Kristin in sight luckily–and a few others.

Jade stopped short and took in a sharp breath. Ariana looked at her friend and followed her eyes to see Ian emerging from the house. Although Jade and Ian were on the rocks, jealousy overtook Ariana for a moment–Ian was still *trying* to talk to Jade–he still cared. There was a certain calculated coldness to the fact that Lukas hadn't even attempted to explain himself or make sure she was okay. The thought twisted like a knife in her gut, but at the same time was slightly liberating. If he didn't care, why should she?

At almost the same moment, Ariana's phone began to vibrate. Her hands shook–somehow, she just knew it was him. Lukas had a knack for calling in those moments when she felt as though she were on the precipice of something–of making progress in forgetting him or getting over him, of coming to some realization about their situation... Right at those moments Lukas always seemed to drag her back to square one.

Ariana flipped over her phone and sure enough, Lukas' name showed on the screen. Her chest grew hot and her legs went weak. She almost answered but then paused. Lukas' call signaled that she still had some kind of hold over him. She had to–he was taking a risk by calling her and he must've been taking risks by hanging out with her, because surely Olivia wouldn't be happy with any of it. Ariana's whole body relaxed as she came to the realization that she wasn't powerless in this situation. And he deserved to suffer.

Ariana pressed the ignore button on her phone and smiled.

CHAPTER 21

Jade

Jade was still panicking on the inside as she calmly walked across the party, completely ignoring Ian along the way. She made a beeline to Taron just to shove it in Ian's face that Taron could still talk to her and hug her, whilst Ian no longer had that privilege.

"Jade, you look gorgeous," Taron said, his eyes devouring her. Taron hugged her with his whole body, pulling her into his chest and lingering for a few moments too long. Jade almost laughed out loud–Taron's timing couldn't have been more perfect. This was *exactly* the kind of thing Ian should witness right now.

"Thanks T," Jade said with a smile, but then pulled away. Taron had taken Jade's dismissal considerably well over the past few weeks and she didn't want to give him any ideas.

Jade could feel Ian's eyes melting into her back all the while as she stepped out of Taron's vicinity and over to Reigh. Melodie lingered nearby, examining her nails.

"Hey J," Reigh said. Her cheekbones shone in the glow from the lanterns, highlighted by a golden shimmer. Jade thought Reigh must've looked into some insane contouring videos to make the outlines of her facial structure look so severe.

"Hey, cool makeup," Jade said, smiling.

"Thanks," Reigh said. "I got some new highlighter I'm in love with–"

Jade tried to pay attention but Ian had walked over to talk to some juniors behind Reigh, and she accidentally looked straight at him. All of the air left Jade as a fierce and painful longing struck in her gut. Ian's eyes seemed to speak to her, relaying his regret. Jade wrenched her eyes away and back to Reigh, although she still couldn't hear a word she was saying.

Although Ian had done the unforgivable in lying about having sex with Kristin, it didn't hurt to feel that he still cared about her. Shit, it wasn't as if there were some magical fairy that had swooped in and erased her feelings for him the minute he'd fucked up. *That's probably the worst part about it,* Jade thought to herself: *you begin to have feelings for someone, then* they *fuck up, then* you're *supposed to instantaneously turn your feelings off, which just isn't plausible.*

"Jade," a husky voice from behind her interrupted. "Can I talk to you for a second?"

Jade's stomach dropped to the ground as she turned to find Ian standing before her in all of his glory. Up close, she noticed his hair had been cut recently and styled. He was wearing a dark blue shirt that brought out his eyes and made Jade's heart hurt. He looked so good, and there was no possibility of a future for them now. Ian took a step forward, looking like he wanted to reach out and touch her, which Jade didn't know if she could handle at the moment.

"Um... yes," Jade mumbled as she took a step backward. Ian was now closer to her than he'd been in weeks.

Ian led the way inside. Jade studied him while he walked, trying not to look at the sexy curve of his tan neck and broad shoulders. Inside, he stopped by the kitchen counter and Jade was momentarily taken back to the memory of when he first flirted with her there, before she'd ever known about him hooking up with Kristin... before she'd known he was a liar.

"I can't believe you," Jade hissed, crossing her arms, keeping a safe distance from him. "How disappointing."

"Look, Jade," Ian said, his words tumbling out on top of one another. "I didn't tell you about hooking up with Kristin because you and I had just started...whatever it was we were doing... and I didn't want to fuck that up. I would've told you eventually. I just didn't want you to go running for the hills, like you did. I didn't want to lose you."

Jade dug her fingers into her arms. "You lied to me from the beginning–that's not good. And it wasn't some little lie. It was huge."

"I didn't know what else to do! I didn't lie about the fact that I don't have any feelings for Kristin whatsoever. To be honest, I was already crushing on you, but it was right after you and Taron hooked up so I thought you were into him, and Kristin was just there. We were really drunk when it happened."

"Wait... it only happened once?" Jade asked, confused.

"Yes," Ian said, his eyes widening. "Only once, and we didn't even have sex. I'm not saying that I wouldn't have, I don't want to lie to you ever again even if it'll hurt you a bit–but I was so wasted I couldn't have had sex with her, even if I'd tried."

Jade took a step back, disoriented. But Dani had said they were fucking...

She wanted to cry, the betrayal by Dani stinging her heart. *Maybe Dani had heard rumors and believed them as well,* Jade reasoned with herself, trying to give her sister the benefit of the doubt.

"But when I asked you, you didn't deny it," Jade said.

"All you said was 'I know about you and Kristin'–you never asked for any specifics, Jade!" Ian pushed a hand through his hair in distress.

Jade considered this. She'd been so angry when she'd found out that she couldn't remember exactly what she'd said, but that sounded right. She mulled the situation over in her mind. Ian and

Kristin hadn't been having sex all along... they'd only hooked up once. Her heart soared for a moment, but then sunk again.

"Ian, it was with Kristin though, who comes after me time and time again. You knew how I felt about her."

"Not when it happened! I didn't know. I still don't know the extent of it."

Jade bit her lip, trying to decide how much to reveal. "She's a bully," she said quietly. "I don't care if saying that makes me look weak. She's spread rumors about me giving a guy three years older than me a blowjob outside of a fast food restaurant that the majority of the school believed because she "swore by it". That's fucked up, Ian. And it's embarrassing. Just because I don't go around crying about these things doesn't mean they aren't hurtful and *wrong*."

Ian's eyes fell. "I didn't know that was her. I'm so sorry."

Jade softened; he seemed sincere. She hadn't known it was a one-off thing, fueled by alcohol and bad decisions. And she couldn't help but compare her situation to Ariana's with Lukas. Ian was standing here in front of her, laying it all out on the line. She could see how much he'd been hurting, and he had never given up on trying to get to her.

"Is there any way this can work again? Jade, I just want to be with you–we don't have to do anything at all." Ian looked defeated. "I just want to be with you."

Jade melted at the longing in his voice. She reconsidered the situation. What was holding onto this anger doing for her, other than hurting herself and Ian? So, he'd made a mistake. If she didn't forgive him now, Kristin really would be winning. Ian wasn't perfect, but who was? She'd certainly made a few mistakes herself. And at least he was trying to make things right.

Jade took a deep breath and willfully let her anger go. "Okay."

Ian looked up, shocked. "Okay?" he repeated, unsure.

"Yes, okay." Jade allowed a small smile to reach her lips.

At the sight of Jade's smile, Ian's entire face lit up. He grabbed her by the waist and pulled her to him, kissing her feverishly, causing Jade's body to fill with joy, relief, and desire simultaneously. She'd forgotten how strong of an effect he had on her and it was wonderful reliving it again, intensified by their separation. Jade knew this was one of those moments she would never forget–no matter what the future held for them.

"Oh, sorry," Ian said, pulling away from Jade as he seemed to remember himself. "I forgot we're still in public."

Jade immediately reached out and put her hand behind his neck, pulling Ian's face back to hers. "I don't care anymore," she said before kissing him again. Jade could feel his smile against her lips as he kissed her back.

"So," Ian pulled away for a moment. "Does that mean you'll be with me?"

"Like be your girlfriend?"

Ian nodded. "Yes, my girlfriend."

Jade's stomach tightened up. Normally that word scared the shit out of her, but the way it rolled off of Ian's tongue sounded sexy. Also, that would mean he would be hers officially. No more Kristin hanging all over him, no more hiding their feelings for each other, no more getting hit on by Taron and other unwanted guys. At the last thought, a hint of panic shot through her. That would also mean no more casual flirting, no more doing whatever she wanted whenever she wanted, no more secret sneaking off to make out with Ian since they could just do it in plain view of everyone now–she would sincerely miss all of those things.

Jade studied Ian's handsome features. His eyes were lit up a brilliant blue; his stare so intense that she was finding it hard to concentrate. She'd forced herself to forget how much she wanted him, but it was all crashing back into her now. Ian's hands were clenched into fists as if he wanted to touch her again but seemed to understand she needed a moment. Jade could see how much he wanted her, and it only made her lust for him stronger. She had always valued her freedom, but she realized now that she wanted Ian more.

Jade grinned at him. "That doesn't sound so bad."

Ian grabbed Jade by the waist again, only this time he didn't hold back. He lifted her onto the counter so that he stood between her legs, his body pressing into hers. Jade was so turned on she nearly forgot where they were. Her hands were in Ian's hair and under his shirt; she traced the outlines of his six-pack as they continued kissing each other, barely stopping for air.

Ian pulled back for a moment and looked at Jade. "This kitchen seems to be a special place for us, huh?" He smiled. "We've had some good moments here."

"Mhmm."

The door swung open and they scrambled. Ian attempted to straighten his clothing while Jade hopped off the counter and ran a hand through her hair.

Kiara turned the corner and floated to one of the barstools by the kitchen countertop, looking like she was in a dream.

"You two!" she squealed, giggling like crazy. "I love you two."

Jade and Ian looked at each other, then broke into laughter at Kiara's marijuana and MDMA-infused state.

"Kiara, want me to make you a drink?" Ian offered. "Jade, tell her I'm the best bartender you've ever met."

Jade walked around the kitchen counter and perched on a barstool next to Kiara. Ian looked so sexy with his hair ruffled from their make-out session. She laughed to herself at the drastic change of events. Mere minutes ago she hadn't been able to see any way that she and Ian could ever be together, and now he was hers completely.

Jade smirked at him."Sure, sure. He's alright."

"I'll show you alright," Ian said, his voice laced with promise meant for only her to understand. They locked eyes and Jade's groin felt like it was on fire.

Oh yes, he was *all* hers.

CHAPTER 22

K, A, J

Kiara lounged at the kitchen bar while Ian whipped up two non-alcoholic drinks. Ariana had lectured them about staying away from alcohol while on Molly–not that Kiara needed to be told not to drink. She was realizing more and more how much she disliked alcohol in general–not only because of the high calorie content, but also because she hated being hung over and making stupid mistakes. Jade was on to something with her choice not to partake. Not to mention the MDMA felt so good that she didn't need or want to add it in.

"Here you go," Ian said as he handed Jade and Kiara each a cran-orange concoction.

"Thank you," Kiara said, although she wasn't sure Ian heard her at all.

Ian's eyes had barely left Jade since Kiara had wandered into the kitchen, and she was about 99% positive that she had interrupted a serious make out session, but she had been in dire need of hydration. *Better get out of here and leave them to it*, Kiara thought. She didn't even need Jade's explanation of what caused them to make up; Kiara could assume that Ian had made a huge mistake by hooking up with Kristin–it was good that Jade had forgiven him. Honestly, he probably didn't need to be tortured any more after *that* decision.

Kiara laughed into her red solo cup at her joke. Ian finally broke his eyes away from Jade for a moment to stare at Kiara, his eyebrows raised.

Jade let out a laugh. "Feeling good?"

Kiara looked into Jade's green eyes and smiled wide.

"I'm happy," Kiara said truthfully, thinking about Teague and her progress with the weight thoughts. It had been a while since she had felt happiness. It wasn't like she was anywhere close to being over the body image issues–she knew that it was going to be a process–but she'd started taking small steps toward recovery and finding things that worked for her, and that was what mattered more than anything. "But I'm still worried about Ariana."

"I'll meet you outside, Jade," Ian said, giving them a few moments alone. Jade blew Ian a kiss in response as he headed out the door.

"That was quick," Kiara said, teasing her.

"Have you not seen his abs?" Jade joked. "No, but seriously, a lot of it was a misunderstanding. He hooked up with Kristin once and they didn't have sex. I believe him–I mean, either he's being sincere or he's an incredibly convincing liar. Either way, I want to give it a shot for real and do it right this time," Jade said, breaking into a pretty grin that covered her face. "So I'm kinda his girlfriend now."

"What? Oh my God, Jade!" Kiara threw her arms around Jade's neck to hug her.

In the spur of the moment, Kiara ran to the door to find Ariana–it was only right she was here for this too.

"Ariana!" Kiara yelled into the party. The crowd looked bigger than when she'd left the backyard minutes ago, but she spotted Ariana easily enough talking to Weston and Aubrey.

"She looks incredibly cool in the outfit I picked out," Kiara said with a proud grin.

Ariana trotted through the kitchen door seconds later, smiling. "I missed you two!" she said, her cheeks flushed.

Kiara sat on the barstool. "Tell her, Jade."

Jade paused, her dark brows furrowing as she seemed to weigh whether or not telling Ariana was such a good idea right now.

"You and Ian are back together?" Ariana said with a smile, right on target.

"You know, it's kind of scary when you do that sometimes," Jade said.

Ariana gave a knowing shake of her head. "So, what happened with him and Kristin?"

"I mean they hooked up, but it wasn't what I thought," Jade explained. "I'll tell you more about it later. But the moral of the story is, don't believe everything you hear, especially not when it's coming from Dani."

Ariana nodded in agreement. She stepped forward and swiped Kiara's drink from the counter, taking a whiff. "Good, no alcohol."

"Geez, mom," Kiara said.

"By the way," Ariana said, ignoring her teasing. "I have come to a conclusion about my situation with Lukas."

"Which is?" Jade asked.

"Fuck him... figuratively, that is. He deserves to suffer," Ariana said matter-of-factly.

Jade laughed. "Memoir title?"

Kiara put her arms in the air in celebration. "Fuck YES Ari. What brought this on?"

"He's been trying to call me tonight. Twice now, and I didn't answer either of them. Each time I don't answer I feel more in control, as painful as it is," Ariana said, staring at her phone on the counter as she spoke. "And the fact that he's calling must mean that he still has some sort of feelings for me right? So I wasn't just a joke to him..."

"Ariana, how could you be a joke to anyone?" Kiara said. "He was just a guy who wanted to have his cake and eat it too. You're a catch, and you caught him off guard, like he said. I'm sure that part was true."

"Well, whatever parts were actually true, I doubt if I'll ever know," Ariana said. "But I'm not going to sit around and wait on him anymore, jumping at his phone calls, pining over him. He doesn't deserve that kind of attention from me."

"I'm so proud of you," Kiara said earnestly.

"I am too," Jade said.

"Tell me more about Ian, J," Ariana said, as she slid her arm through Jade's and sat next to her.

Kiara noticed Ariana's phone vibrating ominously on the kitchen counter, signaling someone trying to reach her. She had a feeling this was only the beginning of Ariana's battle, and that Lukas, who had shown that he would go to great lengths to do and get whatever he wanted, wasn't quite ready to let her go yet.

* * *

"Are you sure you don't want us to stay with you?" Jade asked as she and Kiara walked to the door.

They had turned back to look at her, and Ariana couldn't help but think how beautiful her two best friends were in their own disparate ways. Kiara's long, ash-blonde hair poured over her bare back, her deep blue-green eyes contrasting with her otherwise light features. Jade's cheekbones and red, lush lips were emphasized by her summer tan, and the muted lights made her dark beauty more pronounced.

"No, I'm good. You two go ahead and I'll catch up," Ariana said.

She'd told them she wanted to make another juice drink and take a moment while they rejoined the party. But as soon as the door closed and she was alone with her thoughts for more than thirty seconds, Ariana regretted her decision. A deafening silence rang out around her. *Oh,* she thought, *this is my first time being alone since the end of Lukas.* She looked over at her phone and an overwhelming urge to call him rocketed through her. Was it so wrong to want to hear his voice? To hear what he had to say? She continued to stare at her phone, unblinking. If only he would call her again... not so that she could pick up–but so she could at least see he was thinking of her.

It was so much easier to be strong with Jade and Kiara around. *But I don't need babysitters,* Ariana told herself. *I'm going to be fine.* Besides, Lukas had Olivia now–they were together and he shouldn't even *be* calling her. That last thought, no, that last piece of *truth* finally seemed to sink in, piercing through her bravado like an arrow. She crumpled to the kitchen floor, hot tears streaming down her cheeks.

"Fuck!" Ariana cried out, not caring if anyone heard or saw her at that moment.

Her hands clutched at her stomach, desperately trying to make the pain go away. How was it that she could be completely fine one minute, and then feel like she was *never* going to be okay again the next? She'd just come to another realization as well–she was now pining for a guy who was in a relationship. She'd somehow become the bad guy in the scenario, and Lukas hadn't even cared that he had done this to her–that he had knowingly put her in this position. How could he be so impossibly selfish? And why wasn't that enough to make her stop yearning for him? Ariana put her head in her hands. She couldn't believe she'd been reduced to tears on Taron's kitchen floor at a party, even while on Molly. *This* is what love had done to her.

The back door cracked open and Ariana flinched, but she didn't move.

"Ari?" Alora's voice called out.

"Hey," Ariana said meekly. She thought of how pathetic she must look, slumped on the kitchen floor with large dark splotches dotting her dress from the tears.

Alora's head popped around the door, her face filled with concern.

"Hey," Alora said as she made her way to Ariana. She knelt on the floor next to her.

"What's wrong with me?" Ariana asked, crying quietly through her question.

"Nothing's wrong with you," Alora said. "You fell for a shitty guy. It happens to the best of us."

"I keep thinking I'm okay, but then I fall apart again," Ariana admitted. "The memories of him are haunting me. Like the first time he kissed me. I nearly lost my breath, and I was so happy I thought my heart was going to explode. It felt like it was only us in the world. I knew at that moment that this feeling is what all the love songs are written about–this, right here, is what romance novels are about. I never wanted to be without him again. Seeing him was like the air would come back into my lungs." Ariana stopped, feeling the weight and bliss of the memory suffocate her for a moment. "And now how am I supposed to live without that?"

Alora paused for a moment before she answered, tucking her raven hair behind her ears. "Here's the truth though, Ari, whether you want to hear it or not: he was seeing Olivia too when he kissed you like that. You weren't the only girl in his life, and I doubt you ever would be if you'd ended up with him."

Ariana squeezed her eyes shut to try and block out the pain while processing the facts.

"Also, stop asking yourself shitty questions like what's wrong with me. Maybe think of someone you look up to and ask yourself what they would do in your situation instead," Alora said.

"That's a good idea. I have a lot of characters from my books that I would love to be more like." Ariana thought for a moment. "Alright. So–better question: what can I do to help myself through this right now?"

"Why don't you focus on bettering yourself? And have the most fun you possibly can while you do it. Living well is the best form of revenge anyway," Alora said. "...Oh, and looking super, super hot when he's around."

Ariana laughed, a small hiccup escaping her lips.

"So I vote we not be depressed on the kitchen floor for the rest of the night. Are you in?" Alora said.

"Definitely."

* * *

"Ohmygod Melodie, come here, your dress is so cute!" Kristin Long screeched from across the backyard.

Jade shuddered. It was bad enough that Kristin and her gang had shown up to the party, but the thought of Melodie and Kristin getting chummy gave her the all-out chills.

More people continued to trickle in, bringing the small get-together closer to a rager. Dani and her friends danced near the keg on the patio. Even though Dani's group was surrounding the one source of beer at the party, everyone left them a 5-foot radius and gave them questioning looks before walking up to get refills–almost as if asking for permission. Jade had to admit, although Dani could be cruel, her power was impressive.

Ian was standing close to Jade but they weren't touching, causing her body to hum where it was near his. His arm kept grazing hers at random moments, sending small charges of electricity through her veins. They had somehow gotten stuck standing next to each other but talking to different people, when all Jade wanted to do was kiss him more. She let out a sigh, trying to figure out a way to get them out of the conversations they were trapped in.

"Any challengers up for a game of beer pong against me and Jade?" Ian shouted, as if reading her mind. He pulled Jade into his side. "Being this close and not touching you is torture," he whispered, his lips tickling her ear.

Jade blushed at his words and the attention they were getting. A few curious eyes lingered on them. Jade smiled shyly up at Ian, his eyes piercing into hers in a way that made her want to be alone with him all over again... preferably in a bedroom.

"I know better than to take that on," Weston called back, breaking the moment. "Jade is too distracting to play against."

Jade groaned internally. Now? Out of all the moments Weston could choose to hit on her–*oh, not so subtly*–he chose now? Jade rolled her eyes and looked back at Weston, surprised to find that he didn't look like he was joking. She turned to Ian to see if he'd noticed, but Ian still had a huge grin plastered on his face. He was radiating happiness.

"Agreed," Ian said with a laugh, surprising her. "That's why she's on my team."

In one graceful move, Ian ducked and kissed Jade full on the lips in front of everyone, taking her breath away. A couple standing close to them gasped and people nearby began talking in hushed voices. Jade winced. Was Kristin in the crowd?

Ian pulled back and looked at her. "You okay?"

Jade stared at Ian's handsome, concerned features and tuned out the rest of the party. She took a deep breath. Kristin wasn't going to do anything any worse than usual, she convinced herself. Jade nodded, letting her mouth slide slowly back into a grin.

"God, you're beautiful," Ian murmured.

"Hey, love birds!" Kiara shouted, standing across the table with Haiden. "We'll take you on."

Jade grinned at Kiara. She was actively choosing to ignore the hushed voices circulating who knew what through the party about her. "Okay, but the boys have to drink all the beer. Actually, not you Haide. Only water for you too," she said, laughing when Haiden gave her a sour face.

Ian made the first few cups, shooting the score up to 6-0 in about five minutes flat. Kiara and Haiden's hand-eye coordination skills weren't the best on a good day, and when Taron brought a bong outside and they each took a rip mid-turn, the rest was history. Jade couldn't stop laughing at their shots, each one getting further and further from the cups as the weed killed what little coordination they had left.

Kiara set her face in determination as she pulled her arm back to take their final shot. She bit down on her lip as she flung the ball toward the opposing cups, but instead it whizzed by Jade's ear. "Oops!"

Ian laughed and kissed Jade on the cheek. "I think that's the game. All the beer is going straight through me. I'll be back."

Haiden high-fived Kiara, which they both almost missed, before sprinting inside behind Ian. Kiara came over to Jade's side of the table and they plopped onto two cushioned lounge chairs, looking out at the color-changing water.

"How're you feeling?" Kiara asked.

"Like I hate to see Ian go but I love to watch him leave," Jade joked, staring after Ian as he made his way inside. Even the simple kiss he'd given her on the cheek had left her with a wonderful giddy feeling, albeit she was still slightly nervous.

Kiara laughed. "Seriously, though. I know this is a big deal for you."

"Yeah, but it feels right, you know? Like, I knew as soon as he talked to me earlier that he was genuine, and my feelings for him haven't come and gone like usual. When I'm with him I feel like he's home base almost... Does that make sense?"

Kiara nodded, the corners of her eyes crinkling from her smile.

"So now that I'm sure this wasn't some fling, I'm ready to be official with him, even if that means I have to be ready for whatever Kristin and her crew throw at me."

"I'm proud of you. You're brave, J. Not everyone would knowingly invoke the wrath of the bitchiest clique in school."

"Hmm, *is* this bravery, or is it stupidity?"

"Eh, it's a fine line," Kiara said with a shrug, laughing. "I'm gonna go find Teague. Are you good here?"

Jade nodded and Kiara stood up, kissing Jade on the head. "See you in a bit," she said before she bounded off.

Jade took a deep breath, reliving the past hour and all that had transpired. She had Ian again. How funny life was... one minute she could barely stand to be near him, and the next they had somehow come back to each other. Jade couldn't help herself–she got up and followed the path Ian had taken to the back door, thinking she would surprise him with another make-out session in the kitchen. She grinned devilishly to herself, excited just thinking about it.

Out of the corner of her eye, Jade saw a flash of yellow-blond hair coming straight for her. Kristin was walking into Jade's path, her black, robe-like dress hitting the top of the grass with each step. Two of her loyal followers trailed a couple of steps behind. Kristin's eyes were squinted, her mouth pressed in a thin, hard line. "Hey, slut," Kristin called to Jade, her friends laughing loudly behind her on cue.

For the second time that night, Jade heard people nearby gasp and titter. Her cheeks burned, but instead of fighting back she simply shook her head and went to step around the girls. Kristin followed her movement and stepped in front of her so that they were mere inches apart. Jade's breathing sped up, her fight-or-flight instincts kicking in.

"*Move*," Jade said, looking Kristin dead in the eye.

"I don't take orders from whores," Kristin said loudly, her mouth twisting into a smirk.

Jade glanced around. She was outnumbered, and her friends were nowhere in sight. "Kristin, get out of my way."

"I don't think you heard me, Jade," Kristin said, raising her voice close to a shout. "*I said* I don't take orders from whores. From *trash*, like you."

Kristin was causing a scene; half of the party stopped what they were doing and stared at the girls. Jade's hands started to shake. She'd been in fights before, and recognized the distinct feeling that things were close to getting physical.

Kristin dropped her voice to a whisper. "By the way, I know about your dad."

The air drained out of Jade. How did she know? Only a few people at their school knew the truth...

Just like that, Jade knew she'd lost. But she wouldn't go down easily. Jade squared her shoulders and raised her chin. "Move or I'll make you."

Kristin opened her mouth, but before anything came out, Dani stepped in front of Jade, towering over Kristin's 5'5 build. Jade clamped her mouth shut–she must have been too distracted to notice Dani walking up.

"Kristin?" Dani said, her voice thick with venom. Jade looked from Dani to Kristin, confused. Was Dani about to stick up for her? That didn't make any sense, but there was no mistaking the tone of Dani's voice–Jade knew to run for the hills when she heard that tone. It was quite something else to hear it directed at one of her enemies. "Didn't anyone ever tell you? It's not smart to be unattractive *and* a bitch–you should have at least one thing going for you."

"Fuck you, Dani," Kristin shot back. Kristin glanced around her, but her crew was already backing away. "I'm sure it runs in the family."

Jade recoiled. Dani didn't understand the meaning of that comment yet, because she didn't know that Kristin knew.

"You just look really jealous right now Kristin, and it's sad," Dani retorted with a sigh, sounding bored with the interaction already. "Come on, Jade."

Kristin retaliated with a hateful comment, but it got lost in the wind as Dani steered Jade to the other side of the patio where the keg stood. She poured herself a beer and took a long sip.

"What was that?" Jade asked, still partially in a daze.

"What?" Dani said, irritation already back in her voice. She combed a hand through her strawberry blonde hair.

"*That*, Dani. C'mon, you know what I'm talking about."

"I don't know, I saw her stalking you like a vulture and getting weirdly close to you. Everyone knows how obsessed she is with Ian, and clearly, you didn't listen to my warning about him."

Jade's insides turned. She didn't want to think about Dani lying to her now. But could that have been Dani's strange way of protecting her? "Well, thank you."

Dani shrugged.

Jade struggled to say the next few words, afraid that Dani would be angry even though it wasn't her fault. "Dani? She knows about Dad. I don't know how, but she knows."

Dani's eyes flashed. "What, is she holding it over you with Ian?" Jade wondered how Dani figured out Kristin's motives so quickly. *Oh*, Jade thought in realization, *it's because that's something Dani would do.*

"I think she's going to."

"Don't let her," Dani said, holding Jade's eyes. "Tell him."

Jade nodded, fear flooding her stomach. So Ian would have to see all of her.

"You can go back to leaving me alone now," Dani said, interrupting her thoughts.

Jade nodded and walked away from Dani's group. After a few steps, she peered back at her sister, catching her eye. Jade thought of Dani sticking up for her and gave a small smile, to which Dani snorted and rolled her eyes, turning her back on Jade.

Jade laughed. She began to walk back inside when she felt a tap on her shoulder.

She turned to see a short brunette close up in her field of vision, and Jade realized she was staring directly into Holly's freckled face. Jade took an involuntary step back. The last time she'd spoken to Holly on the bleachers after school had not been pretty. She wondered for a moment if Holly's dad had given up the drugs or not, or if her parents had separated yet.

"Hey, Jade," Holly said, picking at a red cup in her hand.

"Holly, I've been meaning to talk to you." She had wanted to apologize, but so much had happened over the last few weeks she totally forgot. "I wanted to say I'm sorry for the way I treated you after school that day."

"Oh, well, you don't need to be. I... um, I'm the one that should be sorry. I kind of hated you for a while."

Jade cocked her head and raised an eyebrow. "What? Why?"

"Honestly, I thought you had this great life. Like everything just comes so easy to you, and you're beautiful and perfect, and I wanted to take you down a few notches. I'm sorry." Holly stared at the grass.

Jade didn't know how to react, so she touched Holly's shoulder. *Better go for humor*, she thought. "Oh. Well, um, you don't need to be sorry. And I don't know if you witnessed that little altercation just now but my life is definitely not perfect, so don't worry about that anymore either."

Holly didn't laugh. "I saw. I–I think some of it's my fault. I'm the one that spread that rumor about you. Or helped it spread. A lot."

Jade's eyes widened as her hand dropped, going limp by her side. "What?"

Holly's words came out in a rush. "People were already saying you hooked up with Taron, so I just said I saw it and that you actually hooked up with him *and* his friend, and then everyone kinda ran with it, and it became this big thing."

"But you weren't even there, were you?"

"No, but everyone was so ready to believe it, it was almost too easy," Holly said, and Jade winced at the implication. "I'm so sorry. I've been going through a lot and I just wasn't in my right mind. It's eating me up. I'm not a bad person, I swear. Can you forgive me?"

Jade looked at Holly's bowed head and was surprised to find she didn't feel any anger. Instead, she felt understanding. And why not give Holly a little break?

Jade took a deep breath. "I forgive you."

"Really?" Holly looked up at Jade with hope in her eyes.

"Yeah," Jade said, surprising herself again by laughing. "We all do stupid shit sometimes when we're hurting. Just... don't do it again okay? Come and talk to me first? I'll be able to tell you first-hand all of the messed up stuff I'm dealing with too. We're all human."

Holly nodded furiously and turned on her heel. "I'll make it up to you."

"That's not necessary!" Jade called out, but Holly was already walking away.

Jade stood there for a few moments, bewildered by the sequence of events. Then she let out a small laugh to herself... What the fuck had just happened?

CHAPTER 23
Kiara

Kiara and Teague were sprawled out in the grassy area of Taron's backyard, far away from everyone and lost in their own world. Kiara lay between Teague's legs with her head rolled back against his shoulder while he hummed a melody into her neck. His lips brushed her skin as he moved, lulling her into a blissful trance. It had been a long time since Kiara had felt this connected to him. She tried to think back–possibly since their first time together? But no, even then he hadn't known what was going on in her head, so although their bodies had never been closer at that moment, she hadn't completely let him in yet.

Kiara had a burst of inspiration. She sat up straight, whipping her head around to look Teague in the eyes. "Hey," she said, letting the mischievous thoughts in her head play out on her face.

"Hey," Teague responded with a lazy smile. "What's that look for?"

"I know we've been taking it slow, but I really want to be with you right now."

"You *are* with me," Teague said with a small laugh. "Speaking of... Have I told you how great it is to have my girl back?"

Teague pressed his soft lips to hers. She kissed him for a while, then pulled away and blinked her eyes open, focusing on his features. She'd missed so many little things about him, like the way he kept his eyes closed for a couple of seconds after they kissed, almost as if he was swimming in the moment, letting it overtake him. It was in moments like this that she knew how much he loved her.

"What was it like for you when we broke up?" Kiara asked.

Teague opened his eyes and a flash of sadness crossed his face. "I was so angry at first. I didn't know what to think–I went back and forth between wondering if you were cheating on me, to knowing something was seriously wrong but you didn't trust me enough to tell me what. I never would've guessed you were in so much pain. You hid it so well..." Teague said. He touched her face and the sorrow returned to his eyes. "I used the anger to keep myself from reaching out, even though there was nothing I wanted more than to talk to you. And then you weren't at school that day and I couldn't help it–I had to make sure you were okay."

Kiara tried to imagine the situation from his point of view. Guilt dripped into her stomach–she would have gone mad if she knew he was hiding something but wouldn't tell her what.

"Kiara, I don't know if I've told you this or not, but it means the world to me that you opened up about everything. I know you're still embarrassed to talk about it, but just know that I think you're beautiful and you don't need to change your body."

"Thank you," Kiara said. Teague reached up to wipe a tear from her face–she hadn't realized she'd started crying at his words. Kiara pushed her lips to his, hard, kissing him with an urgency that even she didn't understand. Kiara figured she should have felt sad in this moment–they had almost lost each other–but all she could feel was the desire scorching across her entire body, perhaps *because* they had almost lost each other. Kiara twisted her hands in Teague's hair and straddled him, pushing him down on the grass. Teague's body responded to her movement, and he grabbed her hips and pushed his pelvis up to her, causing Kiara to feel how turned on he was through his jeans.

"*This* is what I meant when I said I wanted to be with you..." Kiara leaned forward and whispered, her hair falling around Teague's face.

"OH." Teague's eyes opened wide as he registered her words. He grinned. "I want you too, *so* bad–but here? At Taron's?"

"Mhmm," Kiara said as Teague moved her hips up and down. "Bathroom."

Kiara stood and pulled him with her, practically dragging him inside to the master bathroom. As soon as the door was locked, Teague's mouth was on hers, grabbing her breasts as he kissed her. Kiara unzipped his pants and pushed them around his ankles. Without missing a beat, she hoisted up her dress and pulled her nude boyshorts down. She leaned over the bathroom counter, ready for him.

"Oh my God..." Teague groaned. "What did I do to deserve you?"

Kiara heard the condom package rip open and watched Teague in the mirror as he tore off his shirt and positioned himself behind her. She could feel how wet she was as he pushed himself inside of her, causing them both to moan in pleasure.

"I've missed you," Teague said.

Kiara groaned in response as she watched him in the mirror, his abs clenching each time he pushed into her. After only a few minutes it was enough to make her orgasm, calling out his name as she came. This seemed to push Teague over the edge, and he came seconds after her, making a noise so sexy in his climax that Kiara committed it to memory, right then and there.

Somehow they wound up on the cool tile floor, limbs twisted together and panting heavily in their post-coital bliss. Kiara had never experienced pleasure that intense before in her life.

"I don't ever want to know what it's like to be without you again," Teague whispered.

Kiara snuggled into him and sighed. She traced her fingers on the line down the middle of his dark chest, between his muscles. "I'm sorry, you know," she said. "For what I put you through. I never meant to hurt you. I was so lost in it all that I didn't stop to think about how it was affecting you."

"It's okay, baby," Teague murmured, kissing her on the forehead. He shifted his weight so that he was resting his head on his hand, his other arm draped over her hips. "How have you been doing?"

Kiara thought for a while. How *was* she doing? She knew she wasn't great yet, but she was getting better.

"You know, sometimes I'm good, and sometimes I'm not," she began with a sigh. "I don't think this is something I'm going to get over immediately–there's no miracle cure for it, as much as I want there to be. Like Ari said, 'nothing worthwhile is ever easy'. So I guess," Kiara held up her hand and ticked off her fingers for each item as she spoke. "I'm just going to pay attention to when my thoughts are becoming critical or mean to myself and change my focus to something good instead until the bad mood passes. Look at food as a way to nourish and heal myself, not as something terrifying that's going to make me gain weight. Love and celebrate my body and be good to it, like doing fun workouts and feeling how strong I'm becoming instead of trying to see how skinny I can get. Be honest with you guys about what I'm thinking and feeling, and try to be gentle with myself. I've also found it helps when I dance. It gets me out of my head funnily enough. That's the best I can do for now."

Teague ran a hand over her hair with a smile on his face. "What kind of good stuff do you focus on instead, besides me?"

Kiara laughed and kissed him. "Small or big things that I'm happy to have in my life. It could be something as simple as a moment when I held the door open for a little old man at the store and he smiled at me, to recognizing how lucky I am to have such understanding parents. And then it just flows from there, like the other day I realized I was grateful for the fact that I make myself laugh so much–that's a gift."

"How'd you figure all this out?"

"I've been listening to podcasts and reading books and paying attention to what feels like it's helping and what isn't, then making sure to do more of whatever works for me. But I couldn't have figured it all out without my friends, parents, and wonderful boyfriend."

Kiara blushed a bit when the word "boyfriend" fell out of her mouth; they still hadn't talked about being back together officially, but she figured their recent bathroom tryst had pretty much sealed the deal.

"I'm so proud of you, baby. You just let me know when and how I can help," Teague said, happiness radiating in his tone–he must have caught the boyfriend slip. He nuzzled his head into her neck, warming her skin with his breath.

A knock on the bathroom door made them both jump.

"Just a sec!" Kiara yelled. She sat up in a flash, grabbing at her clothes, then looked at Teague. At the sight of him, she cracked up into her hand–Teague was wearing her panties on his head like a bandana as he jumped around the bathroom.

"Teague!" She shot at him in a whisper. "What're you doing!?"

Teague smiled at her and danced around, throwing her bra around his head as well. "You said dancing helps you, right? So let's dance!"

She took his hand and he pulled her into a ridiculous tango across the bathroom. She spun away from him and he twirled her back in, then spun her out and around until she couldn't see straight and was breathless with laughter.

The knocking grew more impatient, but Kiara couldn't stop laughing. Teague did a ridiculous final leap and then burst out laughing himself. Kiara didn't know if it was because it felt so good for them to be together again, or that there was such a level of relief that they had cleared the distrust between them, but they laughed so hard that they cried, and even then they couldn't stop.

There was a mutter of obscenities from outside the door and

then the sound of retreating footsteps. Kiara finally caught her breath and looked at Teague, happy tears still streaming down her face as she smiled at him.

God, it felt good to laugh again.

CHAPTER 24
A, J, K

Ariana walked around the backyard in a tranquil daze, enjoying the serene harmonics by Shallou emanating from the speakers. A full moon hung low over the party, casting a soft glow on the grass. Ariana looked for Kiara and Jade as she wandered; she hadn't seen much of her two best friends since earlier and was beginning to miss them. Ariana had always felt as though soul mates weren't necessarily significant others–soul mates could appear in the form of friends, and that's what Kiara and Jade were: two of her soul mates. No matter how often they hung out, she still inevitably missed them when they were gone. Ariana came to a stop by the deep end of the pool and sat on the edge, carefully taking her white tennis shoes off before she dipped her feet in. The cool water felt so good she silently wished she'd brought a bathing suit so she could dive in.

"Ari!" A voice shouted from behind her. Ariana brightened as she turned to see Daire walking up. He looked handsome. He was wearing jeans and a tighter than usual shirt–*had he been spending more time in the gym lately?* she wondered. His brown hair was slightly messy in a way that looked like he'd just rolled out of bed, and it worked for him.

"Hey, you! I heard you were here," Daire said as he sat next to her, tearing his shoes off before lowering his legs in the pool. He pulled Ariana into a hug and she breathed in his cologne, feeling at home. How was it so incredibly simple to hang out with Daire? There was no fear, no sudden mood swings from him–a welcome change from her tumultuous relationship with Lukas. The simple thought of Lukas made her want to drown out her mind. She was tired of him being her main focus.

A spurt of impish inspiration washed over Ariana, and her lips turned up into a mischievous smile.

"Can I tell you a secret?" Ariana asked while discreetly sliding her phone away from the ledge. Daire nodded and she put her arms around his neck, leaning in toward his ear. He breathed deeply, and she wondered momentarily if he was enjoying the smell of her perfume.

"I just really, *really* want to get in the pool," Ariana whispered as she leaned with all of her might, causing them both to fall sideways into the water.

"Ariana!" Daire yelled as they went in.

Ariana stilled underwater, relaxing her body and welcoming the silence that came from being submerged. She opened her eyes in the mild saltwater and flipped onto her back, watching the bubbles zigzag to the surface, up toward the world she wasn't quite ready to re-enter yet.

After a few moments Daire appeared as a blurry outline looming over her, and then his strong arms were lifting her out of the water. Ariana took in a huge gulp of air.

"I knew your phone was waterproof!" Ariana squealed as soon as she could, hoping Daire wasn't too mad. She opened her eyes to a slight stinging sensation from the salt water and found Daire's face close to hers, his expression a mixture of amusement and something else... desire? Ariana realized he was still holding her tight, cradled in his arms.

Daire leaned down, and Ariana caught on a second too late to what was happening. His mouth found hers; his lips were gentle and soft, and not unpleasant in the least. Ariana was surprised to find that she felt something in the kiss, although it was lightyears away from when Lukas kissed her. After a moment she pulled back, gently placing a hand on Daire's chest. He set her in the pool, gazing at her expectantly.

Ariana put her hands to her face. "D...I can't..."

"Why not?"

They stood facing each other in the color-changing water–it vacillated from dark green to purple to pink to blue as Ariana flew through several excuses in her mind, quickly assessing which one would remove her from the sticky situation while explaining herself somewhat accurately.

"I just got out of something..." she began. "With a guy from another school–you don't know him–but he basically played me. I found out he had a girlfriend the entire time we were talking, but I fell for him before I knew that and I'm still in love with him. I'm not ready for anything else yet. Like you weren't, when we first met."

Daire's face fell, but he nodded. "I get it."

He took a few moments, his face displaying several emotions as he thought through the situation. "But..." Daire started, his face finally breaking out into a grin. "I am now committed to helping you get over this dude. Like you helped me–you had my back, now I'll have yours. Anytime you're sad or down or missing this guy you just call me, alright? And I won't hit on you anymore... not till you ask me to."

Ariana faltered. "That won't bother you?"

Daire shrugged. "Eh. I'm still benefiting from this scenario. I'm not *that* selfless."

They laughed, and Ariana tuned back into the party around them. Several of their friends nearby *must* have seen them kiss. She wondered if Lukas would hear about it, but then redirected her attention to how lucky she was to have such a good guy willing to be there for her, even if their relationship would probably get a little complicated at times. Ariana couldn't help but feel a million times better when Daire was around, and she needed that right now, just like he'd needed her companionship when getting over his first love.

"Ready for another dip?" Daire swooped her up in his arms and threw her in the air, then caught her in a cradle while she screamed and laughed.

"No!! D!"

He threw her in the air again, higher this time, and she heard laughter and whoops from the partygoers around the pool. Taron ran over, beer in hand, yelling "Cannonball!" as he jumped into the deep end next to them. Ariana burst out laughing–Taron had managed to keep his beer above the water the entire time and when he reemerged, he immediately took a sip. "POOL PARTY!" he screamed a second later.

At Taron's command, everyone threw their phones on the tables and began jumping into the pool. A few brave souls even stripped down to their underwear before diving in. Jade and Alora made a beeline for them, nearly jumping on top of Ariana in the water. Ariana clapped her hands in childlike delight when the girls came up for air, gasping and hugging and laughing.

This was *exactly* what she needed.

It was nearly 3 a.m. when they made it back to Kiara's house. The walk home had been pleasant at first, but now all three girls were beginning to come down off of the MDMA.

"Oh my god, this is *horrible*," Kiara said as they trudged in the front door.

"Uggggghhh," Jade groaned in response.

Ariana wiped a hand across her sweat-covered forehead as she made her way up the stairs behind Kiara and Jade. A feverish chill ran through her body and her mouth began to water, which only happened before she threw up. Ariana gagged; then clapped a hand over her mouth. She wondered momentarily if she was going to make it up the stairs without puking. Ariana clutched at her stomach, willing the nausea to die down. Her mind was racing as well, back and forth between every worst possible scenario she could think of in her life.

She should've known, a feeling that incredible would of course have an opposite reaction to match its intensity. Ariana wanted to take a shower to wash off the sweat and chlorine, but the comedown was making her so depressed that she could do nothing more than strip down to her underwear and crawl under Kiara's sheets. Jade and Kiara did the same, no one saying a word as they got into bed.

The room was as quiet as a crypt as the girls tried to sleep, but unfortunately the drug still acted as an upper, keeping them awake. Ariana was sinking slowly into a deep, deep, gloom. She hadn't anticipated how scary and horrible a comedown could be. She tried to recall the triumph and celebration she'd felt earlier when she had ignored three of Lukas' calls, but all that came was an onslaught of despair. Ariana groaned. The comedown was still increasing in intensity, and an overwhelmingly terrifying thought ran through her mind–what if she never felt happy again?

"Never again," Ariana said, mostly to herself, but partly to let Jade and Kiara know too. Never again would she touch that drug. It wasn't worth it.

"Agreed," Jade said.

Kiara groaned in response.

Ariana squeezed her eyes shut and attempted to battle the feelings of hopelessness, knowing it was going to be a long night ahead.

Jade woke up Sunday evening with the fading daylight streaming in the windows–a gentle reminder that an entire day had been lost to her comedown. She agreed with Ariana: never again would she touch that stuff. The high was fun and all, but the aftermath was *so* not worth it. She sat up and stretched her tanned arms toward the ceiling.

Someone had left a large jug of water and a glass of green juice on the bedside table, and a blue sticky note next to the drinks read, "Drink up!" in Kiara's curvy script. Jade smiled, immediately thankful she could even smile again after the long night of hell they'd endured. None of the girls were able to sleep for a few hours after they'd gotten home, and Jade had spent the night tossing and turning in a miserable mental agony, worrying what Ian would think of her once she told him about her past. Jade grimaced as she remembered those wretched hours, feeling as though she was never going to get out of the depression and cursing herself for trying the damn drug in the first place.

A soft vibration emanated from the bedside table. The edges of Jade's mouth turned upward as she guessed who was contacting her. Even with the worry, the thought of Ian still warmed her. And to think, she'd nearly written him off for good before last night. Jade opened her phone to a multitude of texts and missed calls. She would deal with her mom first, she decided. She pressed call.

"Jade, honey, why didn't you answer your phone?" Her mother said immediately, her voice clipped. "Dani told me you almost got into an altercation."

"Yeah, Mom. It was fine though. I'm sorry I didn't call but... Dani actually stepped in to help me. She's the reason there *wasn't* an altercation."

"She... What?"

Jade laughed. "Dani defended me."

"Oh, Jade!" All anger left her mother's voice. "I'm so glad. I'm so relieved! You don't know how happy this makes me."

"I know, Mom. It makes me happy too."

"Okay, honey. Have fun with your friends. I'll see you tomorrow?"

"Yes. Love you, Mom. Oh, and by the way, you just might meet Ian after all."

She hung up after another minute of Lenee gushing about how happy she was at the turn of events. Jade couldn't shake the smile from her face. She looked through the texts from her friends, saving Ian's for last. Alora and Haiden had made it home safely. Jade had expected to hear from West, but there was nothing from him. The sides of her mouth dropped for a second, but then she remembered she still had Ian's texts to read.

4:16 a.m. Ian: I can't stop thinking about your lips.
1:23 p.m. Ian: I know you're probably sleeping in today. Give me a call when you're up

Jade's stomach did a flip as she read. Life was so exciting with Ian in it–she could hardly wait to see him. Maybe she could hold off from telling him for one more day, and just enjoy him before he looked at her with pity, or like she wasn't okay; like she might break. She shook her head and jumped out of bed, hurrying downstairs to find Ariana and Kiara in the living room, wrapped in blankets on the couch watching TV.

"Hey, sleepyhead," Kiara said. She looked adorable with her blonde hair pulled into a disheveled bun on the top of her head and dark blue framed glasses perched on her nose. "How're you feeling?"

"*Much* better," Jade said. "I can't believe how miserable that was."

"Right?" Ariana said. "Worst morning of my life. I'm so glad the bad part is done now, but I can't believe it's six. We wasted an entire day!"

"Good thing it's a three-day weekend!" Kiara said. She hopped up, seemingly reenergized. "So, J, we were about to call Lukas back and see what he has to say."

Jade took a seat on the couch and wrapped herself in a blanket. "Stop it. Really? Has he said anything else?"

"He texted me today asking to 'please talk'," Ariana said. "I'm curious as to what in the hell his explanation is going to be."

"Same. You should have him come over so that K and I can egg his truck while you're inside talking," Jade said.

Kiara laughed. "That's not a bad idea."

"Also, can Ian maybe come over later?"

"Yes!" Kiara said. "Teague's coming over later too."

Ariana sighed. "Great, now I have to get used to the fact that I'll forever be fifth-wheeling."

Jade narrowed her eyes at Ariana. "You will not be *forever* fifth-wheeling. Don't say that, you're just putting bullshit into your head."

Ariana put her hands up in defense and laughed. "Okay, okay, I won't."

"What about Daire? You could invite him over," Kiara said.

Jade had nearly forgotten that Daire kissed Ariana last night. She'd been pleasantly surprised, although it wasn't completely unexpected. Jade scooted over on the couch to curl up next to Ariana, who seemed to be mulling Kiara's proposition over in her mind.

"It's not like he doesn't live a few minutes away," Ariana said, tilting her head. A few golden tendrils of hair fell into her amber eyes. "And he did tell me to call him when I needed his help."

Kiara jumped up again. "Problem solved!"

The girls laughed and Jade pulled her phone out to text Ian back.

6:16 p.m. Jade: Don't laugh–I just woke up. I'd love to see you too. Want to come over to Kiara's in a bit?

Jade set her phone on the glass coffee table while butterflies danced in her stomach. Last night had been full of so many surprises that she still hadn't processed everything. She never would've guessed Dani would be the one to stick up for her when Kristin was out for blood. It was funny, Jade couldn't remember the last time Dani had done anything nice for her, yet she had been there when Jade needed her the most.

Jade had been ready, as always, to defend herself, but she knew somehow that Dani stepping in had been way more effective at holding Kristin off than anything she could've done on her own. Plus, it made Jade look as though she and Dani were a united front, even though that was the farthest thing from the truth. But even that wouldn't hold Kristin off forever, Jade knew. She would tell Ian her secret first, she decided, before Kristin could twist it.

Her cell phone vibrated from the coffee table, and Jade sucked in her breath at the ID photo. She forgot she'd assigned a new photo to Ian's contact last night–a shirtless picture of him she found on his social media, his muscles glistening with sweat after a long football practice. She picked up, struggling to regain her composure.

"Hi," Jade said, hearing the smile in her own voice.

"Hey," Ian said. "I miss you."

"I'm sure I would miss you too, but I've only been awake for about ten minutes."

"You know you miss me," Ian said with confidence, and Jade's smile widened. He was right–she couldn't wait to see him again.

"Come over to Kiara's in an hour?"

"I'll be there."

"Good. See you soon."

Jade placed her phone on the coffee table, turning her full attention back to Kiara and Ariana, who had been watching her.

"I don't think I've ever seen you so excited about a guy before," Kiara said.

"I don't know, I remember her thinking West was pretty hot freshman year," Ariana said. Jade glanced at Ariana, wondering why she had chosen this moment to bring that up. Did Ariana know something had passed between them before the party yesterday? Jade still had no idea what to make of that, but she was sure it was probably Weston just being Weston–i.e. a man whore.

"Very funny," Jade said. "I thought we promised never to talk about the fact that I *ever* had a crush on West."

"You *tried* to make us promise that," Kiara said.

Jade let out a laugh. "I'll never live it down."

She looked at her hands, scared to bring up what was on her

mind. "Guys, Kristin knows about what my Dad did. I don't know how, but she knows."

"What?" Ariana said. Kiara pursed her lips.

"Yeah, I guess I have to tell Ian even though I'm scared. That way she won't have anything over me."

"I understand why you'd want to keep that private, but Jade, what's the worst that could happen if Ian knew? If anyone knew? Why are you afraid?" Ariana asked.

"Because," Jade said, sucking in a deep breath. "Once someone knows your dad killed himself from a mental health thing, they might look at you differently. I don't want that. Or anyone to think I'm going to end up like him because I have his genes. Or that I'm not enough because he didn't think I was enough to stick around for." All at once Jade was crying. She couldn't believe it. She tasted the tears as they rushed down her face and slipped into the sides of her mouth.

"Jade, do you think that?" Ariana said, her face contorted with shock and sadness.

"I don't know, maybe sometimes," Jade said, her voice muffled. "It's always been there, in the back of my mind. That maybe I wasn't lovable enough to stay on this planet for."

"That's not true," Kiara said.

Jade kept going, unable to stop now that she'd admitted to her deepest fear. She looked at the ground while she spoke. "And if other people find out that I wasn't enough for my own dad, they'll finally know the truth. That I'm not lovable. I'm not good enough. Behind the beauty bullshit that they think they love me for."

Jade couldn't look up. She couldn't look into their eyes now that she'd put it out there. Her stomach coiled and she felt like she might puke. She twisted the black leather bracelet on her wrist. "Sometimes I don't even understand why you guys love me. It's weird," she said, her voice so low it was barely audible.

"Jade," Kiara said, her voice like a sad sigh. Ariana was crying then, her arms around Jade's neck so fast that it was almost painful. Then Kiara was holding her too, holding them both. "You're brave and loyal and hilarious, how could you ever think that? Everyone wants to be friends with you."

"You're more than enough. There's never been a doubt in my mind about that. But you have to know that for yourself," Ariana said into her shoulder.

Their words made Jade cry harder, and they sat there, holding on to each other for what felt like hours. She cried into their arms until the hot heat in her stomach cooled. The tears started to slow, and Jade finally nodded, lighter from her confession somehow. "Thank you."

"If you don't want to tell him yet you don't have to. Just know that none of what you just said is true. I love you more than you'll ever know," Kiara said.

"Me too," Ariana said.

Jade nodded again. "I love you both. I'm gonna go shower and make my decision."

"We're right here," Kiara said as Jade climbed the steps.

"We're not going anywhere," Ariana said.

* * *

"I can't believe Jade could ever think like that," Kiara said, still in partial shock.

"I think we're all learning that no one really knows what's going on in someone else's mind. Even when it's your best friends."

"You can say that again." Kiara readjusted the bun on her head. "Do you want some tea?"

"Tea is *so* needed right now."

Kiara made her way into the kitchen with Bob licking at her heels the entire way. She stretched her arms to the ceiling, relieving the soreness in her body from her rendezvous with Teague in the bathroom. Every time she moved and her muscles stung, she was brought back to the delicious moments from the night before.

She bit her lip and blushed as she thought about leaning over the counter with Teague moving behind her, his muscles flexing with each push–she would savor that memory for the rest of her life.

Kiara grabbed a turquoise and gold teapot from the cabinet, humming as she set about to make pumpkin spice tea. Something about making tea in the kettle soothed her–maybe because her mother used to make tea when it stormed and they would cuddle up and enjoy the sound of raindrops hitting their roof as they sipped from clay teacups.

A low rumbling came from Kiara's stomach, reminding her that everyone needed to eat. She grabbed fresh apples, strawberries, and bananas and began chopping them up. The music app on her phone switched to Let Go by Frou Frou, one of her mom's favorites. Kiara smiled as she turned up the portable speaker.

"What're you doing in there?" Ariana called.

"Come and see!"

Kiara pulled pasture-raised organic eggs, avocados, and gluten-free English muffins from the fridge, her arms full as Ariana wandered over. "Ohh! Breakfast for dinner? My *favorite.*"

Kiara smiled again, the happiness that had been lost to the horrible comedown seeping back into her body. After such a terrible night, she was finding it easy to appreciate all the good she had in her life: parents who loved her, a home that her two best friends could come over to at any time, a wonderful boyfriend who cherished her, and she was figuring out her mental health. Her new approach of looking at food as a way to nurture her body was making a substantial difference with how she viewed eating... could it actually be exciting?

"I think I want to start learning how to cook really healthy stuff," Kiara said as she cracked the eggs and poured them into a pan. "And like, make videos of me cooking and talking about how each ingredient is good for you. Maybe I could help other people like me."

Ariana clapped her hands. "That's an incredible idea, K."

"Yeah, it's like, when I ask myself whether or not certain foods are going to nourish my body, I make much better choices, and feel less like I want to throw up. The eggs and avocado are high in protein and healthy fats that support brain function, clarity, and a better overall mood. And the fruit is good for fiber, calcium, and a lot of different vitamins. I'm also better able to keep my mind in check and keep the food down when I know exactly *how* it's good for me."

Ariana nodded. "Yes. I love it."

"It's wild how simple changes in my thoughts have had such a profound effect on my life. I want to share that."

Ariana beamed. "Let me know how I can help."

An excited noise of approval came from the stairs and Jade reappeared. "Do I smell breakfast?"

"Mhmm," Kiara murmured as the eggs sizzled in the pan. Ariana began cutting the avocados while Jade took a seat on the barstool.

"Did you decide?" Kiara asked. How in the world someone like Jade could believe she wasn't enough to be loved was beyond her. And to think, Kiara had yelled at them the other day, thinking they could never understand how she felt when she thought she wasn't lovable at her current weight.

"I decided I'm gonna see how I feel when he gets here," Jade said. "I feel much better about it all now though. After saying it out loud. I don't know... I think it took some of the power away from it."

"That's amazing," Ariana said.

"Did you call Lukas yet?" Jade asked.

"No." Ariana sighed. "I can't stop looking at the text from him though, hence why I need to be doing something else with my hands right now."

"How many times did he end up calling you?" Jade asked while scrunching her hair in the towel. Kiara studied Jade as she spoke. Her bravado was back on full force, but Kiara knew now that Jade had worked to become as strong as she was. She was a fighter.

"Four times total."

Kiara clenched her jaw. She'd known Lukas wouldn't let Ariana get over him so easily. She wondered what his excuse would be this time, and what would happen now that he was officially with Olivia. Would he try and string Ariana along? "What an assface," Kiara muttered.

"That's definitely the title of his memoir," Ariana said.

Kiara and Jade both let out a hard laugh.

"Well, at least eat something before you call him. You'll be more rational on a full stomach," Jade said.

"Aww, J. I love it when *you're* the one that goes into Mom mode," Kiara teased.

"Hey!" Ariana said, putting on a fake pout.

Kiara did her best old English woman accent and announced, "Breakfast is ready girrrllls!" as she assembled avocado and egg on each English muffin. She placed the bowl of chopped fruit in the middle of the table and poured tea as Ariana and Jade took their seats. They dug in, making noises of appreciation as they ate. Kiara kept her attention on the nutrients the meal was providing to her body and mind, and didn't have the slightest urge to throw it up. She smiled to herself, basking in the seemingly simple yet monumental moment.

"I'm afraid," Ariana said, picking up their conversation from earlier. "What if he's with Olivia when I call?"

"Hopefully he is!" Kiara said. "She deserves to know what he's doing too."

"That's not my place though," Ariana said. "Besides, she would most likely stay with him and end up hating me."

"Why do people do that?" Jade questioned. "Hate the other person when the guy is caught cheating, I mean. It's ridiculous. Clearly the common denominator is the asshole you're dating."

"Maybe it's easier than facing the truth," Ariana said with a sigh.

"Either way," Kiara said. "Don't be afraid to call. Whatever happens is his mess to deal with."

Ariana blew the air out from her cheeks and reached for her phone with a trembling hand. "Screw it, right?"

Kiara nodded in support as Ariana paced around the kitchen with the phone pressed to her ear. She found herself nervous *for* Ariana... whatever was going to happen, Kiara didn't see how it could end well–not when it involved Lukas.

CHAPTER 25

Ariana

The shrill ringing from the other end of the line permeated Ariana's eardrum as she waited to see whether or not Lukas would pick up. Any modicum of power she'd held had vanished the instant she pressed dial. Ariana picked at her white-pink nail polish while her heart pounded out of control. She gave a small start when the line clicked–truthfully, she hadn't expected him to answer.

"Hey," Lukas said, his voice draining the feeling from her limbs. "Where are you right now?"

Ariana hesitated–she hadn't been expecting an immediate question, let alone that one. "Uh, Kiara's, why?"

"I'm coming over."

"What? No!"

She gripped the phone, battling with herself–of course she desperately wanted to see him, but that was the point–she didn't have control over herself when it came to Lukas. If she saw him in person, she didn't know what she'd do.

"It's too late, I'm on the way," Lukas said. "I'll see you soon."

The line disconnected and Ariana stood in a daze for a few moments, the phone still pressed to her ear. Jade and Kiara stared at her expectantly.

She lowered the phone to the table, numb. "He's on his way over."

Jade's eyes got so wide they looked like they were about to pop out of her head. "What!? I was joking when I said for him to come over!"

"You heard me Jade! I didn't invite him. UGH, he is SO infuriating!"

Ariana stomped away from the table and charged upstairs to change out of her pajamas. Once in Kiara's room, she sunk onto the bed and put her head in her hands, wondering how she was going to face Lukas now that he had a girlfriend. She rocked herself back and forth, attempting to soothe the conflicting emotions running through her. She wasn't ready to see him yet–it would be too painful to look at him and know he wasn't hers. That he wasn't ever going to be. And yet, in a confusing way she was still excited that she'd be near him soon.

She stood and shook her body out. She decided not to change out of her pajama shorts and tank top or get ready for Lukas in any sort of way. She splashed some cold water on her face and brushed her teeth to feel refreshed.

"There," Ariana said, attempting to calm her brain. "I'm ready."

She took a deep breath and grabbed her phone right as it vibrated. She looked out the window and her heart did a flip. There was Lukas' truck, waiting for her like so many times before, only this time everything was wrong and broken.

"Ari?" Kiara called.

"I know!" Ariana called back as she raced down the stairs. "I'll be back in a bit."

Jade scowled at the front window. "Good luck. Stay strong."

"We're here," Kiara said, frowning.

Ariana tried to give them a smile, but it was too difficult to muster with the anxiety dancing in her veins. She settled on a nod instead and headed for the front door, doing her best to control her emotions. *How wild is it*, Ariana thought, *that no matter how much your friends support you or are there for you, you still have to do the hardest things alone*?

Ariana walked up to Lukas' truck without really looking at it and hopped inside in one swift move. The electricity between them instantly came to life, a current purring through her before she even shut the door. Ariana kept her head facing the window–she couldn't bring herself to look at him just yet. How was that feeling still there after everything he'd done? She almost asked where Olivia was to be rude, but it hurt too much to say her name–to admit that Lukas had someone else waiting for him.

She could feel him watching her. She heard him open his mouth to say something but then close it again. He sighed. She turned toward him. The moment his dark eyes caught hers, she regretted it. An overpowering longing took hold of her, followed by sorrow. Ariana willed herself to recall her anger, remembering his blatant stare at her across the cafeteria after kissing Olivia, and felt the fire return behind her eyes.

"Talk," she said gruffly.

"Ariana," Lukas pleaded. "Can I please drive us somewhere so we can get out and talk comfortably? I don't want to have this conversation sitting in my truck."

Lukas looked hotter than ever she realized, and Ariana wondered briefly if he had done that on purpose. A new flood of fury ran through her and gave her strength. "I'm not going *anywhere* with you. We can sit in Kiara's backyard."

Lukas glanced up and down the street. Ariana let out a loud laugh when she realized the truth: Lukas was worried someone would recognize his truck at Kiara's house, which would raise questions with Olivia. How funny that she now knew what his then-puzzling actions meant. Ariana raised her eyebrows, challenging him, but he didn't say a word. Was everything he did thoroughly self-serving?

Ariana stepped down from the truck while sending a text to Jade and Kiara, letting them know the situation. Lukas trailed behind her, and Ariana used the few moments of silence to regain her composure. They settled into the wicker patio chairs that overlooked Kiara's backyard and Ariana allowed herself to look at him again. He was dressed in a tight-fitting white t-shirt, his hair perfectly in disarray. He was so casually handsome that it hurt–before, she would have thought about their possibilities together. Now all she could see was Olivia's hands all over him.

"I don't know how to start," Lukas began. "Or where."

"How about the part where you lied repeatedly? Or the part where you told me you loved me while you were seeing someone else?" She flinched at the last words.

Lukas' head snapped up and he stared at her, his eyebrows furrowed. "Look, I was trying to protect both of you but I got in over my head. I don't know what I thought would happen but I just knew I couldn't give either of you up. I'm in love with two people... Do you believe that's possible? I didn't until it happened to me."

Ariana blanched at his confession but said nothing. She hadn't failed to notice that Lukas' "apology" was all about him.

"Ariana," Lukas begged. Her eyes stung. She missed the way he said her name. "I still love you," he said.

Her head spun–her heart rejoiced while her mind remained devastated. She shook her head. *I know better now*, she thought. *Lukas' confessions of love don't hold any promises.* "I'm new to this, but I'm pretty sure that's not how you treat someone you love. And maybe you can be in love with two people, but I guess you chose which one you love more. So please, leave me alone and let me move on."

"I wasn't trying to choose. It just happened, really." Lukas said, somehow looking like he was telling the truth. "Is that what you really want? For me to leave you alone?"

Ariana stilled. It just happened? The fuck did that mean? She willed herself to say the word yes–just a simple "yes" and nothing further, but she couldn't. If she was being honest with herself, she didn't want him to leave her alone. Not now, not ever.

"Ari?" Lukas said.

"Only my friends can call me Ari," she snapped, her voice turning to ice. It was as though she were channeling Jade.

Lukas looked like he'd been slapped, and she almost laughed. The whole situation was so impossibly complicated now. And he had done it. He had done all of it.

"Of course that's not what I want, Lukas, but I need to move on," she said, the words tumbling out now. "I wanted to be with you–how could I not want to be around you? Every inch of me is screaming how much I want you right now, but that's so wrong. You've made it so that it's wrong for us to even be speaking like this. You can't imagine how this feels."

"I *can* imagine," Lukas said, lowering his voice. "Daire came over today and told me about how he kissed you. I couldn't say or do *anything*. I had to sit there and listen."

Triumph washed over her. So Daire had inadvertently given Lukas a taste of his own medicine–he deserved that. The smallest smile crept to her lips. She hoped it had hurt.

"Are you going to start dating him?" Lukas asked. He looked pained.

She scowled at him. "I don't know, I don't usually switch that quickly from guy to guy."

Lukas made a face at the jab but then softened, looking her in the eye. Ariana waited for him to say something, but he only continued to stare at her, his eyes exploring hers. And despite the screaming in her head telling her to turn her back on him, she couldn't make herself look away.

Instead, she took the next few moments to get her fill of his face: she looked from his neck to his angular jaw to his full lips, then finally back to his brown eyes, stopping there. Something was passing between them; maybe an understanding of what they would miss or an acknowledgment of what wouldn't be. Her stomach tightened and her eyes stung as she began to mourn the loss of him. Lukas must have seen it in her face, because he reached his hand out and tucked a strand of hair behind her ear. Ariana didn't move away immediately–she couldn't–she was relatively sure this was the last contact they would have, and decided to allow herself the moment.

Lukas leaned over and Ariana froze. He brushed his lips to her cheek. "I'm never going to stop loving you. Even if you don't believe me."

Ariana's insides snapped. This goodbye was torturous and he wasn't fighting fair. But then again, he never had. She knew though that whatever they were or had been, however magical and incredible and intense, needed to be over.

"I don't trust you." Ariana put a hand on his chest and pushed him away. "I think we're done here."

"Please. I–"

"Just one question. All those times when you had to leave me abruptly, or your phone kept going off, or you canceled our plans... that was all Olivia, wasn't it?"

Lukas involuntarily flexed his jaw.

"I didn't see you before, but I see you now," Ariana said. She stood and walked inside, leaving Lukas alone with his mistakes.

The moment she closed the door tears cascaded down her cheeks. She knew she'd done the right thing, but it was still too painful to feel like it. Minutes later she heard his engine roar to life and retreat down the street. Her phone vibrated and she took it out slowly, fearful that it was from him and fearful that it wasn't.

7:35 p.m. Lukas: you'll be my greatest tragedy.
7:36 p.m. Ariana: I hope it hurts.

Ariana let out a sob and deleted the texts.

CHAPTER 26

J, K, A

Jade sat on the couch with Ariana's head in her lap, lazily running her fingers through her hair, twisting and braiding the long waves. Kiara was sprawled out on the adjacent sofa, still in her pajamas and cradling a bowl of Himalayan pink sea salt popcorn. The girls had decided to put on a movie, and Ariana demanded they watch the furthest thing from a romance possible, so they had gone with Jade's all-time favorite classic: Fight Club. Jade could totally argue that Fight Club was a romance, but she kept her mouth shut.

"I swear, this is the only instance where I like the movie better than the book," Ariana said.

"You're definitely the only person I know who's even read the book," Kiara said, letting out a laugh.

Jade smiled while continuing to run her fingers over Ariana's scalp, hoping to soothe her. Ariana appeared to be doing all right considering she'd walked away from Lukas, seemingly for good. Jade was proud it'd been Ariana who left Lukas instead of vice versa for a change. When Ariana came back inside earlier after their goodbye, she'd cried for a while, but she hadn't been hysterical, which Jade took as a good sign.

The doorbell rang and Kiara popped up to answer it. "Boys

are here!" she trilled. Jade shifted in her seat, eager to see Ian's handsome face. Ariana raised her head off Jade's lap.

"You excited, wiggle worm?" Ariana joked.

Jade nodded while looking into Ariana's eyes. She seemed to be telling Jade something without saying a word–that she loved her, and that she had nothing to worry about. That they would all be there for each other, no matter what came at them. Jade smiled. She felt like she could take on the world, and she knew she was drawing strength from Ariana.

Ian stepped around the corner and a pleasant stinging sensation ran across Jade's stomach. He was so gorgeous when he smiled, staring at Jade like he hadn't seen her in days. She stood and threw her arms around his neck, breathing in his mouthwatering cologne.

Ariana excused herself to make more tea, giving them some privacy. Kiara and Teague's laughter echoed from the front hall while Edward Norton was on screen, desperately trying to figure out the origin of the Fight Clubs across the country.

"I love this movie," Ian said as he took a seat on the couch, smiling shyly at her with his blue eyes shining. "It's good to see you."

Jade stood still for a moment, fighting the urge to straddle him right then and there. Instead, she gave him a mischievous smile and took a seat on his lap. Ian let out a groan that was half surprise and half pleasure and closed his arms around her.

"It's good to see you, too," Jade said, her face inches from his.

Ian seemed to be in a bit of a shock from having Jade on his lap, but he quickly recovered. "If I'd known we could be like this, I would've come after you a long time ago."

He tilted his chin and kissed her gently. Jade felt dizzy for a moment; she hadn't realized how much she'd been craving Ian's lips on hers.

"I think it's best we got together when we did. I don't know if I was ready to face Kristin and her gang head-on my freshman year," Jade said.

"I'm sorry again about last night," Ian said, clenching his jaw. "I can't believe Kristin came after you like that."

"I can. Easily." She picked at her hair, not wanting to meet Ian's eyes.

"I'm going to have a talk with her and make sure it doesn't happen again," Ian said, his brow set in determination. Jade froze. If Ian tried to have a talk with Kristin, she would definitely tell him everything.

"No offense, but I don't think you have as much influence over her as you might think. Thank you for the offer though."

"Well, either way, she'll only look stupid since we're together now," Ian said, a crooked smile returning to his lips.

"That's true," Jade said, smiling back. A small voice in her head was still worrying though, chattering away that Jade might've won this battle, but her defeat over Kristin would have its repercussions. Kristin had looked like a fool in front of a crowd, and there was no way she'd let that be the last word. She would try and hurt or sabotage Jade at some point, there was no doubt about it. So should she just tell Ian now? Would she only be telling him out of fear if she did?

At that last thought, Jade realized she didn't want to tell him yet. She wouldn't let fear run her emotions. She wanted him to know her, *sure*, but not out of panic. Not on someone else's time-line. With that decision, a peace settled over her. She wouldn't be reactive, no matter the circumstances.

And at least when the time did come, Dani supported her telling Ian, which made it a little easier. Who could've guessed that Kristin Long would be the one to cause Dani to act like a sister again? Jade chuckled to herself, joyous at the thought. No matter how fleeting the moment had been, Dani's actions last night had shown Jade that she *did* care on some level, and here Jade had thought that Dani had nothing left but hate for her. It was a huge step for their relationship.

Jade slid off of Ian's lap to lie on the couch, leaving her legs over his thighs. Ian looked disappointed for a moment, but then grinned again. Jade studied his sexy uneven smile, wondering what it would be like for Ian to know everything about her–her likes, dislikes, fears, truths, secrets... *everything*, and she him. For the first time, she was *excited* about it.

"I want to know you more," Ian said, reading her mind.

"I want to know you, too."

"So can I take you on another date?"

"I think that can be arranged," Jade said sweetly, sitting up to plant another kiss on his lips, feeling like she would never get enough.

* * *

Kiara looked up at the pale half moon, enjoying the evening air and sounds of nocturnal nature coming to life around her back patio. A few minutes ago she suggested they leave the boys inside to get some privacy and talk, mainly to check in on Ariana.

As they sat in comfortable silence, Kiara swirled her tea around with a spoon, dripping a few drops of honey into the whirling chamomile, testing herself to see if it made her anxious or not. She sat still, watching the honey float to the bottom of the turquoise teacup. To her greatest pleasure, as long as she kept in mind the health benefits of honey, and that it was okay to have some good sugar every once in a while, she didn't find it such a big deal.

She let out a breath of relief. She knew she still had a long way to go on the road of her recovery, but every day she was feeling stronger. Even when she did fall into a panic, she was getting herself out of it much faster now. Baby steps were key, she was realizing–learning and implementing small changes each day led to the biggest change and overall improvement. Through her health and self-improvement books and podcasts she was learning ways to become healthier and slim down over a prolonged amount of time rather than a shortcut like throwing up meals or meticulously counting calories. In life, those kinds of quick fixes usually ended up doing more harm than good later on down the road. Like putting a Band-Aid on a broken leg–they just weren't sustainable. But most importantly, she was realizing that her body was healthy and beautiful the way it was. No one was harder on her than she was on herself. And now that she'd braved the onslaught of bad thoughts a few times without throwing up and knew that there was always eventually an end to the episodes, she could tell herself it would be over soon, and knew it to be true, even if it didn't feel like the truth in the moment.

Kiara was still struggling with counting calories, which had become so ingrained in her that she almost did it without a thought, but somehow she knew she would figure out a way to stop it all together eventually–she had faith. What she'd learned from her ordeal, above all else, was that positive results took belief–belief in herself and belief that this tribulation in her life was there to teach her something.

Laughter rang out from inside the house, and Kiara turned to see Teague and Ian bonding over some video game. As if he sensed her gaze, Teague turned toward the window and a slow grin spread over his face when he saw her looking at him. Her stomach and groin clenched in a pleasant way, and she thought back to last night, when she and Teague had raced out of the bathroom after finally getting dressed, leaving a few very confused looking people staring after them. They'd run straight into the pool, joining the impromptu pool party Ariana had inadvertently started with Daire.

Kiara smiled into her tea at the memory, then realized what a huge step it was that she'd allowed herself some honey in the tea without any guilt. Two weeks ago she wouldn't have *dared.* She laughed out loud at the absurdity of the thought. Who would've guessed something as simple as honey in tea would become a triumph for her?

Jade and Ariana laughed at Kiara's sudden outburst of laughter, and she grinned at them. Ariana's answering smile faltered at the edges. Kiara wanted to help Ariana as much as she'd helped her, but she didn't yet have an experience of truly losing love. Maybe what she'd learned from the eating disorders could help though.

"Ari, if I've learned anything from all this, it's that everything gets easier with time. Whatever you're feeling now–it'll heal. It may not happen as quickly as you want it to, but it *will* heal, and you'll move on, and be happier than you thought you could be," Kiara said. "But now is the hard part, the beginning of the healing, and this is when you're probably going to be tested. No one ever wants to say that, but it's true. So brace yourself, and know that we're going to be here for you one hundred percent of the way."

Ariana sniffed and nodded her head solemnly. "I'm so glad you're doing better, K. I was scared for you."

"I was too," Jade said softly.

"I know," Kiara said. "I was scared too. I wasn't in control anymore. But you two saved me when I couldn't help myself."

"No," Jade said. "You were ready to save yourself; you just needed a little prodding. I'm sure you would've stopped yourself eventually, even if Ari hadn't forced you to break. She just sped up the process."

"Speaking of," Kiara said. "There's actually someone else I know who still throws up. I don't think she's as unhappy as I was, but I want to help her if I can. She's the one that taught me how to... you know."

"Who taught you?" Jade snapped, her eyes darkening.

Kiara pressed her lips together and shook her head, letting Jade know she wasn't going to reveal Reigh's identity. Jade gave a frustrated sigh and crossed her arms.

After a few moments, Ariana cleared her throat. "K, I know you want to help this person, but maybe take a little more time working on yourself first? You just started getting better and I wouldn't want anything to mess that up. You have to help yourself before you can help anyone else."

"It's just hard to know the right thing to do," Kiara said with a sigh.

"You'll help her. Work on yourself first, then we can revisit the idea," Ariana said again with a sweet smile.

Kiara nodded and brought her mug to her lips, savoring the sweet smells of chamomile and crisp evening air. Had she stopped noticing the little things the past couple of months? She couldn't remember appreciating anything other than a downward fluctuation on the scale. *Well, not anymore*, she thought to herself, a sense of hope filling her.

* * *

Ariana chose to relax in the cool night air a bit longer while Kiara and Jade went inside to make sure the boys weren't tearing the house down. Pangs of envy struck in her gut–now Jade had Ian, too. Ariana looked at the moon, wondering if Lukas was thinking of her at that moment. Tears burned behind her eyes. Had she hurt him even a fraction of how much he'd hurt her? She grabbed her phone and opened past texts from him, knowing this wasn't the best idea, but not being able to stop herself. She looked over her favorite ones, preparing herself for what she was about to do. She read over them once more and relived each of the memories in turn. Then, she braced herself and began deleting.

(Three weeks ago) Lukas: I dreamt we were older last night. We had a white house on the beach. I came up behind you and kissed your neck. You were so beautiful.
Delete.
(Two weeks ago) Lukas: Listen to The Trapeze Swinger by Iron & Wine. It reminds me of you.
Delete.
(Thursday) Lukas: I think we were made for each other.
Delete.

Ariana kept going, one by one deleting the memories, one by one deleting the lies. Or who knew if he'd been telling his own truths, in some fucked up way. A dizzying thought struck her–how was she going to face Lukas and Olivia at school? Would she have to watch them together every day? Her breathing began to accelerate and shots of panic whizzed through her. In an instant, she knew–an anxiety attack was coming.

"*No*," Ariana said defiantly. She would not let herself be reduced to attacks over him anymore.

She tried to relax her breathing, inhaling for five counts, holding for seven counts, and then exhaling for eight counts, but she found her racing mind was too overbearing. She stood and wildly shook her arms and legs–all she knew was that she had to expel the anxious energy somehow. She jumped up, threw her arms in the air and shouted. She hopped around the backyard until her legs hurt, as if trying to distance herself from the anxiety through movement. Feeling like she was onto something, she started dancing and moving her body to an imaginary beat until she finally collapsed on a chair and let out a laugh at the thought of how absurd she must look. She put her hands over her heart and closed her eyes. She thought of her loved ones, the people she had in her life that she could count on, whom she was so lucky to have. She thought of Kiara and her ridiculous antics that were always cracking everyone up, her out-of-nowhere laughter that kept everyone smiling. She thought of Jade, who would go to bat for her in the blink of an eye, who could be counted on to stick up for her at any time, whether Ariana was in the right or wrong. She remembered all of the times the three of them had laughed so hard together they'd cried, and a smile crept onto her lips. She thought of when they'd fallen asleep holding each other when one of them had been hurt. She thought of when they'd pulled each other up over and over again when it felt like the only way to go was down. She let her love for them overtake any other thought in her mind.

Ariana realized she'd stilled, and a subdued calm was replacing the fear. "HAH!" she yelled. Sure, she probably looked like she'd accidentally sat on an anthill earlier, but she was doing it! Ariana looked to the sky and focused harder now, thinking of her mom and each of her friends in turn, feeling so grateful for everyone and everything she had. Next, she thought of small moments, humming a calming tune to herself as she did–the wind on her face on a warm summer afternoon, the fresh smells of autumn, the beauty of sunsets over the lake. Excited by the results, she kept going through her memories, bringing gratitude to the foreground in each. Her breathing slowed gradually, and her lips turned up into a smile. Then, to her surprise, she started to laugh. Had she just stopped an attack?

"What good does it bring me to dwell on him, and what may or may not happen?" she asked herself.

None.

That was the answer that reverberated in her soul, and she knew it was true. She had so much to learn, to experience, to explore. And she didn't need Lukas to do any of it. In fact, he probably only would've dragged her down with all of his lying and games.

Ariana felt as though she'd just experienced a breakthrough. Gleefully, she contemplated what she'd done and wondered if it could work every time she felt the panic rising. If it'd worked once then surely she could figure it out again?

If it took losing Lukas to find a way to overcome the anxiety attacks, then surely it wasn't all for nothing. What other good would come from this disaster? Ariana remembered something Alora had mentioned once about turning a broken heart into art. Didn't some artists' best work come from getting their hearts broken? She'd always wanted to write a book, to give back what other writers had given to her. Maybe it was a gift she could repay to a generation below her. And what better time to start than now?

Ariana grinned. She felt unstoppable. She decided right then and there that if anything, she would be the one breaking hearts from now on.

With a huge inhale of cool air, Ariana stood up with renewed energy. The rest of her sophomore year would *not* suck because of this–she refused to let it. The smile on her face widened. As a matter of fact, she had a feeling that it may turn into one of her best years yet.

Afterword

Although I've had intense bouts of anxiety for as long as I can remember, my first full-fledged anxiety attack was in sixth grade. I hyperventilated until I nearly passed out, and then spent an hour sobbing in my closet and rocking myself back and forth, desperately trying to stop whatever was happening.

One of the only remedies I found for escaping the crushing waves of panic was reading fiction. I picked up the first Gossip Girl book at age thirteen and was instantly obsessed: Serena and Blair became my idols. As I got older, however, I realized they may not be the *best* role models (lol). And then I thought: What if I could create something that felt just as fun, with a story that made readers fall just as in love with the characters as Gossip Girl did, but instead had kind, positive girls in the limelight who actually learned some valuable life lessons?

And that's how Ariana, Kiara, and Jade were born. The three of them are based on different parts of me and things I've experienced, mixed with some characteristics of my friends and some traits I found attractive or aspired to have at that age.

My hope is that Ariana, Kiara, and Jade will stay with you and that you'll bring them to mind when you feel alone, hopeless, or afraid. Because we all feel those ways sometimes, and therefore we're never truly alone.

The girls may not be perfect, but their hearts are in the right place. The lessons they learn are some that massively helped (and still help) me in my life. Kiara's trials with eating disorders and how she begins to heal are based on my own. As are Ariana's battles with anxiety and how Jade works through why people react with malice and negativity toward humans they don't fully know.

I tell this next part not for pity, but to illustrate a point: As I'm sure many of you experienced in your lives, I was bullied growing up and in high school. One time I asked one of the perpetrators why, and they said because my life was "good". In reality, I was battling crippling anxiety and depression, the loss of my father to suicide, and debilitating eating disorders.

We're all fighting unseen battles.

With that piece of truth in mind, I strive to be kinder to strangers, kinder to those with opposing viewpoints from my own–kinder to everyone. In the end, no matter what our views, backgrounds, beliefs, or race, we're going to have to rely on one another to save this planet. Except for those who block the bike lane. F*** those people. I'm joking, but seriously, stop blocking the bike lane—it's dangerous!

I do want to note that my anxiety has gotten astronomically better over the years, through work I've done on myself and figuring out what works for me personally (e.g. ecstatic dancing & shaking, talking to and connecting with others on how I'm truly feeling, doing kind things for other humans, different types of therapies, and sometimes just waiting it out and knowing the feeling won't last forever, even though it can feel like it will). I still have yet to take medication for my anxiety (after being put on Wellbutrin in high school and hating it), but I also know others who have been helped by antidepressants and meds specific to their mental health needs.

This is not medical advice by any means and the choice, ultimately, is yours. There is no one-size-fits-all cure for anything, and I hope (if needed) you take the time to figure out and experiment (safely) with what will allow you to live your best life.

- Diana

P.S. You can find further resources on my website! (www.Dianahawk.com)

Acknowledgments

Thank you to my parents for everything y'all have done for me. I love you both so incredibly much.

Thank you to Lindsey Morgan for sitting next to me on my first day of fifth grade at a new school even though I was the furthest thing from cool. And for recording the audiobook despite all of the time restrictions and obstacles (how were there so many?!), and for being my muse for Alora.

Thank you to Kyndera Keithley for being my ride-or-die in high school, and my soul sister who always saw through my bravado when I was actually hurting. Kiara became the character she is because of your silly antics and ability to keep everyone laughing.

A huge thank you to those who read the early version, gave me feedback, and encouraged me: Caroline Schley, Carmen Skok, Lindsey Morgan, Milly Pain, Alli Schaper, Rebecca Skovron, Lindsey Metselaar, Jordan Metzman, Kort M. Lee, Setare Taboodi, and Jennifer Wilson.

Thank you to my sister, Meryl Hawk, for coming to my rescue in the times it mattered the most.

Thank you to my partner, Nigell Barlis, for helping me with the cover design, websites, and (most of all) moral support. And for putting up with my jokes.

In no particular order, thank you to those who have gone out of their way to encourage my writing or helped me in the process: Kyaire Hywnn, Elizabeth Walker, Jamie Quarnstrom, Noa Griffel, Lexie Lowell, Zoe Haney, Chris Makrides, Adam Greenfield, Dan Hunt, Cynthia Vlad, Richie Bonilla, Adam Devine, Zachary Zane, Hayley Stevens, Andrew Drucker, Ryan Daniels, Malcolm Friedman, and Dr. Jay Heller.

Thank you to Adam Tilzer for the studio time for the audiobook (and not to mention providing such a safe space for me and Lindsey to create in! And thanks to Floyd, Adam's emotional support corgi.) And thanks to Lexie for introducing us.

Thank you to Sam Auch for letting me borrow your jeep (even though everyone else you've ever let borrow it has gotten in an accident) to get me and Lindsey back and forth safely from the studio.

Thank you to my family in Texas—I love y'all.

Thank you to everyone who voted on Weston's name on social media!

This one may sound silly, but I wanted to give a thank you to myself. For sticking with this damn thing and figuring it all out and having the courage to put everything I wanted in here and going for it with self-publishing. I didn't know if I was going to make it for a while there (in all ways), and I'm so proud I was brave enough to keep going and see it all through.

Last, and certainly not least, thank you to every person who ever cheered me on or made it a big deal when I told you I had written a book. I needed and appreciated that encouragement more than you'll ever know!

About the Author

Diana Hawk was raised in Texas and lives in Brooklyn, New York (for now). After rage quitting her corporate job as a hedge fund headhunter, she is grateful to work as Head of Community for an incredible startup. She doesn't have any writing awards to boast about here and essentially taught herself how to write fiction by reading her favorite books again and again and attempting to emulate them. This was fueled by a fierce desire to create the book she'd wanted to read growing up. And thus, her first novel, *As beautiful as it seems,* was born. When she's not reading or writing, she enjoys connecting with other humans, improv comedy, playing video games, taking on too many projects at once, and procrastinating.

Her mom said she should put "at least one thing that you do well in here, like cooking eggs!" So there it is, Mom.

Learn more at www.DianaHawk.com or on Twitter (@diana_hawk), Instagram (@dianahawk), TikTok (@diana_hawk)

Also by Diana Hawk

New York Stories - I take real New York experiences—the magical, the wild, the sexy, the absurd—that happened to me and people I know and make them read like fiction vignettes.

Content warning: (in certain stories) sex, drug use, drinking, bullying, and the beauty of NYC in general.

(https://dianahawk.substack.com/)

The most personal thing I've ever written - content warning: I talk about suicidal ideations and how I got myself out of a heavy depression period.

(https://www.dianahawk.com/personal-blog/the-most-personal-thing-i-have-ever-written)